GENTLE JOURNEY

ELAINE LYONS BACH

Outskirts Press, Inc.
Denver, Colorado

This is a work of fiction. The events and characters described here are imaginary and are not intended to refer to specific places or living persons. The opinions expressed in this manuscript are solely the opinions of the author and do not represent the opinions or thoughts of the publisher. The author represents and warrants that s/he either owns or has the legal right to publish all material in this book.

Gentle Journey
All Rights Reserved
Copyright © 2007 Elaine Lyons Bach
V 0.0 R 1.1
Cover Image © 2007 JupiterImages Corporation
All Rights Reserved. Used With Permission.

This book may not be reproduced, transmitted, or stored in whole or in part by any means, including graphic, electronic, or mechanical without the express written consent of the publisher except in the case of brief quotations embodied in critical articles and reviews.

Outskirts Press
http://www.outskirtspress.com

ISBN-10: 1-59800-904-4
ISBN-13: 978-1-59800-904-0

Outskirts Press and the "OP" logo are trademarks belonging to
Outskirts Press, Inc.

Printed in the United States of America

*Thanks to Mom and Dad,
My husband, Ken,
And my sons, Blair and Brandon,
For all their love and support.
To God be the glory and honor and praise!*

CHAPTER I

"I'll go mad, Mary," Eden said. "If I have to spend one more day at the Mowbrays' trying to teach their three daughters anything at all, I'll go stark raving mad! Don't you dare laugh at me, little sister. You know how their parents have always undermined me. The girls are so spoiled that they think I'm there for their personal amusement to torture to their heart's content. Good Lord! Yesterday, Priscilla and Janine tried to hold my arms while Evelina had the scissors poised to crop my hair. I had to kick their shins to get away." Eden jumped down from the Landau, forcing her hesitant sister to follow.

Mary indicated with a lift of her pointed chin the ramshackle barn they were facing. "I understand your wanting to leave service there, but this is jumping out of the frying pan into the fire. Or is this the wrong address?"

Adjusting her twice-turned coach dress, Eden took a deep breath to calm herself. Unfortunately the fetid aroma of slops and centuries of animal wastes filled her lungs as well. She coughed violently, causing a button to pop on the too tight spenser jacket. Not for the first time she wished she had Mary's figure: slender, graceful, with just the hint of bosom instead of the well-endowed one God had chosen to give her. Her voluptuous shape had been a great embarrassment to Eden, especially when neighbor boys taunted her when she was younger by pointing at her and calling, "Come, Bossy the cow, will you give your cream today?" The taunt had shortened to a sneer and, "Hello, Bossy," as the boys grew older.

Eden glanced at Mary with a weak smile, attempting to calm her sister's fears with false bravado. "Mr. Pierpoint wrote that his studio was a converted barn. He said the large open space allowed the brush-cleaning solvents to dissipate."

"Which reminds me," Mary said. "How did you carry on a correspondence with a stranger without mother knowing?"

"With a great deal of subterfuge which I don't have time to relate right now." Eden turned to the coachman, "John, could you please, please linger here until Matthew comes along?" John Coachman rubbed his chin. "Got to get Molly on into town to start her errands, Miss Barrett. Don't want the horses standin' neither."

Eden glanced at Molly's pockmarked, horse-toothed face through the carriage window. The skinny maid was the only person she would miss at Sir William's residence. The poor girl had often lingered at the schoolroom door to hear the stories they were acting out. Eden had offered to teach her to read, and Molly had been most eager to learn, but was so overworked that the time could never be found. Eden also knew that Molly was anxious to get to the butcher's where she had a secret follower waiting for her in the form of the butcher's son.

"Just long enough to see if we're safe?" Eden begged the coachman.

John nodded and added, "I'll just turn them round and walk 'em a bit."

"Thank you," Eden said, "and please be sure when you do return to Glen Haven to thank Sir William again for me for allowing us the use of his carriage." Again the coachman nodded.

As Eden moved to step through the half-opened gate, Mary clutched her arm to stop her. "Please, Eden, let's go no further. I have a bad feeling about this. The man does not even bother to hide his empty wine bottles." Eden glanced at the mound of empties half hidden in a clump of dead grass and snow behind the bedraggled fence. She took a corner of her lower lip between her teeth. She didn't like it either, but this was her only chance to fulfill her dream of becoming an artist. She could never afford the tuition of a student. Over the years, she had written to so many other artists for work as an assistant or apprentice, and Mr. Pierpoint had been the only one to answer in the positive, knowing full well that she was female. He had said her sex did not matter to him, and due to his many commissions, he needed more assistants to prepare canvases and paint and eventually to learn to fill in backgrounds for him so that he could spend his time on the subjects. He'd written that the sample she had sent of her work showed much promise. Eden found herself having to adopt an air of optimism for Mary's sake. "Oh, that's just the artistic spirit. All mundane things are forgotten in the frenzy of getting the idea on canvas. Besides, we don't know that he drank all of those, or even if he drank any. Come on."

"At least wait for Matthew."

"We have no idea when he will arrive, and I need to get this over with now, before I lose my courage. The family needs what little money I can earn, and board is included as well, so that will be more room and food for the rest of you." Eden pushed on ahead, grasping the knotted rope that formed the handle of the ancient barn door. The rusty hinges screeched loudly as she thrust the door open. Inside, hazy bright shafts of mote-ridden light pierced the gloom through great gaps in the ceiling boards. Eden was immediately arrested by the vibrant colors and scenes of hunts and farm life displayed on giant canvases standing on makeshift easels all about the cavernous barn. So taken was she by the initial assault of the impression of the paintings that she did not at first notice the boys and the artist himself at work until she tripped over the prone body of an apprentice sleeping on a pile of oil soaked rags.

"Pardon me!" Eden cried, but the boy only grunted and rolled out of the way. The artist turned round at the sound of a stranger's voice in that silent cavern. A painfully slender man, he was clothed in a biscuit colored smock, trousers, and unbuttoned Benjamin overcoat, all splotched with various colors of paint. "Ah, who have we here?" Mr. Pierpoint said. Eden noted the unkempt hair and beard and flushed face of her prospective employer and felt a knot tighten in her stomach.

"Miss Eden Barrett, Sir. I believe you were expecting me."

"Ah, the budding artist who wishes to learn about color. Yes, I can use you alright. You'll get room and board and eight pounds per annum. I'll expect you to clean brushes and palettes and dishes and pots. Can you cook?"

"Somewhat, but I..."

Mr. Pierpoint came closer, still holding his palette and brush. The smell of unwashed body and spirits filled Eden's sensitive nose. "You said in the letter you was desperate to be an artist. That's how I started, cooking and washing pots and pans for another artist." His smile was so unnatural it was unnerving. Eden glanced at a painting close to her. Though the colors were striking yet harmonious and the technique was good, the figures seemed poorly drawn. The poor horse appeared distorted. She wondered if a student had painted it or Mr. Pierpoint himself.

"Who's this?" Mr. Pierpoint nodded to Mary. "I can use her too. I could use both of you as models, though I'm thinking I could sell more of you," he said to Eden, allowing his gaze to drift below her face.

"This is my sister. We are waiting for our brother," Eden said, taking a few steps backwards. She decided to add, "He is meeting us here… with some army friends of his. We need his approval. I'll have to think on it."

"I understood that you had accepted the offer for certain," the artist said, annoyance in his expression as well as his voice.

Eden ignored this, "Where would my sleeping quarters be?"

Mr. Pierpoint shrugged, "Wherever you like. We have only the one big room here. We merely find somewhere comfortable and sleep when we're tired."

"My sister and I will just step outside and tell the coachman he may go and see if my brother and his friends have arrived yet," Eden told him. She turned and headed toward the door, over which hung several portraits she had not noticed earlier because she was facing the other way. They were portraits of reclining nudes, garishly done. Now it was her turn to grab Mary's arm and drag her through the door.

"Thank God," Mary said. "John Coachman is still here, and there's Matthew in the curricle down the road. Eden, I was never so frightened in my life."

"Of him? I… I… don't think he would have hurt us."

"No, I was frightened you were going to take the position. I know how much you hunger to be an artist. And don't tell me you weren't uneasy. I notice you felt it necessary to mention Matthew, the coachman, and a few non-existent army friends to boot." Conversation was suspended between the two young ladies while the coachman took his leave, and Matthew, sans army friends, greeted his sisters and helped them up into his equipage. "Well?" he asked.

Eden shook her head, "No. Definitely not suitable."

"Good. I didn't know how I was supposed to explain coming home with Mary and not you. Momma would have sent me back post haste to get you, and I fear her more than I fear my Captain. Now what, sister? You usually have a number of alternate plans all worked out."

The daughter of a country vicar, Eden had cut her teeth on stories from the bible and the lives of the saints. The oldest child, and favorite of her father, Eden had gone with him on his pastoral visits as he distributed food, clothing, advice, and solace to those of his fold in need. She had thus been witness to most of the bad effects of an unfair class society on the lower classes. She was determined that she would emulate the saints and her father by somehow making a difference in the world with her life.

It seemed to her that the existing systems of caring for the parish poor did little to solve more than their immediate problems. The poorhouses were cruel places where families were separated. Husband and wife were denied the right to even speak to each other, for fear the result would be yet another dependent on the parish tithes. The workhouses were used by manufacturers to provide inexpensive, almost slave, labor for their factories. She was not exactly sure how she was going to advance the condition of man, but she was resolved to do something, and she saw her art as a possible way to achieve it.

When her father died, it was Eden who taught her three sisters and two brothers; when the family finances failed, Eden found employment with Sir William Mowbray. She taught his girls during the day and returned home to help her mother with the housework each evening. Sir William and his wife, however much they loved Eden and her family, spoiled their children, interfering in any discipline and dismissing any attempts at getting the girls to apply themselves. She originally thought that teaching could be a step toward her goal. It could be a way of inspiring the next generation to see knowledge as a weapon against social ills, but not if all her students were like the Mowbray girls.

Eden thought if she could get noticed as an artist, she might eventually be able to charge a high commission and use the money to find the power to enact reform. Hannah Moore had become known as a writer of plays before she began writing religious tracts, some of them blasting the theatre as evil. Hogarth had brought considerable attention to social ills through his engravings and paintings. Though they could often be offensive in their seediness, his works had had an effect. Hogarth himself had organized charitable societies and donated much of his own money to them. Surely this was her calling. But how to go about it? She wasn't getting any younger.

"The only thing I can arrange immediately is another governess position."

"Oh, Eden," Mary said.

"This might not be so bad, Mary. Sir William knows I am unhappy there, and he says he doesn't blame me. He told me that Lord Edmund mentioned in a letter that he had been looking for a governess for his only daughter. His Lordship is rich and has an elaborate estate according to Sir William, and this time it will be only one child."

"Wasn't Lord Edmund at the musical evening last June?"

"The same."

"He had gout, and he had to be at least in his sixties. How could he have a young child? At least he didn't look like the type to spoil one."

"My thoughts, exactly. Matthew, how long do you have on furlough?"

"Two weeks, but I'll need a week of that to carry out my plan of changing regiments and becoming a Captain." The two girls exclaimed over this news and grilled Matthew on how it was to be brought about. Sir William had offered to sponsor him, Matthew told his sisters. He would sell out and buy the Captaincy that had become available in a different regiment. The girls wanted to know where the lovely curricle had come from. When Matthew explained that he would have to deliver it to his previous superior's family in Bath, Eden said, "That wouldn't be too far out of the way to take me to Chadilane, the estate of Lord Edmund, if Sir William can arrange an interview - if the position is still open."

"But Eden, are you giving up too easily on your dream?" Matthew chided.

"I refuse to give up. If God has given me this talent, He intends me to use it, does He not? Surely with only the one child and without the chores and responsibilities I have at home, I will have more time to myself to practice my art?"

"You could marry," her sister said.

"*Et tu*, Mary? Isn't Mother's constant urging and haranguing enough? She called me unnatural again last night because I refused to consider our second cousin Harold as a prospect. Harold! She's frantic to get me out of the house, and I'm frantic to move out. Momma's stipend will last so much better once you and I are no longer being fed by it, and I could send home most of what I earn. I'm so glad that you look forward to your marriage, Mary. Mr. Tobias loves and appreciates you and will take good care of you."

"But you have a sweetheart, Eden. All you need do is encourage him."

Genuinely baffled, Eden asked, "Of whom can you be speaking?"

"Oh, don't play coy with me. You know I mean a certain sergeant in the militia."

"I don't know why everyone keeps linking me with him," Eden scowled.

"Perhaps because the two of you were caught kissing behind the barn," Matthew suggested.

"Yes and he bragged about it to the whole town. Not very gentlemanly of him. That was ages ago, and we were merely experimenting. It was pretty pathetic too. I was immature then. Besides he would never do. I really can't imagine marriage for me, ever. I just don't think I'm made for it. I love my freedom too much. I don't have the right temperament. You do, Mary. You're calm, demure, sweet-natured. I fly off the handle if I think someone has been wronged."

Matthew chuckled, "You get that from Mother. Surely there is some man who could find that endearing in you."

"Don't be ridiculous. I can't see myself forever submitting to the will of another, except God's will, of course. The decision to marry may be the last decision a lady is ever allowed to make, and she's usually coerced into that from the cradle by society. I don't look forward as you do, Mary, to childbearing and childrearing and all the duties of home and hearth. Where is the time to think and plan, much less paint? You know I wish to be active in social reforms as well. What man would stand for that?"

"I agree, Eden. Be free. Be an old maid. Be a governess to other people's children or starve in a garret painting ugly people's pictures. That is much more romantic," Matthew offered sarcastically.

"There is no such thing as an ugly person. And either of those choices is far more agreeable to me than becoming one with a master I couldn't admire, for master my husband would be in this society. No, marriage would be compromise. It's asking me to settle for less than I can be. Compromise is giving up before I begin; I detest the very word."

"Detest it all you like. It's the only way to get on in the world," Matthew said.

"It is not my aim merely to 'get on' in the world, but to leave an impression in it," Eden told him, allowing a mild resentment to show.

"You'll never have power to accomplish anything if you don't compromise. But, let us be friends. Humor us, Eden. Describe for us the man you could admire," Matthew said. "Who knows? Perhaps it will enlighten me as to the type of man that I should aspire to be."

Eden laughed at his mocking tone, "I doubt the man exists. I have certainly not met anyone close to being like him so far."

"No, you will not duck the question, Eden. What man would please you, if you were willing to be pleased?" Mary insisted.

"Oh... He would have to be very well educated, genuinely interested in the arts, with an open mind. He must care about the welfare of others. He must have integrity, be considerate, decisive yet tender, have a good sense of humor, and above all..."

"Go on. Above all..." Mary encouraged.

"Never mind. You'll only laugh at me."

"I'm already laughing at you," Matthew said, "I couldn't possibly aspire to that lofty creature. It would take me a lifetime. Except perhaps the sense of humor."

"The closest thing I know to your dream man is Poppa," Mary chuckled. "No wonder you despair of ever finding him."

"You bait me by saying I despair of finding him, when I've tried to explain that I'm not looking for him."

Mary said sweetly, "You must admit you paint a very clear portrait of the one you're not looking for."

"It's not that I haven't given it thought. What were you looking for, Mary, before you found Mr. Tobias?" Eden asked, attempting to steer the questioning away from herself.

"Well, my standards were much less awesome than yours. Perhaps that's why I was able to fill them. I was looking for a man who could provide well for me and for our children. He must love me and be in love with me at the same time. He must come up behind me when I am brewing beer and wrap his arms about me and kiss my neck. He must compliment me on my looks, my housekeeping, and my common sense, and never speak of me in company except with pride."

Eden's smile at the scene evoked by Mary was tinged with rue: Mary's picture could never have been applied to their parents' relationship. Her father had often given from the family larder when the poor box was empty, explaining, "The Lord provides." He regretted aloud the fact that he could not do more. Yet he resisted when his pragmatic and increasingly desperate wife tried to force him to climb the clerical ladder to success. He was happy where he was. Mrs. Barrett became bitter and aimed acerbic comments at her husband often. He blithely ignored her and joyfully remained a mere vicar, though his family existed on the barest of means.

Eden did not admit to herself that her parent's marriage had had the greatest influence on her distaste for matrimony. Nor did she realize she had inherited as much ambition from her mother as she had altruism from her father. "I truly hope you have found him, Mary," Eden said.

"I have," Mary smiled.

"Well, aren't you going to ask me what I look for in a wife?" Matthew said, pretending hurt.

"Certainly, Matthew. Perhaps I can learn how to be a good wife," Mary said with incomplete innocence. She knew her brother too well.

"I am looking for a sweet little armful who will think everything I say and do is inspired and jump to do my bidding every moment of the day… and night."

"May you never find her," Mary said. "You would remain incorrigible."

Matthew shifted the reins and clasped his right hand to his heart with a thud, "I 'm stricken."

"Don't ever try the stage, Matthew. There are too many hams there as it is," Eden told him.

"And don't think I didn't notice your ploy, Eden. You avoided answering my last question. What was the 'above all' you mentioned?" Mary asked.

"Very well, but… Well, you remember Father's sermons about the horse hitched with a donkey being better than two prime bits of blood being hitch together but faced in opposite directions?"

"I remember I used to laugh at the picture it made in my mind. I was too young to understand," Mary said. "But what does Father's sermon have to do with your dream beau?"

"Above all, he must have a living, breathing, faith in God."

CHAPTER II

Eden stretched and twisted in the curricle, trying to relieve the stiffness of four hours on the road in the early morning hours of a brisk January day. Matthew glanced at her and gave her his lopsided smile before looking back over the horses' heads. The Somerset countryside was a blur of snow-covered hills, bare-branched trees, and steel gray skies.

The only humans they had passed had been a deformed little man leading a skeleton of a donkey with two filthy boys astride. From the assortment of shovels, brushes, buckets and ropes the boys held, Eden surmised their trade was chimney sweeping. The boys probably never saw a schoolroom and their feet were bare. There should be a law, Eden thought. She wished her brother and she had not already shared the meal they had brought with them. She could have offered it to the boys.

She unfolded again the note Sir William had received from Lord Edmund, and she tried to imagine the nature of its author. The hand was firm, the letters clear and precise. The diction was elegant, the address formal and polite. He sounds intelligent, she thought. She could not have guessed this to be written by the man she had briefly met at Sir William's last spring. She had noticed a slight palsy in his right hand and gruffness in his address, perhaps because of the gouty foot he was resting on a pillow. He had seemed interested only in hunting and hounds, subjects Eden could discuss only in general terms.

Sir William had written a glowing character reference and arranged an interview with his Lordship at his country estate. Eden had packed the few serviceable clothes she had, as well as a portfolio of her watercolors, brushes and completed paintings. She had expected resistance from her mother, but the thought of Eden residing in an earl's home had sent Mrs. Barrett into transports. "Think what an opportunity! There will be educated, eligible young men about the place - agents, secretaries, perhaps a young vicar! This may be just the thing," she had cried. "I always regretted that we could not give you a season in London. Had you had a greater opportunity to meet a variety of beau...."

Eden had started to protest, but thought better of it. Her mother's mind ran in a carriage wheel rut as far as marrying off her daughters was concerned. One would think she would be satisfied with planning for Mary's impending nuptials, but...

"That looks like a gatehouse up ahead," Matthew broke into her thoughts. "I'll wait for you to finish your interview. If for any reason you decide you don't want the position, or if it is not offered to you, I can take you on to Bath with me. You can stay with Aunt Esther until you arrange for a ride back home. It should be fun, Eden. You've never been to Bath."

"I've never been anywhere but Longacre," she said.

The curricle slowed as Matthew pulled up in front of a small castle. The gatekeeper came out to inquire as to their identity. Satisfied with their answers, he pulled back on the heavy, ornate iron gate. It moved easily and noiselessly. "The manor is on up this road about five miles," the gatekeeper told them. The horses' hooves crunched on the thick gravel as Eden exclaimed at the height of the ancient poplars that lined the path, obscuring the view for the first mile or so. "If that was the gatehouse, what must the main house be?" she wondered aloud.

"Can hardly wait to see it!" Matthew answered. "Hope I can find a good horse in Bath. I'll need to make a mad dash to Lyme if I'm to have time to be fitted for my new military uniform before I board the frigate that's to take me to Aviero to join my new regiment."

"I'll never understand your enlisting at all. Not when Sir William was willing to sponsor your education if you had wanted to follow in Father's footsteps. You already know the Bible backwards and forwards."

Matthew cast his sister a doubtful glance. "Can you really see me in orders? And I needed to be earning my own bread. I know soldiering is a dreary, senseless existence most of the time, but it's a living that lets me travel and see the world. I've no other inclination right now. War time is the best time to enlist; advancement is rapid."

"Because of vacancies through fellow officer's deaths," Eden said. "It's so mercenary."

Matthew shrugged. "Fact of life."

Fact of death, she thought, but held her tongue. As the curricle rounded a bend and the view opened up before them, Matthew began to comment on the beauty and charm of the manor parkland. The farm cottages were well kept. "Look," he said. "I wonder if that could be your new charge. Up on that knoll. She must be. That one could be trouble."

Eden looked up and saw a girl of about twelve astride a fat white pony with a shaggy winter coat. The girl sat tall and proud in her side-saddle with her deep blue velvet riding dress fanned out across the pony's rump and side. She was a large-framed child of no figure. She wore her waist-length smoky-brown hair tied away from her face with a single ribbon. The girl was a little too far away to discern her facial features. As they drew closer, the girl signaled her pony with her knee, and it turned abruptly and raced away.

When Matthew brought the team to a standstill in front of the enormous, sprawling Hamstone mansion, an hostler met them and took the horses' heads. Two footmen in silver and garnet livery exited the house and came swiftly to the side of the carriage. As Matthew jumped down, one footman handed Eden down and the other reached for her portmanteau and easel. Eden took her portfolio herself, saying that she might need it for the interview. She asked the footmen not to take her things up to a room right away, as she was not certain she was staying.

"I never dreamed," she whispered in awe to Mathew. Sir William Mowbray's home had been the largest estate in Longacre and it was a hovel compared to this: Chadilane Manor.

Matthew stayed with the curricle as Eden strolled on behind the footmen up to the massive entry doors. One footman asked for her card, opened the door and led her in.

Inside, he gave her card to the housekeeper, introducing her as Mrs. York.

"Yes, Miss. His Lordship asked to see you immediately you arrived." The rough, red, pudgy little face of a middle-aged woman smiled up at her. The housekeeper moved her round little figure abruptly to a side-table in the hall to retrieve a silver tray arranged with a distinctive silver coffee service. As she glanced up the grand double stairway to a group of men who stood talking earnestly on the landing, Mrs. York said, "If you'll wait here, Miss, I'll let His Lordship know you're here." She then mounted the staircase in a very determined way that would have been bustle if she had moved faster.

Eden's eyes greedily took in the elegance of the wainscoted walls, marble floors, and carved mahogany banisters. When one of the men assembled above laughed, she thought it might be directed at her, and her eyes were drawn toward the sound. The group was composed of five men of indeterminate middle age and one man who seemed to be in his late twenties. This younger man arrested her glance. Taller than the others, he stood with his head tilted to one side giving full attention to the companion who was speaking. If he were not so tall, and built so slender, he would have stood out merely by the mass of over-long, curling raven locks that framed a poet's face with a solemn expression. Eden could see that his mouth was turned down at the corners like one perpetually dissatisfied with life.

By now the housekeeper had reached the gentlemen. She spoke to the younger man, then moved on down the hall. The older men followed her. The raven-haired poet moved away from the group and began to descend the staircase. *He moves like a great cat,* Eden thought: *Controlled, deliberate, yet easy – like power restrained.*

As he came closer to Eden, their eyes met. She felt a distinct chill. His eyes were positively eerie. The color was such a pale blue as to appear almost clear. The lashes were so thick and dark they underscored the paleness of the irises. The effect was of some soulless being approaching.

Eden tore her eyes from his and looked down at the carpet. *He'll think me bold*, she thought. But the young man had noticed no impropriety. Instead he had been occupied with comparing her eyes to the large, mild eyes of a doe. He was, in fact, disappointed when she hid them from him.

When he reached the bottom of the stairs, he stopped before her. "Miss Barrett?" he asked in a velvet voice that seemed to originate from some deep well within him.

"Yes," said the lady with her eyes firmly on the carpet.

"I'm pleased to make your acquaintance."

Eden was so engrossed in listening to the deep, resonant voice, that she knew the sentence was over only because the sound had stopped. "Oh. And you are?"

He raised an eyebrow, but just the hint of chagrin was allowed to tinge his expression. *Please, not another flustered goose.* "I am Colin Ashton, Seventh Earl of Edmund."

"The Lord Edmund I am to see?"

"Currently the only Lord Edmund."

"I'm sorry if I appear confused," Eden stammered, "but when Sir William mentioned Lord Edmund needed a governess, I was certain he was an older gentleman I had the pleasure of meeting at Glen Haven in Longacre last spring."

"My father."

"Oh," she said, but her expression revealed incomplete understanding.

"I lost my father not long after the assembly you speak of. An accident involving a fall from his horse. Sir William had not heard."

"I'm sorry, I…" Eden began to compose condolences in her mind, but he evidently did not think them necessary.

"Stewart," he said to the footman nearest him, "Find Lady Diana and bring her to me now. Then tell Mrs. York to engage a sweep for the music room. I want it readied for Saturday." To Eden, he said, "We'll talk in here." He led the way to a drawing room and indicated a sofa for her to sit on. He remained standing. "Sir William writes that you are an exceptional teacher. I wish to leave for London at the end of the month. I have much business to conduct, and I will take my seat in the House. London is not a healthy place for children. I don't wish to leave my sister without a companion more suited to her than those she has now. Her nurse was my mother's nurse also. Her age and health limit her ability to tame the girl. She will appreciate your help. You may find Diana a bit rough about the edges. She has not had a governess these past five years though she has had many teachers. She needs a friend who will help her adjust from an unstructured childhood into young womanhood. Perhaps you would like to tell me the qualities and accomplishments you feel you possess which would make you qualified to mold my sister."

Eden attempted to compose herself, but nothing was as she had imagined. She had never expected the manor to be so grand, or its master to be so young. She could feel herself trembling. She was sure she was making a terrible impression. Doubts found a way into her hastily constructed fortress. *Was the girl an animal that she needed taming?* She dove in and listed the usual required skills. "I am proficient in reading, grammar, spelling, ornamental penmanship, the reading of maps and globes, embroidery, appliqué, and all manner of fine needlework, charcoal sketching and watercolors. My world history though is only tolerable; my mathematics encompasses only the books of Euclid and simple equations in algebra. I can transcribe Latin and Greek fairly well. My French, I'm afraid, is very limited. I have read extensively the classics and philosophers as well as the Bible. I am afraid I play no instruments, but I am rather good at dances, protocol and posture."

His expression showed amusement by the hint of a smile that transformed his face. "You seek to recommend yourself to me by telling me what you cannot do and what you do not know - a novel approach, Miss Barrett."

Eden's chin came up. *He needn't laugh at me as well as hover over me.* She was already feeling intimidated, an emotion unfamiliar to her. "I'm far from ignorant, yet I do not profess to be a genius. However, what I lack in education, I feel I make up for in enthusiasm, stamina, patience, and imagination. I am young enough not to have forgotten all of how a child's mind works or how dull lessons can be if not presented with some degree of creativity," she assured him.

"Sir William has written that you are a paragon; I begin to believe him. Is that a portfolio?"

"Yes, I thought you might wish to see examples of my work. I constructed the dress I am presently wearing and tatted the lace. I've brought a few inks, charcoals, and watercolors. I was able to sell some of my paintings in Longacre: some china paintings and miniature portraits."

He took the folio held out to him and sat down to glance through the pictures. Eden watched his face for a reaction, but the greatest reaction was her own. His expression revealed no regard at all. There was nothing of distaste, but neither was there the least admiration for these, the carefully chosen best of her work. *It can be embarrassing when people praise you, but this treatment is hard to take*, she thought. *He's not the least bit impressed.*

The Earl closed the folio, stood and handed it to her, and strolled over to the door, making no comment on what he had observed. Eden was sure she was not going to like this callous young man, but she swiftly chided herself for allowing her pride to be so easily wounded.

"In here, Diana," the Earl said.

The very girl Matthew had pointed out from the curricle stepped inside the doorframe. She didn't look like an ogre. Her face was a pleasing mixture of round cheeks and retrousse' nose on a heart shaped face. Her skin was a warm tan, flecked with a healthy handful of freckles. Her eyes, a hazel bordering on gold, were clear and intelligent. She said nothing, but studied Eden closely as if sizing her up

"As I was approaching the house, I saw you astride quite a noble looking beast. You ride beautifully," Eden offered, exuding as much warmth as she could to break down any negative preconceptions the child might have toward those of her profession.

"Do you ride?" Diana asked.

"I used to when I was your age. I've not had the opportunity for a long time though. I'm sure I'm quite rusty."

"Mr. Stagg is our head groom and my instructor. He is very good. I'm sure he would enjoy teaching you. We could ride together sometimes," Diana offered hopefully.

"I would adore it. Come here, and I will tell you a secret that will prove just how much." The child looked surprised, but came quickly and bent down to hear. Eden tossed a sly glance at His Lordship as he stood by the door, then whispered to Diana, "Don't tell, but when I was a girl, I used to pretend I was a blooded stallion and gallop snorting all over the downs looking for brood mares. I would paw the ground and challenge all comers."

The child was enchanted and sat down for a lively discussion of horseflesh. When Eden proved knowledgeable, Diana said that she was getting too heavy for her pony and that her brother had promised to take her to choose her own horse soon. "I hope to find a piebald, a hunter. Do you have a favorite kind of horse, Miss Barrett?"

"I did see a particularly beautiful two year old mare at a fair last summer. She must have contained Arabian blood, for her head was small while her neck was long and arched. She held her tail high naturally as she pranced about the paddock. She was of the most striking blood bay color with glossy black stockings, main and tail, and a glowing white blaze down her forehead. I thought I had never seen anything more beautiful in my life. I spent an hour just looking at her and talking to her. I quite forgot the fair. I believe a Lord Beaumont bought her for his mother."

"I like her, Colin. She'll do," Diana told her brother.

The earl had been earnestly observing the interchange, studying the faces of the two to detect their true attitudes toward each other. He had noted the genuine warmth in Eden's voice, and decided that though she might not have the striking features of some of the reigning belles of the ton, she did have a quiet, smoldering sort of beauty. Her general expression was one of delight. Her lively brown eyes were quick to light up with a smile. That generous mouth hinted at an earthy sensuality. And that demure little morning dress she wore could not completely hide her very pleasing figure. *Oh damn, how long have they been looking at me?*

Colin cleared his throat and told his sister, "Go and change out of your riding habit, Diana. After I have seen to my guests, I'll have exactly one hour before I dress for supper. You have me completely at your disposal for that one hour. I dine at Lord and Lady Welham's this evening."

Eden caught a look of exasperation and then resignation on her new charge's face.

Diana stood and offered her hand to Eden. "It was a pleasure meeting you, Miss Barrett. I hope you will agree to stay."

Eden rose and followed Diana to the door. After the child left, she turned and looked up into the eerie eyes of Lord Edmund. Again she felt a chill. "Her manners are delightful," she told him.

"I am offering the position to you, Miss Barrett. Do we have an agreement?"

"Before I accept, my lord, may I speak with your housekeeper a moment?" she asked.

His expression was obvious puzzlement, but amusement. One corner of his mouth drew up to form a deep furrow in his cheek. "As you wish." To a footman, he said, "Connors, take Miss Barrett to Mrs. York for me, please. I'll be in the blue salon with my guests. When Miss Barrett has completed her interview with Mrs. York, put her in the library and notify me." The earl nodded to her and left.

The footman led Eden through the vast kitchens to the servants' hall where they found Mrs. York. "Miss Barrett requests an audience with you, ma'am," Connors said.

"Alone, if you please," Eden told Connors, who nodded and removed himself immediately.

Mrs. York led Eden to a small parlor in the servants' quarters and turned to her expectantly. "What can I do for you?"

"His Lordship has not mentioned a wife. Has he one?" Eden asked.

"Not yet, though the household expects to hear that he is engaged as soon as his year of mourning is over."

"Forgive me for being so frank, Mrs. York, but you are in charge of all the female servants. Have any of them ever complained of ungentlemanly conduct on the part of the earl?"

Mrs. York's face screwed up into a rather prim expression at the imagined insult to her master. "As you are contemplating moving into the home of an unmarried man, I understand one cannot be too careful, but I am delighted to say that His Lordship has never been anything but a gentleman of the first order." She added with bit of devilment in her eyes, "Of course, he has not been home above two months out of any year, and we have not had so pretty a lass as you among the staff in a long time."

"You are not setting my mind at ease by qualifying your statement, Mrs. York," Eden cautioned her.

"Well, Miss Barrett. In truth, I doubt you'll see much of His Lordship. He intends to take his seat in Parliament when it convenes next month, and he does have a sweetheart of long standing who usually lives in London. I am sure that you are aware of the diseases, both physical and social which are rampant in that city. His Lordship insists the manor is a more suitable place for Lady Diana to be raised in. That is why he has been so persistent in his search for the right governess. He is aware that he will be leaving his sister completely in her hands."

"He has interviewed many?" Eden asked.

"Many," the housekeeper confirmed.

Eden thanked the housekeeper, found the footman, and followed him to the library.

Left there to await Lord Edmund, Eden was again taken aback at the splendor of the place. The library might have made an excellent museum, but surely never a room one could relax in. It consisted of three adjoining rooms fitted floor to ceiling with cabinets with glazed doors. These were crammed with books of matching leather binding or loaded with objects of art, many with historical significance. On one desk was a group of books so fresh from the printer, the pages had not yet been cut. Eden wondered whether His Lordship was a collector and intended to leave the books uncut to insure a higher value.

Most of the furniture was large, heavy, and dark in contrast to the light Hepplewhite furniture so popular these days. Eden spent a long time examining the frieze of a chariot race that hung over the enormous fireplace. The interweaving flow of bulging, strained muscles of horses and men was intriguing. She turned her glance to the objects behind locked glass doors in the center of the west wall. There were delicate Meissen figurines, repousse' silver pieces, and collections of Staffordshire pottery and Sevres china.

"And did we pass muster, Miss Barrett?" Lord Edmund's baritone voice echoed in the vast empty rooms.

Eden turned to smile at him. "There was never any doubt about your sister, My lord," she told him with such a saucy air that she surprised herself.

He smiled back. "And your decision?"

"I shall be pleased to take the position offered."

"Good. Mrs. York will show you your room and the schoolroom. I would like to see some sort of written plan for your first week's curriculum. Have it ready in the morning." Then the earl's tone changed to a more serious one, "Miss Barrett... You are the daughter of a vicar, a man whose sermons I was privileged to hear as a boy, a very convincing orator. That fact may make your employ more desirable to some. To me it is an impediment. I fear you may have inherited the propensity to sermonize. You will teach my sister the usual material without references to matters of faith if you please. My sister and I are not religious, and I will not have her badgered into a belief against her will."

Eden swallowed hard. What did he think she was? She would never think of forcing her opinions on anyone. She managed a genuine look in the slight smile she gave him. "Thank you, my lord, for being direct. I promise to tread softly."

"As long as we understand each other. And keep in mind, my sister has a very good memory, and she tells me absolutely everything."

Was that a threat? Eden nodded, curtsied and left the room before she said something she would be sorry for later. She walked swiftly out the entrance and across the terrace to her brother.

Colin wandered over to the window overlooking the front of the house. He had the distinct impression that Miss Barrett thought she was doing him the favor of taking the position rather than he doing her the favor by offering it. He was about to turn to ask a footman whose curricle he saw standing on the path when Eden came out the front door and ran toward it. Previously hidden by the hedgerows, a striking young militiaman came forward to meet her. In his letter, Sir William had said Miss Barrett was thought to be saving her heart for a certain soldier or she would have been snapped up years ago. Colin watched the two with interest. He couldn't hear their conversation at the end of the terrace, but the two held hands and she smiled up into his face.

"Do you remember when Father used to call you 'Bonnie Prince Charlie' because you used to strut about like royalty in a big paper hat carrying a stick for a sword? It was when you had that Scots tutor, and you thought that all things Scotland were romantic."

"I was very little, but I do remember not liking the 'Bonnie' part. I thought it more suited to a milksop."

"Well, if you ever looked like a 'Bonnie Prince' anybody, you do today--- all decked out in your regimentals."

"Wait 'til you see me in the captain's uniform of my new regiment. Now that's a smart outfit... I almost forgot…" He removed a ring from the third finger of his hand.

"Father's ring. I want you to keep it for me until I return. I'm likely to see action this time, and I'm told the human vultures who glean the battlefield after a fray will cut off a finger to get at a ring that fits as tightly as this. And it doesn't matter to them if the soldier is still alive."

Eden winced. "What a horrid thing to say at a time like this, but of course I will keep it for you."

In the library, Colin watched the soldier take a ring from his finger and give it to the governess. She tried it on a finger, but settled for stringing it on a gold chain with a lapis cross that she wore. The soldier fastened the chain at the back of her neck in a familiar way. The two clasped hands and strolled on closer to the house until their observer could recognize the stripes of a lieutenant and hear their conversation. He knew better, but he listened anyway.

"I can't bear to see you go off to war. The idea of thousands of young men mutilating each other because of the ideas of a few is too hideous."

"Well, we didn't start this war, but you bloody well can't expect us to sit on our tails picking our teeth while that French Toad attempts to claim the very ground beneath our feet."

"I suppose your right. He's made it clear he'll take the world if he can. We must defend ourselves. But why can't the leaders just fight it out among themselves and leave their subjects out of it?" she scowled.

"That would make too much sense."

"Write often my Charlie. I'll be impatient for every letter."

"As often as I can, Eden."

"Much more often than that."

"I'd best be off to Bath. One last swing-round for old time's sake?"

"No! I'll not have you putting on a display. We're not known here. What would they say?"

"Your lips say 'no', but your eyes say 'yes'," he teased. Matthew grabbed his sister before she could escape and swung her in a full circle about him while she squealed with delight. Then as she stumbled from dizziness, he embraced her, holding her face to his breast and kissing the top of her head.

After a moment the governess broke away, wiped at her eyes, straightened to attention and saluted. "Goodbye my proud soldier. Goodbye my Charlie," she said.

The soldier saluted and the two parted.

Lord Edmund came away from the window with the only conclusion possible: Sir William was right. Miss Barrett actually had given her heart to a young soldier.

CHAPTER III

"Surely there's some mistake. This room is far too fine for a mere governess," Eden said in dismay as she looked about the chamber Mrs. York was showing her.

"That's what I told His Lordship," Mrs. York agreed. "I says, 'Shouldn't you be puttin' her on third floor, next to schoolroom?' But His Lordship says you fancy yourself an artist an' the situation of this room is perfect for a studio. Said the views from the window here and the north light in the sitting room were particular suited to painting. 'No sense keeping the rooms in the family wing in order,' he says, 'if no one is to enjoy 'em.' I suppose as Nurse Warren resides in nursery, it's just as well. The schoolroom is just down this corridor, turn left and up the stairs. These old bones don't like all these stairs so much. Think you can find it yourself?"

"I'm sure I can. Might Nurse Warren prefer to have this room? I could have hers."

"Dear me, no, Miss. Nurse Warren has lived in that room for over forty year. She'll not be wantin' to move now. His Lordship said put you in here, and here you'll stay."

Eden looked about her new home. Fresh cut flowers had been placed in vases on the dresser and the night table by the bed. *They must have come from a conservatory to be blooming in January,* she thought. The windows were open to air the room. New logs stood by the fireplace.

"We weren't certain when to expect you, or the fire would be made up already," Mrs. York explained as she drew the windows shut. "What time would you like your bath water sent up? Six o' the morning is convenient for us in kitchen, unless you don't mind an evening bath, in which case nine is more convenient."

"Where am I too bathe?" Eden asked.

In answer, Mrs. York opened a door to what Eden had thought was a closet. It was an entire room with a vanity full of perfume bottles, a cheval glass, and a wooden biddy. "You can bathe in dressing room here, or Nathan and Connors can move the tub into your room in front of the fire. And there's no need to use the chamber pot neither; there's a water closet under each set of stairs in each wing, on each floor. We're quite modern here," she said with pride. "There's even gas light in the dining room and the ballroom.

"Breakfast is ready at eight. Her Ladyship takes breakfast as she pleases; sometimes with His Lordship, or if he's left before she's up, she may have it in her room or with Nurse. Nora is chambermaid for this wing. She'll bring fresh water for your pitcher at half past six. If you lock your door, she'll have to knock and wake you to stay on her schedule. His Lordship said you was to spend the day settlin' in. Any questions on the schedule of the house, see me; any questions on your duties, see Mr. Grey." Mrs. York waited for questions; none came. "When would you be wantin' bath, Miss?"

"The evening sounds delicious," Eden answered, thinking of the metal hipbath the family used in the kitchen at home. The siblings had all used the same water, taking turns being the first.

"Yes, Miss. If you need anything else, this is servant's bell pull," Mrs. York added. Eden thanked her for her kind attentions. The housekeeper excused herself and left.

Eden set out her brush and comb on the vanity, fondly hung her three dresses in the oak clothespress, and placed her unmentionables and nightwear in the spacious drawers of the tallboy. Though she only used the top drawer, her clothes looked lost in it. She took a look behind the door opposite the dressing room and found a sparsely decorated sitting room. It looked as if a few pieces of furniture and paintings had been removed recently. She went over to the window seat and agreed with the owner that the view and the light were exceptional. Remembering that particular choice of words brought another choice of words to her memory. Mrs. York had said the earl said she 'fancied herself' an artist. Had he said that before or after he had viewed her work? Or had he actually used that phrase at all? She shrugged it off and set about exploring.

In the schoolroom, Eden found long tables with eight chairs. There were enough maps, globes, pencils, slates, paper, ink, quills, and books for a hundred children. A closer examination found some of the books objectionable to her, especially the works of Mrs. Sherwood. They contained such harsh descriptions of things that could happen to naughty children: punishments that far outweighed the crime. Little boys who drew on walls were swallowed up by grotesque monsters and never seen again. Eden could only imagine inciting nightmares by reading these books.

After spending several hours looking through the textbooks and taking notes on what she would discuss and do in her first few lessons, Eden decided to stretch a bit and explore the ground floor. Her wandering led her to a conservatory that boasted the amazing new bending glass on the roof. Outside were a bleak, steel-gray sky and the blinding whiteness of snow. Inside was a tropical forest complete with palms and towering ferns and orchids of great variety and other rare species of plants from foreign parts of the world. Surely Eden could find many excuses to hold lessons here.

Another exciting find was a vast room with a tennis net strung across its center. Along the sides of the walls were fencing, boxing, skating, croquet, and cricket equipment. Eden's mind began to run ahead, planning mathematics lessons that could be applied to these games. The room was freezing, though, and she saw no way of heating it. It would have to wait until the weather was warmer.

After a long nap in her big, comfy, canopied bed, Eden set up her easel in the sitting room. Diana came and invited her to take supper with Nurse Warren in the nursery. At least she knew where she would be having her meal this time. The staff seemed nervous about her being in the servants' hall since she was gently bred, and Eden didn't feel it was right to suppose that she would eat with the family although she had at Sir Mallory's. Eden quickly understood why Lord Edmund had felt it necessary to speak to her about preaching. Nurse Warren, a thin, gray-skinned, white-haired, watery-eyed invalid, had "got religion" and used every excuse to give it to everyone else.

"And you must get Lady Diana to attend Sunday services, Miss Barrett. There is a chapel here on the estate, but the clergy are no longer encouraged to come here since the late earl died. Now the servants must go into town of a Sunday to attend, and that's five miles off, so... When her father was alive, he made her go to chapel. He knew what was best for a child," Miss Warren told Eden while glaring at Diana.

"Her brother was so good as a boy, quiet and well-mannered. He was so bright, you only had to tell him something once, and he never forgot. He used to attend service every Sunday until his mother died and he was sent away to Eton. Now he never goes, and he says she needn't either unless she asks to go." Miss Warren's eyes narrowed as they speared Diana, on the left of her, "Of course, children don't know what's good for them until it's too late…"

Eden interrupted Miss Warren's diatribe fearing that Diana would think by her silence that she concurred completely. "Faith is a gift, Miss Warren. It cannot be forced upon one like a bitter draught."

"You're comparison fits my purpose, Miss Barrett. No child wants to take his medicine, but it's for the good of his body, like church is for the good of his soul."

Miss Warren was not above interrupting as well.

"Faith should be a sweet wine: not something dreaded, but anticipated with joy," Eden said.

"Some things cannot be sugar coated," the spinster warned, "and duty is one of them. Lord knows I've tried putting the fear of the Lord into her, but…"

Eden glanced at Diana and raised her brows in commiseration. *But have you tried putting the love of the Lord into her?*

"I'm not so sure I even believe there is a God," Diana ventured.

Miss Warren's jaw dropped to her chest. "Never say such a thing child. You've been listening to that brother of yours!"

"Colin says I must make up my own mind," Diana said.

"Your brother is wise," Eden interjected.

"Shall I not be sent to perdition when I die because I say I am not sure?"

"No. As long as you question God's existence actively with an open mind and determination to have your questions answered, for then you will find your answers. There are many who say they doubt out of sheer laziness and self interest and make no attempt to find out. If there is no God, they will not have to put themselves out to please Him. On the other hand, there are people who say they believe because society looks on them in a better light for it, yet they exhibit no difference in their lives because of this professed belief. To say that you believe in God is not enough. Satan believes in God. Satan quotes scripture. Belief in God must make us better beings, or it is in vain."

Back in her room, Eden found a log fire glowing softly. Promptly at nine, there was a knock at her door. Two young men introduced themselves as Nathan and Joseph. They carried in huge copper cans full of water for the bath. They emptied the water into it and disappeared.

A girl of about sixteen introduced herself as Nora and welcomed Eden. She had brought up a reed basket filled with fresh-laundered, lilac-scented towels, as well as powder, sponges, and a tablet of Windsor soap. These she set out, and then busied herself about the room drawing the curtains and turning back the bed. Joseph and Nathan reappeared with the cans full of water again, steaming this time. They poured each into the tub ceremoniously, testing the temperature with a wrist. "Is that about right," Joseph asked her.

"Perfect," Eden smiled at him, embarrassed to have male strangers having any knowledge of her bath at all, much less pouring it and testing it for her. The servants were gone as quickly as they came.

Eden threw the bolt on her door. She took up the tablet of soap. It was translucent and deliciously scented; unlike the itchy lye soap they often had to make at home with ashes and animal fat. She shed her clothes quickly and stepped into the warm water. The sumptuous experience of a bath before a fire in a beautiful room with a canopied bed started her on a reverie about being a fairy princess. She indulged herself completely.

After dressing, which she found difficult with only a button hook and no sibling to help her do up the five buttons on the back of her dress, Eden lingered in front of the mirror brushing her long, luxuriant, sable-brown mane. Though her hair was not cut in the current fashion, it was her pride. She imagined it made her look sultry as it lay along her shoulders, and she practiced a few enticing looks in the mirror before laughing at herself.

Hoping to find at least some folios of etchings she might study, Eden went in search of the library. She stood at the door and looked in to see if anyone was there. Finding the rooms empty, she snuck inside. Eden began to read the titles to try to determine what system, if any, was used to categorize the books. In the process, she came across a title that was all the talk in Bath just now according to the last letter from Aunt Esther. Eden took the book down and settled close to an oil lamp and the fading fire.

She meant to read a few paragraphs to see if the author could catch her interest.

Wide-awake as a result of the nap and bath, Eden got quite far into *Sense and Sensibility* without noticing the time. When the lamp next to her sputtered out, the room went almost black. The candles in the branchioles had been snuffed out by a servant without her noticing. Eden stood and stretched. She found a vase of fresh tapers on the mantelpiece and lit one from the embers of the fire. Beeswax instead of tallow, Eden mused. Even the candles were expensive.

On the way back to her room, Eden stopped to investigate the stone sculptures on pedestals that lined the hall. She blew out her own candle because the branchioles in this part of the hall were still lit, and she didn't want to risk hot candle wax dripping onto her hand. One particularly well-executed marble bust arrested her attention. The subject was not so fine, but the artist had been. The face of it was so lifelike, even to the delicate veins that stood out on the temples, that Eden imagined the stone flesh would be warm. She extended her fingers to touch the brow. It was cold. She was absorbed in tracing the features with her fingers when a shadow fell across the statue. Eden drew in a sharp breath and turned around. The earl stood close behind her, grinning down at her.

"Don't stop on my account," he said. "Knowing the history of my great uncle there, he's probably enjoying it."

The embarrassment at being discovered and her fear of the earl kept her from finding any humor in his address. "I'm sorry. It looked so real, I thought to find a pulse in this vein."

Lord Edmund chuckled, "Lord, I hope not. He has only a quarter of his body there." When the governess only looked at him, he continued, "Please, don't apologize. I took you unawares. Snuck up on you actually. Thought you were a thief. I'm usually the only one who wanders these halls at night. I'm gratified to have someone appreciate the sculptures. Most of the visitors here give the hangings and art pieces no more notice than the walls. The artist who sculpted that one was a student of Grindling Gibbons. Do you fancy yourself a sculptress as well?"

He did use that phrase, even after viewing her work. He knows art, and does not think much of mine, she thought. "I've not had the opportunity, but I would like to try my hand at it once in my life," she answered. "I noticed several books on sculpting techniques in your library. Are you interested in sculpting?"

"No. The sketches you showed me this morning - they are of your family?"

Eden nodded, "Convenient and inexpensive models."

"Your entire family?"

"All except my oldest brother who has been in service these past three years. My mother had the only sketch he would sit still for long enough framed."

"Where is he stationed?"

"Lyme. He expects to set sail for Portugal in the next few days."

"His detachment is?"

"He is a captain in the third Hussars?"

"A captain? His name?"

"Matthew. You speak as if you might know him."

"No, I have not that pleasure. Merely curious."

"I would not have believed I would miss my family so soon. This is the first night I have ever spent without them about me. The first night since she was born that I will sleep without my sister Mary beside me. Everything seems so strange, like a dream."

"You are blessed with a large family; you cannot have much experience of loneliness."

"Actually, one can feel quite alone in a crowd of people."

"True."

His steady serious gaze was unnerving to Eden. He had turned the conversation deeper and more intimate than she would have expected between a servant and her employer. It seemed he had nothing more to say; yet they were both averse to leaving it at that, so she continued for him, "However, for me, there is a cure for loneliness, and that is solitude."

"One can quickly tire of that. Especially if it is forced upon one."

Eden could feel her heart beating in her throat. The skin about her neck and jaw had tightened. She was afraid she was blushing. He made her feel extremely uncomfortable, but why? They were only talking, but what did he mean speaking of loneliness and solitude and standing so close that he towered over her? She said, "Until today, my only experience of solitude has been in searching for it."

"In that case you will find all that you want of it. So much of it exists in this place," he said abstractedly. Then he drew breath and shook off his mood. "You have been in the schoolroom?" he asked.

Eden nodded.

"How do you find it? Is anything wanting?"

"Nothing I can think of at this time. It seems you've provided enough material for a century of schooling. I've written my plans as you asked; I can begin tomorrow."

"Diana has been informed to be in the schoolroom at ten. Three hours of instruction should be sufficient unless and until you deem more time necessary. Make yourself available to my sister for some outdoor exercise each day as the weather permits. If any problems arise which you feel should be brought to my attention, please do not hesitate to do so."

"Thank you for your concern. You've been most thorough."

But Eden felt her hopes for a good working experience shrink and constrict her stomach as he continued, "Miss Barrett, you have been in my household a single day, and you have been warned not to preach, yet after I returned this evening, Diana imparted a few maxims evidently learned from your lips at supper."

Eden turned those enormous brown orbs of hers up at him in amazement. A shadow of blue outlined his cheeks where his beard would grow if he would allow it. Eden's portraitist's eye absorbed the hue and texture of the flesh, unconsciously storing the visual information for further use. Then she realized she was staring and blurted out, "I was merely replying to Miss Warren…"

He interrupted, "I can imagine. From this point on, I prefer that Diana and you take your meals in the family dining hall." He smiled, "At least you told her I was wise. I'll walk you to your room."

"No, please. I can find my way."

"Then I take your leave. Good evening, Miss Barrett."

"My lord."

Eden walked away without looking back lest he be watching her. He was a mystery to her. His tone had changed from cordial to moody to formal and back again. Now she was in his employ, he was trying to maintain a professional attitude. That must be it.

CHAPTER IV

In the morning, Diana came to Eden's room to go down to breakfast with her. As they walked downstairs, the girl kept up a steady stream of conversation. Yesterday, Eden had judged her a quiet, reserve sort of child. Today she was extremely animated. Perhaps her moods were as mercurial as her brother's.

"Colin tells me I must eat with you now in family rooms. He said he won't be able to see your plans this morning. He had to ride out with Mr. Grey. He's our agent. Then he's riding over to Bath. There are some purchases to make.

"That's what he told me, but I know it is to see Miss Bradley. They're secretly engaged. My brother has to wait until our year of mourning is over before he announces it though - the engagement, I mean. Cassy is very beautiful and has the dearest disposition. They have been sweethearts since childhood. We always have such fun when her family visits. They are usually in London, but her mother wished to take the waters for her aching knees."

The breakfast room was bright and airy. Decorated in lemon yellow and lime green, it was fitted along one wall with French doors that let in the sun beautifully. The day was bright. Eden and Diana filled their plates from the chafing dishes on the sideboard. They had eaten only a few bites when the house was filled with blood-curdling screams.

Eden sprang from her seat and raced down the hall in the direction of the cries. They seemed to come from the music room. She threw open the door. The furniture, floor, and walls were draped in white sheets. In the center of the room stood two sooty black figures. A wiry little man was viciously cuffing the ears of a boy not much smaller than himself. The boy offered no resistance except to cover his ears and cringe and howl.

Too many times on rounds with her father, Eden had seen the victims of child abuse and neglect. Too many times she had wanted to throttle the guilty persons, but it was accepted as a parent's right, however unfortunate. Something snapped. She ran to the man and grasped the back of his collar and tugged with all her might. She was amazed that she was able to drag him half way across the room, shouting in his ear at the same time, "Stop that this instant!" The room began to fill with servants from the hall. Nathan grasped the man's arm, though he was not sure why.

"'Ere. Get awf me! What's awl this fuss about? 'Oo do you fink you are? Oi ain't done nuffin' wrong!" the sooty little man squealed in a surprisingly high pitched voice.

Eden let go and came around to the front of the man to glare at his face. It was lined deeply, the coal dust gathered in the creases causing him to look like a cartoon. From his voice, she had thought he might also be a boy. "Just what can that child have done to deserve such a beating?"

"Ain't no business o' yourn."

"Throw him out," Eden commanded.

"Woit a minute. Oi were teachin' 'im a lesson. 'E weren't moindin' me. 'Spare the rod and spoil the child' the Bible says."

"Dear God, may I never hear that passage quoted by people like you again in my lifetime! Pick up your gear and get out of here!" Eden commanded.

The sweep turned to Mr. York, "Cawn she do that?"

Eden threw Mr. York a warning glance. Mrs. York's mouth flew open, but her husband nodded.

"I certainly can! I am in charge here," Eden lied.

Because of her cultured accent, the sweep believed her bluff. She might be the mistress of the house for all he knew, though her clothes were not as fine as he would expect. He began to coil a long rope as he grumbled loudly about interfering women and disobedient children.

Eden went to the boy. "Are you alright?" She received a meek affirmative nod, though he continued to hold one ear, and tears streaked through the soot on his pain-distorted face.

"He told me to pin Little Tom, and I couldn't. He's so little, and he's just scared like I used to be," the boy said.

"Who is scared? Who's Little Tom?" Eden asked.

The boy pointed to the fireplace. The end of the rope the sweep was coiling led up into the chimney. Eden called out, "Come on down, Little Tom. You're safe now. No one will hurt you."

Presently the grimy bare feet, then the legs, then the torso, and finally, all of Little Tom appeared. He could not have been older than five.

"Why is there a rope tied about him?" Eden asked the sweep, quickly grasping the knot around the child's waist at the same time and attempting to untie it. She was beginning to get irritated at the servants, who said nothing and looked at her as if she was the one who was out of order. In fact, most of them had trickled back to their meals or work. Mr. and Mrs. York and Nathan remained close to her, with Diana lingering near the door.

The sweep refused to answer, so Nathan explained. "It's in case the boy gets stuck, ma'am. The sweep 'd give the rope a tug, and..."

"Good Lord," Eden interrupted. Then turning to the older boy, "What do you mean you were supposed to pin him?"

He bent and retrieved a large upholsterer's needle from the floor. "I was supposed to stick this in his feet to make him go up higher."

The sweep had placed most of his tools of the trade in or around one large bucket. "Look Lady, pinnin's what we do wif new boys. They's moi wards all legal like. Oi laid out eight guineas a piece for these boys, oi did."

"You may have damaged that boy's ears for life by boxing them that way! Heaven knows what damage you have wrought upon their psyches."

The sweep looked shocked at what she said. "Oi never touched their sikees. What do you toike me for? Me old master cuffed me ears a hunert times when I deserved it, an' Oi ain't deaf now am I?"

"By some miracle. But he certainly knocked some sense out of you," Eden said, knowing she was wasting her breath.

"Look, Oi'm doin' 'im a favor; makin' a man of 'im. Cawn't have no fraidy cats."

"Fraidy cat! How dare you call him that! How much of a man can you be, sending a boy to do a man's work and sticking pins in him when he hesitates?"

Mrs. York spoke up, "Miss Barrett, pinning's not so bad. I've known sweeps as would light a fire under the tyke."

"Please, Mrs. York, you'll give the man ideas!" To the sweep, Eden said, "I won't stand for it. Your services will never be needed here. And I'd leave the neighborhood if I were you. I intend to alert the neighbors as well."

The sweep had been tying the ropes and long brushes upon his back, but when Mrs. York had mentioned Eden's surname, he looked up at the governess. "Barrett are ye? Any kin to Vicar Barrett of Longacre?"

"I am his eldest daughter. You knew him?"

The sweep's splotched charcoal-lined face curled into a sneer. The fingers of one hand went absently to scratch at an inflamed sore. "Me an' the good Vicar goes a long way back. 'E did me quoite a favor wonst. Got me moi very first job too," he told her in a slow snide drawl. His black eyes gleamed. He thought, *So, the son-of-a-bitch's bitch lives here. What fun.* "What about me pay?" he asked.

"I'll settle here and now," said Mr. York, reaching into his waistcoat pocket for the coins.

The sweep took the money and called over his shoulder, "Come on."

The boys started to move. Eden placed herself between them and the sweep, "You boys are staying here."

The sweep turned and flew at her, but seeing the two men move toward him, he chose words above action. "Here that ain't legal!" he screeched at her. "Oi' laid out good blunt for 'em. Saved 'em from flash house Oi did. Oive got uvver jobs. Oi needs 'em. Oi ain't broke no law."

"The magistrate will be sent for immediately, and we will see if we can discover a law you have broken," Eden answered. "They've no shoes or warm clothes, and they're underfed. Surely there is some law against that."

"Oi ain't scared of no magistrate. Oi knows me rights. Oi'll 'ave im pop you in goal, oi will, for stealing me climbin' boys."

"You may wait for the magistrate outside," Eden told him.

The sweep glanced at Nathan and Mr. York, both of whom looked as if they would throw him out bodily if need be. He chose to walk out backwards, hissing at Eden, "You ain't 'eard the last uv me. Oi'll get me boys back, an' you'll get what's comin' to ya, on me muvver's grave, you will."

When Nathan and Mr. York had safely escorted the man out of the house, Eden turned to Mrs. York for help as to what to do next. Mrs. York greeted her with contempt. "Never have I seen a more impudent action or person in all my days! What can you be thinking of? You have no authority whatsoever. What'll His Lordship say? Who gave you the right to order people about? Now who's going to clean the chimney? His Lordship asked especially that it be done. He's to have an assembly."

"Begging your pardon, ma'am," the older child ventured, "The chimney is clean as a whistle. Mr. Crane just thought to give Tom some practice and pass some time so you'd pay what you agreed on."

Undaunted, Eden asked Mrs. York, "Could you get them something to eat and drink, while I get them cleaned up?"

"I'll not be waiting on the likes of them. And they'll not be bedding down anywhere inside this house without His Lordship's express permission, Miss Sanctimonious," the housekeeper said, turned her back, and left.

So shocked was she at the housekeeper's retort, Eden could say nothing for several minutes, but there were children present, including her newest charge, and she must set an example. She mustered a smile and told the boys, "Don't worry about her. Her bark is worse than her bite. Let's get washed up first and see what you look like under all that soot."

She led them out to the stables where yesterday she had seen a water trough for the cattle. Diana followed at a distance. The trough had a water pipe rigged up over it that tapped into a reservoir fed by the rain from the roof. Eden turned the cock to let more water flow in and told the boys to wash their hands, faces, and hair as best they could. As the older boy removed his hand from his ear, Eden saw traces of blood.

"Water's freezin'," Little Tom whined.

"Quiet," the older boy warned his under his breath.

A slender, deliberate-moving man of mid-height came out of the tack room. It was hard to pinpoint his age. His hazel eyes were circled with laugh lines; his dark hair was peppered with gray. His frame was tightly muscled; his skin leathery and deeply tanned, even now in winter. Two deep furrows ran from cheek to chin on each side, dug from constant repression of grins.

The man looked at the boys a moment, then turned around and went back into the tack room. When he came out again, he was carrying towels and soap. He ambled over to the boys. "What have we here? Two sticks a charcoal?" he asked fondly. "Think these might be of any help?"

The boys took the gifts and set to work. Eden beckoned the man out of hearing distance. "I'm Eden Barrett, the new governess for Lady Diana. Do you think, perhaps the boys could make a pallet of hay in the loft somewhere for a few nights?"

"No problem at all, Miss. They can sleep in my room. Name's Stagg... Patrick. Head groom. Wouldn't mind a bit of company. No room in the house?" he asked skeptically.

"Not until His Lordship's return. Mrs. York...well... Could you arrange a warm bath for them in your room then?"

"Done."

"I'll take them in and find them something to eat first, and then bring them out to you. Do you know what a flash house is?"

Patrick gave her a dark look before saying, "Aye, Miss. These boys come from one of them?"

"That's what the sweep said."

Eden went back to the boys and applied the soap to their close-cropped hair, something they had been avoiding. When they were as clean as she could get them without a whole bath, Eden found that their knees and elbows were badly scabbed and various scratches and bruises covered their bodies from climbing in the chimneys. The oldest boy had already begun to walk a little hunched over and with a bowed gait. His eyes were inflamed, and he had a nagging dry wheeze. Both boys' heads were infested with fleas and lice.

Patrick had adopted a proprietary attitude toward them. He secretly assured Eden that he knew just the recipe to take care of the crawlers in their hair. He would mix it up while they ate.

Eden led her new charges into the servants' hall and sat them at the long dining table. Then, she went in search of food. Mrs. York greeted her with, "Well, if it isn't Miss High and Mighty herself, Miss Holier-Than-Thou."

Eden subdued her voice to answer, "Accuse me of what you will, Mrs. York. Only give me something substantial to feed those scarecrows in there."

"You won't be ordering me about as well, young lady."

"No, I'll find something myself."

"Not in my kitchen, you won't."

"Whose kitchen?" Eden asked as she took the silver cover off the wooden biscuit tub and heaped the contents onto a tray. "You didn't truly expect me to stand there and allow the man to continue to beat the child did you?"

"As I see it, it's his concern what he does with the boy. What would the world be if some outsider cut in every time a body went to punish a child? Maybe he were a bit rough, but the boy's nigh grown. Maybe it takes a lot to get him to mind. 'Spare the rod and spoil the child' is what the Good Book says. Are you disputing the bible?"

"'Thou shalt not kill' is also in the Bible, and I believe it takes precedence."

"Oh, he weren't killing the lad."

"You can kill more than just the body, Mrs. York. You can kill the spirit. And the rod it speaks of in the Bible is the rod of correction, and you can correct a child with love instead of blows. Does it not also say, 'Thy rod and Thy staff, they comfort me'?"

The housekeeper ladled a portion of boiled beef and cabbage into two pewter bowls, and put them on the tray. Then she poured out two mugs of cool milk, but her eyes remained narrowed.

"Thank you," Eden said. "One more thing. Are there any clothes that we could fit them with? From the smell of theirs, I doubt they've changed their rags in half a year."

"Briggs is got a boy away at school. He might have some of his old clothes around," she grumbled.

"Thank you again," Eden said with sincerity. She then retreated to the servants' dining hall and placed the food in front of the boys. They stuck an elbow on each side of their meals and hunched over the bowls as they set to, as if afraid someone might come along and snatch the food away.

"Do you think you can find your way back to the stables after you've eaten?" the governess asked. Mouths full, the boys nodded. "The man you met there is Mr. Stagg. You'll be sharing his room for a while. Perhaps he can find something for you to do to help him. Ask him to speak to Mr. Briggs about some shoes and clothes for you. I'm the governess, Miss Barrett. I need to go to work now. I'll look in on you later. Don't worry, you're quite safe here."

As she mounted the stairs with Diana still tagging behind, Eden prayed silently, *Father God, how can I help children like them have a voice? Show me a way. And help me not to judge. Help me to condemn the deed and not the man. Only you know the circumstances of his life, what made him the way he is. Take this situation and turn it for good. Father, comfort those boys; protect them. Help them to grow straight and tall in spirit and not be disfigured by their awful experiences. And, Father, bless Mrs. York. Help me not to judge her. And if I really am a "holier-than-thou," help me not to be. Let me show righteous indignation without being self-righteous.*

As she reached the second landing, Eden felt herself begin to tremble. She swiftly turned around and told Diana to go up to the schoolroom and wait for her. Then she walked to her room and plopped down on the bed. She had to grab onto her arms and bend over to control the shaking. What was wrong with her? She'd seen her mother shake this way after childbirth, but she had done nothing so physically draining herself.

She realized it was the emotional drain she had undergone these past few days that was affecting her: a strange new household, a shift in the social order, a disapproving new master, arguments with the sweep and the housekeeper, those poor boys, and what must her new charge think of her? All of these things assailed her, vying for their place in her consciousness. What would the earl say when he heard what she had done? Pack up and get out? Would the boys be given back? And the sweep. He said he knew her father, but his eyes had burned with such evil when he said it, as if he hated the man. How could anyone possibly hate such a gentle man who had given his life and all that he had to help his parish?

Eden sat upright and took a series of deep breaths to calm herself. She was nervous enough about teaching this new pupil. She must put on a front. Children knew a weak adult like dogs knew a frightened rabbit with the same result: attack. She must be strong and sure of herself, in control. At last she felt ready to go to work at Chadilane.

CHAPTER V

Diana had a mind like a sponge. Her vocabulary was precocious. The morning's excitement had not shocked the child or given her a disgust of her teacher as Eden had feared, but had raised the governess to a level of heroine in the child's eyes.

Eden was again struck by the fact that Diana was a very quiet child, not intimidated, just naturally silent. She listened intently, answered astutely when questioned, and asked questions when she did not understand; but she exhibited no signs of being the rattletrap she had been at breakfast. It was as if she had two personalities.

After dinner, Eden and Diana went out to the stables and found the boys much changed in appearance. They were dressed in clean warm clothes. Shoes had been found to fit both of them. As Eden and Diana approached, Patrick was showing the boys how to clean a horse's hoof with a metal pick. The acrid smell of manure was present, but not overpowering. The stables were extremely clean. Patrick greeted them and took them to feed Diana's pony.

Later in the day, as Eden went over the lessons Diana had written, Nora brought a message that His Lordship was available to see her. She was to bring her report. Eden took that as a positive sign. She would not need to show him her lesson plans if she was to be turned off without a character. She wondered at the rapidity of his return from Bath, but the thought left her as quickly as it came, for Nora was waiting for Eden to get her papers. Once she was ready, Nora led her to the back of the manor to the estate office. The aroma of fresh coffee greeted them as the door was opened. Colin sat behind a huge mahogany desk with an enormous ledger in front of him. Behind the earl a medium-sized, middle-aged, harmless-looking man stood indicating with his index finger something in the book. Colin looked up immediately when Eden entered.

He stood and came around to the front of the desk.

"Miss Barrett, this is Mr. Grey, our estate agent," he said. When the governess and agent had nodded to each other, Colin said, "You may go, Grey. Give my regards to your mother. Ask her if there is anything she needs. Tell her I will be down to see her tomorrow morning to find out how you are treating her."

The agent smiled, said, "Thank you, my lord," and left, almost closing the door behind him, but he caught the earl's eye and his almost imperceptible turn of the head to negate the action. He left it ajar. Colin indicated a chair for Eden and reseated himself behind his desk. His expression was serious. Eden thought he looked tired. She remained standing. "You've been told of my actions regarding the sweep?"

"I have."

"Mrs. York?"

He nodded.

"There are two sides to every issue."

"I'm well aware of that. It is precisely why I am hearing your side now."

"Actually, Mrs. York's account is probably accurate enough; I would not bore you with repetition."

"I'll let you know when you are boring me."

"I lost my temper and my control, and I am ashamed of myself for it. I simply could not allow it to happen, or see those boys forced to go back with him into that life. And Mrs. York practically condoned the sweep's actions, and... I mean, a child being beat about the head..."

"You lose your temper easily, Miss Barrett. I suggest you find it immediately."

How dare he lecture me! Right or not. She swallowed her pride. "I'm usually more tolerant..."

He, as had begun to be a habit between them, interrupted her, "Though we may be in legal difficulties if your sweep is sharp enough, I can understand your actions. It will be handled, but I need one thing from you. Patch it up between you and Mrs. York. I will not stand to suffer for your sins."

Incredulous, Eden's eyes caught his. "You suffer?" she said with a greater tone of astonishment than she would have allowed had she known what her voice would sound like before she spoke.

His brows rose, and just one corner of his mouth curled in the mildest hint of a smile. "Most assuredly. Not so much as a charred roast, but as long as Mrs. York is miffed, I will suffer for it: a little too much salt in the stew, the eggs a tad runny, the potatoes cold. We are conducting this interview in the office because Mrs. York saw fit to oversee the turpentining of the desk in my study. That is never done while I am in residence. The fumes will last several days. When you see her, choose your words carefully; be sure to include 'my fault', 'very sorry', 'forgive me', and 'never again' among them."

Eden chuckled. So his housekeeper bullies him. And he does not mind letting me know it. "Yes, my lord," she said with feigned subservience and a scullery maid's bobbed curtsey, but a knowing smile.

Colin held out his hand. "Your notes please."

Eden placed her written plans in his hand, and took a seat. He gave them a studied perusal, and said, "Satisfactory; more than satisfactory." He put the notes down, an elbow on his desk, and his fingers to his eyes, as if they ached. "I'd like you to find Mrs. Sebastion. She is our seamstress. Nora will take you to her. She'll show you what bolts of cloth there are on the estate. If nothing serves, order what you need from Madame Lacroix this evening. She is coming from Bath to take Diana's measurements and yours. You said that you sew. I would like you to choose for yourself some patterns for new morning dresses, and a riding habit that Mrs. Sebastion and you can make up.

"Madame Lacroix will make an evening gown for you and any other fripperies you might need. She can have four or five girls working on it and have it ready by Saturday. I will be holding a musical evening then before I leave for London. You will attend with Diana. Are there any questions?"

Eden was shocked. "Is that customary, my lord? Providing an evening gown?"

"I supply all my staff's uniforms and clothing. You will be required to attend functions with Diana; therefore, I will dress you for them. Everything about you, of course, will be a reflection on me." He dismissed the subject by rising and walking over to the silver coffee service. "Coffee, Miss Barrett? You pour."

Thus ordered, Eden promptly rose and poured the steaming brew. He took his coffee black, he informed her. He held his cup and watched amused as Eden disguised the contents of her cup with three lumps of sugar and copious amounts of cream.

"I see you take coffee in your cream," he observed.

She thought he stood uncomfortably close. "It is how our mother taught us to like coffee. I never cared to take it any stronger."

He smiled with his eyes. "As I suspected. You've not matured in some ways."

She looked up and felt a constriction in her throat. *What did he mean by that remark? Then again, I may not want to know. It's obvious he doesn't approve of me; he thinks me foolish. He's laughing at me. I wish he'd hurry up and go off to London and leave me alone.* She glanced around the room. Tension increased with each silent second.

"You do not ask me to explain myself," he said.

"I'm not sure I want to know. It wasn't politic of you to say it in the first place," she said.

"Perhaps not, but one who cared less would say nothing. You are rather forward speaking, you know, like a child who doesn't know to guard her tongue. My sister does not need to have that particular attribute strengthened, and she will take her cues from you if you come to be the friends I believe you will."

"Ah, I have to agree with you on that. I'm the oldest in my family and used to telling all my siblings what to do. Taking orders is not natural to me, while giving orders is."

"Convenient for a governess," he said.

The wall opposite her was hung with a map of the district. Each farm, cottage, and shop on estate land was clearly indicated. On the far side of the room was a small fireplace, unlit. Above it were two portraits. One was obviously of his mother. The same clear-colored eyes ringed with curling raven lashes gazed at her from the canvas. Eden took a few steps toward it - a few steps away from him.

"I must admire this portrait. It is of your mother?"

"It is," he affirmed quietly.

"It's singular in its execution. A brooding sort of style, allowing the background and garments to be reduced to a haze, rendering them secondary. Too many portraits seem so busy because the artist gives the scenery as well as the subject equal importance. The treatment of light is amazing, it almost makes her look... ethereal." He said nothing, so she continued. "The artist was obviously intrigued by her eyes and hair, both of which you have inherited. It seems the sons most often inherit the long, thick, dark, curling lashes that the daughters would have preferred for themselves. Your nose and ears also favor hers. This is your father?"

"Yes," he said dully.

"Younger than when I met him. From him, you inherited the strong line of your jaw, the cleft in your chin, and of course your height. Your mouth..." She looked up at those sculpted lips and swallowed. Looking back at the portraits, she shrugged. "Your mouth is your own. I cannot discover whom Diana looks like. Perhaps in a few years... Your mother was a handsome woman."

"She was," he said. Colin could not imagine when his sister's new governess had lifted her eyes from the carpet long enough to recognize so many of his features. The thought that she had done so was somehow gratifying. He supposed that a person had to be a quick study to be an artist.

"My lord."

"Miss Barrett?"

"When you sit in The Lords, could you make a motion that children below a certain age, say ten, might not be forced to work all day; might not be apprenticed..."

"I could make a motion until Hades freezes on that one. With the House as it stands now, it won't pass."

"How can you say that without trying?"

"Similar motions have been tried since I entered politics. No one has the kind of power you seem to think I have, not even the king. You have a child's view of Parliament. It is more complicated than that."

"You could choose the right day and change the House."

"What?"

"You could poll the members at parties; see how they stand. Keep a list. Compare it with those in attendance each day. When more are attending who would vote for the motion than not, present it."

Humor glimmered in his eyes. "You have it all worked out, have you?"

"Just an idea. You might even try stuffing the House by warning those who would be for the motion to be there on the day you intend to present it."

"It won't work."

"Why not?"

"It's been done when the question was more closely debated. The opposition on that particular question is too great. Child labor is cheaper than slave labor. Too many people stand to lose too much money if it's limited the way you suggest."

"Try it anyway."

"Good Lord, woman! What did that vicar feed you for dinner: gall or mule meat?"

"Both."

He laughed. "And where did you learn politics?"

"I read. Somewhere I read that all that is necessary for evil to prevail is for good men to do nothing."

"Are you now accusing me of doing nothing?"

"I didn't mean it that way."

"The devil you didn't! How else could one take it? You may go, Miss Barrett." Eden set her cup down on the silver tray and walked to the door. She could not resist stopping to turn with an impish gleam in her eyes and saying, "At least I accounted you a good man."

"Out!" he shouted, and Eden scurried away.

For a long time Colin stared at the portal where he had last seen her. A sappy grin had invaded his face. He was wondering how one person could look so innocent and trusting and knowing and glowing and mulish and naughty at the same time. When the picture finally faded, he summoned Connors and told him, "Bring those boys to me now."

CHAPTER VI

When Daniel and Thomas arrived at the office, Colin shook their hands and offered them hot chocolate, speaking to them as to any peer. He asked them to take a seat, and attempted to put them at their ease by asking with a smile, "Patrick is not working you too hard, is he?"

The boys shook their heads gravely.

"Are your quarters comfortable?"

Daniel nodded his head; Thomas followed suit.

"You can speak, can you not?"

Daniel answered, "Yes, Sir." Thomas nodded.

Colin directed his remaining questions to Daniel. "Patrick tells me you like the horses a great deal, even seem to be a natural around them."

"Yes, Sir. Lived around them all my life, Sir."

"I'm not a stickler about this; but, for future reference, the proper way to address an earl is 'my lord'."

The boy nodded.

"I am told that you say that Thomas's parents have died, but that yours are still alive."

"Yes, Sir, my lord, Sir."

"Patrick is pleased with the way you conduct yourselves. He says you listen well and work hard."

The boy had no answer.

"I'll tell you why I asked to speak with you. If I can get an idea of where you came from, perhaps I can put you in touch with one of your relatives."

"You don't want us here," Daniel said matter-of-factly.

"Nothing of the kind. I merely thought you would be pleased at the possibility of contacting your family."

Daniel stared in disbelief.

"What were your parents' names?"

"Momma and Papa."

"You don't remember anyone calling them by their Surnames, Mr. or Mrs. Something?"

"The staff called them my lord and my lady."

"Well, that narrows it down considerably. Can you remember anything they took you to see? Did you visit some ruins, a shipyard, a coal or tin mine? I need something which could give me an idea of where your home was located."

"The ocean. Nanny took me to the park by the ocean. It was my favorite spot. She pushed baby in the pram, and I walked."

"Very good. If you were able to walk to the ocean, we have already begun to pinpoint your residence. Can you remember any relatives or anything particular about the house?"

"It was white with three floors. I had a rocking horse with a mane and tail of real horsehair. I had boats to sail in the lily pond. Poppa had a pipe that smelled real good. He liked to play chess. He sat in front of the chess set a long time before he moved a man. The pieces were made of the same stone as that statue." The boy indicated an alabaster figurine on a side table. "Poppa said there was only one of its kind, and it would be mine when I grew up. That's why I asked Mr. Stagg to teach me how to play the game."

"This is all very helpful. Patrick said you told him there was a fox hunt on your grounds."

"Not in the house by the ocean, but by the downs. That's where Poppa kept his stables of hunters. He said I must not come up to a horse from behind, or it might kick me."

"How did you happen to... go to work for Mr. ... the sweep who employed you?"

"Mr. Crane. First the pretty lady came. We were in the park and Nanny was playing with Baby. I threw a stick for Poppy, our dog, to fetch. She couldn't find where it went, so I went to help her. A pretty lady was sitting under a tree. She asked if I wanted a sweetie. She said she had a box of them in her carriage. I could have the whole box if I wanted. But when she opened the carriage door, she pushed me, and a man pulled me inside. The man held my mouth, and the carriage started going. The carriage drove a long time, then they let me sit up if I didn't cry. They drove to a campfire where there were Romanies with wagons. The man and the lady took me there. They told me not to run away or they would get Baby and throw her down a well. The gypsies rode each day and made a campfire at night. If the gypsy boys didn't tease me so much, it would have been fun, but I missed my Momma and Poppa.

"Then Mr. Crane came and bought me. I had to climb in the flues and shovel out the soot. I hated it. The soot got in my eyes. It got hot and hard to breathe. I scraped my hands and elbows and knees all the time. I will work very hard here. Please don't give me back to Mr. Crane. I like Mr. Stagg. He's funny."

"Is Mr. Crane a cruel man?"

"Sometimes. And he couldn't always get work. Then we didn't have food. He said we were his very own boys. He said he would leave us his business when he dies. I don't want his business. I am not his boy. I wish you really could find my parents. Please don't give me back to Mr. Crane."

"I don't intend to. I believe your story and will try to find your Momma and your Poppa or their relatives. I can't promise you I will find them, but I will try."

"Oh thank you, Sir, my lord, Sir. I haven't seen them in such a long time."

"That is quite alright. You may go now, but I may ask to see you again. See if you can remember any more details." Lord Edmund rose and saw his young friends to the door.

* * *

Six miles away, on the edge of Edmundton, Crane sat in a back corner booth in The Nagging Wife Pub. As he waited for his order of bubble and squeak, he toyed with his only memento of his run-away father, a bone-handled knife. He'd been paid today, but it wouldn't last forever. Without his boys, he'd have to find something else to do. He was too old now to do much climbing around in chimneys. Anyway, he'd soon have them back, and she'd get something to think about too. They were his boys. Who'd she think she was? Vicar Barrett's whelp was who. Would he ever get away from that man's grasp? Queer, meetin' her here, and her bossin' him around like that. "Bossy" was what the kids used to call her in Longacre. She must have been orderin' people about back then as well.

GENTLE JOURNEY

Crane set his knife down on the table and began to scratch at one of the scabs on his arm. If it hadn't been for that Vicar, he wouldn't be like this. He could have kids of his own. He liked kids. He would have gone to school. The teacher had thought he was real smart those few months he'd got to go to the private school before he had to go to work. He would have grown up straight and handsome. The ladies would of chased after him, like they did his dad. Now if the ladies ever knew of his condition, they would laugh at him and tease him as those boys did that day.

His mother had put all her trust in that stupid preacher. She said, "Don't worry, boy. The vicar'll help us. He's a holy man, and the Lord doth provide." She used to make him thank God for his food, even when the bread was moldy and the potatoes were half rotten.

When his mother's conscience bothered her so much that she confessed to the Vicar that she'd stolen some pastries from the Mowbray's kitchen, he had given her the penance of restitution. He said she must tell the housekeeper about it, and have her wages as laundress docked to make up the difference, or her sin wouldn't be forgiven. He said honesty might be the harder road, but it was the right road to reward. Her reward when she confessed to the housekeeper had been immediate unemployment without a reference.

"All things work for good for those who know the Lord," the vicar told Crane's mother. "When the Lord closes one door, he opens another." And when no one would give her work, the cleric had found a job chimney sweeping for her little boy. He said it was just temporary, but then his mother got sick and couldn't work anyhow. Crane picked up the knife and drew the blade slowly sideways across the scab on his arm. It collected a few fat drops of pus, which he wiped on his sleeve. How many times since then had he, in the midst of a job, envisioned stuffing the fat little vicar upside down in a chimney?

CHAPTER VII

After tea and after visiting Mrs. York with profuse apologies and visiting Mrs. Sebastion to look over the cloth in the sewing rooms, Eden went for a stroll with Diana. She firmly believed in an evening walk to stimulate the flow of blood and lift the spirits. The family doctor in Longacre had convinced her of this, and experience had taught her that she did feel invigorated after exercise. Rain had set in though, so they took their stroll in the long gallery and then gravitated to the orangerie, where Diana identified the specimens she could recognize, and Eden spied several views she thought would look perfect in watercolors. She decided to set up her easel there at her next moment free. Nora came to get them when Madame Lacroix arrived.

The dressmaker had an entourage composed of a manservant to carry the bolts of cloth and display them, and five girls to cut and do gross and fine needlework. After taking Diana's measurements and commenting on how much she had grown in just the last six months, the couturier brought out a series of sketches of evening wear for *jeune filles*. Diana wanted a red velvet design that Madame deftly steered her away from. "It would make you look plump, mademoiselle."

Then it was Eden's turn. She had not had a new dress since her seventeenth birthday, and that one she'd had no say in. It would have to be a heavy material, a practical color, and a classic design with little ornamentation she told the designer. A pattern was quickly agreed upon. It was an empire line with a slight scoop in the neckline and just a touch of lace at the hem of the sleeves and the neck. The sleeves were to be short and puffed slightly.

Madame tried to convince Eden to lower the neckline saying it was all the rage, but her pleading was to no avail. They also disagreed over color. Eden thought a brown or forest green would wear longer, clean easier, and be more apropos to her station. Madame thought a cream or peach would show her complexion to advantage and be more appropriate to her youth. They finally agreed upon a Clarence blue.

At supper, Eden and Diana ate in the family dining room with Colin. During the congenial conversation, Colin mentioned that he intended to compose an advertisement in which he would describe the circumstances of Daniel's abduction.

"You mean you don't think he's just telling tales?" his sister asked.

"His educated grammar and pronunciation as well as his manners tell me that his beginnings were of the gentry at least. He also provided certain specifics that have the ring of truth about them. Unfortunately he could not recall his surname. It would not hurt to make inquiries, and to that end, Miss Barrett, I have a commission for you."

Colin observed Eden as she drew her eyes, and then her face up, tilting it on that swan's neck to give her attention to him. How like royalty she could move. "If you will sketch Daniel's face for me, perhaps he greatly resembles one of his parents. I can take it to London with me and show it about the ton. Possibly, someone can identify him."

"Absolutely. Tomorrow, in fact," Eden answered. "My lord, I was thinking, while the boys are here, might they not also be schooled?"

Eden was proud that Colin felt no need to deliberate further before saying, "If Diana has no objections, I have none to them being added to the schoolroom, but the disparity of their skills may prove difficult for you."

"I am used to children of different ages and skill levels," she said.

Diana said, "It might be fun having classmates. What if I change my mind though and don't like them?"

Colin chuckled. "Then out they go. Nothing is set in stone. We shall see how you go on..."

Later, word was sent to Mr. Stagg to have the boys ready for instruction by the governess at ten the next day.

In the morning, as Eden entered the schoolroom, she was momentarily shocked. She found Daniel in the act of tying Diana's hands behind her back with a rope.

"What is the meaning of this?" Eden cried, moving purposefully toward the two.

Diana smiled brightly, "I told him to do it. I brought the rope. We have a bet. I can get out of any knots he ties in one minute."

Eden allowed it. When Daniel had finished tying the rope to his satisfaction, he stepped back. Almost instantly, Diana wriggled out of her bonds. When the governess and boys had expressed their surprise, Diana explained the trick. "I learned it in a book about the American Native. I've been dying to try it and it works. You see, when taken prisoner, the American Indians would swell their hands and wrists like this as the enemy tied them. Then when the enemy was not looking, they simply bring their wrists as close together as possible, then turn them this way, and shrink them like this. Then the rope is loose and you can twist right out."

The children were surprised when their teacher asked to try it, never giving up until she could also slip her wrists from the rope. Then Daniel and Thomas had to try it.

Eden was pleased to find that Daniel could already read well. In fact, he could never remember a time when he could not read. He had entertained Mr. Crane and later Little Thomas also by reading from the penny awful magazines that specialized in horror and murder stories. Mr. Crane would buy one every time they were paid for a job.

Little Tom knew how to write the letters 'A', 'O', and 'X'. Daniel had taught him that much with a lump of coal on a flat stone. Thomas looked up to Daniel as if he were a saint, looking for his approval before he so much as sneezed.

As the days progressed, Eden quickly came to love her three students as much as her own brothers and sisters. Daniel was intrigued with Eden's sketch of him and asked if he might have paper and charcoals too. He wanted to try drawing the horses.

All formal instruction ended at one o' clock, when the boys went back to Mr. Stagg for dinner, and Diana and Eden had a simple meal in Eden's sitting room or the family dining room. Then the governess and her charge amused themselves with exploring the house and grounds as Diana told Eden about the history of Chadilane. They often ended up in the stables or the conservatory where they discussed life, love, and happiness or their understanding of them until it was time for tea. Eden preferred that Diana have free reign to introduce the topics for discussion on these rambles, so any problems or misunderstandings that might be important to Diana could surface and be dealt with. Although they most often spoke of characters in books or whether to use a facial wash or not, it did seem there were an inordinate number of times when the child's mind took a morbid turn. She would wonder aloud what it felt like to be dead, what exactly happened to the body after it was buried, if it hurt to die, or if it was possible for a physician to pronounce a person dead when he was only in a dead faint.

Eden treated all such questions as normal and natural. She chose her words carefully, showing neither shock nor disgust for any topic and not afraid to admit not knowing the answers to all things. Though Diana did not mention her father, Eden supposed he was not far from the girl's thoughts, his death having taken place only a few months before. One late afternoon as they strolled among the luxuriant foliage - some species blooming early in the artificial atmosphere - Diana plucked a withered brown blossom from a gardenia bush, twirled it between her palms, brought it to her nose to inhale, then plucked the petals absent-mindedly and cast them in front of her.

"Do you believe in hell?" she asked in an off-hand manner.

"I do not like to think about it, but if I believe the Bible, I believe there is a hell. I do, though, believe it is not that easy to get there. What are your thoughts?"

"I burnt my hand badly once. It hurt for days. I don't think I could ever wish for anyone to burn forever and ever. No matter what they had done."

"Neither could I," Eden said. "Though there are references in the Bible to an everlasting fire, I cannot think it is a physical fire as we know it. A fire as we know it burns out, for one thing. But also, it is the body that feels pain, but the senses are lost when the body dies. It is the soul that is everlasting, and at the last judgment we are given our glorified body, which must be of a different composition. When Christ returned to earth in his glorified body, he walked through a wall. If His glorified body had been as our natural body is, that would have hurt, don't you think? And he disappeared at Emmaus. Can your present body disappear?"

"I wish."

Eden chuckled. "Have you ever heard of a 'burning shame', or 'burning' with anger, or envy, or hatred, or desire? If a soul is faced with the knowledge that it could have spent eternal bliss in the presence of the Creator, yet will never again have that hope because of its own stupidity and stubbornness, mightn't it burn with shame and desire, confusion and loss, and anger and self-hatred?"

"I never thought of that," Diana said. She plucked another gardenia blossom before going on. "How can God, who created us and is supposed to love us so much, send people to hell? He is supposed to be better than us. He is supposed to be merciful and forgive."

"God does all that he can to keep us from going there short of removing our free will, and it is we who don't forgive ourselves. I think souls go to hell because they dare not approach Heaven in their guilty state. They are too ashamed. They send themselves to hell."

"God didn't even have to create the place. Wouldn't it take an evil mind to create such an evil place?"

"God created hell as a place to send Satan and his followers after they disobeyed him. It is the presence of that evil creature that makes it a place of abomination. It is the absence of hope and the unforgiveness, hatred, and selfishness of the residents there that makes it a den of everlasting despair and fear. Just imagine yourself locked forever in a room full of hateful, cruel, self-centered people, and you'll have an idea of what hell is like. Of course these are only my thoughts on the question. We can only know for certain in the next life. I'm convinced too that there are a lot fewer people in hell than the human race suspects. It's Christ who judges, and He suffered and died to save us from our sins and thus from hell. You see, he knows more about us than we do. When Christ judges, he takes into consideration each person's circumstances: his understanding, his experiences, his opportunities. We must leave judgment to Him. I certainly would not presume to say - from my vantage point - that any particular person has gone to hell. No matter what he has done."

After this conversation, Diana did not bring up death again. Eden thought that possibly Diana had feared her Father might be roasting in some eternal agony. She was glad if she had been able to console the child, but she was uneasy about how the earl would take it if he heard about what they had been discussing.

On Friday evening, Colin dined at home again. At table, he told

Diana and Eden that his gatekeeper had found a bony donkey eating at the bark on the trees along the highway. The keeper had thrown a loop around it and coaxed it to the stables. There, Daniel had identified it as belonging to the chimney sweep, Mr. Crane. It was now enjoying a warm mash and a clean stall. "I suppose he decided he could no longer feed the animal. No one has reported seeing this sweep, but there are so many vast, uninhabited areas around here, it would be easy to lose him. Hopefully he went to a city to find other employment."

Eden ventured, "I pray for his sake he is able to find a job." Then, she added, "It seems that Mr. Crane had met my father also and disapproved of him strongly. I don't understand how anyone could dislike my father. He was so loving and charismatic."

"A person in Vicar Barrett's position cannot be too careful in what he says and does. Your father wielded great influence over men's minds and lives. People of such power always manage to have some enemies. It is impossible to please everyone," Colin offered.

"I never thought of Poppa as a man of power, but you are right. So many came to him to ask him to help solve their problems and advise them. Do you truly recall him?"

"He stood in for our own parson several summer Sundays when ours was ill. He was a most convincing speaker: animated, which was a novelty for me at the time."

Eden caught his eyes with hers and asked coyly, "And did he influence you?"

Colin's eyes glazed over and his eyelids fell to half-mast. Not the reaction Eden had expected. "In truth, yes, he did influence me. But in the opposite way he intended, I am sure."

That piqued her interest. "What do you mean?"

This time he glared at her, "Your father helped turn me on the path of Atheism."

Eden could not have been more shocked if he had said her father had murdered a baby. "How so?" she asked.

"It was a long time ago, and I don't wish to discuss it." The earl abruptly turned the conversation to his vehement views on the necessity of repealing the Corn Laws to keep the poor from starving. Diana mentioned that she would like to see Cassy before her family removed to London as well, and Colin told her that they would dine at the Bradley's mansion on Sunday evening.

"You will see Cassy in town also, will you not?" Diana asked sweetly.

"Most certainly," her brother said.

"And will you escort her to routes and balls?"

"As many as she wishes."

"She has turned into a beautiful woman, has she not?"

"Truly beautiful, inside and out." His eyes gleamed with teasing, "You would do well to imitate her and quit your hoydenish ways."

"Then I should not be me."

"True, sister. And I would not like that."

* * *

The evening of the concert arrived. Madame Lacroix had completed the ball gown in the morning. Eden was delighted with the fit, style, and color of her dress. She felt positively regal in it. It was quite the finest dress she had ever owned. Though she took extra care styling her hair, she was no hairdresser. Diana's ladies' maid was adept at arranging hair and had done Diana's coiffure in a partly up and partly down combination with coiled braids. It was perfect, not too mature looking, yet special.

The concert was splendid. Eden had expected a local group, but the members of a full orchestra from London began to arrive at about noon. A bed was found for each member, for they would stay the night. In the evening, thousands of candles lit the main hall, the music room, and a room that had been set up for refreshments. Chairs had been brought from all over the house to accommodate the guests. Most who attended seemed to be cronies of the late earl. Chadilane had hosted musical evenings with some regularity for many years.

After Lady Diana and the earl greeted their guests formally in a line, His Lordship wandered among his guests congenially. They obviously genuinely liked him. Diana came to Eden and preferred to watch the proceedings from the perimeters of the room. An occasional person deigned to stop and speak condescendingly to Diana and nod to the governess when Diana introduced her.

The orchestra began to play at nine o'clock, and Diana was fast asleep on Eden's shoulder by ten. The strains of Haydn were the perfect lullaby. Eden eased the child into a standing position and walked her slowly up the stairs and to her room. Diana swayed groggily as Eden removed the girl's dress and then sat her on the bed. She removed Diana's shoes and let her crawl beneath the covers, never coming fully awake. Finally, she pulled out the pins in her hair that had held the braids coiled, but left the braids, bending to kiss the sleeping child.

Not caring to rejoin the group of strangers, but caring to hear the music, Eden went to her room and removed her gown. She dressed in a warm work-dress and wrapped an old cloak about herself. She went as inconspicuously as possible through the servant's hall to the terrace by the music room. The weather was atypically mild, so she sat down on one of the stone benches, fully prepared to watch the performance through the French windows.

At first she thought it was one of the many cats that roamed the gardens and stables. She ignored the slight sound of twigs breaking, concentrating on the music. Then, out of the corner of her eyes, she saw the dark figure and attempted to run, but it was too late.

With a single sudden movement, the man lunged and grasped Eden's forearm, yanking it behind her and twisting it high, forcing her back onto the bench. He stood over her, his face so close to hers that she could feel the stubble of his beard and smell his dinner. She felt a cold blade against her throat. "Now oo's the Boss, Missy? The one oo' 'olds the knoife, or the one who butts into uvver people's business?" Crane's strident boy's voice hissed in her ear.

Eden's thoughts raced, *Lord, help me to know how to act. He's not taller than me, nor even stronger; but I dare not struggle against the knife. Should I pretend to faint? Then, he may just leave me here.*

"Me boys are still 'ere. Oi seen 'em by the mews. Show me where they sleeps," he growled, tightening his hold and shaking her.

Eden sat frozen, unable to breathe.

"Move or Oi'll cut yer pretty face to red ribbons," he hissed.

Suddenly, Eden had a strong sense that all would be well. He sounded to her like a character in one of those penny murder stories Daniel had told them about. She tried to gather her composure so her voice would be calm. "You won't harm me," she said simply, and as she said it, she was even more certain that it was true. She was not alone in this; she had a protector. And He was there with her.

"Devil' oi won't. This ain't no butter knoife. Oi can end your little loife roit now if I loikes. But you'll be prayin' for death when Oi finishes wit' you. You fink you can order me about? You'll be beggin' me for mercy."

"There is Someone here who will stop you."

She could feel him twisting his neck to look about. "What kind a pea-brain do you toike me for? Move."

"You can't see Him, but He's there."

"Loidy, you're mad! I can't see 'im because there ain't no 'im, but this is real and it's right 'ere." He turned the knife so the point rested on the tip of her nose. "You can see that aright, an' if you don't lead me to me boys, you're gonna feel it real good too." Suddenly the sweep dropped the knife, shoved her aside, and dove into the shrubbery.

"Who the devil was that?" Patrick asked.

Eden was gasping. She couldn't take in enough air to make up for all the time spent holding her breath. She clutched her aching chest. Patrick took her shoulders and guided her towards a bench closer to the house. Eden sat and shivered. Patrick grew more alarmed. "My God, woman! What is it? Who was that?"

"The sweep."

"Crane?"

Eden nodded.

"He threw something on the ground. Do you know what?"

Eden finally caught her breath, but was having difficulty focusing on what she was hearing and seeing. She steeled herself and tried desperately to shake it off. When she thought she had control, she said, "A knife. He wants the boys. I don't know what he would have done if you hadn't come just then. Someone must guard the boys."

Patrick's face blanched. He pulled her into the light and scrutinized her neck and face. "Were you cut at all?" She shook her head, frightened anew by Patrick's fear. He called to Nathan, who was standing just inside the French windows. When the footman came out, Patrick told him, "Take Miss Barrett inside and give her some brandy. That sweep had a knife to her throat. I'm going to the chapel and sound the alarm. Then I'll rouse Daniel and Thomas and keep 'em by me. I saw him dodge into those hedgerows over there." When he'd finished speaking, Patrick took off running.

Nathan took Eden inside the house and sat her down in the hall. He found Joseph and told him to get the master. Joseph disappeared and soon reappeared with the earl. Nathan related what Patrick had told him. Colin glanced at Eden and then dug into his coattail pocket for his keys. He chose one particular key and placed that one in Nathan's hand.

The chapel bell could be heard over the music of the performers. The music stopped. Male servants began to assemble in the hall. "Follow Nathan for your weapons. He'll explain," Colin told his servants. "Stay here," he said to Eden, "I'll have to explain to my guests."

Eden was left alone in the hall, but not for long. Male servants armed with rifles ran past her. When Mr. York opened the entrance doors, Eden could see Mr. Sebastian, the gamekeeper, standing on the threshold with his two big bloodhounds. Nora came out with a glass of brandy for Eden. "His Lordship wants you to drink this, then for us both to go up to Diana's room and stay with her there and bolt the door. He says the man may try to slip into the house," Nora said.

On the ground floor, the guests seemed to think the situation was all very exciting and amusing. It initiated a number of lively discussions of encounters with highwaymen and poachers and previous manhunts the guests had been privileged to experience. Refreshments were put out early and the normally silent and staid group became a noisy, laughing crowd. As the evening wore on, the guests thinned out, but some stayed in hopes of seeing the scoundrel caught and dragged back to the house.

The local constabularies had been alerted and were also on the case. Cook felt it would be excusable if she turned in for the night since she had been up since five helping the baker prepare his special pastries for the feast. She trudged up to the fourth floor female servants' wing. As she entered the door to her cell, her candle revealed a glimpse of something odd in her cheval glass. "Dear me, I've forgot me warm milk," she said aloud as if to herself.

Cook calmly retraced her steps and roused Cathy, whose cell was next to hers. She whispered, "There's a man hiding behind my dressing screen. I saw his face in the mirror, but I don't think he knows I saw him. Go tell master and be quick about it. I'll stand here and watch my door. Hurry now!"

Cathy returned swiftly with Colin. The smithy and a gardener, who had both reported back to the house, were with him. The sweep gave himself up easily. He was unarmed. He said he was searching the servant's wing for his boys when he heard the bell and got scared. He thought he might be charged with trespassing, so he was simply hiding until all was quiet, and then he was going to slip out and leave as soon as he could.

The message circulated that the sweep was found. The sheriff arrived and carted him off. Chadilane settled itself down for the night. The master bid his servants sleep late in the morning as he fully intended to do so himself. Before he turned in, he meant to inform the occupants of his sister's bedchamber that the culprit was in custody and all was well.

A gentle rap on Diana's door brought Eden's quiet, "Who is there?"

For a moment, Colin wondered what to call himself to her. He settled on, "Edmund. We've found Crane. He's in custody. You're safe. You may go to your rooms if you like."

Eden opened the door, "My lord…"

He looked down at her briefly, then away: shaken, trying to control an unfamiliar turbulence of emotion. *If she had been hurt…*

"Is Patrick all right? He seemed so upset. So odd about the knife and looking for a cut, I wondered…"

"You think it unnatural he be upset about an attempted murder? I'm sure he was reminded of his wife, Cathleen."

"She was murdered?"

"Nothing so quick. She cut herself slightly on a knife she was sharpening. A rusty knife. She contracted lockjaw. Yes, I see by your expression you know of the convulsions she went through. They had been married only four months. For such a simple little thing to cause such …"

"I'm so sorry. This whole thing is my fault. If I hadn't…"

"Spilt milk, Miss Barrett. Leave it as it stands."

"Thank you, for everything. I think I'd best stay with Diana for tonight."

"I'll see you in the morning."

GENTLE JOURNEY

* * *

At eight in the morning, Eden was summoned to the estate office. She found Patrick there, as well as Mr. Grey, a constable, Mr. Smith, and Colin. The earl greeted her with, "You're looking more the thing this morning, Miss Barrett. The trial will be held in two days time. As luck would have it, the Assizes here take place this month. The outcome is a forgone conclusion. With your testimony and Patrick's and the knife we found, we'll have no problem putting your chimney sweep away for life… deported to Australia if you like."

"My testimony, my lord?" she asked with feigned innocence.

"Of course, your testimony. It was your life that was threatened."

"When was this?"

Vexation tinged his tone this time. "What game are you playing? You said… Patrick saw the man. He saw the knife to your throat. You were in extreme agitation when he questioned you. You told him your life had been threatened."

Eden looked all amazement, "Did I say that, Patrick? I don't… seem to recall…"

Patrick stammered and Colin interposed, "Miss Barrett, this is serious. Are you saying you won't testify against the man?"

"He could be hanged, or worse sent to prison. Half the men in prison die of 'goal fever'. Men are flogged and left to rot in filthy, over-crowded cells. Mr. Crane has no family to assure him of sufficient food or clothing while he's there. I can't be part of sentencing this man to that. It was my fault he was driven to such extremes."

"What has that to say to anything? Yes, the punishment is too great for some, but this is a grave offense. Would you have him set free to wander the area wielding his knife at innocent citizens? The man has become desperate; it was pure luck you escaped without harm."

Eden said quietly, "You call it luck; I call it Providence."

His Lordship was not so quiet, "Luck! And the next person may not be so lucky. I can't understand your attitude. How can you be so blasé about this?"

"Oh, I assure you, I was not calm last night. But enough time has passed to allow me to view the situation dispassionately. I believe Mr. Crane is not dangerous to others, and he meant only to frighten me."

"You believe! But you don't know!"

"He has never harmed anyone else this way. Daniel told me that Crane was usually kind enough. I wounded his pride. His argument is with me. It unsettled him last night when I wouldn't give in to fear. He didn't know how to act. He meant to punish me by frightening me - which he did. Something festers in his mind..."

"What a lot of swill you spew, Madame!"

"I know it to be true."

"How can you?"

"I just do."

"That's no answer! You're a stubborn, unreasonable, perverse and frustrating creature! Your ideas are not only ridiculous; they are dangerous!"

With great difficulty, Eden suppressed a smile at his description of her, but a dimple gave it away. Colin saw it and said, "I fail to see any humor in this. If no one was ever locked up..."

"I didn't say no one should be locked up. I simply said I would not have a hand in the punishment of this particular individual. His conscience punishes him enough."

"Don't speak such drivel to me. I'm not one of your innocents in awe of your every word. Dammit, woman, the man will be incarcerated. If you don't have the sense to care about your safety, I do. At least I'm responsible for it while you reside under my roof. Which may not be much longer. I can have him goaled on trespassing alone. Good day to you, Ma'am, though you most certainly have spoiled mine."

As Eden backed out of the room, wondering at his display of emotion, she encountered Mrs. York standing just outside the door. She had evidently been listening to the entire conversation, for she gave Eden a black look and walked away.

In the office, Colin turned to Constable Smith. "You know what to do, Sir. Thank you for coming." When Patrick and the officer left the room, Colin turned to Mr. Grey. "Advertise for another governess in the London papers. I'll see them in town. This one won't be around for long."

A little while later, as she sat in the schoolroom, Eden literally felt as well as heard the vibrations of someone abusing with a vengeance the pianoforte in the music room. Though he played furiously, he played well. She realized it was the earl redirecting his frustration into his music, and she knew she was the cause of that frustration.

CHAPTER VIII

Breakfast was uncomfortable for all. The earl spoke coolly, little, and only to Diana. Eden was too intimidated by his manner to speak. She realized she had wounded his pride by embarrassing him in front of his inferiors, she a mere servant arguing with the master in that way. In her thoughts, she composed several pretty apologies, but each time she tried to catch his eye, he would turn from her and speak to his sister, and the words would melt on her tongue and escape her mind. She knew enough of humanity to know not to attempt to discuss anything with an angry man. Though the meal looked delicious, Eden could taste none of it. At last, Colin turned to her and said in a clipped, but quiet manner, "I have a very busy schedule today, Miss Barrett. Diana will be with me most of the day. I would like to speak privately with you at, say, after tea in my office."

"Yes, my lord."

As that was to be the extent of their conversation in front of Diana, she excused herself as soon as possible and escaped to her room. Nora found her there and invited her to accompany a group of the servants who were going in to town to attend Sunday services. She grabbed a bonnet and gloves and went with her. They traveled to town in a long phaeton drawn by four matched sorrels.

Though she thought the sermon and its' delivery uninspired and verbose, Eden lingered to introduce herself to the parson, complement him on the points he had made, and offer such services as she might be able to render without interfering with the duties of her profession. Dr. Trumble surprised her by being ready with an immediate request. Mother Grey, the mother of the estate agent at Chadilane, was nearly blind with cataracts. She had done much sewing for the church before her affliction had grown too great. The parson wished Eden might visit her to read to her sometimes. The agent's cottage was within easy walking distance of the manor. The servants could show it to her on the way back. The parson lowered his voice as he explained that he was giving her this charge because she would have more free time than the rest of the staff at Chadilane, and he imagined that she read better than many of them.

On the way back, Eden had the staff drop her off outside the Grey's home. Nora also jumped down from the phaeton and knocked on the door of the pretty little wattle and daub cottage. "Mother Grey, are you up?" she called.

Mr. Grey came to the door. "Nora, Miss Barrett. What brings you two here?" he asked with a hint of impatience.

"Miss Barrett wished to meet your mother is all. Is she receiving today?"

"One moment." He ducked back inside and closed the door. Nora told the coachman to drive on; she would come home with Miss Barrett. Mr. Grey reappeared and let the ladies in. The roof was low, the sitting room dark. The furniture was well worn but comfortable looking. Embroidered linen draped each end table, protecting it from dust and scratches, or perhaps covering up ancient stains. Many knick-knacks embellished the cozy room. To the right of the room, a single log of timber stood vertically floor to ceiling as if to support a weak beam. Eden wondered at it, but did not get a chance to comment upon it. At the base of the beam was tied a scruffy mop of a dog which growled at Eden and wagged its tail at the same time.

"I'm on my way out," Mr. Grey said to Nora. "See to the tea and the fire."

Nora glared at his retreating figure a moment, but immediately picked up a small log and put it in the middle of the fire, then took a poker and stirred it.

In the center of the room sat Mother Grey. She looked like her name: a plain, well-lined face accustomed to smiles; the delicate, translucent skin of the aged; wonderful white hair done in braids and wound around her crown; a plump, shapeless sort of body.

She looked in the general direction of Eden and said, "You are Miss Barrett. I've heard all about you. I'm glad Lady Diana will have a governess again. It has relieved His Lordship's mind a great deal. He didn't like to take her to London. He says you can't trust the milk there. People put water and chalk in it among other things to cut the costs. Typhus and cholera are rampant there, and robberies, and riots, and fire. It's no place to raise a child.

"Tell Her Ladyship she must come and see me. I have missed her since her brother has been home. Have you come to read to me? Dr. Trumble told me he would find someone to read the Bible for me. My son has little time for me with all the estate business. I don't think he enjoys reading aloud on top of all the reading he must do to keep up with the times. Too much like work. There's tea on, and His Lordship brought honey by yesterday. You must take some if your voice gets tired. It's the best thing for it…"

Eden did get to say a few things to mother Grey, and she did read to her until her voice was tired. Nora hunted in the larder and fixed a meal for Mother Grey, while the other two women spoke. Then she sat and listened to Eden's vocal interpretation of Revelations. When they left, Eden promised Mother Grey that she would return within the next few days with Diana. Nora told Eden that if she did not wish to be a governess, she could make money on the stage. She had so enjoyed the governess' histrionics. She said it was better than going to a play.

The servants were busy with preparations for the earl's journey to London. A cold collation was served for dinner, which Eden took with Nurse Warren. Though the woman complained of many aches and pains and went into great, loving detail when describing the inner workings of her digestive system, she had an enormous appetite.

Finished with her meal, Eden took an apple from the assortment of fruit that had been piled on a platter for the two of them, and went to visit the stables. She found Patrick running a currycomb over Lord Edmund's big gray-white Hanoverian, which he said was named Galahad. The horse nickered and stomped a hoof at her coming. Patrick said he was greeting her. She offered the animal her apple, carefully keeping the palm out flat, remembering that curled fingers could be inadvertently nipped. Galahad eyed her, sniffed the offered gift (blowing hot horse breath on her hand and body), tickled her with his long, stiff whiskers, and then took it gingerly in his mobile lips. He munched away, tossed his head, and then eyed the lady again.

"Sorry Galahad, I only brought one."

The horse snorted in reply and inspected her closer. He seemed certain that she must be hiding something edible somewhere about her person.

"I promise to come back with two apples next time," she said.

The horse gave her a gentle push with his forehead.

"He's one of the most intelligent creatures I've had the pleasure to know," Patrick told her. "His Lordship gentle trained him so as not to break his spirit, but contain it and use it. Brought him here as a colt six years ago. They're thick as thieves, 'Had' and His Lordship. That horse follows his master around like a puppy, even plays 'hide and seek' with him."   When Eden left the stables, Little Tom was enjoying himself polishing a saddle, and Daniel had gotten out the chess set to play with Patrick. In her room, she finished hemming her riding skirt and laid out the pattern for a new morning dress and pinned it to some Galatea fabric of willow green Mrs. Sebastian had given her.

The closer it got to teatime, the more restless she became. His Lordship had hinted she might soon be looking for a new position. Was he really that angry? Was she wasting her time sewing clothing? If he turned her off, would he give her a character? Would he give her transportation back home? If not, how would she manage? She had absolutely no money. *Father in Heaven, You know it does me no good to worry, so I refuse to do so any more. I put this situation in your hands. You take care of it; I trust you. I just wish it were over with.*

At the appointed time, Eden went to the earl's study. The door was open. She looked in. He was standing with his back to her, going over a map on the wall. She entered and took a deep breath. "My lord."

"Miss Barrett, take a seat, please," he said without turning around.

And let you tower over me? She sat.

Presently, he concluded his occupation and turned and sat himself across from her, behind his desk. He placed his elbows upon the desk, steepled his large hands, rested his chin on his thumbs, and gazed at her from that vantage. "We need to resolve a few issues if you are to remain here."

Since he seemed satisfied to allow that statement to sink in and offer no more, Eden began, "You have a right to be angry."

"I'm gratified you think so."

"I realize that my behavior this morning was unacceptable. I should never have raised my voice or expressed myself so boldly in front of others in that way." He said nothing, so she offered, "You did raise your voice first, however."

He smiled briefly at her teasing. "We both were deficient in our behavior, I suppose. I accept your attempt at apologizing. That is not my only concern. It is only that I am too well aware of your kind, ma'am. Because of Diana's pleading, I have decided to retain you for the present, and provide a proper balance to any influence you may have on my sister. She will not suffer from knowing you."

It seemed to Eden that each word that issued from his mouth served to inflame her more, but having just expressed remorse for raising her voice, she was determined not to have to do so again. She turned those enormous brown eyes up at him and said quietly, "Well, I like that. Suffer from knowing me. Pray tell me what is this kind I am lumped in with in your estimation?"

"Religious fanatics, Miss Barrett. The kind who sees only what he wants to see and disregards the rest, blithely unaware of life as it really exists. You live in a dream world where everyone is kind and comfortable. You believe there is a pat answer for every question somewhere in your little Bible. Life is all sweetness and light if you will only love your fellow man. Grow up, Miss Barrett. It is a hard, senseless life out there with many useless and unexplainable evils where people are only too ready to do you an injustice for all your loving them."

Eden almost laughed, but he was serious. She said calmly, "You know me not at all, My lord…"

"I am not blaming you. The daughter of a vicar, you have led a sheltered, insulated life. Even the books you were given would have been chosen for their instruction or at the very least their inoffensiveness."

"I agree to the last, my lord, but I had always been of the same mind with my father that a person reflects what he allows into his mind. Do you prefer that I read trash? I disagree vehemently that I know nothing of the world. In fact, I challenge you to know more of it than I. The clergy is more associated with death and sin and sickness and disease of the mind and body than any profession I know.

"I have known my father to bury, baptize, and marry in the course of one morning, hardly having time to shake off the experience of one to address the next. I have known him called out of his bed to settle family disputes or talk a despondent husband out of pulling the trigger of a huge horse pistol as it was pointed at his temple. He so hated the idea of burying a suicide at a crossroads; he made sure he was successful at it.

"I have known the loss of a beloved sister one year younger than I to scarlet fever. Have you ever had to console a bereaved person, my lord, when the deceased is a child? My father has been there for hundreds. Have you smelled the stench of gangrene in a soldier sent home half-healed? I have. The physician in a rural area cannot dress wounds each day. It is too expensive for the patient, and the physician spends too much time traveling as it is. When there were parishioners without spouses, I often had to help bandage all sorts of hideous injuries. I especially abhor burn wounds, but it must be done without wrinkling the nose and allowing the patient to see how much disgust you have for it.

"I was eighteen when my father died. I had been traveling about with him on calls since I was seven. As I got older he found me a great help. I could take the children away from the house while he counseled or consoled the parents. I could bring soup, or read, or nurse, or provide a shoulder to cry on, or an extra ear to listen when he could not be in two places at once... I... I could go on this way for hours, but I will not. I refuse to continue to excuse myself to you. You come to your conclusions too haphazardly."

Eden stood, forcing Colin to stand as any well-schooled gentleman would in the presence of a lady. "A sheltered, insulated life indeed. Because I refuse to be a pessimist? Good day, my lord."

"Miss Barrett, I'm not finished with you. You will leave when I tell you to." Eden schooled her expression to keep from casting dagger-eyes at him. He had just interfered with her favorite method of delivering a parting shot and then retreating to allow the victim to mull it over. They seated themselves again.

"You are aware that Diana often tells me of the discussions you two have. I am not spying, only politely asking how she spent her day and if she learned anything new. It seems to me that you must spend an inordinate amount of time on matters of faith. Refrain from all theological discussion in future. I have already spoken to you about this."

"It would be futile to attempt to instruct a child who has no sense of purpose, no direction, no morality."

"Those things can be taught without bringing God into it."

"Manmade morality would be imperfect."

Colin glared at her. He was not used to servants who were not privileged by years of association with him daring to question the least article of his authority. "It will have to do," he growled, attempting to quell her, but failing miserably.

"Why settle for less?" she demanded. "In fact, my lord, we have spent a very minute amount of time on such discussions, and only in answer to a direct question posed by your sister. You may follow us about all day and find that it is so. In fact, last evening's questions I considered particularly difficult to answer. Diana wanted to know why the water in the pond looks blue in the summer, yet when you cup it in your hand it is as clear as glass. Then she wanted to know why we dream, and if dogs dream, and if so what about, and if not, then why do they make those little noises as they sleep? I not only don't have any solid answers for these, I don't know where to go to find an answer.

"The fact that Diana reports any conversations we might have had about faith attests to the importance she gives that subject in her mind. I believe in answering children's questions to the best of my ability when they arise. Instead of asking me not to answer her questions, why not ask Diana not to have them?"

"You will not evade me so easily, Ma'am. The same questions were answered for her previously by me."

"Then the answers you gave did not satisfy her."

"I cannot believe you do not guide the conversation toward such questions. They seem to come up with you alone."

"Because I do not guide her away from them. I treat all her questions as worthwhile. I try to be frank and clear, though I do tend to be long-winded. Shall I send her to you when such questions arise?"

"If she must have an answer."

"Are you ready with an answer?"

"You are impertinent, ma'am."

"I mean only that I consider myself a little more grounded in such matters - Vicar's daughter and all... Children do not like hemming and hawing, or being fobbed off."

"I think I can handle the mind of a twelve year old."

"Fine. While you are in London, shall I have her write all her questions down and mail them to you?"

He winced and narrowed his eyes. "That was an unnecessarily low blow."

"You're right, I'm sorry. Only, it appears to me that you wish

Diana to think independently as long as her conclusions concur with yours. How happy do your conclusions make you, my lord? Do they satisfy? May I be excused now?"

"By all means" he answered with a tinge of sarcasm. Yet, when she was completely out of the room, Colin allowed himself a half-smile. The argument had been surprisingly stimulating, especially conducted tête-à-tête with the lively and lovely governess. Few dared disagree with him openly. Women never did. Except Cassandra.

Miss Barrett was quite wrong, of course, but she had her point. So, she was not the mild doe he had thought that first day. She was a cat in a corner with its back arched and hairs on end, hissing and spitting - well able to take care of itself. No, the metaphor would not suit. Colin could not, nor did he care to, imagine Miss Barrett spitting.

How calmly, with what cool assurance she had made her case. No spite, no tantrums, no tears, and no backing down. She was more like an untamed filly; eyes wide, nostrils flared, sure of herself, prancing and sidling away from the halter, but challenging the trainer, standing her ground. It was Plutarch who said, "The wildest colts make the best horses." *I wonder if that applies as well to biped fillies*, he thought.

Eden retreated to her room again. A few deep breaths were in order to calm her confused emotions. As she glanced about her sitting room, she decided she had made her point in a calm manner and had it received with some degree of respect, and she had better not press her luck again because she would really miss this whole situation of lovely rooms, books on art, prospects to paint, gourmet meals served to her, no household chores, and sweet children to inspire.

Though the tasks of the household were normally greatly curtailed on Sundays, allowing it to be a true day of rest, the servants were busy with last minute preparations for the earl's journey. Perrin, his valet, would go with him, of course, as would many others to run the London house. To spare the kitchen help from having to cook, a cold collation was again to be served for supper since Colin and Diana dined out. Eden found herself again eating with Nurse Warren. The mealtime conversation seemed to dwell on The Honorable Miss Cassandra Bradley. The earl and

Diana had taken the carriage along with four outriders to the next town to dine at the home of the Bradleys.

"I'm predicting he'll announce his betrothal by summer, and the marriage will take place at Christmas time. The servants have a pool on it, if you wish to get a date in," the Nurse told her confidentially. "They're both prime for marrying, if you ask me. At nineteen, she's just the right age. At six and twenty, he's a little young, but I believe he's terrible lonely."

"There's lonely and there are loners, Miss Warren," Eden offered.

"His Lordship is no loner. He enjoys the Bradleys immensely when they visit. Miss Bradley can make him so light-hearted. The only time I hear him laugh out loud is when she's here. Oh, his school friend Mr. Blake makes him laugh as well, but he don't count. They were all such good playmates when they were little. I'll never forget when Miss Cassy fell out of the punt, and His Lordship rescued her. What a sight! But she's become a true gentlewoman now, and so sweet to her maid."

It was evident to Eden that Colin had his staff's love and concern as well as respect. She was very interested in seeing this paragon of virtue the servants called Miss Cassy. She returned to her room and wrote several letters home. Then she completed several watercolors she had begun of orchids and Diana. Finally, she went down to the library to replace a huge folio she had borrowed of etchings of scenes of Venice. She had wanted to study the artist's handling of light and shadow. Once in the library, she found a copy of a new novel called *Waverly* written by an anonymous author. She sat and entered its world.

At ten-o-clock as Eden read in the library, she heard a coach pull up out front. She went to the window and watched Colin's big spotted setter disembark, followed by Colin, who turned to hand his sister out of the carriage. She went upstairs to her room to prepare for bed, dressing in her night-rail and wrapper and letting her hair down, giving it fifty strokes and leaving it free. When she tried to sleep, her mind raced with thoughts of the past two days. She had forgotten to bring the book she had been reading from the library, thus denying herself her favorite way to relax before sleep. She got back out of bed and sat on the window ledge looking out. Below her, on the snow-laden lawn, were the figures of the earl and his dog.

Eden thought she would have time to sneak back down to grab her book and dash back to her room before the earl came back in the house. As she was about to leave the library, a log fell in the fireplace. Eden turned at the sound and saw a flurry of sparks float over the fire screen and land on the carpet. She ran over and stomped them out, then searched to make sure none had escaped her. She was looking at the fire, mesmerized by its glow, and trying to decide whether to damp the fire or call a servant at this late hour, or whether His Lordship had asked that it be left burning like this, when she heard the tick-tick-tick of the dog's nails on hardwood floors. She turned to see the setter and then Lord Edmund enter the room, effectively blocking her escape as they did.

He glanced at her, but said nothing. The setter went up to her and pushed a cold, wet nose into her hand. Eden knelt on one knee and stroked its silky head. As she bent to the dog, she realized she was in her nightclothes, which gave her a moment's embarrassment, but what could she do? Still, she was well covered from neck to foot. Ah, well. She looked up at Colin and asked, "What is his name?"

Colin strode over to the fire and put one foot on the fender and both hands on the mantle. In this position, he answered, "Sean." He then stared down at the fire as if in a trance. His countenance was despondent, burdened.

Thinking it might be rude just to walk out, and not willing to venture a topic for conversation when it was obvious the earl was not in a conversant mood, she rose and went to a wing chair facing Colin and sat. The dog chose to walk over to Eden and place his silky muzzle with the prickly whiskers in her lap for a continuation of the caresses she had been administering. Eden began to scratch behind the dog's ears. Sean's face broke into an expression of utter bliss.

His eyes drawn by the movement, Colin stopped staring into the fire and gave his attention to the young lady. He studied the shadows that danced across that lovely face wreathed in an expression of delight. It was a treat to see her glossy mane of long, dark waving hair falling freely about her shoulders in that way. The yellow glow of the firelight upon the scene reminded him of a much-varnished Old Master. He was gazing so intently at her that, when her eyes lifted to his, he involuntarily (and he hoped imperceptibly) lurched. That which he had been amusing himself with as a dream was now returning his look and speaking to him, forcing him back to reality.

"I saw you walking with him. He feathers out and stops now and then to point. Is he trained to hunt?"

He glanced away into the fire again. "He is."

"Do you work him in season?"

"No... I don't hunt."

"Truly? I'm surprised."

His chin lifted. "Are you?"

"How old is he?"

"Twelve."

"He's in excellent condition for that age."

"My father brought him home to me as a pup." He seemed to sneer as if at some private, pathetic joke. Then he straightened and strode to take the chair opposite Eden. After arranging himself in a relaxed pose in the chair, he continued, "I think he meant to soften the blow of my mother's death, as if a dog could take a mother's place. He also meant the dog to be a common point of interest for the two of us. He professed to want to get to know his son. His son certainly wanted to know him at the time." He was silent a moment, then exhaled a deep, audible breath and words came pouring out. He spoke to the fire as if picturing the events he described.

"Father had the dog trained to set and retrieve. He made a great fuss of teaching me to identify, clean, and fire several types of firearms. We practiced loading, firing, and reloading until I could do it with some degree of proficiency. We fired at still targets until I was adept, and then we culped wafers. He'd given me a flint loader, which meant I had to aim far ahead of the target to offset the slow ignition. Never in my life had he spent so much time with his son.

"I couldn't wait to be one of Father's crones; spending the day mucking about in hunting clothes; coming home tired after a day's shoot to brag, over a glass of brandy in the game room, about the performance of the dogs, or the pinpoint accuracy of the shooting; laughing late into the night as any well bred gentleman of leisure.

"Finally, the great day came. I was primed. Father would accompany me on my first sojourn into civilized manhood. I was up and dressed long before the appointed hour. Sean was poetry. When he froze to a point, I felt a rush of excitement. I gave the command to flush. A flash of color fluttered up. I drew a bead, fired, and missed. Father hit his mark. The bird fell and Sean bounded after it. He brought it back, holding it gently in his mouth and dropped it at my feet.

"A pheasant. A magnificent specimen. The iridescent throat feathers shimmered purple and green in the dawn light. It had only been winged. It struggled and up-righted itself, then settled, eyes wild with fear. Its little body pulsed with rapid breathing. I thought, 'God is he beautiful. I can set his wing, nurse him, tame him, make a pet of him.

"I moved to catch the bird, but my father shoved me aside. He shot it point blank. 'Put him out of his misery,' he said. The bird's misery had ended. Mine had begun. Morbid curiosity forced me to stare at the downy little form with shreds of meat where its beautiful head had just been. To my horror, the headless bird began to flop its wings about. I dropped my gun and ran as far as I could to get away from the scene, but every time I closed my eyes, there it was.

"Dear Father. He was so understanding when I finally came home. 'You'll get used to it,' he said. 'In fact, I've arranged a Grand Batteau for Thursday. You'll get plenty of experience then.' I refused to go. He said I'd go of my own volition, or I'd go bound and gagged. No son of his was going to be a damned milksop.

"Father convinced all of the local gentry, and yeomanry to come. The agent rounded up every free rustic to serve as beaters for the brush. Thoroughly intimidated, I agreed to attend, but I refused to shoot. My gun was thrust into my hand. The carnage began. There was no sport in it. There was no place for any kind of creature to hide. Birds of all species and rabbits fell by the hundreds. The continuous close reports of the rifles caused my ears to ring. The smell of gunpowder in the air choked me.

"Finally, I threw down my gun and turned to go home. I didn't care what my father thought of me; I wouldn't be a part of that massacre. My father shouted my name. 'Not one more step,' he said. I turned. His rifle was aimed at me. I told him, 'Go ahead and shoot. Do you think I have the least desire to live with you for a father?' Before I reached the first tree, I was retching my lovely breakfast.

"When I got home, I locked myself in my room. In the evening, Father came to the door and shouted the day's bag: 1,100 pheasant, 1,300 quail, 700 grouse, 600 partridge, and 800 rabbits. For what? Sport?"

For a while, nothing more was said. Eden was thinking, *With a Father like that for a model, no wonder you have trouble fathoming an all-loving Father God.* Then Colin took another deep breath and said bitterly, "What say you now, woman? I am laid open to you. A fine soldier I would make. How fortunate I have an excuse not to join the military. Am I not weak and womanish? A milksop?"

"Absolutely not. How much more masculine to be strong enough of character and conviction at such an early age that you would fly in the face of society's idea of manhood. How much weaker you would have been had you conformed against your sensibilities. I cannot think less of you for it, but more."

"You would turn weakness into strength."

"Because yours originates there."

"You're resolved to think me more than I am."

"Would you have me think you less than I know you are?"

They were silent a few moments before Eden said simply, "So you strove to be perfect in every other way to capture some remnant of his approval."

At this, Colin turned his head sharply to catch her expression. Almost as sharply, he turned his face again to the fire. "Perceptive," he murmured.

"And did you gain his approval in the end?"

The earl shrugged. "I have no idea why I've told you this. Possibly because you chose to reveal a slice of your life to me this afternoon. Though I've relived that day in my mind, I've never before voiced it." He seemed bemused a moment, then continued. "I wonder: was it a need in me or a power in you that brought it forth?" Not waiting for an answer, "Both, I suppose. I was depressed and that depression has lifted."

"I'm glad I could assist your remedy in some way," she said. "People often unburdened their stories upon me. I'm not always certain what to think of my part in these confidences. I'm afraid the speaker expects me to offer some sage advice that I'm incapable of.

"I do feel a sense of pride that one places so much trust in me that he is willing to share personal matters. Often a bond is formed between us, but just as often, the narrator will then avoid me as if ashamed he ever knew me. I hope you will not be one of those. I am not a sage. Yet I feel singled out, somehow."

Colin ventured, "The expression of your eyes and face is attentive, sympathetic, open, approachable. You appear to be one who can be trusted not to impart any of a deep, dark secret. You listen completely, without judging. Therein lies your power."

Eden smiled. "I hope you're right. Let's see if I can divest you of another secret."

He straightened, on his guard, "And what might that be?"

"What has become of the sweep?"

His gentle expression became a cold mask again. "You forfeited that right when you refused to testify."

"Will you forgive me?"

"For what?"

"For differing with you?"

He managed a half-smile. "Never for that!" he said. But the ice was broken. They talked comfortably until very late. He spoke of his admiration for Jeremy Bentham and asked Eden what she thought of that man's philosophy of forming legislation according to whether it could achieve the greatest good for the greatest amount of people.

"It does sound high-minded, but sometimes slogans can be misleading. I would want to know who is to determine what is the greatest good, what right they have, and what their criteria is," she said.

Lord Edmund gave her a book titled *Fragment on Government* and continued to discuss Bentham's ideas as well as politics in general. Eden found herself marveling at the range of expression hidden in the slight raising of an eyebrow or the crinkling of the skin at the corner of an eye of her employer. His eyes glinted with humor, they scowled, they reflected pain and bewilderment and despair; and then they crinkled again in self-deprecation, enlightenment, resolve. Lord Edmund displayed a depth of intelligence, sensitivity, and emotion she had seen in no one since her father. She felt at home in the world once more.

CHAPTER IX

The next morning, Diana, Eden, and Colin breakfasted together. When Joseph announced that all was ready for the earl's departure, they walked out. Diana had brought an odd-looking doll to breakfast with her, and she clutched it now at her brother's parting. Though there were many fancy porcelain dolls in Diana's room, Eden had not noticed her giving them a second glance. This particular doll was a simple cotton one with hair made of mop strands pulled back into a bun at its neck. Tucks in the fabric formed the pinched eyes and nose. Sewn low on the bridge was a pair of spectacles.

As they walked down the corridor, Eden noticed Diana hanging back, wiping at her eyes, and straightening her shoulders, but the ache showed plain enough in the child's face.

On the terrace, Colin gave the staff last minute instructions. Then he took Diana aside and apologized for having to leave her, explaining that he truly did not like to, but felt it unavoidable. He promised to write often while he was away and to travel the entire fourteen hours distance by post horse just to see her as soon as he conceivably could. This treatment did little, however, to erase her woebegone expression.

Colin decided to change his tactics. "What shall I bring you from London? Name anything." Diana's face brightened a little, then gave way to a scowl when she could not think of anything. Colin suggested, "A new doll at least, to keep Miss prim company?"

"No dolls. I'm too old for dolls."

"But here is Miss Prim. She's a doll, is she not?"

"She's different."

"She's different alright," he said as he took the doll from her and held it up to face him. "Your other dolls are so much fancier. Begging your pardon, Miss Prim, but you must know it to be true. Why is she so special?"

The child's face became grave and she evaded the answer, "Nothing that would interest you. I know what I want. A new mount, a horse, not a pony, a piebald jumper; you promised."

"If Patrick tells me your hands are strong enough to handle one, I promised to look in at Tattersall's. And you can't throw me off so easily. Everything about you interests me. Why is Miss Prim so different?"

Diana hung her head, "She reminds me of Father."

Colin held the doll up so that it stared over the rim of its metal glasses into the earl's eyes. "I fail to see the resemblance," he said, grinning.

"That's not fair," Diana scowled.

"You're right. How can I expect you to be open when I make jokes? Please, explain how the doll reminds you of Father."

"When I was little, and Father tried to teach me reading and writing after... Miss Austen..." Brother and sister glanced away from each other. Diana continued, "I sometimes made mistakes and didn't want to work anymore. Then Father would say, 'Very well, I haven't the patience for you, but I know someone strict who will make you work.' Then he would go get Miss Prim. He bought her from a tenant for that purpose. He'd hold her waist and make her go up and down like this, and say in a funny high voice, 'All right, Miss, none of your sauce. You're a bright little girl; you're just lazy. Now show your father what a fool he is and make that 'Q' with no blotches from the pen."

Colin chuckled. "Thank you for telling me this. It sheds new light on Father's character. One thing troubles me though." When his sister did not take the bait and ask what troubled him, he volunteered, "Why did you feel it wouldn't interest me? I found it most amusing and enlightening."

Diana looked aside and said nothing. She seemed to hope the question would simply go away.

"I expect an answer," he prodded.

"You didn't like Father," she accused tentatively.

Lord Edmund straightened at this. He took a moment to compose a reply. "Come here child," he said tenderly as he took her by the hand and led her to a stone bench. He sat himself on it and stood her in front of him so that their eyes were on about the same level. Then he drew a breath. "You are right. I was angry with Father for most of your life. I was wrong to be angry. I know that now when it's too late to tell him.

"We know people are not perfect. Everyone makes mistakes, but when we are little, our parents seem like gods to us. We're certain they know everything. As we grow up, we are in the habit of looking up to them. It's comforting. We continue to demand that they be perfect even though we are not. We ask a great deal of them and give back so little. One day our eyes are opened. We see them making mistakes, behaving stupidly, and it dawns on us that they are no better than us.

"The people we love are too often the very ones we treat with the least courtesy and understanding. They are so close to us we don't see them as a whole: as who they are, but what we want them to be. I felt Father was this way with me, but now I know that I was this way with Father, too. Do you understand what I mean?"

"I think so."

"Will you do me a big favor?"

"What?"

"If I ever start to treat you that way - expect you to be perfect, or take you for granted - will you point it out for me?"

"Of course, and if I expect you to be perfect, you must remind me."

"No need to."

"Why not?"

"Because I am perfect."

"Oh, You!" she laughed and punched him on the shoulder, then threw her arms about him and admonished him, "You'd better get going. John has had to walk the horses round in a circle three times waiting for you. I will see you the first Friday next month. I love you, Colin."

"And I love you always, elf." They kissed each other's cheeks in tandem, and Diana scurried to the safety of her governess.

After watching her brother board the carriage and waiving to him until it was out of sight, Diana could be a brave young lady no more. She embraced Eden and sobbed uncontrollably. When she could at last control her tears, she began to mumble as in a chant, "I mustn't be angry; I mustn't be angry; I mustn't…"

Thinking Diana was referring to the conversation she had just had, Eden said, "It is natural to be angry at times. It is just important to forgive and not stay angry."

Diana looked up at Eden with an expression of fear in her hazel eyes. "You don't understand. I'm not like other people. I must not get angry at all. Never. My power goes out of control. Bad things happen when I get angry." Eden would have asked for further explanation, but Diana ran into the house.

Eden decided to give the girl time alone to calm down and collect herself. In the schoolroom, she put Daniel to reading a history book and Tom to copying a page of letters. When sufficient time had elapsed, she went looking for Diana. She was not in her room. The second and third floor staff did not know where she was. Nurse Warren had not seen her all morning, but she thought of a few of her favorite hiding places - on the roof, in the attic, or in the folly by the water. When Eden opened the attic door a crack, she caught a glimpse of Diana wreathed in sunlight. She was sitting on a bench and gazing out a small window. The governess closed the door and left the girl there to her thoughts.

At noon, Eden took dinner with Nurse Warren. There were two questions she hoped the older servant could answer, and the lonely nanny was a mine of information waiting to explode. But when she spoke of Diana's strange behavior and her mention of powers that went out of control, Nurse Warren's eyes shone. "That gel does have powers. She is correct, she must never get angry."

Eden decided to drop the subject and try the other question she had. "What became of Miss Austen, Diana's last governess?"

Nurse Warren scowled, "I swore to the late Lord Edmund never to speak of it, and I never shall. All the servants will give you the same answer. That baggage, she got what was coming to her. Lord Colin was a fool to give her a second glance. He should have known better. Lady Laura would have told him, if she had lived. Lady Laura was Lord Colin's mother.

"Everyone deals with problems differently. I have my Savior to help me, of course, but some people take to drink, some complain, some try to run away. Lady Laura, she just ignored problems, denied they existed. Life was just one big harvest fair for her. Everyone in her company must always be gay and carefree or she wanted nothing to do with them.

"Real problems never did exist until she took to childbed with Lord Colin. My poor little Lady, how she cried and screamed those nights. The baby was quite large, you see, and Her Ladyship was small and it took two days before she could deliver him. She lost a lot of blood and she was confined to her bed for months. We moved her to that room opposite yours to convalesce. She wanted only to sleep all the time. She didn't have enough milk or energy, so we had to find Lord Colin a wet-nurse, a lady named Sheppard.

"I think Lady Laura blamed little Lord Colin for awhile for causing her so much pain and illness. Then she blamed the late Lord Edmund. You see her husband was so very large ... Not a good start between mother and child. Well, once she was on her feet again, she was frightened of ever having another baby. There was only one way she could make sure of that, so she locked all her doors at night. His Lordship was a virile man, and he wanted at least one more boy - an heir and a spare - so her sleeping in a separate bedroom and behind locked doors caused a rift between them in more ways than one.

"Lord Edmund really loved his little wife. She could charm the birds out of the trees. Always laughing and carefree. He could deny her nothing. She was witty and frivolous and self-serving. Her parents had spoilt her with a passion. It's so odd. The late earl married Lady Laura because he was captivated by her vivacious nature. Then, after the move, he began to despise her for the very same quality.

"She was arranging routes and musical evenings and hunts and picnics. She brought in ballet troupes and opera companies and acting troupes. Dancing was her favorite, though. Her husband wasn't one for dancing, or dressing up if he didn't have to for political parties. He was a farmer at heart, like our poor king. He was always hunting and riding and taking care of the estates.

"At first, he complained about the constant stream of visitors. Then he criticized. Then he found reasons to be elsewhere. Finally he found reasons not to return, spent most of the year in London, Parliament and all. Lord Colin was hardly walking and talking yet, when his father left. The late earl didn't get to know his son - the only one Lady Laura intended to give him.

"When His Lordship was about four, Her Ladyship finally began to pay some attention to her son. She treated him like a little girl treats her dolls. She dressed him up and showed him off and petted him and chatted to him when she thought of it. If he fussed, she handed him to me to take away. Sometimes she let him brush her long black hair. I remember he liked that particularly.

"When he was about seven, he thought he'd play a tune on the piano. Someone in the company commented he just might be another child prodigy on the style of Mozart. They was just havin' fun, but it put an idea into his mother's head. She got him the best music master money could buy and had him rehearse all the time. He didn't seem to mind as long as it meant she was paying attention to him. Turned out he had a real gift too. She was soon trotting him out to perform every time they had company.

"Well, anyway, when His Lordship was about twelve, Lady Laura started fretting about her age. Told her son not to dare make her a grandmother until he was thirty. All her friends couldn't make her happy anymore. She did attend church when the fancy struck her, but it was more to see and be seen and socialize. To turn to God in your need takes a denial of self, and all she had was self. I tried to persuade her to try prayer, but she only pooh-poohed me.

"She began to long for her husband. A woman needs to be held and told she's pretty all the more when her waist begins to thicken and tiny lines about the mouth and eyes don't disappear when the smile does. She needed him, but he wasn't around. There was a certain handsome young man who visited, who flattered her. He was married. I don't believe his wife suspected. After all, it doesn't mean the same to a man as it does to a woman. He can pretend love to attain his object, she allows the object to attain the love."

At this point, Eden began to squirm, not at all certain she should be listening to this and not really agreeing with the last statement, but she could not get a word in. Fortunately, Nurse Warren began to come to the end of her tale. "Too shorten the story, Lady Laura wrote several lengthy letters to her husband and he came home. She moved back in with him, and he stayed. Diana was born eight months after His Lordship's return, but she was so puny she might not have been full term. Lady Laura was fine for three days after the delivery, but the physician insisted she needed cupping. She couldn't survive the blood loss from both the childbirth and the cupping. Doctors are no better than murderers if you ask me. That's why I won't let 'em send for one, no matter how bad I feel."

Since that sounded like the beginning of a segue into Nurse Warren's favorite topic of description of pains, Eden excused herself and left. She had had quite an earful as it was, but it had helped her in forming her opinion of the present Earl of Edmund.

* * *

Time went swiftly that month and the next. Though Eden knew her situation was like a dream come true, two related feelings persisted in haunting her at night when she had read until her eyes closed of their own accord, but before her mind had drifted into dreams: she didn't deserve all this, and she wasn't doing much to improve the quality of life for the poor and abused in the world.

If only she had been born a boy, she could have studied politics and made her way into the House of Commons. In her mind, that was the place to be to change bad laws and enact new, beneficial ones. She was reading to Mother Grey a few times a week now, and she had enlisted the help of Daniel and Tom to carry dinner to the dear lady and do any little chores she might be able to give the boys. But that was just one person. That was the kind of work her father had done, one to one helping. Eden wanted to change the whole human condition, and as soon as possible. It certainly needed changing.

She consoled herself with the thought that by teaching the daughter of an earl, she was sculpting in an even more creative way than with clay. Each new idea that entered Diana's mind changed her inner features ever so slightly. Her soul was the substance taking shape; changing from gross to fine. Diana was the masterpiece Eden was privileged to assist in modeling. And when Diana was near to completion, (for surely humans were never finally completed) the girl would not be satisfied to sit cold and lifeless on a shelf behind the glazed doors of some library in a rich man's castle. She would move about in the world, and the world would be better for it.

Diana was definitely different from most girls of the gentry. She had a distinctive character. She was not as trivial. Also, she loved to act out parts from plays or books she read. With Daniel and Thomas as her new friends, she directed impromptu scenes in which she told the boys who they were and how to move. Robin Hood and King Arthur were favorites with the boys. They also liked to play soldiers or navy men aboard ship. The day's history lesson was sometimes re-enacted on the music room stage or in the courtyard. The boys were very adept at catching a pretend bullet in the heart and twisting about and falling all over the stage where they could then play dead until the cows came home. The only discouraging thing about Diana was her continued insistence that she must never get angry or her "powers" would go out of control.

Colin wrote to Diana often, as he had promised, but when March came, he did not come home. He wrote that some very important things were brewing right then, and he was swamped with work and assignments. Though seeming more preoccupied than usual, Diana took it well, even when the papers brought news of the Earl of Edmund escorting the Honorable Miss Cassandra Bradley and her mother to a certain masquerade. In another account, the three had been spotted at the opera.

"Colin must mix in society; it's his job. He says he must 'cultivate contacts'," Diana told Daniel when he brought her the first article. Mr. York had read it aloud at the breakfast table in the servants' hall.

Another article reported that Lord Edmund had made a speech in the Lords advocating repealing the laws against combination. The writer felt that such a stand would make many enemies for the Earl of Edmund. Trade unions would result if such laws were repealed. If trade unions were allowed, they would demand higher wages and expensive changes made in working conditions. This would mean higher prices for goods. The writer thought prices were high enough now as it was; except, perhaps, for rich earls.

The staff discussed that article all morning. They were ready to hang the writer and leave him for the crows. Stupid people should not be allowed in print. The earl was absolutely right to take such a stand. Eden felt a surge of pride when she read the article. He was not a man who let society form his opinions, and he was concerned for the lower classes.

* * *

One morning late in March, Lady Diana uncharacteristically lingered over her breakfast. She stared into space over her meal and ignored Eden's questions of concern. Eden did not make too much of it because Diana often liked to indulge in daydreams, and ignored everyone when she did. As long as it did not happen while she was supposed to be working, she saw no real harm in it.

The governess had finished eating long ago and was anxious to get up to the schoolroom. When the boys got there first, they tended to explore or tussle. Eden had an experiment set up on her desk, and she was worried they might upset it. She excused herself from the breakfast table, told Diana to hurry because she had a surprise planned for today, and left.

When Eden reached the classroom, she found her fears well founded. Little Tom and Daniel each had a chemists' flask in one hand. Little Thom was sniffing the contents of his. The governess calmly told them to put the flasks down where they had found them and explained how she would use them as soon as Lady Diana arrived. She gave each of the boys a set of sums according to their ability and perched on the edge of her desk waiting and watching the boys work.

Daniel coughed much less now and his color was becoming healthier, though he was still pale. His hair had grown quite a bit and had turned out to be a striking platinum color. His cornflower blue eyes no longer showed any of the coal dust that had rung his lids for so long. The inflammation in his eyes was completely gone. He had an aristocratic face: thin, pointed, thin-lipped, with an aquiline nose. His fingers were the long slender ones of an artist.

And artist he was. His sketches of the horses and people and buildings that made up Chadilane were amazing. Eden had to admit to jealousy toward his work. The sketches were strong and swift and alive. They roared and leapt. Her own sketches were reworked, painfully detailed, soft, sweet, quiet creatures.

Eden had tried studying the sculptures and paintings at Chadilane. With great effort, she could imitate some of the artists admirably, but she did not like her own compositions; she always felt there was something amateurish about them, but could not put her finger on what it was. She had thought if she just had a good teacher, he could help her develop her technique. But Daniel had no instructor, and his artwork showed the hand of a genius. She loved to watch him draw. His hand never stopped. He had no patience for planning; nor did he seem to need any. He looked, and his hand drew. He didn't seem to need to refer to the paper with his eyes. And the finished product looked professional.

Eden looked at Little Thom. The child rarely spoke, and rarely smiled. When he played the part of an Indian or a pirate, he was serious about the whole thing. He liked to help. He would jump up to fetch a book or a blotter or anything. Patrick couldn't find enough things for him to do in the stables.

It was most amazing to Eden that she had come from attempting to teach the three self-important, empty-headed, vindictive chatterboxes of Sir William to the three quiet, hard-working, sensitive, intelligent children at Chadilane. She smiled as she thought of some of the nasty tricks that had been played on her by her former pupils in Longacre.

Then Diana entered the room.

She carried a pewter mug in her hand. She stumbled in, bent at the waist. "Ooh, Miss Barrett. I've done something stupid," she moaned. "Very stupid... I didn't know it would hurt so bad..." Diana's knees buckled, and she dropped heavily to the floor. The mug rolled away from her hand. She drew herself up into the fetal position, clutching her stomach. "Why didn't he come home? It hurts, Miss Barrett."

Eden was down on her knees by the writhing girl. "What is it Diana? What have you done? What hurts?" she cried as her heart pounded in her throat. The girl's eyes were closed and her head twitched violently. She opened her eyes, but they rolled back and showed the whites. Eden turned her head to the side. The boys stood behind her, eyes wide. "Thomas, go tell Mr. York to send for the doctor," she said. Thomas ran.

When Eden looked back, Diana seemed to be having trouble breathing; raspy sounds came from the girl's throat. "Help her, Miss Barrett. Do something!" Daniel cried. Then Diana began to relax. A brief, low moan escaped her lips and she was quiet. Her body went limp.

"Oh my God; my dear sweet Lord!" Eden cried. She placed a hand under Diana's neck to lift it to her knee. The girl's head flopped backward, her mouth gaping open. "Get the hand mirror on my vanity, quick!" Eden told Daniel. To the girl, she cried,

"What have you done?" Eden felt the blood drain from her face. She felt queasy. Gently, she lay the girl down flat again and bent over her; with her ear pressed hard against Diana's chest, she could hear the girl's strong, regular heartbeat.

As she repositioned herself, Eden's knee hit the pewter mug Diana had been carrying. She picked it up and looked in it. It contained a few drops of a milky-looking substance. She brought it to her nose and inhaled. A sharp, chemical odor made her draw back from the mug and cough violently.

Daniel arrived with the mirror. Eden held the glass above Diana's nose telling Daniel that her heart was beating normally. "There's a mist on the mirror. She's breathing, but ever so slightly," Eden said. "I don't know what else to do, except wait for the doctor. I suppose we'll need to put her in a bed. Nathan can help. Maybe Mr. York can tell me what was in this cup."

Thomas came down the hall and into the room. "Joseph's gone for the doctor, ma'am. Now what?"

Eden turned to look at him. Then she heard giggles. She turned toward the sound and saw Diana, eyes still closed, giggling. Then the girl opened her eyes and sat up. "Rat poison," she said. "I put a touch of it in some milk for effect. Then I put some plain milk on the corner of my mouth so it would look like I drank it. You fell for it. You all fell for it. You fell for everything." Diana began to laugh hysterically. "You should have seen your faces! I was superb."

After the initial shock of seeing the pretend dead rise giggling, Eden became angry. She had never been so angry with anyone in her life. "My God, girl. You think it's a joke! My heart is pounding so fast it hurts, and you sit there laughing! Daniel and Thomas and I were frightened out of our wits! We love you. We thought you were in pain. Poor Joseph has been sent on a wild goose chase."

"Oh, stop it. It was all in fun."

"You can't know how cruelly you're behaving! You will be punished for this."

Diana struggled to her feet and glared at her teacher, "You won't punish me, and stop ranting, or I shall hate you. Bad things happen to people I hate. Very bad things. I'm a very bad person, Miss Barrett. Don't make me angry!"

"Oh, stop your nonsense. That's all trash you read somewhere. I've never hit a child, but I'm very close to it right now! Get out of my sight! Go to your room!" Eden's clenched fists and contorted face convinced Diana, who ran out of the room crying, "I mustn't get angry; I mustn't get angry; I mustn't…"

Eden took a few moments to assure Daniel and Thomas that she would not murder Diana. She picked up the mug and accompanied the boys downstairs to alert Mr. York that it had all been an act. Daniel and Thomas were told there would be no school today and to run and ask Mr. Stagg to ride out in search of Joseph. Then Eden turned to Mr. York and asked, "How could Lady Diana get her hands on rat poison?" She held the cup out to him.

He took it and sniffed. "There's some layin' out in attic, but she knows what it is and to keep away from it. I showed her myself. Told her even touching it can make you bad sick. We got to have poison out for the vermin. There's antiques in the attic. The cats and terriers keep 'em down on ground floor, but we can't keep dogs up in there."

Mrs. York glared at Eden. "You're not accusing anyone of anything, are you, Miss? 'Cause His Lordship knows all about it."

"Not at all, ma'am. I was just curious."

Later, when Eden judged herself calm enough to go to Diana, she tried to explain the seriousness of the situation Diana had caused. She apologized for losing her temper, then reminded her of the story of "The Boy Who Cried Wolf" and discussed the fact that the doctor might have been pulled away from a patient who was in real pain to attend what he thought was a more dire case. She gave Diana a long writing assignment and forbid her to leave her room until next morning. All her meals would be taken alone in her room. Then she brought up the subject of Diana's power. "Please try to explain what you mean by your power."

"I have the power to think of something happening, and then it does. If I'm angry enough and just concentrate hard enough and see the thing happening, it will. Don't laugh; the staff knows it's true."

"I'm not laughing. The mind and the will are powerful tools that we don't completely understand. But what you have experienced might have been a coincidence, or a kind of premonition. Something was going to happen, and you just happened to think of it before it did. What specifically do you mean by this 'power' going out of control? What has happened?"

"I can't say. I promised Father not to tell. They might... I can't talk about this, not yet.... Miss Barrett, you said you loved me. I didn't know that. Can you still love me?"

"Of course. Love is much stronger than one misunderstanding. After all the wonderful talks we have had, I feel like you are more a sister to me than most of my own sisters. I love you very much indeed."

"And I love you. You're the best teacher I ever had. Do I still have to be punished?"

"Did you do something wrong?"

"Yes."

"Then if I love you, I must punish you, so you can learn from your mistakes and become a better person. If I didn't love you, I wouldn't really care enough to risk your displeasure in me for punishing you. "

"Rats."

Nora brought Eden a letter from Mary. The date of her wedding was imminent. The banns would be read for the usual three weeks beginning next Sunday. She begged Eden to ask to be allowed to travel home for the wedding.

Enclosed in Mary's note was a letter from Matthew. It was filled with complaint of lack of food, medical supplies and aid, proper footwear, blankets, or clothing for the foot soldiers. It seemed all they did was march, contract dysentery, and wage war on insects when they bivouacked. A story was told around camp of a young captain, the third son of a Marquis, who had been driven by the relentless itching of fleabites to commit suicide by falling on his sword.

Eden knew they had seen action from his references to need for skilled surgeons, but he didn't go so far as to describe or even allude to any skirmishes. Matthew's complaining may have served to lift his spirits by sharing the load, but it was sure to depress the reader.

March had been the lion it always is, with high winds and rain to keep the inhabitants of Chadilane prisoners within its walls. April was dreary with rain. Diana became bored easily, since the weather stopped her from riding. Eden held some classes in the orangerie attached to the side of the south wing. The gardener allotted several flats to the children and let them sweeten the soil and plant their very own seeds. Thomas wanted to water his seeds every hour the first few days.

On quarter day, Eden received her first wages at the manor: fifteen pounds. Part of it was promptly set aside to buy new half boots and undergarments, and part to purchase more oils and canvas. These things could not total more than three pounds together. Eden had wanted to put the rest into an account to save for tuition to a school for portrait painters, but she decided to send the remaining twelve pounds home to apply to repairing the roof for her family.

As April drew to a close, Mrs. York received word from His Lordship to be prepared for a concert on the first Saturday of May. She had Nathan let down the chandeliers for cleaning. Seeing one of them down within easy reach, Eden persuaded the footman to detach a single crystal drop to demonstrate Newton's "white light" experiment in class. The children chorused "ooh's" and 'ah's" as the little rainbows were cast about the room. This done, she returned the precious crystal promptly for fear an enthusiastic child might trip and break it.

* * *

On the morning of the first Friday in May, Nora tapped on Eden's door. "His Lordship has arrived. He wishes to see you and Diana in the drawing room now."

Lord Edmund looked cheerful as he held out his arms to his sister. "Home again."

Diana stood her ground, looked at the carpet and said in a flat voice, "Well, hurrah. For how long this time?"

Colin lowered his arms and looked hurt, but exaggeratedly so. "Is this the reception I get from my own sister? My very blood? Of whom I have thought every day of my absence, and to whom I've written almost as often. How shabbily she treats me. She does not run to me with hugs and kisses as she always has before."

"I'm too old for that. I'm growing up."

"I'll allow you to grow up, Diana, but please don't grow away. I need one ally in this miserable excuse for a world. Have you nothing for me when I have something nice for you?"

As if by prearranged signal, Nathan entered with a large white box tied with various colors of ribbons. Diana's greedy little face relaxed its scowl, "What is it?"

"A gift for you."

Diana reached for it, but Colin took the gift and Nathan drew back and stood by the door. Colin seated himself expectantly. "Kiss first," he said.

"Present first," Diana argued.

"Kiss first."

"Present."

"This is getting nowhere. I'll tell you what, we'll trade kiss for present on the count of three. Agreed?"

"Agreed."

The earl presented his cheek. "One... Two...Three." The exchange was made. Diana took the package to a seat by the windows and made a fuss with the ribbons, not wanting to break them, but eager to get at what they bound.

Colin nodded to Nathan, who left the room. "I've also brought a gift for Miss Barrett."

"Then she must give you a kiss for it too." Diana commanded, secretly watching the reactions of the two.

Colin looked up at Eden to see what she thought of this. He was pleased to see her face flush. But the frown in her brow clearly conveyed she was not about to agree to such a trade. He roasted her a few turns with his grinning eyes, before turning back to Diana. "Miss Barrett has earned her gift by keeping you out of trouble. She need not pay for it a second time." Glancing back at Eden again, he added, "Unless she would like ..." An indignant look from her sliced off the remainder of his sentence. "Perhaps not," he concluded.

Diana had managed to uncover her gift, a large musical round-about with beautifully carved wooden horses. It wound up with the same crank the fair man would have turned if it were a real, full-sized carousel at a fair. Nathan re-entered with two packages, one upon the other. "These quite heavy objects are for you," he told Eden. "Shall I take them up to your room?"

"She has to open them here," Diana commanded.

The footman put the packages down on a side-table. Eden removed the lid of the box above while Diana came over to investigate. The content was swathed in muslin. Diana, in her eagerness, reached her hand into the package and pulled back the cloth. "Is this a joke?" she demanded. "That's a lump of mud."

"Clay, Miss Nosey. Sculptor's clay. And sculpting tools in the box on which it sits. Miss Barrett once told me she would like to try sculpting."

Eden's pleasure could not be contained. She allowed her eyes to smile for him. And how those eyes could sparkle with a fresh delight, a genuine joy he had seen in none of the debutantes in town. His sister never reflected the pleasure that Eden's face was capable of showing.

"I don't believe it," she said. "How thoughtful, how generous. I can't accept...but I will. Thank you, my lord." She thought for a fleeting moment, *I could kiss you after all.*

"How easily you are made happy with a lump of mud, Ma'am. It is very gratifying to watch your face. Take lessons from your teacher, Diana, on the proper way to receive a gift: showing genuine surprise and enjoyment instead of greed; then you shall entice me to give you more for the satisfaction of giving you joy. I have yet to hear a 'thank you' from your lips."

Once Diana had thanked him, the earl told Eden, "Diana is mine for the next two days; no lessons for her. You may join us if you wish at any time, Miss Barrett. I'm famished. Let me change these traveling clothes, and I'll join you both in the breakfast room."

When he left the room, Diana's eyes narrowed. She decided to put her plan further into action.

CHAPTER X

At mid-morning, Eden was summoned to bring her reports to the library. Colin was writing at a desk laden with opened books. Sean lay at his feet. On seeing Eden, the earl stood up, wiped his quill pen on a cloth and stuck it back into its standish, capped the silver ink pot, and held his right hand away from his clothing as he rummaged with the left in his waistcoat pocket for a handkerchief. "Have you ever discovered a way to compose in ink without staining the fingers?" he asked her as he wiped the offending blue digits.

"In the schoolroom, we are still trying to use the pen without staining our clothes, faces, and hair, as well as fingers and arms."

"Hair?"

She put her palms up and shrugged, then held the reports out to him. He took them, bid her take a seat, and reseated himself once she had. After reading every word she had written, he pronounced her work excellent. "Is there anything else you wish to add?"

"No, my lord."

"Anything you need?"

"Not that I can think of at this time, my lord."

"Then we may conclude this meeting." His eyes glittered with wry amusement.

Eden thought, *Damn his eyes. The young ladies at Almack's must fall all over him.* She said aloud, "If you don't mind, I wish to see if I can find a book on game, especially the different species of deer." The earl rose as Eden did. She went to the cabinet that housed most of the books on animals, saying, "Please go back to your work. Don't let me disturb you."

With her back to him, she continued, "The children got into a dispute yesterday and I couldn't settle it for them. The story we were reading spoke of a witch's circle made by the hooves of a deer. Daniel said it was the roe deer that does that; Diana must argue that it is the fallow deer like those in the park here. This is the first I had heard of a witch's circle. I hope I can find the answer. Or possibly set them to work finding it themselves."

She pulled out a few books on the shelf that fell at eye-level when she became aware that he was standing close behind her. She felt the warmth of his breath against her ear. The flesh at the nape of her neck and along her arm prickled.

Quietly, he said, "I recall a book that should…" his fingers scanned a row of books just above those that Eden was perusing. He pulled down an oversized volume, saying, "Ah, here it is. This should contain your answer. The boy is correct, by the by."

Sean stood up and walked to the door, which caused the two at the bookcase to turn in unison. Diana entered with a scowl on her face and bent to pat Sean. She looked suspiciously at her brother and her governess. Neither said a word, and both had guilty expressions. "Why do boys always have to lie about everything?" the girl asked.

"I take umbrage at that, elf." Colin said, though he found it necessary for some reason to clear his throat before he could speak. "Lying is a vice both sexes participate in with equal relish."

"Boys lie bigger."

"We do everything bigger," the earl teased.

"Yes, but we do everything better," his sister countered.

Always waiting for the right question to teach a lesson, Eden didn't want to let this one get away. "To determine why people lie, look to yourself, Diana. Think of the last time you told a fib. Why did you do it?"

Diana made faces to better help herself remember, then came up with, "So I wouldn't get punished."

"Very astute. That is probably the most common reason people lie, to avoid pain," the governess praised.

"But Daniel lies for no reason," Diana said as she took a seat by the fire. "In fact, he's more likely to get into trouble for it."

"What does he say?" Eden took a seat by Diana, while Colin went back to his desk and shuffled papers.

"He says he was stolen by Gypsies, and he had hundreds of blood horses, and a hundred servants, and three estates, and a townhouse."

"If those things were true, you might look up to him."

"So you're saying he does it to impress us, make us think he is more important than he is?"

"Possibly. It's another reason people lie. Why are you so sure he is lying? Your brother thinks it may be true."

"Gypsies don't steal children; that's only in fairy stories," Diana insisted.

Eden thought she understood the problem. "Diana, Daniel was very little when the lady lured him away. He hadn't been told not to talk to strangers yet. You are too grown now ever to approach a stranger. And the park here is a well-protected environment. You don't need to worry about…"

"But Mr. Crane attacked you."

Colin's head came up at that. Eden glanced at him; she had no ready answer for that. He spoke. "The farmers had seen Mr. Crane, but they thought he was still working for us and made no comment. Strangers are not allowed on the estate. And if it is Crane you are afraid of, he is a continent away from here right now."

"Well, but lying is wrong, and if Daniel is lying, he is doing something wrong, and I will not stand for it," Diana insisted.

"We still don't know if he is lying, Diana. But he is young and the archer does not always hit his mark, especially in the beginning. Practice makes perfect. What is important is that we aim in the right direction," Eden offered.

"I have no idea what you mean," the girl said honestly.

"Merely that none of us is perfect. We should not cast stones at others."

"Yes, and why are we not perfect? God is supposed to be perfect. And we are supposed to be made in his image and likeness. Then why are we not perfect?"

"That is indeed a difficult question, and I am not sure I can give you a short answer," Eden said. At this point, a book slammed behind Eden, and she turned to see Colin's narrowed eyes and disapproving brows. He was letting her know she was treading on dangerous ground, but he did look a little comical, and she had to turn away to suppress a smile.

Diana waved a hand at him, dismissing him. "Don't pay any attention to him."

"Perhaps your brother feels he has a better answer for this than mine would be."

Diana turned to her brother. He put his feet up on a stool, folded his arms and prepared to watch the governess squirm. Diana turned back to Eden and said, "I know his answer. I want to hear yours."

"May I hear his: since you know it?"

"There is no God; we're all a big accident," Diana said.

"Rather simplistically put, little sister," Colin defended.

"You don't accept that answer?" Eden asked the girl.

"It's harder for me to believe that there is no God, than that He does exist. Nature is too vast and too ordered for it to be an accident," the girl said.

"You came up with this on your own?" The governess was amazed.

"The idea is not my own, but I agree with it."

Eden turned again to the brother. "You see. Your sister does have her own opinions. Do you mind if I venture my personal interpretation to the question?"

"I am all ears," he answered sarcastically.

Eden began anyway, "It has to do with free will. This is a flawed example, but … do you love your pony?"

"You know I do."

"Do you love your brother?"

Diana flushed. "Most of the time, yes."

"Answer seriously or this won't work. Do you love each equally?"

Diana thought. "I never considered it before, but no."

"Which do you love more?" She had the earl's interest now. You could hear a pin drop.

Diana's tone was incensed as she answered, "Colin, of course. "

"But why?"

"Because he's my brother."

"I hate to disillusion you, but not all siblings love each other, in fact some fight like cats and dogs."

"I guess because he's good to me."

"And your pony is bad to you?"

"I didn't say that. I guess because Colin loves me back again."

"And your pony does not return your affection?"

"It's not the same. If ponies can love, then I think Tony loves me back. He neighs when he sees me and tosses his head and begins to move about his stall."

"Then what is the difference?" Eden asked.

"You tell me."

"No. You think about it."

"I think I know what you want me to say."

"I want you to say what you think."

"But you have an answer in mind."

Eden shook her head and stole a glance at Colin. "Your sister is too sharp for me. Are you certain she is only twelve?"

Colin chuckled, "We were always a family of precocious children."

"I'm almost thirteen," Diana corrected.

"Very well, what answer do you think I have in mind?"

"That Tony loves me because I feed and exercise him, and Colin loves me because he just does."

"Precisely. Which is more precious: love forced or love volunteered?"

"You can't force someone to love you, can you?"

"No. Because they have a free will. Without it, we would be nothing but puppets. Because God wants us to come to him freely, willingly, He must create us with a free will and therefore a free choice. We can choose truth, right, the good: God - or the opposite. If God interfered every time we chose to act wrongly, would we really have a free choice? If I told you to choose a cup of tea or a glass of wine for refreshment, yet each time you reached for the wine, I moved it out of your grasp, how do you think you would feel?"

"What ground we have covered: lying, tolerance, and free will. That's enough serious conversation for one day. Give it time to sink in. Let's quit disturbing your brother," Eden said as she rose to leave.

Lord Edmund thought 'disturbing' an appropriate word to describe what the governess was doing to him. He said, "Come, Diana, I promised you a ride into town. Shall you invite your governess to go with us?"

"Do I have to?"

His Lordship said wryly, "You have just learned you have a free will and a choice."

"Then my answer is no."

"I beg your pardon?"

"No, Colin. I see Miss Barrett every day. I see you so little; I want you all to myself. After all, I love you more than my pony."

"Your wish is my command. Miss Barrett, guests will arrive at about eight. You will attend."

"Do I have a choice?"

"No."

"Very well."

"You give in easily today."
"I am no fool."
"I will see you then."

* * *

Later, Mr. York handed Eden a letter. This one had come directly from Matthew. On the sixth of April, he had fought in a bloody battle. Many of his comrades had fallen beside him. "I write frankly to you, Eden, in hopes you will show this letter to Lord Edmund and beg him to use his influence to get Parliament to loosen its purse-strings and provide us with trained sappers and miners. The infantry was forced to do the work of mine and shell.

"You cannot believe the bravery of our soldiers. I saw men grasp the bayonet of the enemy with their bare hands. When officers fell in the line of battle, their servants insisted on taking their master's place in the ranks. We could win this war so much faster and with so fewer losses of lives if only the treasury could back us."

Matthew feared for his sanity. He begged her to continue writing her chatty letters filled with the news of the children for they were shared with the entire camp. "They're saying we have Boney on the run, but I can't see it from where I sit. Tell me, sister, do children really have such great trials as a wiggly tooth that defies falling out, or indecision about whether to spend their copper on a gingerbread or a penny loaf? Or are they as the children here: dirty, scab-infested, runny-nosed, mat-haired, flea-bitten, and shoeless? Do they constantly whine and beg and search the litter for their supper? Are there really debutantes who wonder which gown will best show off their coloring to impress a certain foppish beau? Or are the girls here the real ones. Girls of thirteen who wander about in the stench of their unwashed bodies with blouses pulled down bellow their shoulders and faces painted like clowns, attaching themselves to anything in uniform? Are there people who still value human life? Does anyone ever sit down? Do they really sleep in feather beds? Is my life real, or is yours? Or is reality something in between? I feel as if I'm existing in a tangible nightmare.

* * *

The evening's entertainment boasted a soprano, tenor, alto, baritone, pianist, cellist, and harpist. Diana had begged off the event, and her brother did not insist she attend. Eden had no comrade to sit beside her in the party of strangers who ignored her so obviously. She smiled and watched others joking and drinking as if they were all part of a dream; removed from her - unreal.

When the performers took their places on stage and those assembled began to fill up the chairs in the music room, Eden placed herself well away from the French windows. From her position, she was able to watch the earl unobserved as he made the rounds among his guests. Each time she looked his way, he stood listening to a different person, often with a look of veiled disinterest. She found some consolation in knowing he took about as much pleasure in the present company as she did. He looked as if he would just as soon be engaged in one of his solitary pursuits.

On Sunday, Colin slept until noon. When Eden returned from services, the earl and Lady Diana had gone visiting. Eden spent her usual time with Mother Grey and wrote letters. She took an early supper with Nurse Warren and prepared for bed, giving her long hair its fifty strokes, but refusing to braid it or cover it with a nightcap, as was the custom. She lit the lamp on the table beside her bed and climbed in with a copy of *Rasselas*. The day had seemed to take an eternity to pass.

At about ten-o-clock, a storm came up. The wind moaned and wailed insistently about the manor. The high-ceilinged rooms seemed to trap and magnify the eerie wails. Open doors shut. Windows that were shut rattled. Several close, deafening cracks of thunder caused Eden to flinch in her bed as she attempted to read. She decided to check on Diana to see if the noises had frightened her. She pulled her wrapper around her and tied its belt, walking barefoot out of her room.

Diana's sitting room door was open, and Eden saw her standing in the center of the room in her nightgown. She went to the girl, saying, "Diana, are you all right?"

Colin, who was kneeling at the fireplace fussing with the damper, stood up and turned around. He was dressed in a burgundy velvet robe and slippers.

"You must stay, Miss Barrett. Colin is about to tell ghost stories. He does it extremely well."

"This wasn't my idea," Lord Edmund apologized. "I don't ordinarily approve of frightening little girls, but my unnatural sister here enjoys a good scare."

"Sit here, Miss Barrett," Diana ordered. She picked up a toasting fork and speared a slab of bread. "Toast?" Eden declined. "Isn't it a perfect night for ghost stories?" the girl asked with a spooky gleam in her eyes.

"It is the worst sort of night for ghastly tales. It renders them more believable by the ambiance," Colin said in a macabre tone that promised theatrics with the storytelling. He handed Eden a cup of hot chocolate. He then made a great show of blowing out all the lamps in the room until there was only one candle left flickering. The embers in the fireplace afforded a dim glow as only a few fagots of twigs had been lit to warm the chocolate and toast the bread, the weather being mild.

Colin brought the remaining candle with him, seated himself on a stool before the two females, and placed the candle below him on the floor. The effect of the wavering shadows the candle cast upon his face from that angle was positively fiendish.

Diana settled herself closer to Eden and asked her brother, "Shall you tell a new one?"

"If you like."

"I like."

"Very well." He then proceeded to tell a convoluted tale of unrequited love and revenge that was calculated to frighten only slightly and to lead to an exquisitely suspenseful climax that placed the heroine in grave danger. At the most climactic moment, he leaned forward and blew out the candle. Diana squealed with delight and clutched Eden's arm, which caused her to lurch. Colin laughed and finished the story, stood, and relit the oil lamps. When he returned to the two on the settee, he said to Diana, "Hello young man, have you seen my sister?"

Diana looked to Eden for enlightenment. "Your brother refers to the fact that you have grown a chocolate mustache," she informed her. Diana promptly shaved the mustache with her pink tongue.

"Isn't he the best story teller?"

"I can see where you get your acting talent from," Eden said. "Thank you for the diversion, but I need to get my beauty sleep. As the storm has now died down, I suggest you do the same."

Diana kissed her brother and ran into her room. He rose and followed the two ladies into Diana's bedchamber. The governess bent over the bed to kiss his sister's nose. Eden's waist-long, silky sable hair fanned out across her back and onto the bed. She straightened and tossed her head to move the mane back out of her way. As she turned, she saw that he was watching and smiled up at him, "Next time you're telling stories, please remember to invite me. I wouldn't miss it for the world."

As she walked away, his eyes followed her. Diana recognized the look of fascination in her brother's expression, though he tried to disguise it. She was reminded of Miss Austen and a similar look of regard on his face. At first she had encouraged that budding romance, hoping to have the attention of both her brother and her governess, but it had backfired. They soon had eyes only for each other and found excuses to leave her with the nanny. She had felt odd-man-out and disgusted by their displays of affection when they thought no one saw.

She told Father then. And she had used her power against Miss Austen that night. It must not happen again. She liked Miss Barrett. If lies were not enough to keep them apart, she must not, under any circumstance, use her power. But she was afraid she might get angry and accidentally use it.

Colin turned back to his sister and positioned himself on the edge of her bed. "How goes it with you and your governess?"

"Oh, we get on famously. Miss Barrett is fun."

"What useful bit of information does she teach my favorite sister now?"

"I am your only sister, and she is teaching me the waltz."

"But Mr. Beauchamp is your dancing master."

"He says the waltz is too fast and refuses to teach it to me."

"It is now considered acceptable at Almack's, with a sponsor's permission, of course. Therefore it can no longer be considered fast."

"Miss Barrett's very words."

"And who takes the part of the gentleman when you practice these waltz lessons?"

"Miss Barrett, of course, so I may learn my part."

"And who plays the music?"

"Miss Barrett sings it."

"And how do you find her voice?"

"Tolerable. Are you falling in love with Miss Barrett?"

"Good Heavens, no!" he answered a little too quickly.

"That's good because she is secretly engaged to a soldier. She is head-over-ears in love with him. They are only waiting until he gets an advancement and can support her to announce the banns. She wears his signet ring around her neck with her cross."

"I know. I've seen it and him."

"You have!"

"He drove her here in a curricle the day she first arrived. I saw him give her the ring."

Diana realized he meant Eden's brother. This was going to be easier than she had thought. "What does he look like? Is he really handsome?"

"What does Miss Barrett say?"

"She says he is exquisite. But all ladies think their fiancés are."

"He is tall... blonde... I suppose good-looking; I didn't see him close up."

"She pines for him, especially when she gets a letter from Bath."

He thought, *He'll never see the enemy in Bath. Perhaps he'll get reassigned and killed in action. Perhaps I can get him reassigned. Now that's beneath me. Shades of David and Bathsheba.* He changed the subject. "Does Miss Barrett ever lecture you like Nurse Warren?"

"If I misbehave."

"Do you misbehave?"

"Sometimes."

"Well, don't. What I meant was does she try to get you to go to Sunday service and talk about sin? You know..."

Diana did know. She debated her answer. If she said 'yes', he would dislike her governess, but he would also surely sack her, and Diana was not certain she would like the person who took Miss Barrett's place. "No. She's not stuffy at all. But I have been considering going sometimes to service. May I?"

"That is up to you. Now, goodnight. I must get my handsome sleep. I leave in the morning."

* * *

At the same time that Colin was drawing the soft goose-down counterpane over his sister, a grizzled sailor was yanking a damp, scratchy wool blanket off a wiry man who had curled up on the deck of the H.M.S. Warhorse. He kicked the prone figure. "Get off your bloody arss. You can get twenty lashes for sleeping on watch."

Crane groaned and opened his bleary eyes. The steady moan and creak and grumble of the boards sounded like the inside of a starving dragon's belly. The salt air assailed his nostrils. He remembered where he was.

He had puked for two weeks when they first brought him on board. Now he was seaworthy. The work was hard at times, especially since he'd had to use muscles that hadn't been used in a long time, but he was getting stronger. At other times, they lay about counting the hours. That was when Crane's mind went back to Daniel. Daniel would always entertain him by reading to him. He could barely read himself. But, at least he was fed regular now, and the Navy had given him a newish set of clothes. It wasn't as bad as it could have been if they'd tossed him in goal.

But he had to be careful and keep himself away from others. They mustn't find out about his affliction, or he'd never hear the end of it. They were a rough lot.

Crane pulled himself upright. "Thanks moite. That bloody rollin' back and forth puts me to sleep loike a babe in the cradle. D'you know where we're 'eaded?"

"Not headed anywhere. We're sittin' still. That line of dark gray just off the bow there is Portugal."

"Cor, never thought oid see the world."

"Well, look all you want now. If we do put in to port, you'll be locked in the hold with the rest of the prisoners. They won't be lettin' the likes of you touch land. They don't trust you yet to ever come back."

"Won't be able to spend me blunt then. I'll have a tidy sum 'o back pay when the war's over," Crane said. He thought, *Plenty enough money to get me back to that town Edmunton. Then Oil be payin' back a certain vicar's bitch.*

CHAPTER XI

At breakfast the three comrades were solemn. Eden informed the earl of her sister's wedding in three weeks' time. He insisted she must attend and offered her the use of a carriage and driver. He then assured Diana he would come back to Chadilane to keep her company on those days her governess was away. Thus encouraged, Eden pulled out her brother's letter and handed it to Colin. "It's from my brother. He asked that I let you read it. He makes a request of you."

The earl glanced at the addresses on the letter. It had come through Weymouth. Her brother was in Badajos, half a world away from Bath. He read the entire letter with his meal before him, but not touching it. "I don't know how they do it. I suppose one does what one must, but I could never be a soldier. I am proud of our men, but I don't envy them. Only a fool would. I'll see what I can do. I can speak to a number of people in the Ministry of War. I can't promise anything though."

"It is more than enough," Eden said.

After His Lordship returned to London, the days went back to normal for Eden and Diana. The weather broke and tender green things began to push up and out, relieving the all grays and browns in the landscape. Diana and Eden did a lot of riding. Sometimes Patrick would allow Daniel to come with them, acting as groom instead of himself. Little Thomas did not have the hang of handling the reins as yet, but Eden insisted he could go too, and she held a leading rope. The four friends would picnic by the lower pond where Diana introduced them to the pair of swans. The birds would come hissing congenially when called and accept disdainfully any leftover baked goods that had been brought along. "Colin brought them home two years ago from Abbotsbury. They still had their dirty gray feathers then," Diana said. "I had hoped they would nest, but they don't seem interested. They hardly look at each other."

"Swans take longer to mature than most birds. They don't breed until about three or four years old. But once they have chosen a mate, they stay faithful to each other for life, and that can be a half century for some swans," Eden told them. "Did you know the Greeks thought that swans were the souls of dead poets, so strikingly pure and white they are? Have you ever heard the story of Lohengrin?" The children shook their heads. Eden promptly told it to them.

* * *

The third week in May, Eden was delivered to the door of her mother's cottage in an opulent black coach, the doors of which were emblazoned with the Edmund crest. She was hugged until her chest ached by the two younger sisters and one brother who remained at home. Though her mother was still cool to her, except to ask if there were any prospects at the manor, the siblings' excited chatter kept the conversation warm late into the night.

Mary was a beautiful bride. From his own store, Mr. Tobias, who was a linen draper, had provided the beautiful satin and lace fabrics Mary had used to sew her bridal gown. Eden had used the curling tongs to give her sister a stylish coiffure. A silver sovereign had been tucked into Mary's slipper for luck. As the ceremony progressed, Eden felt the familiar tightness in her throat. Weddings always made her cry - anyone's wedding - and this was her sister's. She strove vainly not to make a fool of herself when it came time for the exchange of vows. There was Mary, in all her youth and innocence gazing with such pride and trust up into her betrothed's eyes and promising before God and the whole town of guests to "love, honor, and obey him until death do us part." No manner of swallowing and lip biting could keep the tears from streaming down her face. Sir William gave the wedding breakfast, which was served under tents on the church lawn. Finally, old shoes were thrown at the departing couple as they rode out of town in a white curricle drawn by two white horses. Then Eden boarded the earl's carriage and felt that she was traveling home instead of coming from it.

Colin had estimated the time it would take Patrick to travel to Longacre, stop for refreshments and bring Eden home. He supposed the wedding breakfast would last until noon or so; he hoped no later. He had challenged his sister to a game of croquet on the front lawn. Croquet was a civilized game that required no exertion, thus no sweat. He did not intend to be sweating when Eden arrived. Nor did he want his nosey sister to suspect how eager he was to encounter her governess. Not yet.

He appeared engrossed in the game while keeping an eye on the path the coach would take. When he saw dust rising in the near distance, he applied his mallet a little too forcefully causing the ball to roll down the hill and over the road. He told Diana to wait there while he retrieved it. She offered to help, but he said he didn't need help as he could see the ball very well by himself. Then he timed his stroll so that he reached the ball in time to intersect the carriage.

As Patrick drew up, Colin motioned to him to stop. He opened the door and let down the steps himself, then waited for the appearance of the occupant. When Eden stood on the top step, he tossed his mallet down and held out a hand to assist her. But when she reached to take it, both his hands went directly to her waist. He then hoisted her high in the air to rest her waist upon his right shoulder.

"Put me down now," Eden demanded coolly, steadying herself by holding on to his head.

"Diana," he managed to call, "look what I found."

"Sir, you are embarrassing me and you know it."

"Am I? Good. It is your punishment and you will take it. You are a vile, wicked creature who runs off for weeks at a time without so much as a backward glance at your master. Did you call me Sir?"

"My lord would not do this, and I was only gone three days with your permission. Please put me down or we shall both fall."

"There is no danger of that if you will stop kicking. A partridge weighs no more than you." He brought her slowly to the ground, sliding her along the length of him. He left his hands about her waist. "You are too thin. Shall I have to feed you?" She glared at him. "You won't shame me," he said, "I cannot come any lower. I am reduced to playing croquet with a little girl. Have you any idea how boring croquet is?"

"If you insist on trifling with me, I tender my resignation now."

He instantly released her like hands release a hot potato and bent to pick up his mallet. "You are indeed hard, but I have missed my sparring partner. Diana has missed you too."

Eden started up toward Diana, who was approaching, but the earl stopped her with a hand on her wrist. "Your family, they are well?"

"All of them. Deliriously so."

"The wedding was a success? The guests enjoyed themselves?"

"Some a little too much. My poor sister was embarrassed out of her mind."

"What do you mean?"

"Well, Sir William provided the refreshments for the bridal breakfast, and some of the company took it as license to imbibe too freely. The toasts, of course, got out of hand."

"In what way?"

"You've been to such breakfasts, surely."

"Not lately," he said.

"Well, they went beyond innuendo, especially the Master of Ceremonies, and he should know better."

"I don't understand. What do you refer to?"

"Never mind. I'm sorry I brought it up."

"But you did bring it up, and you will finish what you began."

"You know very well what I refer to. They were teasing her about…what newlyweds do on their honeymoon."

"I hear some even do it after their honeymoon."

"Oh, you odius creature! You set me up for that." She moved away from him swiftly, but he kept apace with her to get in another jibe since a deep dimple in her cheek belied her attempt at not finding him funny.

"What a salacious little mind you have. I was not aware governesses entertained such thoughts."

"Governesses are as human as the rest of the world," she admitted.

"Well, this is news! Very encouraging news, I might add." As Diana had reached them by now, he could not continue in this vein, and another thought came to him, "Was your brother able to attend?"

"No and he was sorely missed."

"Was there any other young man from the military in attendance?"

"There was one, a friend of … the family. Why do you ask?"

"Just wondered." Colin was sorry he had asked. He was very sorry he had to return to London again the next day, but at least he had the excuse of the musical evening to return in a week's time.

* * *

GENTLE JOURNEY

The first Friday in June, Eden escorted the children down to the lower pond. The plantation was like a fairytale garden now. The pear, cherry, peach, and plum trees were laden with tiny pink or white blossoms. The air was heavy with sweet scents. The rhododendron and hawthorn added their own deep shades of pink. She had brought her wooden case of watercolors to capture spring.

Diana and Thomas painted swiftly and haphazardly. They then turned in their handiwork for praise. Thomas got down to the more exciting business of catching pollywogs. What he intended to do with them after catching them was anyone's guess. Diana fashioned a very pretty wreath of wildflowers. When she finished with this, she pleaded with Eden to let down her hair and wear the colorful circlet. Then she commanded Daniel to paint Eden as a barefoot medieval maiden. He agreed eagerly.

Eden was persuaded to remove her half boots and sit on a boulder with her knees up just so with the willows and the lake behind her. This she didn't mind so much because her shoes had been pinching her. Daniel became absorbed in his work and executed a fine piece. When he had finished, he suddenly realized how hungry he was. They had not brought lunch along knowing that the earl would return today, and there would be many fine things baking for the evenings' repast for the guests. The children just might be needed for tasting. As the governess was not hungry, Daniel offered to carry the art supplies and herd the other two children if Miss Barrett wished to stay. On the way back, they wanted to glimpse the badger set and the rabbit warren they had discovered a few days before. Partly because it meant taking the long way around and partly because the beauty of nature was calling Eden to commune with her Creator, she agreed that she did wish to stay a little longer.

When they had gone, she removed her stockings, stuffed them in her boots, tossed them beneath a bush and went to wade in the cool water. Her aching feet now relieved, she chose a grassy area that afforded a clear view of the lake. Here she sat down and drew her knees beneath her chin, clasping her arms loosely about her legs. She was praising and thanking God for all that He had done when she drifted off in a daydream.

She neither saw nor heard Colin's approach as he stretched his legs after the long carriage ride from London. He'd been told where his sister was and strode out on the usual path to meet her, but the children had taken the alternate route through the woods and missed him.

Sean, who had been trotting along beside him, became engrossed in something under a bush until Colin came up to investigate. He picked up the shoes the dog was nosing and held them behind him while he went in search of the owner. When he spied her, he gave Sean the hand signal to 'down' and 'stay.' He hesitated a moment before shifting the boots to his left hand. Then he bent and broke off a blade of tall grass. Treading softly until he was close enough, he extended the straw leaf until it just touched Eden's neck.

This, of course, made her flinch and strike her neck, thinking it was an insect. When she turned and saw the earl, she drew her bare feet up under her skirts. "Very amusing," she attempted to quell him.

"Mistook you for a wood nymph. Had to test and see if you were mortal," he explained. She felt stupid being found barefoot and wreathed in wildflowers, but it was too late. When she didn't answer him, he asked, "Where are the children?"

"They went up to eat."

"And left you to play dress up?"

"Daniel was painting my portrait. It came out quite well, I might add. I'm supposed to be a medieval maiden."

"You look more like a wood nymph to me. You were too pensive; what were you thinking about?"

Eden looked back at the big Mute swans gliding sedately near shore. "I was watching your swans, my lord, and identifying with them."

"In what way?"

"They are pinioned, are they not?"

"The pen's wings are pinioned. The cob stays of his own volition."

"Then they reverse the roles humans play. With people, it is usually thought to be the male whose wings must be clipped to keep him from straying."

"Not when the female is worth staying home for," he grinned.

Eden smiled at his quick riposte. "To answer your question, I am feeling a little like that pen out there. God has given me the desire to fly, but society has clipped my wings. I'm paddling about in a much larger, more fulfilling, more captivating lake here at Chadilane, but I'm still not flying.

"You're not walking either."

Eden turned back to look at him, "I beg your pardon?" He held up the boots to explain. She stood then and made a single attempt to take them, but he yanked them high above his head. She found herself uncomfortably close to him. "Please, give them to me. You can have no use for them."

"Wood nymphs don't wear boots."

"But I do."

"I think I'll conduct a little experiment. How far do you think I can throw these, and how long will it take for them to sink to the bottom of the lake?"

"You wouldn't"

His chin came up at that. "How can you know what I would do? If you want them returned safely to you, what ransom are you willing to pay?"

"They're not worth much."

"To me they are. They look brand new, and well constructed. Why, what have we here? Stockings! Why, Miss Barrett, I'm shocked."

"Very well. What do you consider a suitable ransom?"

"Why the privilege of watching you put them on, stockings included."

The gleam in his eyes caused Eden to glance about for an escape route even more than his words had. Her cheeks were aflame. "How can you suggest such a thing?"

"So, I'm a scoundrel, am I?"

"If you insist on pursuing this course, yes. Let me by,"

"Oh, very well. Take your old boots," he said, holding them in front of him. When she reached to take them, his left hand darted out and grasped the hair at the nape of her neck. He turned her to face him and stole a gentle, lingering kiss from her generous mouth. Affected but unsatisfied by the first, he tried for a second, but the frightened look on her face stopped him.

The boots dropped to the ground as he grasped her waist and pulled her to him. She didn't struggle; he was far too strong. She simply placed her hands upon his chest and turned her head aside as she stood calmly in his clutches.

"Most ungratifying," he told her. "It would really be much sweeter if you responded. I promise." She was trembling, mortified, on the verge of tears. She blamed herself. She should have been more reserve toward him. Didn't he know this would change everything between them?

He continued stroking her with his voice as he ran his fingers through her hair and crushed the curls. "There's no use pretending that you're ice. I've seen the fire in your eyes. How often I've wanted to touch this hair. It's just as I thought it would be, soft and sleek as an ermine's fur. How long I've wanted to taste that mouth. It is petal soft and warm as I had thought it would be, but refuses to answer my pressure with pressure of its own. Cruel. I ask so little."

Eden felt her breathing and heartbeat accelerate. She felt giddy and warm about the face and neck as one does when drinking brandy. Was he speaking of love or lust? Eden pushed away from his chest, but his powerful arms held her firmly.

"Not just yet," he said. "Perhaps I can melt this armor that surrounds you." He kissed her right temple with a slow reverence, then her ear, then the flesh below her ear. He was rewarded with a shudder. A more forceful kiss a little lower on her neck caused her to squirm against him and groan the quietest little, half-hearted, "Don't. Please don't, my lord. I thought we were friends." Needles and flames spread down the side of her body and made her knees weaken. He lifted his head to look at her face. Tears gathered in the rims of her eyes. She was terrified of him or of herself. He had risked all and lost.

Once he let her go she would fly back to the house and pack her bags to go home. He would never see her again. Well, in that case, he would make it worth his while. "Eden, you never need be afraid of me. I am your friend. I don't know why I…When I saw you with your hair down and the flowers, and I knew we were alone… You are absolutely enchanting you know… I hadn't planned this… I wouldn't hurt you for the world. Don't hate me. I'm going to let you go in just a moment. I promise never to alarm you this way again; I swear it."

"But before I let you go, make it worth the risk I've taken: the loss of your friendship, your trust, your esteem, all of which I value greatly. I intend to kiss you once more. Return it this time, and I will never force my attentions upon you again. You have my word on it." She said nothing.

He tilted her face up to him. She closed her eyes, distress in her face. To look into his pale irises at such close range was too intense for her. He kissed each eyelid, and then claimed her mouth. At first there was no response but he was so gentle, so reverent, she yielded at last - a sweeter surrender than he had thought possible. It would be the only one, so it must last forever if he could manage it. Heart racing, he prolonged the kiss until he thought he would die.

When he finally raised his head, she was breathing fast and shallow and leaning so heavily against him that she would fall if he let her go. He rested her head on his chest and his heart pounded in her ear. As soon as she could think again, she became completely bewildered. Her own body had deserted her reason in favor of what? Emotion? Sensuality? She had found pleasure in responding to him, and what was worse, he must be aware of it. Worse still, she wanted more. How could she ever face him again?

He brought his face close to her ear to tell her something and she misunderstood his movement. Her hands went up to his neck, and she drew his mouth down upon hers for more loving. Colin had no choice but to oblige, taking even greater delight because she had initiated it. When he felt himself becoming aroused beyond control, he broke his lips from hers, and she nestled her head beneath his chin.

She was cherished and by a worthy man! Her mother was wrong; she was not unnatural! Surely this was not something passing. She felt excited and languid at the same time. She thought of the one other time she had kissed a man not related to her. It had been experimental and disappointing. The sergeant friend of her bother's had made some advances that made her ashamed. But her body had certainly not reacted this way at all. Those kisses had meant nothing.

Then she was aware that Colin was saying something to her, but she had been so removed in reflection, she had heard nothing but the depth of his voice. In her confused state, she attempted to apologize for not paying attention to his words. "I'm sorry... I was thinking of someone...someone else, or I should not have..."

She felt herself pushed abruptly away from him. He bent to retrieve her boots and placed them in her hands. She could not see the stricken look in his eyes. Then he turned her to face the manor and said in a gruff voice, "Go home, Eden. Now. We'll speak of this later."

She wandered up the path at a loss, embarrassed, bewildered, and hurt. Now what had she done? Eden glanced back to see the earl sans coat and waistcoat sitting in the grass removing his shoes. The wreath of flowers fell from her crown as she turned back toward the house and began to run. When she heard a splash behind her, she looked back quickly and saw the rippling water where the earl had dived into the lake.

Later, as Colin sloshed his way back to the stables damning himself for a fool, he grumbled aloud, "Thinking of someone else! What does that make me? A stand in for another's embrace. A phantom lover. All that sweet warmth was meant for that soldier I saw you with, that Charlie fellow. What does he have that I don't? Your fidelity evidently." He had protected her from himself by putting her away from him, and she was thinking of someone else. His body still quivered from wanting her, and she was thinking of someone else!

As he approached the stables, the person he wished to speak to appeared from behind the barn door. "Daniel, come here a moment."

Daniel approached taking in the sight of Lord Edmund, hair soaked, clothes dripping, holding his boots and coat away from him. "My lord?"

"Miss Barrett says you did a portrait of her."

"I did. It came out pretty nice, too."

"I'd like to see it after I change."

"You're all wet."

"I know. I took a dip in the lake."

"Mr. Stagg says there's leeches in that water."

"I'm aware of that too. But I had to cool off... fast."

CHAPTER XII

Safe in her room, Eden wrestled with her conflicting thoughts. She had been aware of a mild attraction to him, but had discounted and suppressed it. The staff and his sister believed that the earl was all but publicly betrothed to Cassandra Bradley. Diana had said they were to be married after he was out of black gloves. Either they were mistaken about the engagement, or she was mistaken about his intentions toward herself. Had he fallen out of love with Cassandra and in love with her? Had the engagement been broken off before it was announced? She was not of his rank, but she was of the gentility, at least she had been before she became a governess. A man did not embrace a young lady of her station in the way he had unless he intended to marry her. That is, not if he was a gentleman. But he had not spoken of love, only desire. And he said he had not planned it beforehand. What was she to think?

He had said they would speak of it later, and he had used her given name for the first time. What if he were serious? What if he meant to propose? She must consider this a possibility. He was not a shallow sort of person; he might make jokes, but he was not unprincipled. He was an honorable man. At least she had thought he was until today. If he meant to ask for her hand, she should prepare an answer for him while she was still able to think calmly and clearly. This was too grave to be left to chance. She had been far from rational in his arms.

She began to list in her mind his good attributes. He was an intelligent, sensitive, considerate man. At least he had been. Though he was commanding, he was not dictatorial. If she disagreed with him, he heard her out. He had stood on her side in the incident with the climbing boys. He had allowed them a place at Chadilane without batting an eye. He did seem to value her opinion on things. The discussions they had enjoyed proved this to her. He was rich and powerful. Though she was ashamed to admit it to herself because it seemed so mercenary, this was a definite plus. It could cut years off her scheme to earn a reputation. As his countess, she would instantly become a part of that social realm which could be cultivated to participate in and donate to the philanthropic societies she could organize. That is if the ton would even accept her. Or would she be a detriment to his political aspirations because of her current position?

She asked God to help her discern the right and good in this situation. Promptly she was reminded that he espoused atheism. He seemed to respect her beliefs and not attempt to change her, but there would be children. Her own convictions were so central to who she was, she found it impossible to think of becoming one with someone whose beliefs ran counter to hers. How could she be a parent without sharing her faith with her children? Her faith was herself. It was the most important thing in the world to give a child. No riches, no power, no beauty, no knowledge could sustain like faith. He would not support her in this. He would imbue his children with his negative, no absolutes, and no purpose to life attitude. She must never entertain any designs upon him. How often her father had preached from the pulpit that a marriage must be composed of three people: a husband, a wife, and God. God was the force that held the other two together, guiding them, keeping them whole and safe in hard times, and rewarding them with joyful times.

But Eden fell into remembering his expressive face as she listened to him hold forth on a political problem, or the easy way he had with his sister, and his wry smile, and a hundred other moments with him. Then she knew that she was not just attracted to him, she was already in love with him. She had put up walls; he had dug beneath them. He was like that setter dog of his. It would push its silky muzzle gently against your hand until you were forced to pet him, whether you wanted to or not. He was as perfect a suitor as she could imagine, except for that one giant mark against him. She hadn't asked to fall in love, but she had, and she would like nothing better than to run into the circle of his strong arms again and feel that sweet lethargy overtake her senses. She was sorely tempted to say 'yes' and spend the rest of her life trying to change him, but she knew that never worked. He would have to change first, or there could be no joining to him.

Having reluctantly decided this, Eden realized she would need to guard her heart with the keen awareness of a sentry on duty. They could never again be as comfortable as they had become together. Why had he ruined it all? She set about preparing for the evening's entertainment. If he did choose to make a proposal before supper, she would be ready to receive him. She would have to let him down gently. She laid out the lavender satin gown she had just finished sewing, arranged for an early bath, went down to the still room for flowers to put in her hair, and scanned the pages of "La Belle Assemblee" for a suitable upswept hairstyle.

As the eight-o-clock hour approached, Eden viewed herself in the cheval glass and was pleased with the results. Never had she taken so much time arranging her hair. She had just put the finishing touches on the style with a sprig of Baby's Breath and was experimenting with velvet ribbons about her long neck, when she heard the knock at her sitting room door. Recognizing it as his, the mass of butterflies in her stomach fluttered madly for an escape. She took several deep breaths to calm herself. She went through to the sitting room, careful to close her chamber door behind her.

When the door opened and she turned that lovely smiling visage up to him, he drew an audible breath, then looked almost as if someone had punched him in the stomach. *Why must she look so amazing?* He schooled his expression before he spoke. "You are absolutely stunning this evening," he said gallantly but coolly.

"Come in." She turned and moved further into the room.

"You forgot this," he said, holding out to her the wreath of flowers.

She bit her lower lip and looked at the carpet, and he placed the wreath on the closest table and stood before her like a schoolboy. "Miss Barrett, Eden. I must know. Are your... Would you say that your affections are presently engaged?"

She turned her back to him. She had never admitted anything so momentous, so intimate as this to anyone - had only just admitted it to herself. *He wants to propose, but he wants to secure my feelings first before imposing upon me. He doubts his power over me. How sweet. If I admit my feelings for him, will that not incite him, encourage him to stronger feelings for me? But I cannot have him think that I allowed... participated in his attentions this afternoon when they meant nothing to me. Honesty is the best policy.* "Yes, My lord. I am afraid they are."

"And if the object of your affections were to ask for your hand in marriage, would you accept him?"

What is this? He wants to know the answer to his question before he asks the question? How very shy he is in this. "Not at this point. There is an impediment…"

"And if this impediment were removed?"

"I'd rather not say until I am asked."

"Is it likely you will be?"

Pique showed in her voice as she turned to face him, "How should I know?"

"I'm sorry, it is not my… About this afternoon… It was a stupid, clumsy mistake. The entire episode must be erased from your memory. It must not be allowed to interfere with our friendship, which is worth so much more than the disgusting lack of circumspection I showed you… Please do not leave us. I could never replace you in Diana's heart, and I should miss my ally, my sounding board…" He continued deprecating his action, saying all that he thought she wished to hear and none of what she had anticipated with joy. Every word cut her and convinced her that he had been trifling with her, and the entire episode was nothing to him but a great embarrassment.

He left her alone when she found her voice and interrupted his monologue to say, "Yes, of course. Think no more of it. Please, attend your guests."

Once beyond her door, Colin strode to his own rooms, removed a small box from his waistcoat pocket, and placed it in a bureau drawer. He then took up a fanciful watercolor painting of a beautiful wood nymph complete with masses of sable tresses, a ringlet of flowers, and bare feet, and signed 'Daniel'. After gazing at it for a while, he placed it in the same drawer and closed it.

Once her door was closed, Eden allowed the tears to burst their dam. What a blow to her femininity. She had misread every sign. He had seemed so sincere by the lake. She could not help thinking she had been tried - and found wanting. She certainly found herself wanting - wanting him, wanting to die, wanting to break something. After indulging herself in great waves of self-pity, she blew her nose and began to think.

GENTLE JOURNEY

If she didn't attend the assembly, he would want to know why. He must think the episode by the lake meant as little to her as it obviously meant to him. Eden washed her face, collected herself, and went down to join the party. Diana was there to talk to at least.

Something was missing from this evening's entertainment. It took Eden an hour to figure out just what it was. It was the earl's smile. It seemed each time she stole a glance at him, she caught him glaring at her. He was a poor diplomat tonight.

CHAPTER XIII

Colin avoided Eden completely until his departure, and she was glad he did. She could not tell how she would act if she had to face him. She had a suspicion she would break down and cry and make a fool of herself in front of him, and she hated the thought of not being in control of her emotions that way. But when he had gone, she was on tenterhooks with missing him. *It is my punishment*, she thought. *I was tempted, and I yielded, not just to his caresses, that was not so bad, but to even considering marriage with him. What a fool he must think me. What an idiot I am.*

In the next week, Eden received a letter from Evelina Mowbray, Sir William's fourteen-year-old daughter. "Please, please Miss Barrett, we beg of you to come back to us. Our new governess, Miss Turner (we call her Turnip), is nasty to us. She lies to us and plays tricks on us, and when we tell father, she says we are imagining things, and she makes us take medicine all the time. She is very sneaky.

"You know Molly, the scullery maid? Well, Father found out she was breeding because she got a fat belly and he turned her off. When we asked why, he said she was a bad influence, and he'd better never hear of us kissing a boy before we're married because he'd send us off to finishing school, and we'd never be allowed home again. He was so furious; I got scared. You must, you really must write and tell us how babies are made because I thought I had an idea, but now I'm not so sure, and it might be too late for when we went to the fair last week, Celina Varney dared me to kiss John Rumplesleeve on the mouth. I ran up and kissed him hard and said, 'I'll do anything on a dare.' We asked Miss Turner if kissing was what made a baby start growing in you and she said, "It sure does." But she doesn't always tell the truth like you did.

"Molly had a baby growing in her for half a year or more and nobody even knew it. If she weren't such a bony thing, we still wouldn't know. Please, at least write and tell me if I have got a baby."

The letter was promptly answered.

* * *

Though Parliament was scheduled to rise in July until the fall session, the earl returned two weeks earlier than expected. Diana was deliriously happy and insisted that he take her to the shore at Sand Point. He suggested they make a picnic of it and include Daniel and Thomas and the governess as well. The motley group set out the next morning with Eden crushed inside the Landau with the three children. The top was down, but they intended to put it up for the ride home to keep from getting burned since they would spend the whole day in the sun. Colin rode on Galahad, with Connors driving and Patrick and Joseph as outriders.

It was glorious to stroll along the pebbly shore against the wind, shouting to each other over the roar of the surf. The children watched the sandpipers' antics playing tag with the waves. Then they ran about finding all sorts of flotsam and exotic life in the tide pools. After they availed themselves of the nuncheon Mrs. York had packed, and made certain all persons in the party including servants were stuffed to the gills, they found that the greedy gulls would gladly accept leftovers, catching them on the fly as the children tossed them up in the air. Then Thomas and Daniel fashioned ships of driftwood and set an armada afloat, only the ocean kept sending the ships back, so then the children attempted to build a stone castle since there was not enough material for the sand variety. Eden and Colin said little to each other, but they stood or sat comfortably side-by-side watching the antics of the children and commenting upon discoveries as they were brought to them for appreciation.

When they returned, Colin asked Daniel and Thomas to join them for tea. When all were served, the earl spoke to Daniel. "Do you remember the sketch you drew of what you remembered as your home? Diana sent it to me in London."

Daniel nodded.

"It is a very good likeness of Darrow Hall in Cornwall. At least that is what Lord Everly tells me. I circulated the picture among members of the ton to see if someone could identify it. It seems that Lord and Lady Darrow have been in India these past three years. Lord Darrow is ambassador to that country. Several people who knew him well were able to tell me that his only son had been reported missing while in his nanny's care about eight years ago. The boy was four at the time. They searched for him for years until Lady Darrow's health became poor. Lord Darrow only accepted the ambassadorship in hopes that a warmer climate would bring Her Ladyship back to good health."

"And did it?"

"I believe so, yes. I've written to them and sent them both your sketch and the watercolor Miss Barrett did of you. I received from them a very long letter and several sketches of them in case you might recognize their faces. These were done by Lord Darrow himself; you will see that he is as talented as you. You must realize that they are older now than when you saw them last." Colin rose and withdrew the letter from his inside coat pocket. "When I saw these pictures, I knew they must be your parents; you are the image of Lady Darrow." He unfolded the sketches and held them out to Daniel. "Lord Darrow is winding up a few things, and they will travel here as soon as he can be ready."

Daniel took the pictures and looked at them as if he were looking at ghosts. His face drained to white, and he ran from the room.

Thomas stood and put his plate and saucer on the side table. "May I see?" Colin showed them to him. "Yes the lady looks like Daniel. I wonder if they will let me visit him. Thank you for tea. It was delicious. May I please leave now?" His voice broke at the last.

Colin excused him. He looked questioningly to Eden, "I thought I was imparting happy news. I admit it was sudden, but I won't get a chance to see him for several weeks."

Diana turned an accusing face upon him and demanded, "You're leaving again! You just got here!"

"Yes, dear sister, but before you bite my head off, I came to take you back with me."

"To London!"

"To London."

"You always say it's not a good place for children."

"Well, since we will be holding a house party here after parliament rises, we would only be staying there for two weeks. I think you can survive the city for that long."

"Truly?"

"Truly, elf."

"Yes! Yes! Yes!" Diana shouted and jumped up and threw her arms about her brother. "When do we leave?"

"Cock's-crow tomorrow, so start packing now. Long sleeves and wool stockings, we stay at Aunt Chadwick's."

"Why not the townhouse?"

"It's being shown to let. I prefer my bachelor quarters when I'm in town; they're much closer to work. The town house was made for assemblies and routes. It is much too big for just myself, and it's a sad waste to see it empty. I promise we will dine out often, and spend as much time as I can spare you at amusements."

"Then Aunt Chadwick's should be fun."

"I have one yea, but you go only if Miss Barrett goes to mind you when I am working. What say you, Miss Barrett? Shall you care to leave your exciting classroom duties for the dull and dirty little borough of London?"

"Who else goes with us?"

"Why Patrick and John will drive; Connors will postillion; Joseph will outride; and Perrin will foot. I had thought to take Nora as a sort of Abigail for you ladies, but she has asked to visit her ailing father. I'm not really sorry she cannot come. Three will be a crush on such a journey as it is. I take up a lot of room. Should you prefer that I find another female to lend propriety, or is Diana duenna enough for you?"

"By earning a wage, I am no longer due a lady's consideration."

"Nonsense. You are a lady in my book, and due every consideration."

"Prettily said, my lord. As you are a gentleman in my book, Diana shall be chaperone enough for me. Thank you for the invitation."

"Good. I must warn you, my aunt has many household pets and tries to keep the flea population down, but with varied success, thus the need for long sleeves. If you stay on the upper floors, though, you can avoid the pests. Connors has gone ahead with the bays for the second part of the journey."

Eden had a worried look. "You don't travel there in one day?"

"On horseback I do, but it is quite a long journey, and I have arranged to meet some of my tenants in outlying areas at the Blue Lion just outside Farnborough, so we will put up there one night. Separate rooms have been arranged for all of us, if that is what worries you." His eyes gleamed with ribbing her.

She looked away at that, unable to meet his gaze. He continued, "We will make the trip in easy stages."

"Is Miss Fitzwarren still at the townhouse?" Diana asked.

"She's there."

"May I see her?"

"If you like. Now go pack. I have work to do."

Diana and Eden rose and went out to examine their wardrobes. As they mounted the stairs, Diana told Eden, "I am going to will Miss Fitzwarren to make her wonderful gingerbread. You'll see. Its aroma will fill the air when we arrive at the townhouse."

"You describe things like an author, Diana. Perhaps you should write a book."

* * *

Great quantities of cold water splashed about the face were needed to get governess and charge into action the next morning. Both had been too excited to merely fall asleep. They resolved together not to take coffee or any other liquid until it was absolutely necessary. The thought of causing six grown men to have to stand about while they "bloomed behind the bushes" was daunting.

The coach was packed and on the road before daybreak. Though their eyes were pinched, Diana and Eden's minds were racing with the sheer novelty of their adventure. Diana reveled in the position of tutor as she regaled Eden with impressions of her last London visit when her father had taken her. The vignettes she described were more suited to a child's mind, but they were exceedingly refreshing. Diana could vividly recapture such moments as when the dromedary at the Zoological Gardens had spit right in Father's eye, and what foul smelling stuff the saliva was.

"A hurdy-gurdy man came round to our door with a little monkey in a red suit with gold braid that danced round and round and took a penny from my hand. He bit the coin to see if it was real and then gave it to his owner. Then he tipped his cap and showed all his teeth. The monkey I mean, not the owner.

"Colin, you must take us to a Punch and Judy show in the park. I'm too old for puppets, but Miss Barrett would like them. And I want to see a play this time. Father refused to take me to the theatre."

"I hesitate myself, Diana. The theatre can be rough for a lady of your tender years. Even with box seats, one has to push in with the crush when the doors are opened or get trampled. And once you are safely in your seat, I cannot guarantee you will hear any of what's happening on stage. The audience is often louder than the performers, especially if they don't approve of the performance. It's a mixed bag that go to theatre, Diana. I've seen them pelt the actors and each other with nutshells and orange rinds. The opera usually affords a better conducted audience," Colin cautioned his sister.

"You make the theatre sound fun. We must buy nuts and oranges there for ammunition. Besides, I've heard enough opera at the musical evenings at Chadilane to last me a lifetime."

"We'll see what's offered when we arrive. Kean may still be doing Shylock."

"No Shakespeare!"

At one point Diana actually wound down, looked out the window, and was quiet for a spell. Colin took this opportunity to tell Eden, "Have you been to London?"

"No. Have I missed anything in particular?"

"You will like the museums I think, especially Somerset House, and I have something planned which I will not let you in on until it is finalized. But to my mind, one could live a full and satisfying life without ever venturing there."

"You don't care for London."

"It's tolerable as cities go - if they could only eliminate the masses of people that congregate there."

"You don't like the people?"

"Oh, I like most people very well: I just don't like them all grouped in one spot like that."

"You would have them distributed about the countryside?"

"I would."

"Then there would be no city."

"You take my meaning."

* * *

At about ten o' clock, John turned the horses onto the gravel drive of a tidy little posting inn. The occupants of the Berline spilled out and stretched their legs. The gentler sex dashed inside and directed pleading looks to the first female they saw. The maid pointed to a privy in the fields beyond the garden. When they reached the privy, Eden said, "Age before beauty."

Diana said, "Rank before age."

"Well, hurry then," she was told.

When they returned, they were informed that breakfast would be served promptly in the private room above. The ladies kept His Lordship company while he downed a hearty meal. Diana had hot chocolate and nibbled at a sweet bun. She feared travel sickness if the roads got rougher or the day too hot and humid in the mid-afternoon sun. Eden's stomach was queasy already, but she said nothing, not wanting to spoil the journey by unnecessary concern.

With fresh horses, the troop was off again. On this leg of the journey, Colin entertained his sister with conundrums and twenty questions until the combination of early rising and the constant swaying of the vehicle caused the girl's eyelids to become heavy. Because she was sitting on the same side as Eden, she leaned against her governess, who adjusted her position, putting an arm around her, so that the girl rested comfortably against her bosom. The child fell promptly into a deep sleep. Eden suppressed several yawns of her own before laying her head atop Diana's and succumbing to a light slumber.

Colin thought ruefully that it was just like his companions to desert him in this way, but he took full advantage of the opportunity to study Eden's face as he had never dared before. Her countenance was serene. When those large, dark eyes were open, all other features were forgotten by the viewer. Now with those mesmerizing orbs safely concealed, Colin was free to consider her other charms to his heart's content. Her generous, naturally rose-tinted mouth tended to part slightly in repose, rendering it most provocative. The nose was small, exquisite, slightly turned up. A few wisps of dark hair had worked loose from their prison of pins and played about her round chin and amazing swan-like neck. He approved her complexion; it was clear and tanned, not the ghostly white fashionable at present. Colin was pleased that the governess shunned the use of a bonnet so often. When his eyes came to rest on the place where his sister cushioned her head,

GENTLE JOURNEY

envy invaded the depths of his irises, and he schooled his glance back up to her face least Eden wake and find him staring.

More than an hour was spent in this fashion. Then, after much stretching to awaken herself (which Colin immensely enjoyed watching), Eden took her turn to amuse the group. This she did by quizzing the other two on types of flora and fauna she saw and recalling little episodes of her younger years that showed her to be no saint.

It was about five o' clock when the carriage turned on to the drive of the Blue Lion. At the top of his lungs, Patrick called, "House there." The posting inn was a picturesque white wattle and daub building with a deep brown scalloped-edged, thatched roof. A high, well-trimmed hedge enclosed the tidy yard. The innkeeper, his wife, and the tapster lined up outside the door to receive them, while an hostler in corduroy and gaiters ran to take the horses' heads.

Perrin hopped off the boot and let the steps down. He handed the ladies out and followed them into the inn. Colin's deep voice could be heard greeting the innkeeper and telling a great hulking boy to attend the horses. "Get inside and have your mug Patrick. Don't bother about the cattle. Jem here's as good an hostler as you'd care to meet. Got a real way with the big animals he has." The young man referred to gave the biggest, sheepiest of grins possible as he detached the traces from the carriage.

Diana and Eden were shown to a cozy chamber with an adjoining sitting room. They helped each other change out of their dusty carriage costumes and into fresh frocks. As Eden brushed down their travel clothes, Diana washed her face and hands and took out her nightgown and cap. The two then descended the staircase to the coffeehouse. Diana had pleaded with her brother not to have to take her meal in a private parlor where there would be no ambiance.

A bored waiter spread a cloth for them in a box by the window and handed them a bill of fare, then retired to his small pantry to wait. Lord Edmund stood talking to some plainly dressed gentlemen. He excused himself to come over and seat himself with the ladies. Diana and Eden deliberated so long over their choices that Colin threatened to order for them for he was famished and he had business to conduct. Eden decided upon a ragu; Diana, a bird; and Colin, the House Specialty of the Day.

When the waiter had taken their orders from Colin, the earl excused himself from the table until the meal was brought in. He continued to speak to the gentlemen, some of whom became very animated, but not quite heated. At one point, Colin took a pad of foolscap and a pencil from his inside coat pocket and wrote down a few notes on what was being said. From some bits of conversation, Eden deduced these to be tenants unhappy with their rent or the way things had not been repaired.

The men must have come to some sort of amicable agreement because they shook hands all round and left with looks on their faces that ranged from satisfaction to disbelief. Colin had just begun to enjoy his food when a second group of locals began to gather at the desk. A spokesman for the men leaned over the desk and said something to the innkeeper, which caused him to look in the direction of the earl's table. The locals milled about, hat in hand, and watched the diners.

Colin hurried his meal and suggested the ladies take their time eating, and then they might care to stretch their limbs in the garden when they finished. Mrs. Sheppard, the innkeeper's wife, could show them around. He excused himself and went to the new group of men and invited them to join him in a tankard of home brew. The men seemed eager for that. When Diana completed her meal, and Eden finished pushing her food around on its pewter plate, they stepped out into the garden.

The innkeeper's wife, a tall, full-figured, friendly-faced woman, introduced herself as Ma Sheppard. "Everyone around here calls me 'Ma'; calls my husband, 'Da'. We started it ourselves when we had Jem. Most 'Mas' have more children of their own than us, but I guess I been wet-nurse to more'n half the youngsters that lives hereabout. Half the folks as stops here thinks of us as ken. We like it that way."

"Do you have any children other than Jem?" Eden asked.

"Another boy, Simon. Goin' on eight," the woman answered. "He's somewhere about, playin' with his battledore, I expect." As Diana skipped ahead, Ma Sheppard allowed some of the concern she felt for her youngest to show on her face. She lowered her voice as she spoke to Eden. "Simon needs some special care I can't always find time to give him. A postin' inn's a busy place all day an' night, an' I don't seem to be able to hold on to help. You get a chambermaid trained up good, an' she gets to thinkin' she could just as well do the same work in London an' be closer to the sights an' shops, so she hops on one a them coaches after quarter day an that's that. London is too close to here. Its pull is too strong. If I could just get me a few extra girls as would stay, I think I could reach Simon.

"He's brain-blessed, you see. Don't speak none, but I know he can hear for he hums the tunes his father whistles. He won't look you straight in the eye, but he knows we're here. He'll put up his arms to have his shirt put on. He's the dearest, sweetest child; amuses himself, ain't no trouble, but I can't help worryin' at times who'll look after him when I'm 'put to sleep with a shovel' as they say."

Ma Sheppard was particularly proud of her husband's rose garden. He had succeeded in crossing two strains to achieve a new variety the color of fresh salmon flesh. He also had a fine vegetable garden lined with a low hedge of herbs. The innkeeper's wife pulled some overripe vegetables out of the garden and led the two ladies to her own particular avocation: pig farming.

The pigs stood on a wooden floor and were extremely clean as were all of the grounds around the barn. Eden had never heard of pigs being raised this way, but they seemed to be happy. Ma Sheppard called them by name and tossed the vegetables to them, talking to them as they ate, urging them on. The creatures seemed to be conversing with her as they grunted back in answer.

Colin joined the ladies for a brief stroll about the plantation. He spoke to Mrs. Sheppard with affection, taking her arm in his and complementing her on the size and color of the young peaches and apples. As the group walked back toward the inn, Diana asked her brother, "Those men you were talking to...Is there a problem?"

"Definitely. But easily resolved."

Although Eden had felt she could not keep her eyes open one minute longer, when, at last, she sank into the linen sheets, no sooner had she closed her eyes than her mind sat up wide awake. Tomorrow she would be in London! She was to accompany Diana on shopping excursions, to the theatre, to Astley's Amphitheatre, to cathedrals, to tearooms, to art and science museums, to the gardens of Hampstead Heath. All the places she had read and heard about. What a feast it must be! Her imagination ran wild.

Several times, Eden got up during the night to pace about the bedroom and look out of the window as coaches drew up noisily to change their spent horses for fresh ones. The newly arrived travelers had little thought for the peace of any boarders who might be trying to sleep. The little food she had managed to eat was not agreeing with Eden, and her eyes burned, her head ached, and her throat was slightly sore. Each time she looked at Diana, the child was sleeping soundly. Eden stretched out on her bed and tried to emulate her pupil's good example. Though she yawned heartily and counted the primroses on the wallpaper, she could not doze off. Not long before dawn, she finally gave in to exhaustion.

At cock's crow, Diana woke and dressed herself. A chambermaid knocked softly at the door, and Diana let her in. She was carrying fresh water for the pitcher and ewer. A second maid entered with hot chocolate and buns, which she set down in the sitting room. Diana ate greedily, and then went in search of her brother.

His chamber door was unlocked, but he was not in bed. Diana called him. No answer came. She looked about the room and realized his articles had been removed. Perrin must have packed her brother's trunk already and brought it down to the carriage. Her brother must be below.

Diana went down the backstairs and into the yard. She saw the horses being backed up to the carriage and went toward it. Before she had taken two steps, she tripped over a pair of legs as they stuck out from beneath a bush. "I'm sorry. I didn't see you there," Diana said. "Do you know where Lord Edmund is?"

A brown-haired boy sat up and began to examine an ant making its way along the soil.

"I say, excuse me, but have you seen my brother, Lord Edmund?" she asked in a slightly louder voice.

The boy drew a circle around the ant with his finger; then a larger circle around the first circle, then one around that.

Diana gave the boy a push on his shoulder. He tensed and drew himself up tight.

"What's the matter with you? Speak when you're spoken too. Look at me. Are you deaf?"

The boy fell back on the soil and stared up at the trees. Diana became frightened and ran back into the inn and up to her room. She shook Eden and cried, "Miss Barrett! Wake up!" The look on Diana's face woke Eden with a start. She jumped out of bed and pulled her dressing gown about her.

"What is it?"

"There's a fey boy in the garden."

"What did he do? Why are you frightened?"

"He wouldn't answer me."

"Perhaps he's deaf. What else?"

"I touched him. He cringed like I'd burned him. He knew I was there, but he stared at the sky."

There was a knock at the door. Eden opened it to Colin. Diana ran to him and took his hand, looking pleadingly at him.

"What is this?" he asked, half surprised, half amused.

"There's a fey boy in the garden," Diana said.

"Leave him alone. What were you doing in the garden?"

"Looking for you. You've seen him?"

"He's harmless. He's the innkeeper's child. He lives in his own world. He doesn't think as we do, but he harms no one. There's no need to be frightened," he told her. Then he picked her up and held her as he said to Eden, "I'll send Connors up to take your luggage in a few minutes. We'll be leaving soon. Mrs. Sheppard has packed us a nuncheon." He glanced at the breakfast on the table and asked Diana if she had eaten. With her affirmative, he carried the girl out of the chamber.

Eden was still dressing in the bedroom when Connors rapped on the sitting room door. She called to him that all was packed and ready in the two trunks. Connors picked up the luggage while a chambermaid took the rolls and chocolate, leaving Eden with no breakfast and no time.

Colin's manner when they set out was subdued. Diana threw off her experience, as children do, and was pestering her brother with excited questions about where they would stop to eat, how much longer it would take to get to London, and what they would do first when they got there.

He answered patiently, smiling wanly at her, but with no attempt to feign great interest. Diana assumed the role of adult and attempted to amuse him out of his blue funk. When he resisted amusement, she asked simply, "Have I done something wrong?"

It was effective. "No, child. I'm preoccupied. That's all. I'd tell you if you'd done something I could not approve of."

"Is it because of those men last night? Some of them looked angry."

"You needn't concern yourself about them. It's estate business; we came to an agreement. They were satisfied."

"But you are sad, Colin."

"No need for you to be, Diana. Sometimes life just depresses me; but as often it brings me joy."

"Tell me," the child asked with true sympathy.

Colin chuckled fondly. She sounded so grown up. "Well, the innkeeper and his wife: two harder working, warmer, more deserving people you would not want to meet. They call themselves 'Ma' and 'Da', but mother and father to what? A full grown man who is so slow of mind he can hardly remember his direction, and a boy who is unaware of communication, has never spoken his mother's name-does not even seem to know people have names. They have been twice cursed."

Out of concern for Diana, Eden offered her view. "To you they may be cursed, my lord, but I know the Sheppards consider themselves twice blessed."

Colin was nettled, as Eden was afraid he might be, though he tried to control it in his voice. "How can it be a blessing to produce a son who can barely add two and two; who can never laugh at jests because he doesn't understand them; who will never be anything more than an hostler because he can't even conceive of a career beyond that?"

"Is that really so bad?" Eden soothed. "I have known intellectuals who tortured themselves with their own knowledge, dreamers who wasted themselves with disappointment when the dream failed. Jem is proud of himself and proud of what he does. His parents need his help. What he does is necessary. He feels needed and wanted because he is.

"As for jests that fly over his head, I'm glad he didn't understand the ones I heard leveled at him by the coachmen last night. They were mean and deflating and sarcastic, and could only anger a man of abler wit. He took them all with a grin and a nod, innocent of their ill intent. Jem is at peace, complacent. He has few worries and much love. How can you call him a curse? Only a cynic could do so."

His Lordship listened condescendingly, a sneer hovering at the corner of his mouth. "Cynic is what a hardened optimist calls a realist. I suppose you are now going to tell me it is a blessing to produce a feeble-minded child, a child who eats what is put in front of him, but otherwise never indicates hunger or thirst, a child who never returns his mother's smiles or embraces? This child shall never be necessary."

"I admit, I'm not as acquainted with the boy as you, but I saw pride and love as well as the concern in his mother's eyes when she spoke of him last evening. I believe that it is possible for good to result even from what we perceive as a bad situation. Where there is life, there is hope, and his mother spoke with hope of reaching the boy in the future. If there is any hope for normalcy for the boy, he has certainly most providentially been placed in the ideal home for him. The overflowing love of the Sheppard's is what can bring him round, if anything can…"

"No. He is a useless burden; it would be better for all if…" Colin's glance at his sister and subsequent altering of his sentence showed he still protected the girl. "If things were different."

"But they are not different, and wishing they were is useless. We must accept the situation as it is, and work from there…"

"I don't need you to tell me that," he growled with a look that rendered any further discussion futile. The two adults stared out opposite windows of the carriage while Diana sat silent between them. She was convinced that the present mood was all her fault. After all, she had willed them apart.

They rode on like this for about half an hour. Finally, Colin broke the air of enmity by raising his walking stick to thump the roof of the Berline. The communicating window was slid aside, and John asked from above, "Milord?"

"This is it. The big chalk boulder on the left," Colin told him.

"Very good, milord," John answered, and slid the window closed again.

The carriage began to slow and turn. It was finally brought to a stop in front of a boulder that stood like a great monolith on the otherwise flat land. After Perrin had handed Diana out, Colin laid a hand on Eden's wrist to stay her. "Let us agree to disagree and refuse to entertain any resentment. If not for our own sakes, since we must remain in close quarters for several more hours, then for the child's sake."

"Of course," she said, giving him her gloved hand to shake on it. But she could not help adding, "You intend to 'accept our situation as it is, and work from there?'"

His eyes narrowed, but his mouth was curled in a grin, "As a lady, you are allowed the last taunting remark, but it was beneath you."

Eden lowered her eyes, but her smile also belied her words. "You have just successfully delivered the last remark and rendered me defenseless, my lord."

They might have continued amicably digging each other all day if Diana had not thrust her head into the carriage and demanded to know why they had stopped when they were not getting out. "Are we going to eat or not? I'm sharp set."

"This is a favored spot of mine for a nuncheon," Colin informed them cheerfully after all had alighted. "There is a picturesque little brook with a miniscule falls just beyond those rushes. The spreading branches of that elm form the perfect shade for reclining picnickers. You might pluck a bouquet of forget-me-nots growing in the moist soil along the banks to bring to Aunt Chadsworthy, Diana."

As the footmen brought out the cloth for the ground and the reed baskets, Lord Edmund led his ladies to the brook to point out the best places to find the pale blue flowers. Diana spied a patch of deep lavender and bright yellow among a tangle of vines and reeds. She tore back some of the vines to expose an enormous delicately ruffled iris blossom glowing luminously from within its dark confines. "Isn't it exquisite?" Diana asked in reverent undertones. "How could it bloom here without sunlight? But look at the stalk: it is so pale. I'll tear away these vines and let the sun shine on it. It's too splendid to cut."

Colin told her, "Remove only one or two vines, Diana. If a plant is accustomed to shade, placing it in direct sunlight will only scorch it. It must be acclimated by stages, to toughen it gradually to the harsher elements."

Eden and Colin left Diana and strolled back toward the elm tree. Within minutes, Diana caught up with them and said in a low tone, "There's an ugly lady sitting on a rock by the water weeping into her arms."

Eden turned immediately around and started back in the direction from which they had come. "Miss Barrett..." Colin began, but she gave him a dark look that said she would brook no argument, and told Diana to stay with her brother. When she followed the stream a bit, she found the pitiful figure hunched over by the water's edge. She went to the woman and placed a hand on her thin shoulder. She was never so surprised as when the face that turned up to her turned out to be that of the Mowbray's scullery maid, Molly.

CHAPTER XIV

When Colin followed Eden's path a moment later to make sure she was in no danger, he found her embracing the stranger. The two women were talking nineteen to the dozen like old acquaintances. He looked up and down the water's edge to see if there was any sign of footpads lurking about. Satisfied she was safe, he left the ladies to themselves. Diana had begun to eat, so Colin joined her and told the servants to begin also.

Molly broke down with relief and fatigue in Eden's embrace. "How did you get here?" the governess asked.

"I was tryin' to get to London. I've a sister in service to a family there. I had only enough money saved for a outside seat on the coach as far as Basingstoke. Then I got a ride on the back of a farm tumbril, but the man had to turn at the crossroads to Chilton so he put me down there, and I just started walking. When I saw this stream, I came to get a drink and wash in it 'cause the day got so hot. I thought I better stay here until I could get another ride because of the water. Several coaches went by, but they won't stop or they won't let me on 'cause I have no money. I been waitin' here since yesterday with only a biscuit to eat."

When Eden heard this, she interrupted Molly's tale to call Connors to bring her meal. He brought her a china plate of cold ham and chicken, with a meat pie and sweet buns, and a glass of wine. Eden set these before Molly, who blessed her profusely. "Please take as much as you want," Eden said. "You see how they feed me far too much."

Between eating ravenously and wiping away tears, Molly told her old friend, "I didn't know what to do when they turned me off. I just couldn't go home and let my parents see me like this. How could I face those sweet, perfect people and tell them their pride and joy was no better than a strumpet?"

"No, Molly, they would never think that way. Everyone makes mistakes..."

"Some just make bigger mistakes than others. Spare me the sermons, Miss Eden. Pretty girls like you - girls of higher class - can't possibly imagine what it's like to be ugly. And a scullery maid is the lowest of the low. People don't treat you the same. They don't even look at you if they bother to speak to you, and that's only if they're givin' orders. Pretty girls can say 'no' to a man because they know they'll be asked again. He said it was what people in love do, but now I know he just said that to get his pleasure.

"I knew what could happen. I hear plenty a tales, but I chose to do what I knew was wrong. I thought it might not be so bad if a baby did come. I would tell him, and he would marry me. I'd make a good wife. I likes little babies. But when I told him, he said it prob'ly belonged to one of my other followers. I said, 'You know I ain't got no other followers.' He said, 'All my chums'll say they been with you. You think I'm gonna let myself be leg-shackled for good with a witch like you? Don't give away the cream and come around expecting me to buy the cow cause it's heavy with calf.'" At this she broke down again.

"Hush now," Eden consoled, "You're among friends. Your sister - do you know her direction in London?"

"Only that she's workin' for a fam'ly name of Haxton."

"Did you send your parents a note so they wouldn't worry?"

"I can't write that good, and they can't read. I asked cook to tell me parents where I was goin'."

"I'll write to them when I reach my destination this afternoon just to tell them you're fine. Someone will read it to them. Molly, I wouldn't like to send you on to London without knowing if you'll be able to find your sister or employment there. London is very big, and there are thieves as well as others who will be looking out for a girl alone to take advantage of. But, I do have an idea if you will agree to it." Eden explained Mrs. Sheppard's needs to Molly and assured her she would be well treated at the Blue Lion while they looked for her sister in London. Molly was glad of any hope brought her way.

Colin heard what he needed to from Eden. "What would you have me do?" he asked. When she told him, he took out his writing case and penned a letter of explanation to the innkeeper of the Blue Lion assuring him that, should he not need Molly's services, the earl would bear all expenses for her room and board until he returned. He folded the letter, melted the wax, and set his seal to it. Then he pressed ten guineas along with the missive into Molly's hand. He instructed Joseph to wait with Molly and see her safely on an inside seat of a coach stopping at the Blue Lion. He could catch up with them later.

After she had embraced and reassured Molly sufficiently, Eden was handed into the Berline. She waved to the pathetic figure of the scullery maid as the horses drew away. When at last she turned to her companions, she found Colin's pale eyes regarding her with a tinge of disbelief.

"How could you?" he said.

"How could I what?"

"How could you let such a perfect opportunity slip through your fingers like that?"

"You mean to be severe, but I'll humor you. What are you speaking of?"

"No remonstrations, no sermons on the evils of sin and the efficacy of walking on the right path? You let the girl off without a single attempt to instruct. You made no accusations. You simply helped her. Are you slipping, Miss Barrett?"

"If a man falls into a well, my lord, he needs no lectures about the dangers of wells or his stupidity for falling into one. What he needs is for someone to throw him a rope. Strong arms are also useful. It is most likely he will then avoid wells in future. Charity is still a Christian virtue, my lord."

"Ah. I had hoped it was a sign you were now above sermonizing. I see you save that for me."

Eden could see by the playful gleam in his eyes that he was ribbing her. "You asked for it, my lord."

"And I got it; didn't I just?" he chuckled.

Until they reached London, the tourists were quiet and reflective, but not resentful as they had been before the stop.

CHAPTER XV

Lady Chadwick's townhouse was almost as interesting as the lady herself. Her plump figure did not hide the fact that she had once been a very pretty woman. Her voice in conversation had a two-octave range, especially when making innuendos, but it mostly stayed at the higher register. Her face harbored a perpetual insincere smile. She spoke sharply to her servants. Her hair was the same thick mass of black curls as her nephew's, but it had lost its luster and seemed unnatural as if dyed.

Her home was on a fashionable street, and the architecture showed it was once fashionable itself. Lady Chadwick's tastes ran to the gilt, gaudy, and ornate, and plenty of it. The décor could have been excused had it not been that her Ladyship insisted on sharing her home with every unwanted animal she met on the streets. The animals were given the run of the house to the point that it became uncomfortable, if not unfit for human habitation.

The air of the house was permeated with the smell of old dog and old dog urine. Every soft cushion a human might sit on was already occupied by a feline or a canine. A stroll through the first floor reception rooms resulted in an accumulation of various lengths and colors of hair on the clothing. If an inch of flesh was not covered with clothing, it soon would be - with fleas.

Conversation was difficult because it was punctuated by the raucous screeches of two huge Macaws or the hurdy-gurdy man's monkey that had bit one too many children.

Lady Chadwick felt creatures should not be caged. That would be cruel. She did, however, like to talk despite the noise. She asked questions she did not wait for an answer to, and gave advice that was not asked for.

The only escape from her overpowering society was broken when

Diana asked to be shown to her room for a little lie-down before supper. She explained she had been awake all night with excitement and was afraid she would fall asleep in her soup if she could not rest now. "Of course, my child. Nesbitt will show you the way. I'd come up with you, as well; but my heart, you know, can't take the stairs. Haven't been up them in years. Made a bedchamber of one of the sitting rooms here on the ground floor for myself. Show the governess her room as well, Nesbitt."

Nothing at all inhabited the first floor. Since her Ladyship did not come up here, the animals didn't either. Most of them looked too old and infirm to make it up the stairs anyway. Diana was shown a lovely room on that floor, but Eden was led even higher to a cubicle on the third floor. The furniture in the room consisted of an iron cot, a nightstand, and an ancient, warped clothespress. Concealed beneath the nightstand was a cracked chamber pot. On the nightstand stood a simple white ewer and basin with a frayed linen cloth for washing, and a tallow candle.

Eden opened the casement in the unaired cell and looked out over the city. From this vantage point, she was privileged to see miles of rooftops with hundreds of smoking chimney pots. She tried washing herself by dampening one corner of the cloth and using the other half to dry. She had not been provided with a tablet of soap.

When Eden had slipped into a pretty violet lute string frock (chosen for its long sleeves) and was struggling with the buttons at the back, Diana came in. She offered to help Eden with her buttons and then sat on the edge of the bed. "This room is not very cheerful, is it?" she understated.

"It'll be simple to keep clean. Did you dress yourself?"

"No. Nesbitt helped. Miss Barrett, you said I may talk with you about absolutely anything, and that it's better to ask and find out than to wonder and worry?"

"Yes, I did. What is it?"

"That lady today - the one we left with Joseph - she was uh... breeding; was she not?"

"Yes, she was."

"She wore no wedding ring. Did she loose it?"

"She wasn't married."

"That's what I was afraid of."

"Afraid?"

"How could she get a baby in her without a husband?"

"She had relations with a man as if he were her husband. Do you understand what I mean by 'had relations'?"

"Nanny Warren told me." Diana screwed up her face, "It sounds disgusting, and she said people must do that only if they're married, then God makes a baby from it. But God gave her a baby anyway, and that lady wasn't married. Isn't it wicked to make a baby and not be married?"

"It is God's plan that only a husband and wife have relations with each other. That way the marriage is kept beautiful, secret, and sacred, and if a baby results, the child will have a mother and a father and God to love him and care for him and provide for him and teach him what he needs to know. Babies are a big responsibility, and it is easier when there are two parents to share the work of raising them."

"Then she is a wicked lady, and you were nice to her."

"She is human and made a mistake. It is not our place to do the judging. People make mistakes and learn from them. It is between her and God, and He promises us forgiveness if we ask for it."

"Did she get a disease? Is that why she was crying?"

"Disease?"

"Nurse Warren said if anybody did it without getting married first, God punishes them by sending them a horrible disease that drives them mad. Baron Bradley got the pox and went mad, and they had to put him in Bedlam."

"Nurse Warren drives me mad with some of the things she tells you. I don't believe diseases come from God. He is pure good; bad cannot come from Him. It's truer to say disease comes because of Satan. We put ourselves in the power of evil when we choose to cut ourselves off from God by preferring sin to His Law of Love. Sometimes God allows sickness to overtake someone for the good of their soul, but He did not create disease. But this is something wiser ones than I have tackled. It's one of those things you need to believe on faith. Jesus went about healing all those who believed when He was here on earth, and He said, 'Whoever sees me, sees the Father who sent me'."

"If God did not create disease, where did it come from?"

"A question I too have wondered about. I warn you, this is my own thought on the matter. It may be wrong or incomplete, but Satan has taken so many things that God intended for good and twisted them to bad, like when he twists love into lust, that I think he has done the same with health. God gave us foods of all kinds and a healthy desire for nourishment, yet Satan entices people to Gluttony, eating even after the need is fulfilled. Gluttony ruins the health of many people. Another example of Satan changing what was meant for our good into something bad with our cooperation would be the physician uses laudanum to ease pain. That's a good use for it, but the devil entices people to continue to use it even after they don't need it until they actually experience pain if they try to stop using it. Many people become a slave to laudanum and lose all desire to eat or even move, thus ruining their health."

Diana thought about that for a moment before asking, "Why would Nurse Warren say something so awful if it weren't so?"

"I suppose in an attempt to make certain you remain chaste until you are married. There are better, more positive reasons for remaining pure, though. One reason is so that the married couple can always trust one another, something very important to a marriage."

"But Baron Bradley got a disease because he did it with bad women."

"There are some diseases associated with the sexual act, but never when both people involved are chaste, clinging only to each other."

"When I get married, I'll adopt babies from a foundling home if I want some."

That seems a generous plan. But first make sure your husband-to-be agrees with you," Eden said as she began to unbraid Diana's hair.

"Then we won't have to do it at all."

Eden forced back a chuckle as she brushed the girl's locks. "Oh, but husband and wife don't have relations just because they want to have children."

Diana was appalled. "Then why else would they do such a disgusting thing?"

"The marriage act is far from disgusting when two people truly love each other. It is a gift from God to his beloved creation, mankind. It's joining your body with someone you love as much as your life - becoming one with him. God has given a very pleasurable sensation to the experience; one you will long to share with your life's partner, as you will wish to share all of your other joys and your sorrows as well with him.

"You're right; it is a very intimate thing. But there should be no embarrassment between husband and wife if they truly respect each other, as they should. Don't fret about it now. You have years to go. As you mature, you'll understand better."

"That lady did it, and it made her cry."

"She was crying because she felt confused, sorry, and afraid of the consequences she will now have to face. She thought the father of the baby would marry her, but he refused. Life will be difficult for her as a lone parent and for her child as natural born. God meant sex to be beautiful, special, sacred, and he meant for each and every one of his newborn children to be welcomed into the world as a joy, not a hardship. But if a person does not have the proper reverence for sex, then it becomes a trap. We must learn to accept with gratitude and esteem all of God's gifts in order to get the most enjoyment from them."

The appearance of Nesbitt brought an abrupt end to the conversation. The servant told Diana, "You're wanted downstairs, Your Ladyship. His Lordship is going out."

Eden followed Diana and Nesbitt down to the first floor landing. As they approached it, she heard the beautiful musical trill of a lady's laugh. She halted at the top of the stairs. Diana yelled, "Cassy, Dory!" and ran down the steps to them.

Colin was elegantly dressed in black evening clothes. He held the delicate cream porcelain hand of a gorgeous, tall, willowy, fair-haired, modishly attired young lady. A blonde-haired, mustached young man in regimentals stood with them. After greeting Diana, the soldier glanced up and saw Eden at the top of the stairs. He ran his eyes languorously over her from her face to her feet and back up again, before smirking and saying, "Bless me, Colin. Are you hiding something from me?"

When the earl looked up at her, he did not seem pleased. "Come down, Miss Barrett, and meet my friends."

When Cassandra was introduced, she offered Eden her other creamy hand and a lovely smile that lit beautiful summer-sky blue eyes. When Major Dorian Bradley was introduced, he clutched her hand longer than propriety dictated and said, "Not bad. Not bad at all."

The three friends and Diana would be dining out and attending the ballet afterward. Lady Chadwick had been invited, but declined. No mention was made of what Eden would do. When the young people had left, Eden turned to go upstairs.

Lady Chadwick turned cold eyes to her and said, "Miss... A word..."

Eden turned again, thinking to be invited to a meal, if only in the servants' hall.

"I feel it fair to warn you," Colin's Aunt began, "Don't bother casting out lures to my nephew. And don't look so stupid; I saw the way you look at him. You forget; you are a nobody with no connections. He will marry Miss Bradley, and that is that. Anyone can see they are deeply in love. My nephew may exhibit a predilection for governesses, but he does not marry them. Miss Austen found that out soon enough. As you will also if you overstep the bounds."

Though Eden wished to ask what had happened to Miss Austen, she also did not wish to grace Her Ladyship's comments with a reply. She nodded, turned, and started back up the stairs. Suddenly, she was extremely tired and achy and the stairs went on for miles.

Eden's first night in London was miserable. Sleep was fitful. She had thought the long hours of confinement in the carriage had caused her aching bones, but she now realized she also had a fever. If the night watchman did not wake her by bawling out, "Twelve o' the Clock, a clear night, and all's we-ell," in stentorian tones, the gurgling noises of her stomach did. Iron horseshoes clopped on the cobblestones, and coaches and drays rumbled and clinked by all night long. Did no one ever sleep here? At the earliest rays of light, the milkmaids and muffin-men began to call-sing their wares.

In the morning, Diana woke Eden up. "Get up and get dressed Miss Lazy Barrett. We go to the mantua-maker on Bond Street at ten. Colin has gone out on business, but he is to collect us at noon and we'll go to Cox's museum and then dine at a teashop. Tonight we go to Astley's Amphitheatre for the equestrian circus. Colin says we must stay inside the shop and not walk up and down the street until he comes for us. I have to go have my bath now. We'll breakfast at the dressmaker's. They always have the most delicious hot chocolate and pastries. Aunt Chadwick doesn't care to come. It'll be you and I."

Eden got up slowly. She felt light-headed. If the earl had not already left, she would have begged off. But, after splashing her face with the same tepid water that was in her ewer last night, she felt up to the excursion. When His Lordship came to get them, she would let him know that she was ill.

At the dressmaker's, Diana was seated on a plush red velvet chair and fawned over and plied with pastries and encouraged to try on bonnets and gloves and see the dresses she chose modeled on a young girl of just her size. Eden felt much better after several cups of hot chocolate and half a sweet roll, but she found Diana's excitement, egged on by the mantua-maker and her assistants, taxing in the extreme. Two hours of commenting on the styles and colors and decoration of clothing took their toll. Eden wanted nothing more than bed.

When Colin finally rescued them, he was hurried and brusque. He drove a low hung, two seated phaeton. He handed both ladies up into the front seat with him. "Diana, I'm taking you back to our Aunt's for now," he began. "I know this is not what we planned, but it is necessary. Something has come up which I must see to immediately. I've instructed Perrin to take you about to the amusements we spoke of."

Diana's eyes narrowed and her lower lip jutted out. "I knew you were going to do this. It's always business. You just don't care about me. Well I don't care about you!"

Lord Edmund's hands tightened about the reins, his jaw clenched, and he swallowed an angry retort. He refused to speak until he had control of his temper. With gentleness, he told his sister, "I know I made a promise. And promises mean a great deal to me. But you are old enough, Diana, to understand that important circumstances arise that can interfere with a person keeping a promise, no matter how much they would like to do so."

"What circumstances?" she demanded.

"You are also old enough to realize that for every pampered child in London, there are twenty forgotten waifs. You know I'm on the board of several subscription foundling homes. We decided, for good reason, to pay an unannounced visit this morning to one of those homes. We were investigating a report made of the death of several children from cholera. We found a freshly painted building on a newly scythed lawn. Outside, children dressed in their clean red uniforms were weeding the garden. Inside, we first inspected the larder. We found rotting potatoes and rat leavings in the moldy grain, no other food at all. The kitchen was filthy.

"When we went to the boy's dorms, we found the stench unbearable. Many boys were lying on straw pallets in their own vomit, but that would not account for the odor. Upon further investigation, we found that the cesspit that we had known existed directly under the boy's wing was still in use and overflowing. We had already given the director a hefty some of money to dig a new, larger cesspit in a safer place on the grounds and to have new plumbing installed. None of this was done, and the man could not account for a groat of the funds. They seem to have disappeared.

"We sent for a physician and ordered the attendants to clean up the children who lay ill. Several boys were taken to hospital. The other boys must be moved while the cesspit is cleaned and filled in and another one dug elsewhere. No one had any good suggestions of where to move them meanwhile. The hospitals are overcrowded already. The other members were afraid to bring illness into their families. My townhouse stands empty. Joseph is there now helping Mrs. Fitzwarren bring mattresses down to make a sort of infirmary in the servant's hall. She felt it best to have them there because the stone floors are easily mopped, and it is close to the kitchen, and no stair climbing.

"Easy," he said to the horses as he maneuvered them away from a flower cart that had just been pushed into the street by a blind seller. "I will go now to get the last few boys. We've already brought some of the girls over. I'd come nowhere near you had not the doctor assured me that the illness is not the infectious type. It's the bilious cholera that originates in spoiled food or bad water. Now, Sister, would you prefer that I spend the day gazing at jewel-encrusted gadgets at Cox's with you?"

Diana looked away from him and sighed, "No."

By this time, the phaeton had come to a stop in front of Lady Chadwick's townhouse. Connors was waiting to take Diana's hand. He looked up for Eden's. She turned to Colin and asked if she might help him in any way.

"Entertain Diana," he said.

"I don't need entertaining, Colin," Diana said firmly. "I can't enjoy amusements without you, so I'll just read one of the books Aunt gave me until you return. We can still go to supper and Astley's if you have time.

Don't worry about me. I'm not angry. I'll see you when you come."

"Are you quite sure?" he asked Diana. When he received a decided nod from her, he said to Eden, "Then, yes, I need you. I was trying to determine how to transport a certain small bundle, but if I have you with me, you can hold it." He saw his sister into the house, raised the ribbons and brought them down, and the horses started off. The occupants of the phaeton said nothing to each other as they rode through town, though Colin cast a few glances at the governess next to him as she absorbed the sights wide-eyed.

At one point, they left the flower-filled window boxes of the spotless fashionable lanes and turned on to a street of run down shops. A trench ran along the center of the street and an old woman threw slops into it from her doorstep. Most of the houses further down the road had at least one broken window stuffed with newspaper or rags. Several barefoot urchins were kicking a ball around in the middle of the street. When Colin had to pull his team up to keep from running over one of the boys, he growled, "Bloody hell" beneath his breath. A few moments later, he was cut off by a dray driven by a bellowing drunk. He mumbled, "They'll let anything get behind a horse."

When they arrived at the foundling home, Colin brought the carriage up the drive close to the entrance. A young man came over to take the horses' heads, and Colin jumped down to tell him something quietly. Then he walked over to the side of his vehicle and looked up at Eden. "Stay here. I won't be long."

Almost as quickly as he disappeared into the home, Colin reappeared with a boy in his arms followed by the physician, who also held a child. Eden jumped out of the carriage by herself, though the jolt to her feet was greater than she thought since no one had put down the steps. She ignored the pain and moved to assist them in making the boys comfortable in the back seat. She noticed some small, encrusted sores on the scalp of one of the boys. The other one's hair was cropped quite close. He did not exhibit the same wounds.

Colin and the physician, Mr. Ranleigh, made a second trip inside the home. When they returned, the doctor held a burden wrapped in cloth against his shoulder. Colin handed Eden up into the front seat, then turned to take the bundle from the other man. "I have something here for you to hold," he said. When Eden had adjusted herself in the seat, and turned to reach down to him, he handed her a toddler wrapped in a thin cotton blanket.

The length of the child would place him at about two years: a time when most children look like the fat little cherubs that decorated the ceiling at Chadilane. The bundled child seemed weightless in her arms. The normal two year old is curious, adventurous, and rebellious. This child was stiff and apathetic. The skin was drawn tight over his face. The eyes, circumscribed with bluish tinged flesh, appeared enormous. His face resembled Lady Chadwick's monkey, or perhaps a miniature ancient sage for there was a wisdom of the world in his eyes.

At first, upon being handed up to the governess, the little face constricted and the lower lip trembled as if he would cry. But he controlled the need, and a cloud came over his expression. As they rode back over the streets they had come on, Eden asked Colin if he had noticed the patches of inflammation on the boy's scalp. He said he had. "I'm not familiar with the disease that would cause that," she said.

" A disease of society," he said. "Someone has yanked the hair out of his head by fistfuls."

"Oh God, my God…." Eden groaned.

He supplied, "Why hast thou forsaken these?"

CHAPTER XVI

She was so preoccupied with the urgency of transferring the children from the carriage to the vast servant's hall that Eden barely noticed the appearance of the Ashton townhouse and completely forgot that she had been ill. She worked easily with the housekeeper, who quietly gave orders with an air of dignified authority. Patrick had been sent to buy new nightshirts for all the children. Mrs. Fitzwarren insisted on burning all the clothing they had on. "Cholera might be in them," she said firmly.

Colin not only offered his home to the children and transported them there, but he made himself available to his housekeeper, continually asking how he might help. She did not shoo him out of the way and tell him the servants should do it, but found work for him as well. He removed his coat and waistcoat and stirred the fire up, added new logs, filled and carried the kettle, and peeled potatoes for the soup that Mrs. Fitzwarren felt would draw out all the poisons.

The housekeeper, her daughter Verity, and Eden divided the nine children between them and cleaned them up as best they could. The children were not completely neglected, but the double bind of cholera, which manifested itself in vomit and diarrhea, plus the fact that the school nurse had dosed them with laudanum had left the children so weak they could barely move. Mrs. Fitzwarren said they must get as much water as possible back into the children to offset the continuous loss of it.

As the day wore on, the effects of the drug began to wear off, and the children came more awake. The adults were gratified to find that these children had, as the doctor had assured them, passed through the worst of it and were on the mend. They confirmed this by being hungry. The first children to taste the thick soup and biscuits encouraged their comrades to eat also by marveling at the fine texture and whiteness of the bread, never having had any but coarse brown.

At one point in the day, Mrs. Fitzwarren and Verity sat at the table spooning soup into the mouths of the two smallest children. The housekeeper was holding the smallest baby. When the little one batted out at the spoon, he caused her to spill some of the warm liquid into her lap. She called the earl and held the child out to him, who took the infant gingerly. Because of the sharpness of Mrs. Fitzwarren's movement in handing him to another, the baby began to cry.

Colin looked apprehensive for a moment, but soon began to commiserate with his charge in a soothing voice. He cradled the child upon his breast and it started to quiet down. Suddenly the toddler lost all of the supper he had just eaten all over the person upon whom he was cradled. This startled both the child and the earl so that the baby let out an ear-piercing scream, and Colin looked as if he would join him.

Lord Edmund could not cradle the infant again as the front of his shirt was covered with the late meal, so he held the kicking body at arm's length and ask the child, "This is how you repay me?" Mrs. Fitzwarren bustled back from the kitchen and took the baby. Verity thrust the one she had been feeding into Eden's hands so that she could hunt up a fresh shirt for His Lordship.

"Forgive me ladies if I offend, but this shirt is not staying on me one second more!" he warned as he pulled it over his head and slung it into the fire. He then went into the kitchen to bathe.

Eden was astonished at the brief view of her masters' bared broad shoulders. His back was covered with fine, curling, dark hair. *Almost like an ape*, she thought. *And his muscles are quite well developed. His hips are so slender that I just supposed the rest of him was. Those tailored coats he wears fit him so well, I thought the shoulders to be stuffed with cotton wadding. I should have known his figure would be masculine; he is forever fencing, riding, rowing, walking or swimming when he is at home. Still I always think of him behind his desk or reclining with a book on the long, red velvet Grecian Ottoman in the Library.* But then Eden remembered the vice-like strength of his arms as he held her by the lake, and her face flushed with embarrassment, and she busied herself with stroking the cheek and hair of the child in her arms.

GENTLE JOURNEY

Mrs. Fitzwarren brought the governess back out of her reverie, grumbling, "He didn't have to throw it in the fire; I could have washed it easy enough. What a waste of fine fabric and stitching."

After he had dressed himself, Colin came back to the servant's hall to find everything quiet. He pulled on his waistcoat and coat. "Miss Barrett, if you can extricate yourself from that sleeping child without upsetting her, we will be leaving now. Mrs. Fitz, could you do with the aid of any more of my staff for the night? When Connors gets back with the supplies you asked for, his instructions are to remain here to obey your commands."

"I'm sure we'll be able to handle it from here, milord. Thank you. The children are all settled down now. Between Verity and Connors and myself, we can handle any situation that might arise until morning. If not, I'll send him around to enlist more aid."

Eden had managed to lay the child on a mattress without waking her. She was completely worn out. She followed Colin into the hall where she stopped him with a hand on his arm. He placed a warm hand over hers and looked deeply in her face, questioning and contemplating it.

"My lord, may I not stay here the night? The children have slept in fits for most of the day; I feel sure they will have difficulty sleeping the entire night as well. They are too well rested and in a strange environment. If truth be known, my muscles ache with fatigue. I cringe at the thought of yet another carriage ride. I spied an inviting porcelain bathtub down the hall off the kitchen. Ever since I saw it, I've entertained dreams of the first free moment I might have to make full use of it. I am too tired to go on."

That did the trick: she did indeed look tired. "As you wish," Colin told her. "I'll send Joseph over with your portmanteau." He then took her hand into his and led her back to the kitchen. "Mrs. Fitz, this young lady refuses to leave, wants none of my company. Do you think you can put up with her for the night?"

The housekeeper smiled broadly and nodded.

"If she gives you any trouble, let me know."

Again a grin and a nod.

Colin turned to Eden and brought her hand up to his chest pulling her in close. Quietly, he said, "I have one grave request to make of you before I agree to let you stay."

"What is that, my lord?"

"Eat and sleep."

"Gladly, my lord."

He increased the volume slightly, "Mrs. Fitz, see that Miss Barrett eats. I've not seen her take nourishment in three days. She may, however, be sneaking food into her room as Diana used to do."

"Don't worry about me," Eden said, pushing him toward the door. "Go rescue your sister." The earl studied her face a moment longer, eyes lit with affection. Then he gave her an eloquent smile of approval, and left.

Eden alerted Mrs. Fitzwarren to her desire, and the housekeeper and Verity helped her fill the huge tub. She was handed one of Verity's soft white linen nightgowns, some fine linen towels with lace edging, and a tablet of pears soap. Verity stepped out into the garden to gather a huge handful of Sweetbriar rose petals to float in the bath water and release their fragrance.

Eden let her hair down to wash as well. She did not believe in the old saying, "Wash the hands often, the body seldom, and the head never." As often as she had washed her hair, she had never caught the quinsy from it yet. Cleaning her hair with hair bran or ivory powder - as so many others preferred - could never make it feel as full and silky as soap and water did.

When the governess had finished her warm bath and slipped into Verity's gown, she squeezed the water out of her hair, wound it in a towel, and went back into the kitchen. Since Verity was taller and wider than Eden, the gown dragged on the tiles. Verity saw this and went in search of something to use as a belt. She returned with a soft gold cord. Eden belted the gown with it and bloused the waist to take up the length.

At last Eden sat and took coffee and toast with the ladies. They spoke of Verity's upcoming marriage to a fireman. Mrs. Fitzwarren advised her daughter to make him coffee with eggshell in it to ward off bitterness. "Making good coffee and tea is a tricky business, but very important to the men. Not too strong, not too weak, smooth tasting."

When Eden commended her on the spotless condition of the kitchen, Mrs. Fitzwarren glowed. One of the secrets the housekeeper was willing to confide was the terrier she kept in the garden, and the hedgehog indoors. The hedgehog ate up any beetles or roaches, and the terrier would not lie down to rest until he had assured himself that there were no mice or rats that might take up residence. Should he happen to find one wandering in from another yard, he would grab the rodent by the neck and shake it to death. He was also good for eating scraps of leftover food so that there was nothing left about to spoil.

"Which reminds me," Verity said solicitously, "You've not eaten enough to satisfy a linnet, Miss Barrett. You heard what his Lordship said. You must eat."

"I don't think I can eat any more. All that has happened this afternoon has left me ill to the stomach. I know wishing is useless, but I wish I were in a position to do more for children like these. So many people suffer needlessly, and I feel powerless to help them. If I were rich…"

"If wishes were horses, Miss Barrett… You can't eat yourself up with worryin' about what you can't control. The best we can do in this world is to do what we can, with what we have, where we are. The good Lord put us right where he knows we can do the most good, and He knows what He's doin'. We have to trust Him. Big people can make big splashes, and little people can only make little splashes, but the splashes make ripples, and the ripples make wider ripples, and only God knows how far all those ripples travel, maybe all the way across the wide sea."

Eden must have heard something like it many times before, but if Moses had come down from the sky in a chariot and handed her Mrs. Fitzwarren's words engraved on a golden tablet, they could not have made a greater impression on her. She had needed to hear it one more time for it to become clear to her. She was just like her father, eating herself up with what she had no control over. The Bible told her to be at peace, to have no fear, but how could she with the world the way it was? She could trust the creator of the world implicitly. She must consider this idea further.

"You are absolutely right, Mrs. Fitz. And now I'd better wash my dress before any stains set in, though the ripples I'll create there will be confined to the sink."

The housekeeper went to sleep in her quarters after showing Eden a room she could use. Verity sat watch over the children. Eden washed and rinsed out her dress, emptied her bath water and the wash water, then squeezed out her dress and arranged it over the back of a chair in front of the fire. She took a second chair to the fireside and sat with her back to it brushing her long mane.

As long as she had been needed during the day, Eden had somehow been filled with the energy to do what must be done. The bath and the coffee had revived her again, but now the effort of brushing her hair felt so great that her arm fell limp at her side. Verity saw this and came to offer help. "Verity, you go to bed now. When my hair is dry, I'll call you to take over the watch," Eden said.

The servant had been yawning violently, so the governess was not surprised when her offer was accepted. After the housekeeper's daughter left, Eden sat with her chin propped up between her palms until sleep overcame her.

The nagging cough of a child soon caused Eden to open her eyes again. She saw a boy of about eight years sit bolt upright and shout, "No!" His wide-open eyes seemed still to see the nightmare and not the room he was in. Eden went to him and knelt before him. "It's only a dream," she said. He began to whimper. "Does something hurt?" she asked. He looked at her now and struggled pitifully to stifle his tears until he succeeded.

"You're among friends here. No one will harm you. You had a bad dream. Oh, child, life has been miserable for you, but from today on, you will find that there are good people in the world too, people who care about you and your comfort. Can I get you something?"

The boy bit his lip and shook his head. He shook his head to all of her suggestions: a glass of water, a blanket, something to eat. She was moved by his obvious fear and reached out to reassure him, but he recoiled from her and she didn't press him.

The little toddler in the bed next to the boy began to heave in his sleep. His stomach was already empty though, so he was only able to bring up a little water and bile. Eden fetched a soft, clean cloth and a cup of water. The toddler began to cry. When he did, several other children called out in their sleep, "Be still!" One child put his pillow over his head to muffle the noise.

Eden positioned herself on the mattress with her back against the wall. She picked up the infant, dabbed his mouth with the cloth and offered him the cup. She then cradled the wretched creature in her arms and spoke soothingly to him. The baby fell back to sleep mumbling something about Dan Evil.

GENTLE JOURNEY

The first boy watched all this with interest. He inched his way closer to the pretty stranger. She didn't snap at him to go to sleep. He crawled to her feet. She smiled at him. " 'At's my bruvver," he said to her.

"Well, he's a brave little boy, just like you."

" 'E was thinkin' of Dan Evil."

"And who is that?"

" 'E's a rat what lives at the 'ome. 'E comes out at noight and boites us on the toes."

"The housekeeper assures me there are no rats here."

"They might be 'oidin', cause of the fire."

"Mrs. Fitz has a dog named Fred who is very good at finding and killing rats."

"Where is 'e then?"

"In the garden."

"Can I see 'im?"

"In the morning."

"Does 'e boites children?"

"I don't think so."

"Are you a angel?"

"What?"

"Are you a angel?"

Eden chuckled, "No."

"You look like the statues a angels in the churchyard. 'Cept you got no wings."

"I expect it's this oversized gown."

"An' your long 'air. Me muvver is a angel."

"Is she? That's wonderful."

"She said she would wait for us in 'eaven and watch over us from there. Do you fink she knows where we are?"

"I think your mother knows exactly where you are, and she led us to you."

"If you're not a angel, why're you bein' noice to us?"

"Because it is right for people to help each other out."

"Why di'n't you 'elp us before?"

"We didn't know where you were."

The boy yawned, "Cawn't sleep. Oi 'ave dreams."

"Do you want to tell me about it?"

"It's about the man who 'anged. Mr. Proctor took us to Lincoln's

Inn Field to see a man get 'anged. They 'ad to pull on 'is legs 'cause it was toikin' to long for 'im to die. 'Is oiyes bulged out. Jake said 'is face turnt black, but Oi wouldn't look no more. Mr. Proctor said if we broke fings, 'e would tell the runners and they would 'ang us. Oi broked a bowl. We sneaked the pieces outside and buried them in the garden. Oi wished 'e 'ad told the runners on me, but William wouldn't 'ave nobody to look out for 'im then. Peter used to look out for me after muvver went to be a angel."

"And who is Peter?"

"Me big bruvver. 'E were a link boy. Press gang jumped out of a cart and snatched 'im away to the Noivy. 'E wanted to be a fireman, but 'e weren't old enough. Press men don't bother firemans."

"Did Peter have a second name? The same as your mother's?"

"Black. Same as me an' William. Peter Black."

"What is your name, child?"

"Christopher."

"Well Christopher, if you will just make yourself comfortable right here next to me, I'll tell you a secret that is guaranteed to keep you from having bad dreams." She shifted little William so that he rested against her side as her left arm encircled him. She then held her right arm out to Christopher. When he had turned about until his head was pillowed against her, Eden stroked his hair as she continued, "When you say your prayers, ask God to let your mother keep a special guard over your dreams. Ask Him to allow only good dreams to come in your mind, so you can sleep in peace. He'll do it. You'll see. He loves to answer children's prayers."

She listened to the child's simple cockney prayers then. When he asked God to allow only good dreams, she was asking with him. When he finally fell asleep, she could no longer hold back the weeping. She was afraid to tremble or sob lest she wake the boys. As each arm was occupied, she had no free hand to wipe away her tears.

Morning came too soon for Eden. She felt Verity take the children out of her arms one at a time, but did not open her eyes. Connors had arrived quite late last night and Joseph was also there to help. The occasional clinks and rings of dishes and pots and the quiet voices of the servants infiltrated Eden's dreams and finally roused her. She sat forward on the mattress slowly and rubbed her eyes. Her very bones ached. She felt like she weighed a ton. She waited for sleep to subside and total consciousness to take over.

As in a fog, Eden heard the entrance door open and close, but it meant nothing to her. Then she heard Mrs. Fitzwarren's cheerful voice. "We didn't expect you so early, milord. Have you breakfasted yet?"

Eden was startled into awareness. "He mustn't see me like this," Eden said to Verity as she rose abruptly from the mattress. Almost as abruptly, she moaned and crumbled back down onto the bed in a faint. Lord Edmund saw the falling figure as he entered the kitchen. He went swiftly to her, knelt beside her, and gathered her in his arms.

CHAPTER XVII

Colin carried her upstairs to the bedroom he was most used to entering - his own. If Mrs. Fitzwarren thought this odd, she said nothing. She turned back the counterpane and plumped the pillows as the earl stood holding the governess.

He had been surprised at how light and yielding her limp form was. Immediate concern had given him strength, but the warmth of her against him, as he stood waiting for his housekeeper to adjust the satin sheets, caused him to experience a weakening sensation. Her head nestled on his breast aroused a powerful protective instinct in him. He began to blame himself and magnify the seriousness of her condition.

When the housekeeper was satisfied that all was comfy, Colin sat on the edge of the bed and held Eden in his lap. He called Mrs. Fitzwarren over to feel her forehead. "She is feverish, is she not?"

"A little warm, milord. She's just exhausted. I couldn't compel her to go to bed last night. Neither would she take more than two bites of toast. I did try," the housekeeper explained.

"I completely understand. Miss Barrett is not one who can be coerced into doing anything against her will. Send Joseph to fetch Mr. Ranleigh. He was to examine the children at ten, but I want him here now."

The housekeeper left the room, hesitating only a second or two and casting him a worried look, which he did not notice, oblivious as he was of anything but the woman he held so close. Colin studied the face of his sister's governess for a long time. She looked so vulnerable, so beautiful, and so perfectly peaceful. *In the arms of Morpheus*, he thought. Well, he would be content to play that god of dreams for quite a while longer, but he knew Mrs. Fitzwarren would have something to say if she came back and found him still holding paradise in his embrace.

He breathed in the rose scent of her hair and took the liberty of pressing his lips to her crown before he turned and placed his burden in the center of the bed. Tenderly, he pulled the counterpane up over Eden and arranged her long hair so that it did not bunch up beneath her neck and cause discomfort. Eden, who had come out of the faint the moment his hands first touched her, had pretended continued unconsciousness out of embarrassment and confusion and exhaustion. She was acutely aware of all his loving ministrations and felt abandoned when he left her. She allowed herself to drift back into sleep without opening her eyes.

Colin went downstairs to pen a few brief notes of apology to people with whom he had appointments. Looking in on the children, he noted with satisfaction that they were already exhibiting signs of full recovery. There were no games, nor even smiles; yet the little one's eyes were now beaming with wonder at their new lodgings and situation and especially food.

At last, Mr. Ranleigh arrived. Colin gave his notes to Connors and bid him take breakfast before he delivered them. He then led the physician up to Eden, where he hovered over the doctor and made a nuisance of himself until he was told to leave the room.

His examination completed, Mr. Ranleigh spoke quietly to Colin in the hall. The doctor concluded it was not the cholera at all, but exhaustion and the end of a flu or bad cold. Complete rest was all her body needed to cure itself. Colin suggested that she was feverish and in need of cloths damped in lilac water and pressed to her forehead. That had been very beneficial to him on more than one occasion of fever. Mr. Ranleigh argued that the fever was mild, and cold cloths would only wake her when he especially wanted her to sleep. Colin had his doubts, but the physician, in his eagerness to see other patients, walked away from further debate.

Mr. Ranleigh convinced Lord Edmund that all in the house were on the mend and none in need of his services, and he left. Colin wrote a note to the proprietor of the toyshop on Bishop'sgate Street to charge a quantity of their most popular indoor toys to his name. He included the ages of the children involved. This he sent with Perrin.

In the meantime, he ferreted out some string suitable for playing 'Cat's Cradle' with the children himself. Soon tiring of this, he amused them with a game of his own invention. He lined up a number of utensils on the long servants' hall table and asked the children to close their eyes. When they did, he swiftly removed an article and hid it in a drawer. The children were told to open their eyes again and identify what had been removed.

Colin considered it a real triumph when, by dinnertime, one little girl became brave enough to put out a hand to touch his cheek. He caught the little hand in his and kissed it loudly. She was at first alarmed by his sudden movement, but then she giggled and said, "You're funny. I like you."

"And I like you," he said, "very much." When he held out his arms to her, she deliberated an entire minute before crawling into his lap.

After dinner was served, Perrin arrived with shuttlecocks, marbles, bilbocatches, spillikins, dolls, music boxes, mechanical toys, and tin soldiers enough to fill two toy stores. Colin helped distribute the toys and spent some time teaching a group of boys a game with marbles. When all the servants and children were busy enjoying the toys, Colin snuck out and mounted the stairs to expedite Eden's progress by watching her. When he could watch no longer without touching her, he drew his chair close to the head of the bed and proceeded to determine, once and for all, if she had a fever. He did this by stroking the stray locks away from her face and resting his palm on her forehead for a few moments.

This had the surprising effect of causing her to stir. She brought both hands up to her mouth to cover a rather musical yawn. She then stretched her arms and body most seductively to the mind of her sole viewer. At last, she opened her eyes to find herself in a massive four-poster Elizabethan bed. The last thing Eden expected to see upon awakening and looking about was her employer. She averted her eyes and blushed, pulling the counterpane up to her chin, as any demure maiden would in a similar situation.

Equally embarrassed at being found there, Colin began to tease. "Well, are you finally arrived from the land of dreams, Miss Lazybones? That was very inconsiderate of you to go off in that way and leave us mortals to worry about you. How dare you lie about all day and leave the work of entertaining a pack of children to people with no experience whatever. I almost amputated my finger trying to get the hang of 'Cat's Cradle.' My knees are positively raw from playing 'Ring Taw' on the hard tile floor.

"You see, I insisted on playing until I had won because I refuse to give anyone just cause to say I have lost my marbles. See..." he said, retrieving a handful of commoneys from his waistcoat pocket and displaying them. "I have every one."

Eden did not answer or move even, but she could not completely suppress the smile that gave her away. She was thinking that he certainly had lost his marbles and those in his hand had been purchased to replace them.

"So you won't budge will you?" he continued. "Ah, I suspect you are now waiting to be served breakfast in bed. All right, very well, have it your way then. If that is the only way I can get you back on your feet working, breakfast in bed it shall be." Colin rose and strode over to the bell pull and gave it an exaggerated tug.

"I am a little hungry," Eden admitted weakly.

"She speaks! And she hungers. Both excellent signs of returning health. Your wish is my housekeeper's command. What exotic dish can I offer to seduce your sensitive palate?"

"If there is any of the potato soup left over..."

"What! Surely my larder can provide something more palatable than that!"

"I'm afraid I couldn't keep anything more extravagant down. When I can eat nothing else, I can eat that. And Mrs. Fitz swears it takes out all the poisons."

"Potato soup it shall be."

The invalid stirred, and Colin fairly jumped to prop her pillows up behind her so she was comfortably positioned. When Verity appeared, Eden motioned the servant to her side and asked in hushed tones if she could find her a bed jacket or dressing gown from the portmanteau Connors had brought in last night; then she gave the servant her meal order.

Colin passed the time it took to prepare the dish in a running monologue about the progress of the children and the comments of his sister at Astley's last night. "Diana has agreed to go to see *The Merchant of Venice* tonight if we can see Grimaldi tomorrow to make up for the culture she might accidentally absorb there." Eden was not at all certain what to think of His Lordship's animated, solicitous attitude, so she resolved not to remark on it. Heaven knew he could be silent and withdrawn enough. There could be no sense in discouraging him by noticing aloud the curiousness of his present mood.

Verity arrived with china dishes of soup and rolls arranged on a white painted bed tray of woven rush. She carefully placed the tray over Eden's lap, laid the bed jacket at the foot of the bed, bobbed a curtsy, and left.

Eden pushed her soup about in the bowl hoping the earl would take a hint and leave. Then she could at least pull the jacket on. The soup stirred, but His Lordship did not. He demanded quizzically, "Do you intend to eat that, or did you order it to play with it?"

"It's hot just yet."

Colin took the spoon from her hand and placed it in the bowl. He sat on the chair by the bed and lifted the tray from her lap and placed it over his own. "If it's too hot, I'll just have to cool it for you. And if you won't feed yourself, I'll have to see to that personally as well. I'm not leaving this room until I've seen you eat every bit of this bland looking stuff."

He tipped the spoon into the creamy liquid, raised it to his lips and blew gently across it. Then he offered the spoon to her expectantly.

"My lord, you are embarrassing me."

"And you, young lady, are embarrassing me. Why, it must be all over town by now through the physician that I starve my staff and work them to the point of exhaustion. Now eat this before I spill it on you."

"I can't eat and laugh at the same time. Surely I'll choke."

"Serve you right. Here it comes." Colin brought the spoon confidently to Eden's lips, but she refused to open them. "Miss Barrett, don't force me to give them a lot more to talk about below stairs. I have no recourse now but to beat you soundly if you won't behave like a good girl."

"You wouldn't dare!" But she wasn't so sure. "You, who are too tenderhearted to strike your horse…"

"He gives me no cause. He does as he is told."

Eden steadied Colin's hand with her own, though the physical contact with his warm flesh disconcerted her further. Together they thrust the spoon into her mouth. Colin fed her several more spoonfuls until she pulled the tray back from him and satisfied him by finishing on her own.

GENTLE JOURNEY

The conversation as she ate took several twists and he mentioned that his Aunt Chadwick had the gall to disapprove of his housing the foundlings at his own townhouse, or in allowing Eden to leave her charge to attend them. He went on to describe the ridiculous sweater his aunt was knitting for one of her dogs. "I can't begrudge Muffin the sweater. He's so pitifully old and balding that he shivers from fall to spring. But must she begrudge the children space at my empty home? Most street urchins don't live as long as her dogs.

"I suppose you believe, as so many others have told me, that had she born children to pour her surplus affection upon, dear Aunt would be more fulfilled at this point in her life and less eccentric." Eden's only answer was a half smile. "I interpret that look to mean you prefer to keep your opinions to yourself to spare me from injured feelings. I may have an opposite opinion myself."

"I don't think all women were meant to be mothers. It takes a certain kind of love to nurture children," she ventured.

"This promises to be diverting. Continue. What kind of love?"

"Animals are easy to love. They're dependant and forgiving. They live in the moment. All things that went on before are forgotten. They don't worry about the future. They do as they are told when they understand, and they wish only to please. They can also be forgotten for a time as long as their basic needs are provided for.

"Children are not so easy to love. They can be selfish and independent. There are so many variables to their character you can never be sure where you stand with them. They are subject to the sullens and tantrums. No matter what advantages you contrive to provide for them, they are rarely satisfied.

"They mature as they please. Even in the cradle no two react to the same stimulus in the same way. One cries at the rattle's noise, another laughs. They're a puzzle.

"I'm not saying they are impossible to love or undeserving of love. Some deserve much more than they'll ever get. I'm saying it must be the deep sort of love which asks and expects nothing in return, yet is open to receive and marvel at returns if they present themselves."

"Something like yours, Miss Barrett?"

"I beg your pardon?"

"Your sort of love?"

Her eyes fell away, "I was speaking in a general vein, my lord. I had no one in mind."

"Nevertheless, you describe yourself well."

"No. You mistake. Training another's children is one thing; raising your own children is different. You expect so much more of your own because they are a reflection of your values and beliefs... I have trouble with patience, though I see the need of it. I am afraid I might make a poor parent."

"I beg to differ with you."

"As usual, my lord. Forgive me. I am very tired."

"Too tired to argue?"

"Far too tired to argue."

"Then you must indeed be tired and not merely dismissing me. Very well," he said, standing and taking the tray from her, "Get your rest."

CHAPTER XVIII

Diana came to visit Eden after tea and before the theatre. When she arrived, the house was filled with the aroma of fresh baked gingerbread. Colin forbid Eden to leave her sickroom, and told Diana to entertain her, which she did gladly until time to go. Diana and Colin's luggage had been transported to the earl's townhouse as well to facilitate the staff so they would not have to travel back and forth. The next day, however, Colin was threatening to lock Eden in her cell to force her to rest, and both his sister and Eden were threatening to crawl out the window if he did. He gave in and packed them off to Somerset House for a showing of the Royal Academy.

Eden could have passed a week standing in front of the works of the masters. The paintings seemed to breathe at the same time they took your breath away. They were not a moment captured in time; they were alive at that moment. Rembrandt's use of light and shadow held her in awe. How did he do this? Could it be learned? Who could possibly teach the mechanics of this kind of painting? Were there mechanics, or was it merely magic? She had not realized from the etchings she had seen in books that his works had the paint applied so thickly in some places that it became three dimensional.

The Rubens' canvases were flat and attached to the walls, but she could swear the figures moved and through a third dimension. How did Watteau capture the sheen of the fine silk material? Why did he mix fine detail with muddled obscurity? Van Dyke, Cuyp, Lelys, and Reynolds: each had his own personal style; each excited her. These were geniuses. How much did they owe to learned techniques, and how much to their own outstanding talent? She did not have genius. She never would. But for her, nothing less would do. Suddenly her artistic aspirations fell as an eagle falls from a precipice when it sees prey.

Diana could not understand her teacher's absorption in a bunch of paintings. Real life was right outside. Colin had his hands full amusing her to allow Eden time to have her fill. As the three of them were leaving the exhibit, they met the Honorable Cassandra Bradley, Major Bradley, and Lady Bradley with a party of their friends. "I look forward to seeing you at Chadilane next week," Cassy told Colin as their party continued on their way. Major Bradley moved close to Eden and *sotto voce* repeated the same sentiment word for word to her, but with an emphasis on the 'you.'

"We'll walk over to the tea rooms," His Lordship said. With Diana on one side of Colin and Eden on the other, the earl offered his ladies his elbows and they accepted with gloved hands making a chain of three links as they walked. "I needn't ask, but did you enjoy it?" he said to Eden.

"It was glorious. Thank you forever and ever," she said.

He chuckled. "I had originally arranged a studio visit so that you might be able to watch Mr. Thomas Lawrence at work, but unfortunately that was for yesterday when you were not well, and he had to travel to Winchester this morning for an appointment. As painter-in-ordinary, he is at the command of the king and his court. Then I tried to arrange the same thing with another artist for today or tomorrow, a Mr. Turner, but he was painting at the home of his subjects, a husband and wife, and they had requested no students or observers be invited as they felt they could not accommodate them. I'm sorry I could not…"

Eden halted there in the street and stared up at him stupefied. *Are you serious? Yes, he looks perfectly serious.* "I am speechless at your consideration. It would have been the dream of a lifetime to watch such as them. You are amazingly kind to me, my lord."

"It is not kindness, it is a pleasure. I was not going to say anything, lest you regret your illness, but I didn't want you to think I had brought you all this way just for the regular amusements or to put you to work caring for my foundlings. I may still be able to arrange something with Lawrence. Perhaps later in the year. He is always quite busy."

"Since he was six years old, I hear," she said.

They walked on then, and Eden was glad for something to do. She was so flustered at his revelation of his obvious regard for her felicity, she felt foolish, giddy, confused, and flushed. These were not things she wished to feel while her hand was hooked in the crook of his arm, and she was trapped in such close proximity to his masculine form.

After a leisurely tea, Colin brought them back to the town house to dress for an evening at the Royal Opera House since a box for Grimaldi could not be got for several days. The earl warned his sister she must hold hands with one or the other of them at all times so she would not get lost in the crowd or knocked over in the rush for the doors when they were opened. He also felt obliged to hire two hefty sedan chairmen to ride in the boot of the chaise as protection against footpads, and three linkboys to run ahead of the chaise with their torches for protection against the dark.

The three tourists spent so much time seeing the sights of London that when they boarded the Berline on its trek homeward, each did so with a sense of relief. Mrs. Fitzwarren had prepared a breakfast of muffins, cakes, and fresh fruit. They ate in the servant's hall, much to the housekeeper's shock and disapproval; after all, the master should keep his place. It was homier there, though, and Colin wanted to spend some time with the orphans before he left. Three extra girls had been hired to help Mrs. Fitzwarren and Verity with the children until the foundling home was fit to receive them again with a new director.

Several letters had been handed to Colin as he entered the carriage, and he read them as the Berline rocked along. Eden and Diana lost themselves in their own thoughts and impressions. The ride was very quiet, except for the clopping of hooves and the ring of carriage wheels until they were out of town and on a dirt road. Then there was the dust to contend with and whether to have the windows up or down. After about an hour, Diana began to look ill. She begged her brother to have the carriage stop immediately. He relayed the message to John, and the horses were pulled up swiftly.

Eden jumped out with Diana and held her while she heaved over a hedge. Colin emerged from the carriage and walked with his sister until she was feeling more the thing. He gave Eden a questioning look. "I think its only motion sickness after that big breakfast," she said.

Diana begged to be allowed to ride on the box with Patrick and John for a while. "I only get sick because closed up in the carriage, I feel like I'm in a room, and the room is moving. On the box, I can see that I'm outside, and it is like riding my pony," she explained. It evidently made perfect sense to Colin for he granted her wish. Eden tied Diana's bonnet under her chin and handed her a parasol, though it was still morning.

The two inside the carriage rode in silence seated on the same forward facing seat until Colin turned to examine Eden's face. "You are depressed?" he asked.

"No. Resigned I think. I realize now I'll never be a professional artist. I don't have that flame of real genius that I've been privileged to see this week. I could never be satisfied to be average. I thought anything could be achieved by hard work, but talent is a gift. Being an artist has been a dream of mine for a long time. Now I realize it may have been my dream alone and not God's dream for me. Knowing that, the vision has been wrenched from me. It leaves a hole that waits to be refilled. I am trying to discern God's will in my life, what He wants me to fill the space with."

"Are you certain? I would hate to think I have anything to do with squashing your aspirations."

"No, it was not just this trip. I think I knew all along. Good Lord, Daniel is a better artist than I, and he's had no lessons. Mr. Lawrence was selling pastel portraits at the age of six and keeping his fifteen brothers and sisters and his parents well fed."

He leaned back against the velvet squabs and said nothing further. She regarded his downcast visage and told him, "It is you who are despondent. You are troubled. Tell me."

He shifted his entire torso to face her. His expression was one of puzzlement and disbelief. "And you," he said, "are not."

"Do you want me to be?"

He pulled one of the letters out of the cloth pocket in the side of the coach and held it up. "An answer to the note I sent round to the war office: Christopher Black's brother was killed in action two days after the press gang forced him to board a Navy frigate. The Navy hadn't even had time to teach him to load a gun to defend himself. All he could do was hide in the hold and cry. Where is your all-knowing, all-loving, all-just God, Miss Barrett?"

"Here, everywhere. Are you so set against Him? Is there no room in your mind for the possibility that He does exist?"

"Oh, it is possible, perhaps even probable. But God and I have our differences, you see. I do not like Him, or the way He runs things. Religion is pap, food for babies."

"Religiosity, perhaps. But not true faith."

"And you would put your faith in a God who sits up in His heaven with his arms folded doing nothing while innocents suffer? Babies who don't know the meaning of the word 'sin' are abused and neglected everyday, and you sit there at peace in the knowledge of a God who cares? I might even be able to understand the suffering of an adult as capable of purifying, but defenseless babies don't need cleansing from guilt!"

Eden's first reaction was defensive, but his face was distorted with anger - not at her, but at God. *You can't be angry with someone you don't believe exists,* she thought. He wanted to understand. She prayed she would not fail him. This subject was something far greater minds than hers had debated for centuries. "You and I are coming at this from such opposing angles; I fear we can never agree. You are reasoning with your mind."

"And you are not?" A wry laugh escaped him. "I should have guessed."

"I may begin with my mind, but I end with my heart."

"The heart was not meant for reasoning."

"No. It was meant for knowing."

"A pretty answer, which means absolutely nothing."

"To me it does. You want to understand the mind of God, which stretches beyond the last star of the universe, with your mind - a mere grain of sand in comparison. You might as well try to teach politics to your dog. I believe God can infuse your soul with the knowledge it needs if you are open to His teaching you the kind of wisdom that you cannot find in books, unless it is the Bible, or the writings of the saints. And there are some things that are so beyond our ability to understand that we must accept them on faith, because God said it. The heart helps us to know which things. I accept that God loves us, because He was willing to suffer excruciating pain and to die for us."

He shifted back away from her and leaned back against the squabs. "You are willfully blind."

"I know of the world, and it breaks my heart. But this world is not what He wants for us. It's what we have done to ourselves. We've chosen to turn our backs on God and His laws, and we've set ourselves up as His equals. Because He gave us free will, He can't work this world through us until we allow Him to by giving up our will to His. And many do, but not enough. It's you who are blind when you choose only to look at the bad, see only the evil. There is so much more good than evil in this world. And that is amazingly in spite of our basic self-centeredness.

"I don't pretend to understand, but suffering serves some purpose. I know that the Father suffers when His children do, just like any good father on earth, only more so for His understanding and love of His children is fathomless. I know that good can come of bad situations."

He glared at her then, "What good can come of the things those children have gone through?"

"I don't know how to put this without seeming callous, except to preface it by saying that I too have known suffering as a child, though not anything as bad as they. People who have suffered are often more intense, more motivated, more understanding of others' failures, more sensitive to the needs of others. They've been forced to question and searched until answers were found, thus becoming stronger. It's not what happens to you in life, but how you react to and interpret what happens to you. Affliction can be an opportunity to access one's values, determine what is truly important in life."

She stopped to let him rebut, but he said nothing, so she continued, "Remember the iris your sister found in the tangle of weeds by the brook? It bloomed in the midst of adversity. What did you tell her? Remove some of the weeds, but not all, least the plant be weakened by too much sun and no support for its fragile stalk.

"My sister Mary used to keep a pot of geraniums in the kitchen window of our cottage. She watered it and turned the pot so that it would not want for sunlight. Not only did the plant never bloom, it fell prey to a blight. She finally gave up and emptied the pot out onto the dung heap behind the mews. Imagine her surprise a few weeks later when she found a riot of red blossoms peaking out at her from among the refuse."

We are not speaking of plants here, we are speaking of humans, he thought angrily. He did not help her as a listener does with eye contact and nods of the head. He glared at the opposing wall of the carriage with jaws clenched as if daring her to say something sensible. She was terrified that she was not saying it right; that her words had the ring of hollowness to them; that she was failing God. Tears welled in her eyes, but she willed them to stop. She would just have to trust God to put the right words into her mouth.

"I am no seer," Eden continued, "I can't say how the children will be affected. I know they have been, and it will be a determining factor in the adults they become. I also know that what you have done for them will influence the shaping of their personalities. Children are far more resilient than flowers. Having aided them will be an element in forming your life as well. Faith is a great source of comfort and strength in a time of adversity."

"Faith. Sweet Faith." He spit the words out like foul food. "I heard a sermon on faith once. Our own parson was ill. Vicar Barrett kindly rode over to the village church to preach in his place. He said that faith could move mountains. He said God loved us and answered prayer. I believed him. I believed all that rot then.

"I was thirteen. They wouldn't let me see Mother. She was very ill. I asked God to make her well. It was the first and only time I asked Him for anything. As each hour passed, I believed she would get well again. I had faith. I made sure I was very, very good. Things were finally going well. Father was finally staying home. I had a new baby sister to love. Why must my mother get sick now? She was never sick. Don't take her, God. Please, don't take her. That little baby girl needs her. I need her. I'll be so good. I'll do whatever you want me to. I'll repay you with my life. Let her live, God. You love us. I believe. I have faith. Please, let her live.

"But, no. She died. I didn't want to move a mountain; the mountains are fine right where they are. I just wanted one little insignificant life to recover and remain here a while longer. At first, I blamed myself; I had failed; I didn't have enough faith to keep her alive; I must have done something wrong; maybe I didn't say the words right; there must be some trick to it.

"Then I blamed the baby - if she hadn't sapped my mother's life with her own - but she was so tiny, so innocent. So I blamed my father. If he had loved her enough, if he'd not been away all those years, if he'd called a different physician, she'd still be here. Finally, I put the blame where it belonged - on God. And there it stuck. He didn't answer my prayers because He didn't exist. I'd put my faith in a lie. And I saw the lie for what it was more clearly still when I was sent to school. The way the older boys tormented the younger. Horror stories I won't repeat. No God intervened to save them. A walk down any unfashionable street in London will show you more any hour of any day. There is no God. There is no sense at all to life."

Moved by his emotion, Eden swallowed to keep from sobbing. "There is a God, and He answers every prayer, but we mustn't try to control Him. We must ask for things in line with His will for us. He is not Father Christmas dispensing gifts. He may not give us the answer we wanted at the time, but He gives us the answer that is best for our welfare, and that of all concerned."

"His answer to my only request was, 'No'."

"His answer was, 'I have a better plan for you'. You see it that He took her because He did not love you enough; I see it she was taken because He loved you both infinitely."

Colin turned from her and glared out the window at nothing, effectively erecting a wall between them. Eden suffered for him, feeling certain she had failed him, but not sure what else to say. He clomped a booted foot up on the seat facing them and sat his hat forward over his brow as if preparing to sleep. "You are now boring me, Miss Barrett." Silence filled the carriage and magnified the sounds outside, until the earl's deep voice broke it again. "How shocked you shall be when you die and find nothingness beyond the grave."

When Eden glanced at him, she saw a distinct sneer, as if he were enjoying the idea of her death. "By then it would no longer matter, would it? For my entire journey through life should have been made bearable, even enjoyable, gentled by the belief that I am here for a purpose, that things happen for a purpose, that my God created me because He loved me, and He sent His beloved Son who died for me and triumphed over evil and death for me, and holds a mansion in everlasting light for me. I shall have traveled with hope, peace, and true joy: three companions I should never have met except in the presence of faith in God."

Colin slammed the communicating window open so hard that Eden jumped with fear that he meant to slap her. He barked at John, "Stop the carriage now! Diana will ride inside. I ride on the box. It's too damned stuffy in here!"

CHAPTER XIX

Molly came out to stand in line with the Sheppards and the tapster when the carriage pulled in to the Blue Lion's gravel drive. She was radiant. Eden could hardly wait for the steps to be let down to exit her prison and run to Molly's arms. The maid had, as Eden knew she would be, been accepted into the family like a long lost daughter. Mrs. Sheppard had written to Molly's parents assuring them of their daughter's comfort, security, and usefulness here in her new position. Ten days had changed Molly's out look from despair to great promise.

Ma Sheppard met Diana and Eden in the garden after they had seen to their needs and walked with them as they stretched their cramped limbs. She showed them a white and rust spotted spaniel bitch heavy with milk and yet-to-be-born puppies. The dog's owner had stayed the night and snuck off early without paying his tab, leaving the dog in his room. "I believe she may be some good to me in reaching Simon," Mother Sheppard said. "She crawls all over him and licks him without shame whenever he sits down out here. At first he cringed, but now he doesn't seem to mind it one bit, in fact he smiles.

"And Molly is a love. She is so industrious. When there is naught for her to do, she plays with my Simon for she says she must get in practice. She feeds him for me, for she has an idea about getting him to look at her by drawin' the spoon in front of her face and saying the name of the food each time before she lets him take a bite. I hope it works. It makes sense like. He does like his food."

In the morning, when they were boarding the coach again, Eden caught a very shy, conspiratorial smile passing between Jem and Molly. It warmed her heart for the final length of the journey. Colin was grave and preoccupied but conciliating. He answered Diana's questions and saw to Eden and Diana's comfort with his customary all-encompassing consideration, but without his usual warmth. He did not initiate any discussions except with Diana, but neither was he resentful in what he did say.

Finally, the coach pulled up out of the drizzle under the *porte-cochere* at Chadilane. Colin's first command was to Mr. York. "Send Grey to my office at once." His tone was ominous. Later, when Nora came up with fresh towels for Eden, she told her it was all about in the servants' hall that His Lordship had turned Mr. Grey off without so much as a by-your-leave. The man had been agent on the estate for twenty years. He was a trusted upper servant with his own cottage, and he was on the verge of taking a new wife. What could he have done to be treated so shabbily? If he could be dismissed so perfunctorily, then perhaps others would soon find themselves out on their ear as well.

Eden said she was sure His Lordship had not made a hasty decision, and she would find out what had caused the dismissal for the sake of the staff's peace of mind. Before she could take a step, though, Nathan came to her door. "His Lordship's compliments, Ma'am. And you're to accompany Her Ladyship to meet a guest in the billiard room," he told her.

As Diana entered the billiard room with Eden, she screamed, ran, and threw herself into the waiting arms of an auburn-haired gentleman. He caught her and raised her up off the ground. She clasped her legs round his waist and remained there. "Jeremy! I love it! How long do you stay?"

"I've only just got here, Elf. Diana, I fear I must find a new name for you. You are getting rather heavy for an elf."

"Am I too heavy for you to hold now?"

"Not just yet, but soon. Here, get down and introduce me to that demure vision that accompanies you."

Colin stood in the background, clutching his cue, and watching silently as Diana performed the introductions. The freckle-faced, pug-nosed, boyish-looking young man was introduced as Mr. Jeremy Blake. When Eden's name was made known to him, he took her hand, bowed low over it, and pressed his lips to her fingers with graceful gallantry. Instantly Eden liked him thoroughly.

"So you are the fair governess I've heard so much about," he said.

Eden smiled shyly, "You can have heard nothing of me."

"I've just come from London, where absolutely everyone I met had one identical question to ask me, 'Who is that sable-haired goddess Edmund is escorting about?' I simply had to come find out for myself."

"I'm on my guard against you, Sir. For I see the very devil in your eyes," she replied archly and truthfully.

"Who ma'am? Me ma'am? Oh, no. The devil is said to have been the very handsomest of God's angels and bedecked in jewels. I could tempt no one with this face, and the only jewels I own are paste. But you are right. I'm teasing. I hear you don't like teasing."

Eden shot a quick look toward Colin, but he was examining the shine on the toes of his Hessians with a sudden all-consuming interest. She immediately knew where Mr. Blake had gotten any information he might have about her. At one point, when Mr. Blake and Diana were talking nineteen to the dozen, Eden managed to come close enough to Colin to tell him she would like to speak to him alone and soon. He raised a curious brow, but told her he would come to her suite to collect her a half hour after the bell rang to dress for supper, if that was convenient. She would be expected to dine with the company.

When the earl rapped on her sitting room door, Eden was still shoving pins in her hair. She let him in. "The staff is upset because you turned Mr. Grey off without telling him why," she said bluntly.

"He knows damned well why! Pardon me. He was behaving as usual to the tenants here about the estate, but he raised the rents of tenants on the properties that lie in further districts without recording the raise or the difference. He also recorded repair bills to things that were not repaired. My guess is, since I had put no time in meeting my other tenants and left all the running of the estates to him since my father's death, he felt I would never find out. When confronted with the evidence, the man had not the decency to own up to his own guilt, but must lay the blame on his fiancé, saying she put him up to it.

"I would not have known it at all, had not a desperate tenant finally written a letter of outrage to me. He thought Grey was acting for me in good stead, and that I was an unreasonable landlord. I lifted the names of other tenants in that area from the estate ledgers and had Mr. Sheppard notify the men that I wished to meet with them. Only then did they tell me what has been going on for eight months.

"By turning him off without going over the books for outlying properties, I've put myself in a pickle. I will not be much help to the next person I hire in deciphering those accounts. The ledgers dealing with the immediate estate and the township, I am familiar with. But to entertain that thief in my presence one minute longer after I was convinced of his dishonesty would have been compromise to me. Compromise is something I cannot abide."

Eden chuckled, "That is surprising. As a politician you must see the wisdom in compromise. It is often the only way of gaining where two parties come to an impasse."

"Yes, but each party must give up something. There I have a problem. Do you now presume to counsel me on compromise? You can know nothing of it; you who hold stubbornly to your views like a terrier to the neck of a rat," he said smiling warmly.

"I thought I was open-minded, but not so much that the wind enters one ear and blows my conclusions out the other. One cannot always be with children without seeing the value of compromise. I admit it is one lesson I am still learning." He only smiled. She changed her tone. "This was really not a matter which I had a right to bring up with you. You have been kind to explain it."

"I trust you will put the staff at ease for me?"

"You could do it yourself."

"I shouldn't need to."

"I agree."

"As I have told you something which is none of your concern, you must do the same for me." Eden looked askance at him. He ignored the look. "The chain with the cross and ring: you are not wearing it. Lost?"

"It does not suit the evening dress. I would never lose it or part with it for the world," she said with love in her voice.

"Mm," he grunted and left.

* * *

Mr. Blake proved a cheerful addition to the household. His vocation was Member of Parliament for a borough in Wiltshire. His avocation was legerdemain. He delighted in pulling coins, eggs, and flowers from the oddest places. It seemed he was able to make anything disappear and reappear elsewhere as he chattered glibly of the latest political *on dit*.

After dismissing class the next afternoon, Eden was invited to join the gentlemen with Diana. They enjoyed a row on the lake and an exhibition of the gentlemen's fencing prowess on the indoor tennis court. When a close thrust on the part of Mr. Blake toward Colin tore a scream from Eden's throat, Jeremy laughed. "See how much she cares for you, Edmund. Don't worry pretty lady. The foils have buttons on them. I could never harm Edmund. He saved me from many a cruel thrashing at Eton. I am ever in his debt."

Colin had whipped his head round in the direction of the cry. Catching his breath a moment, he held Eden's gaze with his own. Beads of perspiration dripped down his neck, and he grabbed a towel to mop them. His lips curled in a droll smile. "So you do care."

Unnerved as always beneath his unrelenting stare, she must come back with, "As I would care for any living creature I thought about to be run through before my very eyes!"

He chuckled.

"This is too intense for me," Eden said, rising from her chair on the side. "Diana shall we go riding?"

Diana remained seated, "No. I'm enjoying this."

"*En Garde*," Colin called to Jeremy, suiting the stance to the challenge.

"No thank you, Edmund," Jeremy said. "With that look on your face, surely I shall be the one who is run through. Riding it is, Miss Barrett."

In the evening, Colin played the pianoforte, and Jeremy and Diana performed a trick. They used a silver serving-tray with a domed cover. First, with great fanfare, they placed two live Pouter Pigeons on the tray and covered them with the lid, assuring Eden the birds would not be harmed. But when Jeremy raised the cover again, flames shot out from under it causing her to cry out a second time that day. He replaced the cover immediately. Diana re-removed the cover to reveal two roasted birds. Eden was not laughing, so Diana replaced the cover. Jeremy swiftly removed the cover one last time to reveal the two original pigeons completely unharmed. Now Eden applauded, but asked them never to do such a thing to her heart again.

The next day and evening were spent in like vein. Eden was sent for after classes to accompany the group on horseback. As she descended the stairs in her stylish riding outfit, she noticed the bustle of industry among the servants. They were getting ready for more visitors. On the third day, Eden was disappointed when she was not sent for. She had looked forward to being entertained by Jeremy again. He was eternally ebullient, and it was infectious. While in the library searching out the answer to a history question, she had just sat down with a book when she heard the sounds of approaching carriages. She went to the window to watch the arrivals. When the first coach pulled up to a stop in front of the terrace steps, Lord Edmund himself opened the door and let down the steps. Cassandra Bradley hesitated on the top step and then fairly jumped into his arms. Colin swung her half way about and kissed her soundly. It might have been on the mouth. It was a little hard to tell from Eden's vantage point. The lovely blonde did not seem to find his display of affection odd in the least. The earl left one arm tight about her waist as he greeted the remaining occupants while they disembarked aided by the footmen.

Eden left the window. It had to be true. Colin would never act so freely with a gently bred lady in front of her own family, unless there was a definite understanding between them. She thought of the day by the lake and then of his profuse, embarrassed apology. Suddenly, Eden felt rather tired and strange, almost ill. She headed for the solace of her room. Laughter traveled up to her as the company approached the entry doors downstairs. One laugh was especially memorable for its beautiful musical trill.

The manor came alive with the commotion of moving the guests into their rooms. The single ladies were situated in the same hall Eden's suite occupied. The single men occupied the opposite wing of the house on the same floor. Eden took her books to her room and remained there until tea. She heard the voices of the guests several times as they passed through the hall. The voice she could identify as Cassandra's was warm and delightful. Each time Eden heard the voice, she tried to catch the point being made so that she could judge the character of its owner.

At teatime, Diana came to Eden with a message. "Colin says I'm to take tea with the guests. He asks a favor of you. When Mr. Grey left, he neglected to take his mother with him. Colin told her she might stay in the cottage as long as she likes. She said she might be able to move in with her daughter in town now that her grandchildren are grown. In the meantime, since she already knows you and likes you, Colin hopes you will keep her company for tea and see that she has all she needs. He says you may use your mount or the curricle if you like. John can go with you."

"I think I'll walk. I could use the exercise."

As Eden walked toward the center staircase she passed the little balcony where ensembles usually set up to play over the dance floor for balls. The sounds of a man's and a woman's voices in song drifted up to her. The timber of the man's voice was unmistakably that of her master. Amazed and a little amused at first, Eden soon found herself entranced. *Why should I be so surprised at his talent? Had I not always thought his speaking voice melodic?* It was just that in all the months she had been here, Eden had never heard him sing before. She leaned on the railing of the overlook onto the dance floor and watched the couple from above.

The song they sang was a haunting ballad written in a minor key. From her vantage point, Eden could see Colin's back as he played the piano and Cassandra's radiant expression as she faced him. Eden could not help feeling the couple delighted in one another. The familiar interplay of smiles and touches as they chose a second song testified to it. They made a handsome couple. They were in love. *I'm glad for him; he needs someone.* But she could not help thinking if only she had met him first. *It should have made no difference. I would still be classed as beneath him, and he would still be antagonistic toward my beliefs.*

Eden's walk to Mother Grey's cottage was not her usual lighthearted stroll; it was closer to a trudge. She had brought teacakes and sandwiches from the kitchens and made and poured the tea and visited and walked the little mop of a dog and fed him and made a stew to leave warming on the stove for later. When the sky grew dark, Eden prepared to return to the manor. "Will you feel safe all alone out here?" she asked the old woman.

"Oh, I'm fine. Mr. Sebastion dropped by last evening. He says he's keeping an eye on my place as well as the rest of the grounds. He'll be by later to sup with me, and if I need help, he's around."

"I'll see you the same time tomorrow then."

When she entered the house, Nora was waiting to tell her she was to take supper with Nurse Warren. Though she had not really expected to be included with the guests, Eden could not help feeling rejected. After supper with the nanny, Eden collected the dishes on the tray and took them to the silent butler. She was returning from there when she heard, "Ah-ha! There you are." She lurched. "Come here this instant fair sylph and join the party. I have been looking for you all day."

Eden turned to see Major Bradley grinning at her. She hesitated, but then Colin appeared behind him and said, "By all means, Miss Barrett. Come down and join the party."

"I'm not appropriately dressed."

"Nonsense. You look fine. We're all comfortable," the major argued.

Eden obeyed her employer and followed the two men downstairs. The guests were gathered in the music room. Eden was introduced to Miss Wentnick and her parents and to Lady Bradley and a Mr. and Mrs. Denton. "Miss Bradley, Major Bradley, and Mr. Blake you already know," Colin said, adding in a voice loud enough for all to hear, "I must warn you to be on your guard against the Major here. His intentions toward you are strictly dishonorable."

The gathering of friends laughed heartily, and Eden curtsied and thanked Colin archly for the warning. On hearing that she was the governess, Lady Bradley and her sister, Mrs. Denton, lost all interest. Major Bradley, however, used the information as a starting point for conversation. He was completely charming and at ease with her. Mr. Blake soon intruded himself into their conversation to claim Eden's hand and invite her to dance if Cassandra or Colin would play. The carpet was rolled back as the elders chose seats and the younger guests chose partners and Cassandra chose a reel from the music in the piano bench. Eden was able to enjoy the exhilaration of a set with an accomplished dancer. Mr. Blake then led her to the punch bowl and offered her refreshment.

Before she could receive the cup, however, Major Bradley snatched Eden's wrist and insisted, "I will not allow Blake to take you away from me so easily, even if I have to pull rank on him. You perform admirably, Miss Barrett. Do you waltz? It is acceptable on such informal occasions, you know." Not waiting for an answer, he seized her waist and commanded, "Give us a waltz, Cassy."

Cassandra declined to play and glared at her brother, but Colin slid onto the bench beside her and struck a chord. It all happened so quickly; Eden really had no choice. As Lord Edmund played, he watched with a disgruntled expression the couple getting to know each other. Imperceptibly at first, he began to increase the tempo and volume of the music until at last the dancers were spinning at a dangerous rate.

Jeremy and his partner, Miss Wentnick, left the floor. Major Bradley, an athletic dancer, took it as a challenge, whirling Eden about until they were both quite dizzy, flushed, and out of breath. When the music stopped, Eden could hear Cassy asking Colin what had gotten into him. The couple had to cling to each other even after the music ended, because the room had not stopped spinning.

Mrs. Denton prompted her husband to rescue the little governess. He did so by claiming the next dance after she had had a moment to catch her breath. He chose the more sedate Boulanger. At the close of that dance, Eden felt the way a prize winning rabbit at the fair must feel as it is held by the scruff of the neck and handed about from judge to judge. Mr. Denton drew her by the wrist toward the earl where he sat behind the pianoforte. "Edmund," he said, "you must oblige Miss Barrett with a dance and complete her collection of all the male hearts in present company. I can sincerely recommend her as a partner."

All conversation in the room died. Eden felt her flesh prickle with embarrassment, but also anticipation. Colin rose, gazing resolutely into her eyes as he did so. He said solemnly, "I should like above all things to lead Miss Barrett into a dance." He stepped off the podium and took her hand from the elder man. His voice was liquid gold. "May I have the honor of your company on the floor, Ma'am?" Eden inhaled and blinked. He commanded, "A waltz, Cassy, if you please."

The governess had never performed so miserably. Stirred by his embrace (much tighter than the prescribed inches) she flushed and missed steps all around the room. Eden lifted her eyes to his and was locked in his icy irises. He smiled and murmured, "Perhaps if you would relax a little and follow my lead...or are you too used to doing your own leading? Diana has told me how you take the man's part."

"Perhaps if you would relax your hold, I could relax; though not altogether, for I am wondering just where you are leading…"

"You find my embrace a little too … arousing, perhaps?"

Eden felt all the blood in her body rising to her face. "It is arousing, my lord, - arousing my ire."

He chuckled, and relaxed his hold - a little.

Where does he get the audacity to flirt with me like that while he has his fiancé play the music for us? I don't know him at all. I have heard that the ton practice flirtation often with their spouses present. And I can smell the sweet odor of brandy on his breath. That must be it. He is drinking to excess because of the company. People say all sorts of stupid things when they are in their cups.

Eden was humiliated by the earl's behavior that first night, but from that point on, he completely ignored her, though she attended all the functions at Diana's request. The raven-haired Miss Wentnick was quiet and unassuming. An excellent listener, she had much to listen to. Jeremy partnered her at all of the ensuing events, and Colin squired Cassy. The four made a close-knit group, talking and laughing among themselves or following Colin as he made his rounds among the other guests.

This left Major Bradley to amuse himself with Eden's charms. He seemed more than satisfied with this arrangement. Eden afforded him the same bright interest she paid to any acquaintance: she was open, warm, and attentive. Dorian was neither a sage, nor even a wit, but he was a practiced rake. His air of light flirtation could not help but evoke a certain mirror response in the ladies. And Eden was a lady, and one mildly miffed at the clique of four excluding her from its circle of warmth.

After morning class, Diana invited Eden to join her and the guests at the pavilion by the lake. Daniel and Thomas were invited as well. When she arrived there, she found a party of at least a hundred picnickers. After the meal, the young men tried to set up a game of football. The men on the wrong side of forty were not interested in exercise, especially after indulging in such a repast. Jeremy suggested the boys against the young men. Major Bradley felt it could not be fair due to their size. Daniel said it most certainly would be fair as the men may be larger, but they were also less agile due to their age. At this the young men protested, saying they would show him who was old and feeble.

A field for play was laid out, the spectators dispensed themselves comfortably about on blankets, and the game began. Eden found Cassandra and Judith gravitating towards her as they watched the proceedings. "I was enjoying the privilege of being among some of the wisest young men of my acquaintance," Judith said. "Now I find them behaving like children."

"According to my mother," Cassandra answered her, "boys never really do grow up, they just get taller."

"And stronger."

"And more interesting to look at."

"And to talk to."

"And to dance with."

Judith turned to Eden, "You will think us hardened coquettes, Miss Barrett."

"And you will be right if you do," Cassandra added. The two were quickly sharing observations with Eden and asking her to address them by their first names. There was no false sentiment here, or condescension. The two ladies were perfectly amiable with her. Cassandra told Eden that her birthday was two days hence, and she had persuaded Colin to hold a dinner and competitions in her honor for she would reach her majority then. The entire neighborhood was to be invited; farmers, tenants, and servants included. Eden was encouraged to propose some events.

As the football game progressed, the boys gained an extra goal on the men. This could not be tolerated so the players became seriously competitive. The play had maneuvered directly in front of the three lady spectators, when Jeremy attempted to kick the ball with all his might and landed flat on his back. Everyone laughed at first, but Jeremy did not move. He lay with his eyes closed and a drained expression on his face. Colin bent over him. Cassandra ran to him, crying his name. Judith and Eden followed quietly.

Cassandra fell to her knees and placed her head upon the prone man's heart. "It beats," she said in a distressed but hopeful tone. She began to take his head upon her lap when Jeremy's eyes popped wide open. Cassandra screamed, and Jeremy sat up laughing.

"Oh! You Beast!" Cassy railed at him, "You were posing all along! How dare you play such a cruel joke! You frightened me out of my wits when you opened your eyes just then!"

Jeremy laughed harder, "Cassy would rather I be dead than that I should open my eyes and frighten her."

Cassy's voice lowered to its usual calmness, "Look what you made me do. Grass stains on my dress. They're impossible to get out. It's all your fault. You're an absolute beast."

Jeremy leaned over to her and practically whispered, "You are right; I am an animal, for I am thinking I would like to seize you and put a few more grass stains on that dress."

Cassy put a finger to her lips and said, "Behave."

Though Cassandra may have thought Jeremy a beast, when the game had ended, the two couples promptly formed their bond again. After most of the picnic guests had left and the houseguests began to wander back to the manor for tea, Eden started to split away from them. "You are not leaving us?" Major Bradley came to her side.

"Just for tea. I must visit a dear lady who lives in that cottage over there."

"When will you return?"

"Before it gets too dark."

Jeremy met them and grabbed the major's arm. "Dorian, I propose a bet. I'll wager you fifty pounds, here in front of all these witnesses that I can carry you upon my shoulders the entire way from that fountain down to the willow tree and back again without falling."

"You're out of your mind, Blake. I'm full as heavy as you. You couldn't carry me a stone's throw."

"Nevertheless," Jeremy said, then repeated his bet word for word loudly for the benefit of the guests and over the protest of the ladies that he would do himself some irreparable harm.

"You're on," cried Dorian.

It was decided that Judith would hold the wagers. After placing his fifty pounds in her hand atop Jeremy's, Major Bradley declared himself ready. The group moved to the starting place. Jeremy performed some limbering up exercises and some deep breathing exercises and declared himself ready to begin. When Dorian stepped forward, Jeremy told him nonchalantly, "You may now strip, Sir."

"Strip! What are you talking about?"

"Strip, Sir. Remove all your clothing and be quick about it. We don't want to keep the ladies waiting."

"You're mad! Nothing was said of removing my clothes."

"The wager was I would carry you. Nothing was said of carrying your clothes as well."

Bradley snatched his money from Judith's hands and stomped off toward the house away from the derisive laughter that followed him.

As Eden was laying out her clothing for supper, Cassandra came to her door. "May I lend you my Abigail tonight, Eden? She's a wonder with arranging hair. If you would let her cut yours a little, just below the shoulders, I am sure you would find it easier to manage. It dries so much faster then and doesn't need so many pins to hold it up. Oh, but it would be such a shame in your case. Your hair is so lovely. I retract the suggestion. You will think me silly, won't you? If you need any kohl or lip rouge or burnt cork for your brows, I have them all. I cannot abide painting or powdering the skin except for a light rice powder applied with a hair's foot. All else only upsets the complexion. But darkening lashes discreetly, I can heartily recommend. God has been so unfair. He makes the men so handsome without any need of artifice."

"I can't think I envy them the necessity of shaving," Eden answered.

Cassandra laughed her musical laugh and said, "Oh, I did not think of that. No, I can't envy them their beards. I do like you, Eden. Please excuse me. I must have a lie down with cucumbers on my eyelids before I dress." Then she was gone. It was like the appearance and disappearance of a ray of sunlight in the dark woods.

Nora came up with a spray of tiny wild orchids for Eden's hair. The governess managed to accent her white gown with some lilac ribbon tied about its empire waist and woven through the lace that adorned the little puffed sleeves. She went to Diana's room for the girl's reaction.

As the door to Diana's bedchamber was opened slightly, Eden heard some rather astounding sounds emanating from within. It sounded so much like what noisy and passionate kissing might sound like, that Eden hesitated as she approached the door. "Diana?" she called doubtfully.

The noise stopped. "Enter," Diana answered.

When Eden did so, all was as usual. Diana lay on her bed on her stomach with a book open before her. "What did I just hear?" Eden had to ask.

"I was practicing kissing," Diana said. She then made mad, passionate love with her mouth on her forearm to illustrate.

"Good Heavens! What a noise. You won't practice your piano, but kissing you will practice."

"I've never kissed a man on the mouth before. I wondered what it felt like. I wonder who invented kissing."

"Probably Adam. And I don't think your forearm feels quite the same as a man's mouth."

"What do you think Eve thought when Adam said, 'I want to push my mouth on yours and move it about while sucking at the same time'? She must have screamed."

Eden could not control her laughter, nor was she inclined to. "It certainly sounds repulsive when you put it that way. In that case, I hope he did not warn her. I hope he just kissed her and let her decide for herself if she enjoyed it." Eden peered at the title of the book Diana was reading, another Minerva Press romance. "I see what has sparked your interest in the subject."

"You disapprove?"

"Yes and no."

"Miss Warren says I shouldn't read them. I should only read 'edifying' books. But they usually put me to sleep."

"If fiction is well written, one can escape to another, in a way, truer life. More true because it is condensed to the moments that matter. But if poorly written, you may be getting such an unreal view of life that you are not building a good basis for making important decisions later on."

"Do you believe in love at first sight?"

"No. That's infatuation. It can develop into love or fade."

"How does one know the difference?"

"The young lady who is infatuated thinks: He makes me happy; He makes me proud; and so forth. She puts too much importance on superficial things about him; his appearance, his social standing, the amount of money he has. When it is real love, the lady thinks in terms of what she can do for him, and whether he possesses those lasting values that don't fade with time and serve to make a life together sweet. Things like trustworthiness, gentleness, true kindness, thoughtfulness..."

"Have you ever been in love, Miss Barrett?"

She did not hesitate, "Yes."

"The kind that leads to marriage?"

Eden swallowed and nodded.

"How can you decide if you love a man enough to marry him?"

"I can only answer for myself. If I were ever to accept the hand of a gentleman, I would have to be convinced that living apart from him would somehow diminish me, that I couldn't be whole or happy without him."

"What happened?"

"What do you mean?"

"You didn't marry him."

"Oh, it was unrequited. He simply... did not return my affection."

"I think I'm in love."

"Do you? With Daniel?"

"Is it so obvious?"

Eden shook her head. "Just a guess. He is a worthy young man. Read your Bible to find a description of true love. First Corinthians, Chapter Thirteen is a good place to start."

"We were taking a basket of meat pies and sweet buns to the stables, and Daniel let his finger touch mine on the handle. I looked at him. He knew it was there. He smiled. You're quite pretty tonight, Miss Barrett. Your dress shows off your figure well. The colors agree with your complexion. In fact, I don't think I've ever seen you as pretty as you are tonight."

"Thank you. Are you sure you'll be satisfied to stay in your room?"

"There's no one else for me to talk to. Cassy and Judith are sweet, but children aren't really wanted in grown-up company are they?"

"Grown-ups who think that way are missing a great deal."

"Do you not think Major Bradley handsome and dashing?"

"A delight to the eyes."

"Do you want to kiss him?"

"Did anyone ever tell you some questions are just too personal?"

"That means you do."

"Don't put words in my mouth."

CHAPTER XX

As she went down the hall, Eden heard laughter coming from Cassy's sitting room. It was Jeremy Blake's ridiculous laugh. She tiptoed by the slightly ajar door on the way to the ground floor. The voices of the earl and Jeremy reached her and held her there.

"So when is the honeymoon to be over, so that I may be the first to visit the happy couple?" Jeremy asked.

"I don't intend for the honeymoon ever to be over," Colin's voice replied.

"Oh Lord, I knew it. I knew if you ever fell again, you would fall like a boulder down a mountain. You're thoroughly besotted. There's no hope for you," Jeremy teased.

"I haven't fallen anywhere. Believe me, I've walk into this with my eyes wide open. I have no desire to go back."

"No, Edmund. I can't possibly let you marry in this odious condition."

"You can't stop me."

"The girl has put a gold ring in your nose. You should be training her to be a biddable, obedient wench. If we can't extricate that ring before you're wed, she'll crook her little finger through it, smile seductively, and lead you where she will."

"The seductive smile will be sufficient to do that," Colin retorted.

At this, Jeremy and Cassy could both be heard laughing. Eden turned and walked back to her chamber. She never imagined her master could speak in such a maudlin way. She also had no business listening, nor did she wish to hear another depressing word.

In Cassandra's sitting room, the conversation continued. "If you can't say when the honeymoon will end, then at least tell me the day you have set for it to begin. If you expect the best man to be there, I must plan," Jeremy begged.

"That's even harder to answer," Colin said.

"Is the lady being missish? Take a tip from me, Colin. I'm an authority on these things. Put your foot down. Tell her where and when a curate will be waiting to perform the ceremony. Then say that you, the curate, and the witnesses will wait exactly ten minutes and no more."

"I'll take your advice, Jeremy, just as soon as I've asked her if she'll have me."

Jeremy cried, "You mean to tell me the lady still does not know your intentions?"

Colin shrugged. "What a conceited ass you are," Jeremy smiled, "inviting me to your wedding before you invite the bride."

"There are obstacles."

"I've always known you to be shy, Colin. But this is ridiculous. What obstacles? 'Faint heart ne'er won fair lady' you know."

"I must tread carefully, Jeremy. She's too important to me. You know what people are, including servants - they gossip and speculate if I notice her. The few times I've done anything more than hint at my feelings for her, she's turned cold and pointedly avoided me. Yet, if I behave as no more than a concerned friend, she puts her trust in me. She's not ready for anything more, and I won't frighten her off by forcing my attentions on her. But Jeremy, I don't know how much longer I can mask my emotions in this way."

"You say she pointedly avoids you?"

He nodded.

"Then there are no obstacles. Mark my words. I have far more experience in translating the ways of women. I guarantee if she pointedly avoids you, she is repressing feelings that equal yours. Now if she merely avoided you instead of pointedly avoiding you, it would mean she did not care a fig for you."

"Cassy, I pity you. You are marrying a babbling idiot. You still have time to run," Colin said.

"Though I hate to admit it of someone so conceited that he claims to understand the ways of women, he does make sense," she answered. "And Colin, her eyes are never off you as long as you are not looking in her direction."

"You teach me to hope," Colin said. "Something has to give way. I can't concentrate on estate business. My new agent and my secretary think I am in my dotage already. In the middle of conversations with them on my appointments or whether to drain a field or not, my mind wanders off in search of her."

"And there is something between us. I know it. I have only to look at the nape of her neck - that amazing swan-like neck - as she sits sewing in the salon to make her turn and see who watches. She feels my presence. Still, there is another obstacle, a soldier stationed in Bath."

"You've a rival?" Cassandra asked. Again Colin shrugged. Cassy continued, "She said nothing to me. But, she really had no opportunity. No. I can't believe it. Who is there to rival you?"

"Cassandra, the man's pride is too swelled already without you feeding it more," Jeremy said as he stood to go. "I fear we may be keeping company waiting."

Eden joined the guests gathered in the great hall where Major Bradley at once claimed her for his supper partner as it was an informal evening and rank could be dispensed with. He complimented her on her dress, her hair, and her radiance. His manner was easy and unassuming as he placed her gloved hand on his arm to lead her in to supper. Cassy, Jeremy, and Colin descended the stairs. Eden watched Colin stand dutifully still as Cassy straightened his already perfectly tied cravat.

Dorian's golden brown eyes danced in a merry face that bore an infectious grin. They took seats about mid-table next to his mother. His aunt and uncle faced them. As the footmen offered the dishes, Dorian chose for Eden, then for himself. The feast of comments at table was almost as varied and well seasoned as the dishes of the feast itself.

At the head of the table, Lord Edmund chose for Cassandra and smiled into her eyes. Whenever he could steal a glance toward his governess without appearing partial to her, Colin took pleasure in observing her manner of eating. She savored the food, taking tiny deliberate chews. Then she looked back at her plate, studying her fare before carefully choosing the next morsel. Next to her sat Dorian shoveling into his face whatever his fork brought up and washing each mouthful down with wine.

When the fish course was brought out, Dorian insisted Eden try the lobster, as he had personally arranged for them to be brought in from Bath that afternoon. They had been packed alive in rush baskets with wet seaweed in between each layer. She admitted hesitating for lack of knowledge of a lady-like way to attack the carapace. Dorian was pleased to assume the role of instructor. There was no way to get into the shell without creating a mess, so he did just that. He then plunged his own tiny fork into the white meat, dipped it into melted butter, and held it up to Eden to eat.

As she gingerly took the fork from Dorian's hand, Eden's glance met Colin's. His expression was censorious. She averted her eyes and took a bite. *Now what have I done! He disapproves, but what? I'm only being nice to his guest. Is that not what is expected? I am certainly not flirting; Well maybe a little, but an innocent flirtation.* Eden became indignant. To hide her pique, she pretended not to notice. In order to feign disregard of Colin's look, she appeared a little more interested than she really was in what Dorian had to say, smiling and laughing even more than usual. Dorian took it as encouragement and magnified in his mind Eden's regard for him.

When he asked Eden to pass judgment upon the lobster, she pronounced it, "Delectable."

"The very word I would have chosen," he told her with an expression that let her know that it was not the food he thought delectable, but her. He then used the same fork she had used and licked the tines lasciviously before plunging them deep within the white meat of the lobster. Eden became mildly afraid.

The topics Dorian chose for dinner conversation seemed to center around gambling and racing. When he mentioned a rat match, he asked Eden if she had ever been to one. *Surely he knows no lady would be caught dead at one*, she thought. He laughed heartily when she winced at his description of a terrier that could shake to death as many as fifty rats in the time limit. His mother reproved him with, "Must you speak of rats while I'm eating?"

He answered, "Weak stomach, mother?" Then he delighted in giving a gory description of a bear baiting.

When the ladies removed to allow the gentlemen their strong spirits and tobacco, Eden was relieved. In the parlor, Cassy and Judith distinguished Eden again with their company. Eden was pleasantly surprised at their attention tonight when they had other, higher-ranking guests present. Some of those guests were obviously registering concern over deference being paid to a mere governess at all, but they kept it to their expressions and did not voice it.

As usual at parties of the ton, the Prince Regent came up in conversation. Lady Welham told them that at the last state dinner she had attended, the gold embroidered coat that Prinny had worn was said to weigh as much as it cost.

Cassy made sport of the Prince's regimen aimed at helping him loose some girth. It seemed he put great stock in playing Royal Tennis. "Fewer desserts would also be in order," she said.

"Don't be so smug about his waist," her mother said. "The man is fifty years old. He was a fine figure when he was your age. Once you pass five and twenty, the bodily humors change. It becomes more and more difficult to keep the weight off, especially if you have had children."

"Lady Welham has five grown sons, and she still keeps her girlish figure."

"Lady Welham is an exception. Mark my words. You'll get a taste of what you're snickering at."

"I do not snicker mother, and I say that it is inactivity and overindulgence that put on weight."

"You'll see."

The conversation took its usual twists and turns until someone mentioned the word 'governess'. All eyes turned to Eden to see her reaction. Cassy began to praise her own governess to the skies, saying that she was the warmest, most wonderful, and wisest of jewels she could ever expect to know. "I shall keep her with me always. If she cannot teach my future children, I shall be greatly disappointed."

"Don't I know she was a jewel? I had the worst of luck with Dorian's nurses," Lady Bradley added. "Do you remember? No, you weren't born yet. We hired a nurse who came to us with the highest of recommendations, a very genteel looking older lady. It took us the longest time to discover her taste for gin. I turned his next nurse off when a footman opened a closet one day to find Dorian bound and gagged inside. The next nurse had the gall to take him with her to town and leave him in a teahouse while she ran away with a common foot soldier. I was never so glad as when he was old enough to send away to Harrow."

"Poor Dorian couldn't keep his nurses, tutors, or pets. He insisted on having pets, but he never took care of them, and he could be rather rough. I had an understanding with a tenant to provide me with look-alike linnets. Every time one died, we put a new one in the cage and hoped he didn't notice."

The gentlemen joined the ladies for coffee. Dorian sat with Major Smyth as Eden was between Cassy and Judith on one settee. He did not take coffee. In fact he soon fell asleep. Eden intercepted a conspiratorial smile passing between Colin and Cassy twice during the evening; once, when Lord Welham asked Cassandra if she thought reaching her majority in two days time would bring about any changes in her, and a second time, when Mr. Denton observed that parents should never insist their children act in any particular way, as children always felt compelled to punish their parents by doing the exact opposite.

Eden thought Cassandra took her impending role at Chadilane for granted when she spoke of redecorating the parlor. "Everything here is so old and dark, even during the day. You must take down those heavy curtains, Colin, and let some light in here. I daresay you would find things in corners you hadn't seen for years."

"I thought that was why man builds a house, to get out of the sun. If you want light, go outside. Give me dark corners for hiding in and observing. Besides, I've grown fond of the furniture. I grew up in it," Colin defended himself.

"Oh, men have no imagination. Some nice light Hepplewhite chairs and remove the dark wainscoting…"

"Remove the wainscoting!" he cried. "Just like a woman. Throw out all that superior workmanship because something new is in style." They sounded like the wedding day had taken place years ago. When the guests broke into groups for cards, Eden made her excuses and went to bed.

The next two days were spent in similar amusements. The older guests entertained themselves in a dignified manner with cards, sitting, talking, and eating. The young adults disgraced themselves playing children's games, dancing, singing, walking, riding, shopping, sitting, talking, and eating.

On Cassandra's birthday it drizzled, threatening to spoil all the festivities planned. Cassandra refused to allow the inclement weather to dampen her spirits, so she proposed a game of hide-and-seek in the house. The boundaries were to be the sitting rooms on the ground floor.

When Eden hid behind the Chinese screen in the blue salon, she found herself promptly joined by Major Bradley. He whispered his doubt that they could both fit behind it; but Jeremy, who was 'it', was close on his tail so he would have to try. He facilitated this by placing his hands on Eden's waist and drawing her to him to save space. As she was considering what to do about his forward manner, one of his hands began to slide upward. She jerked and twisted, pulling both his hands off her. The movement almost toppled the screen.

Dorian grinned and teased, 'Ticklish?"

"Extremely!" she quelled him. He laughed aloud.

Fortunately for Eden, Jeremy found them then. The tottering screen and raucous laugh was a dead give away. When the last participant had been found, Jeremy gallantly suggested a game of cards; Eden quickly seconded the motion. Dorian refused, saying he liked the game they were playing, and Jeremy was too dexterous with cards for him. Jeremy asked if that was any hint of a question of his honesty. Judith and Cassandra interposed between the two inflamed males and insisted they had already tired of the game. The mad rush for a hiding place in the humid weather tended to spoil the results of their careful morning's toilet.

The day cleared in time to decorate the pavilion for the country folk. The games were a huge success. Scarves, hams, cheeses, bolts of cloth, and cakes were offered as prizes for racing uphill or rolling downhill or lifting the most weight or closest arrow to the middle of the target, etcetera. When the day came to a close, the biggest surprise yet was unveiled. Colin had arranged for fifty stone of fireworks to be sequestered on one of the islands in the lake. At dusk, the countryside was treated to a display of loud, colorful, and brilliant explosions. Eden watched from Mother Gray's cottage and described the show to the old lady.

After supper, an aide-de-camp rode up to the manor with a message for Majors Bradley and Smyth. They had orders to rejoin their detachments in Portsmouth in three days time. They would set sail for Spain. The officers decided they could stay until next afternoon and easily make it to their ship in time. Lady Welham made the comment that it would be a sin and a shame to have to do without the gentlemen's presence. Mrs. Denton remarked that Miss Barrett might better know if it were a sin or not, as her father had been of the clergy. To this Dorian added *sotto voce* to Major Smyth, "Capital. In my experience, children of the clergy have heard so much about sin they can't wait to try some for themselves."

Major Smyth leered back at him with, "Not your usual type is she? Thought you liked them young."

"Age is not my requirement. Innocence is. If dear Papa taught me anything, he taught me that. No nasty diseases for this Bradley."

"Will the lady be willing?"

"Does it matter?"

"I can help restrain her."

"Go find your own wench."

CHAPTER XXI

The party of guests had their bags packed and loaded onto their coaches. They would spend the next week at Lord and Lady Welham's and then move on. Colin was to accompany them on his favorite gray stallion. He would return the next day.

Major Bradley, Major Smyth, and their batmen set off after dinner to rejoin their detachment. A few miles down the road, before they came to the gatehouse, Dorian told the rest of his party to go on ahead and wait for him at the Nagging Wife in Edmundton.

Major Smyth raised his riding crop into the air and wished him, "Happy hunting." Bradley waited until they were out of sight, doubled back a way, and dismounted, leading his horse deep into a stand of elms and chestnuts and tying it there.

As the guests gathered in the drawing room for tea and leave-taking, Nora came to the door with a message for Eden. "A visitor to see you, Miss."

"A visitor?"

"A young man, a soldier." Nora handed her his card.

Eden glanced at it. Joy transformed her face. She excused herself and ran from the room. Colin secretly followed her. There in the grand hallway, in full view of every footman on duty, he found his Eden locked in an embrace with that damned beau of hers.

Colin could hear the young man telling her he had just arrived on English soil yesterday, but simply must ride up here immediately to put his arms about her once more. Propriety told Colin to withdraw, but he refused. He forced himself to walk across the Harlequined tiles toward the demonstrative couple. Two feet away he drew himself up to his greatest height and waited for an explanation.

Eden's eyes met Colin's directly, but she exhibited no shame. In fact, she seemed pleased to see him there. *Maddening woman*! Then she spoke to him while still clutching his competition. The soldier released her so that now the earl could see that he wore the uniform of a different regiment than before and the decorations of a captain. He also leaned heavily upon a walking stick.

"My lord, may I have the pleasure of introducing to you my brother?"

"Your brother?"

"You've heard me speak of him. I gave you a letter from him. Captain Matthew Barrett."

"Matthew?"

Yes, my lord. May I introduce you to him?"

"Yes, of course."

"Matthew, allow me to introduce Colin Ashton, Seventh Earl of Edmund."

Colin finally found his wits and offered his hand. "It is an honor to make your acquaintance, Captain Barrett." As Matthew reached to take his hand, Colin saw the soldier grimace. "Miss Barrett, I'm sure you and your brother have much to talk over. If you will entertain him in the China salon, I'll have Mrs. York have tea brought in. May I join you later, in quarter of an hour say?"

"How kind of you. Of course you may join us."

"I can only stay a few moments. I have a companion waiting who is also going home, and I hope to make it to Longacre by tonight," Matthew said.

"Miss Barrett, if he is Matthew, then who the deuce is Charlie?" Colin asked her beneath his breath.

"Charlie is the family nickname for him. Did I call him that?"

"Earlier," Colin said. *Much earlier.*

The gentlemen nodded to each other, and the earl moved away. He could hear the scrape and clump of Matthew's pain-filled stride as he followed his sister into the salon.

After comparing notes on the family, avoiding mention of the violence of the war, and downplaying the extent of the injuries that had brought him home to recuperate, Matthew began to tease. "Eden, you've been hiding something from us all."

"What do you mean?"

"Had I known His Lordship was quite so young or handsome, I should never have allowed you to remain here."

"Your consent was never sought."

"Nevertheless, I am head of the family."

"He's harmless."

"Oh really, one of those? He didn't strike me that way."

"One of what? What are you talking about?"

Matthew explained by pantomiming taking snuff in a very prissy way and letting his wrist flop about like a dishcloth.

"You are not amusing, Matthew. And he is nothing of the kind."

"Then he is dangerous. All men of his face, figure, and manner are."

"You posses the same qualities. Are you dangerous?"

"I most certainly am. That's why they sent me to Spain. To preserve the virtues of the English misses."

"Well, he has been the perfect gentleman, even if you have not. Also, he's engaged to someone far prettier than I."

"Nonsense. There is no one prettier than you."

"Now you tell me! Won't you stay the night? I'm sure His Lordship would insist. There is room for your friend as well."

"No. It's his chaise, and he's as anxious to get home as I am. We brought a sailor with us as far as Edmunton. Odd fellow. He was on the Warhorse, the ship that brought us home. Friendly at first, asked us where we were headed. When we told him where, he begged us to take him too though there was little enough room for two. When we said 'yes', he hopped in the chaise, but after we introduced ourselves, he kept mum the whole ride and hopped out in town without a by-your-leave. At least the ride should be less crowded and thus more comfortable from this point on.

Above them in the library, Colin sat mesmerized by the dancing of flames across a huge log. He was allowing the new information to take effect. Was his competitor for her affections imagined? Diana had said... But Diana could not always be trusted to be truthful. He smiled, rose, went to the door, and locked it. He wanted no servants walking in on what he was about to do.

Standing in the center of the room, he spoke aloud quietly as he did when he was reasoning with another peer. "Alright, God, if you listen to mortals: if you are this all-loving, all-knowing, all-forgiving, all-just deity that she believes you to be, don't begrudge me her hand. I swear, if she will have me, there is no one on this earth who will cherish her more than I. Because she calls you Father, I ask your blessing. I promise to encourage her to accomplish what she will, to reach her full potential. I will not hinder her in any way. I'm well aware that I have absolutely no right to ask you for anything; but dear God, I beg of you, give her to me."

As Matthew was making his way toward the great entrance doors, Colin rejoined them. He offered Matthew and his comrade rooms if they wished to stay. No, he could only take his sister in small doses, the soldier joked. Colin exerted himself to draw the young man out and put him at his ease. When Matthew left, the earl saw him out with Eden. Matthew thanked him for his warm hospitality, adding, "It's a good thing for you your heart is otherwise engaged, or I should suspect your motives toward me." Colin smiled and nodded without knowing to what he was referring. Eden walked her brother to the waiting chaise.

When she returned, Lord Edmund was still standing in the great hall, arms folded across his chest. "What was that last comment your brother made to me about, Eden?"

"It is 'Miss Barrett' when my brother is here to defend my honor, and 'Eden' the minute he is out the door?"

"I thought you would prefer it that way, and you did not answer my question."

"What comment?"

"You know very well what comment. I saw you looking conscious as he said it."

"I suppose I let it slip that you...are...engaged to Miss Bradley."

The earl cocked an eyebrow high. "And why do you suppose you told your brother that?"

Laughter interrupted them as the party of friends came toward the entrance doors to leave. Colin turned to face his friends, and Eden took that moment to scurry off to Mother Grey's, effectively avoiding admitting to listening at doors.

The various chaises set off in a caravan with Colin riding beside them. As the horses started off, the sky behind them was a watercolor done in a monochromatic burnt sienna scale with the darker hue at the tree line. After the wash had dried, God had used ink in muted black to add the silhouettes of trees. A single evening star already glittered in the upper left quadrant. The Almighty had chosen to include only a sliver of moon on his canvas this night.

Eden spent a hurried visit with the old lady for she had arrived late. She assured a worried Mother Grey that she could find her way back in the dark by looking up at the lights of the manor. The woman told her to take the little candle lantern that sat in the window by the door. As she said 'goodbye', Mrs. Grey told Eden, "Tomorrow morning early, I go into town to stay with my daughter for about a week, kind of a trial period. If we get on each other's nerves, I'll come back here, but His Lordship is too kind - letting me stay here when I do nothing to earn it, and my son... Well, anyway, you won't be needing to come around any more unless you get word in a week's time."

Eden lit the candle in the lantern with a stick from a fagot of them in the kitchen by the stove, took leave of the old lady, and followed the path that ran by a stream on the way back to the house. She could see the stars and the bit of moon reflected in the water to help her pitiful lantern light. As she passed under the branches of a stand of oaks, Dorian dropped out of the trees to land directly in front of her. This caused her to cry out and drop her lantern, which promptly extinguished.

"Miss Eden Barrett, well bless my soul. I always knew you were a Gallic sylph, and now I find you in your sylvan couch." Dorian spoke in an oily voice.

"Sylphs were soulless beings. I have a soul. Why are you here? You left hours ago. I thought you had to join your detachment."

"Relax, Eden. Get into the spirit. You're no fun this way. I couldn't leave without saying goodbye to my girl could I? I have something serious to ask of you. Diana says you write and receive many letters. I wondered if you might consider writing to me. You have a lively conversational style. Your writing is surely the same, and it would do so much to alleviate the tedium of an officer's existence. I must admit, I'm not likely to answer them often, but news from home means a great deal to a soldier."

"I would consider it an honor Major Bradley. But I don't recall giving you permission to use my Christian name. Do you have a flint to relight my lantern?"

He shook his head. "When I receive a missive from you, I shall horde it here against my heart, to unfold and reread again and again."

Eden moved to go past him, but he blocked her and took her wrist.

She pulled it away. He allowed her to. "You flatter me, Major. You have not read one of my notes. And you have seen so much of the world; I would not know how to entertain you. My descriptions of a hatchling quail trying to stand, or what the children did or said in the schoolroom would only bore a man brought up on routs and races and hunts among the circle of the Prince Regent's friends."

"That is what I love about you, Eden. You see the world through fresh eyes. Someday I must take you traveling with me. It would be like seeing the world anew to see it with you."

"You will turn my head with your pretty phrases," Eden said. *What you're turning is my stomach.*

"My very purpose," he returned.

"But to what end, Major? You'll be a long way from here, and I doubt I'll ever see you again."

"Never say so! I like to think I might take the impression of you with me to call back at will over the campfire. Then, when I return - if I live - I'll look for you here. Edmund and I are childhood friends. Wouldn't you love to go traveling with me, Eden?"

She tried again to pass, but he snatched her forearm up in his gloveless hand, and continued coaxing her, "You'd like that wouldn't you? There are so many things I can show you. You're like a little child. There are wonderful things you haven't seen, done, experienced. You have so much to learn. And I would so love to be your teacher. You're too fine a specimen to stay a governess hidden in your puritan's clothes. You're a beautiful woman."

He would not let her speak; he pulled her closer, tightening his grip. "I must go soon. I may never return alive. Never see another English rose of a girl. Grant me a last request. I've wanted to taste that delectable mouth since the first day I set eyes on you. Grant my wish. Just a kiss. What harm is there in that?"

At last he allowed her to speak. "Major Bradley, you are progressing our relationship further and faster than I wish it to progress. Let me go."

"Only because of my predicament, Eden. I've only just met you, and I won't have time to court you as you deserve. What are you afraid of? It's just a kiss. A harmless kiss. Sweethearts have been doing that since time began. I may be killed in battle. You couldn't let me die without a single chaste kiss from those seductive lips of yours, could you?"

She pulled away, so Dorian yanked her back and held her to him with both arms. He tried to kiss her, but she turned her head. He persuaded, "What are you afraid of? No one knows we're here. No one will tell. No one will think bad of you."

"I don't live my life according to what others know or think of me."

"I'm glad to hear it. Then you can have no objection to what I have in mind." He grasped the chignon at the back of her neck and forced her face into position. He then lowered his mouth upon hers. This was no chaste kiss! It was continuous and possessive and nauseating. His breath was stale with claret and tobacco. Did he ever clean his teeth? Did he intend to let her breathe? When he tried to force his tongue between her teeth, Eden twisted her head, causing excruciating pain to her scalp. Pins came out of her hair and it half-tumbled down her back. "Please, no!" she cried with what breath she could find.

"Stop struggling, Eden. You want to be kissed. You love it. All women do. You would be unnatural otherwise. Just relax." His mouth moved over her neck and throat like a great slimy, sucking leech.

Eden growled, "Let go of me, or I'll scream!"

He straightened, but he held her like a vice. "You're cold and unnatural."

"Do you call yourself natural?"

"The beasts of the field make love without a bit of shame."

"I have never considered myself on the same level as animals, and they do not make love, they mate. Love has nothing to do with it."

"Between us it'll be love, and it will be beautiful, I promise you."

"Love is commitment and sacrifice and cherishing. What I see in your eyes is lust, not love. It doesn't matter for I return neither feeling."

"You're inexperienced. I know how to make you want to be loved as much as I want to love you. Your body will give you away."

"Stop speaking to me of love when you mean the opposite. What you are asking of me is wrong!"

"Wrong? Nonsense. Don't be such a prude. You'll see how right it is. Everyone does it."

"Wrong is wrong. I don't care if the whole world does it; it will not make it right. Besides everyone does not do it; I don't."

"There's no sense discussing it with you. You don't know what you're missing, and I will be sated. You've aroused me too much for me to stop now." He began to violently kiss her neck below the ear. She was disgusted to feel her body responding with a strong chill down her arm and side.

"I warn you. I'll scream," she groaned.

He pulled his head up then, his yellow eyes narrowed as he grinned triumphantly, "Go right ahead. No one will hear." She struggled, but she was no match for male muscle. "Relax damn it, and enjoy it," he hissed. "You can't escape me." His voice was husky; his breathing, rapid. A second time he tried to force his foul tongue inside her mouth. This time she clamped her teeth viciously down on his lower lip. He groaned and pulled her hair until the pain made her unclench her jaw. He held her away from him with one hand while he swiftly drew back the other and delivered with all his might a resounding slap to her face, immediately followed by a second slap of even greater force.

Eden tasted blood. Both times the heavy ring on his finger struck her cheekbone; the second time, it tore the flesh.

He shoved her down on the ground with all his might. A shock ran through the length of her body when the back of her skull hit an exposed root. Before she could move, he fell to his knees and straddled her waist. She cried, "You can't know what you're doing!"

"I know damned well what I'm doing, and so do you," he spat at her. He reached back to grasp the hem of her skirt and dragged it up to her waist. Eden screamed, "Jesus, help me!" before he clamped a hand over her mouth. He positioned his knees to hold her arms down and thrust his face in hers. It was contorted with hatred; His eyes were wild, burning orbs. "The more you struggle, the more I like it." He twisted his torso, and Eden felt his fingers on her inner thigh.

Though her jaw ached horribly, Eden bit hard into the middle finger of the hand over her mouth. The moment he removed his hand, she screeched again, though she had little breath. "You stupid witch." he screamed, "If you bite me again, I'll knock your teeth down your throat."

The barking of bloodhounds in the distance and the voice of Mr. Sebastion calling Miss Barrett found them. Dorian turned his face to the sound, then back to her. "You made me hurt you, you little witch.

I never would have hurt you, if you'd gone along like a good girl. Tell no one about me. Say you tripped in the dark. If you say a word to Edmund about me, I'll say we've met here every single night, but you demanded more money this time." He stood up then and ran into the woods. The moment his weight was off her, Eden scrambled toward the sound of the gatekeeper's voice, spitting Dorian's fetid saliva from her mouth and calling as she went.

* * *

The house party had gone only a few miles beyond the gate when Judith realized she had forgotten her reticule. Colin told them to ride on ahead. On Galahad, he could easily return to the manor house, fetch the purse and rejoin the party before they reached the Wellham's residence. As his horse cantered out of the giant trees and into the open grounds in front of the house, the dim light revealed the stumbling form of Eden, being assisted to the front entrance by his gamekeeper. Colin dismounted, tossed the reins to John, who had run out to meet him, and ran to the house. When he opened the massive door, he saw Eden's back, covered with mud and clinging leaves, as she reached the landing and turned down the corridor. Sebastion almost bumped into him on the way out.

"What goes on here?" the earl demanded.

The gamekeeper looked beyond his master, "She wouldn't say. But I seen that Major hanging around down there earlier, his horse was tied under the young chestnuts, so I thought that was where he was. I was watchin' her walk up to the house from far off like you said, but it was dark tonight, so I went to get my lantern, and then I positioned myself between where the Major's horse was and the path by the river. I saw her go into that little forest of oaks like usual, only tonight she didn't come out the other side so fast. I heard her yell, and then I heard him yell and when I went calling her, she came running out of there like a bat out of you know where, and she tripped and fell. I went to pick her up, and she grabbed my arm and begged me to walk all the way back to the house with her.

Eden had locked her bedchamber door and thrown herself on

her bed to clutch her pillow and weep, forgetting the sitting room door. *It's my fault. I didn't like him, yet I flirted with him. I could tell he was a bounder, but I thought I was safe because he would leave, and I'd never see him again. I led him on. I thought him coarse and stupid, yet I flirted anyway. I should have had someone walk with me at that time of night. Why must I always...*

Colin went straight to her parlor door and on through to her bedchamber. The sight of her sprawled on her bed fully clothed, hair disheveled, clothing soiled, and sniffing and sobbing distressed him. He spoke soothingly, "Eden, what has happened? I must know."

His voice in her room startled her, and she jumped to a sitting position, head hanging down. "Get out," she groaned.

But he was too agitated to be denied. He moved closer to the bed. "What happened between you and Major Bradley?" Eden said nothing. "I demand an explanation!" Eden moved then. She rose from the bed, keeping her face down and hidden, and ran out the door. Colin shouted, "Damn!" to the empty room, before following her.

She was out the front door before him and running down the road. Colin called to John who was leading his horse back to the stables. He kept an eye on Eden while the man brought Galahad back to him. "Send Nora to find Miss Wentnick's reticule. She left it on her vanity she thinks. Then take a horse and catch up with the party. Tell them I may join them later or not at all, but not to worry, just unforeseen business." He took the reins from his groom, mounted Galahad from the ground, and tore off down the road.

As he approached Eden, Colin slowed the horse to a walk and slid from his saddle before the horse came to a standstill. Galahad began to munch on the thick grass as he slowly followed his owner.

"Eden," the earl called softly, but she walked on. He ran to her and gently grasped an arm.

Eden snapped, "Get your hand off me!"

"I will, if you'll just listen to me." She stood still, and he released her and spoke to her back. "I had no right to speak to you that way. I was alarmed, upset. I don't demand anything of you, but I beg you to silence my fears..."

Eden answered dully, "He didn't achieve his goal, if that is what you mean."

Colin let a deep breath escape, bit his lip and swallowed. Eden began to walk again. "Are you alright? Were you harmed?" he asked. Eden continued walking away from him. "Where are you going?"

"Home," she said.

"Home? But that's the wrong direction."

"Home to Longacre."

"Longacre is thirty miles from here. Be reasonable."

"I don't… know…what…" her voice broke.

"He's gone, Eden. We can ride pillion on Had back to the house. If you still want to go home in the morning, my Landau will take you."

She stood still, though her body trembled with contained sobs. He moved to comfort her, but she moved away, saying, "Don't touch me."

He curled his fingers into his palms and clenched them, standing frustrated and confused and angry with Dorian and himself for not protecting her better. She sat down on the ground. He stood above her for a time, finally breaking the silence with, "What would you have me do?"

"Stay," was her answer.

When the breeze began to toss Eden's hair, Colin saw an opportunity to be of some use. "Let me give you my cloak, Eden. It's getting cool." She said nothing, so he went back to his horse, untied the saddlebag, and retrieved his cloak. He brushed the leaves gently from her back and draped the cloak over her shoulders. When Eden didn't move or speak, Colin took a seat on the ground and buried his head in his hands.

Galahad brought his head up, chewing noisily on a clump of grass. Presently, he recognized the scent of the lady who often brought him apples or carrots. He moved slowly to her and put his big hairy forehead against her shoulder and shoved, breathing hot horse breath into her hair. Colin looked up and called, "No, Had." He stood up to move the animal.

Eden stood and stroked the horse's neck, placing her forehead against it. "I'm alright, you funny old thing," she told the animal. "Strange how supposedly unintelligent creatures can exhibit such sensitivity and sympathy. Or do I give you too much credit, Had? Are you really just trying to urge me to let you get home to your stall and food and friends?" She took his reins and began to lead him. "I too long for my cell and sleep."

Colin came alongside her. "Eden, it's a long walk back. Let me put you up on him. I'll walk."

She was tired and her head and jaw throbbed. She nodded her assent, and moved to the horse's right flank, and waited, head down. Colin came and stood in front of her, hesitating with hands held open. "I have to touch you to assist you up," he explained.

Eden took a step forward and lay her aching face on his breast and found seclusion there. His arms closed round her, and he began to stroke her back absently.

She started an apology; "I was horrid to you, for no reason..."

"No. Hush. Don't explain yourself. It is I who am at fault..."

"No. You told me to take someone with me..."

"Don't blame yourself. You couldn't possibly have known. I had a suspicion. That's why I asked Sebastion to keep an eye out for you whenever you were on the grounds alone. I just never really believed he ... not on my own land! You're safe with me now. It was his fault, not yours. Hush." He placed his cheek across the top of her hair and held her closer. As she melted against him, she felt all her repressed fears, anger, anxiety, and confusion melting away to be replaced by a deep peace. Even the pain in her head seemed to ease. *Oh God, he is so loving, so gentle, so understanding. I thank you for him, for being allowed to know him.*

If his embrace was a little too tight, it was exactly what she needed. Emotion distorted his face. He gently, lingeringly kissed the top of her head once, twice, a third time. They stood in their embrace, mesmerized by the steady rising and falling of their breathing and the warmth of their bodies.

As Colin absent-mindedly stroked her back, he found Eden's hair trapped beneath his cloak. He lifted it from its prison and disentangled the remaining pins to let it fall free. Caressing the long silken tresses, he spoke softly, "I do love you, Eden. Oh God, how I love you."

She was still. She said nothing. She did not resist when he began to distribute tender kisses across her temple and forehead. Encouraged by her silence, he tried to tilt her head up to find her mouth with his. She groaned, "No, please." *He mustn't see my face, the cut I know is there.* Much as she might want to, she couldn't possibly receive his kiss. The pain would be too great for her injured jaw.

She would have to be content to stand in the protection of his arms, smelling the delicate musky scent of his cologne, and listening to the wild pounding of his heartbeat against her ear. She thought she could stand like this for the rest of the night, the rest of her life, the next life, too... *But, he is promised to Cassandra. He said he loves me, but what kind of love? The love of a good friend? Is this my destiny, to love unrequited?*

She placed a hand flat against his chest and tentatively pushed away from him. He released her most reluctantly. She turned to Galahad and reached up for his saddle. Colin took her by the waist and lifted her easily up onto the horse. As she lifted one leg over the saddle, her skirts bunched up, exposing a well-turned calf. Colin saw the little kid boot he had once teased her with. He scanned up the porcelain white flesh of her limb to find her face, but it was covered with her dark hair as she leaned forward to catch her foot in the stirrup. "Can you keep your seat without the reins?" he said as he pulled the leather straps over the horse's ears. In answer she curled her fingers into Galahad's thick silver-gray mane. Lord Edmund led his lady home.

CHAPTER XXII

The breakfast gong woke Eden next morning. Every bone in her body ached, and her head throbbed mercilessly. Too weak to rise, she sat on the edge of her bed. Her neck and shoulders were so stiff she couldn't turn her head. The entire left side of her face prickled with heat. Eventually, she rose and poured the water from her ewer into its basin. A cold cloth on her face helped a little.

When she went to the mirror to investigate her injuries, Eden drew back in alarm. Her face was swollen and livid on the left side. The pattern of a palm and fingers was sharply outlined across her temple, cheek, and jaw. Her left eye was swollen and dark. Eden went back to bed. There would be no school today.

The second breakfast gong rang. A little while later, there was a gentle knock on the door. When there was no answer, Nora's voice called, "Miss Barrett, are you ill? Eden dragged herself from the bed and went to the door. She unlocked it and opened it a crack. "I'm not feeling well. I slipped and fell last night and don't feel up to coming down today. Please tell the children for me."

"Can I bring you something to eat?"

"Perhaps later, thank you."

In a few moments, Nora was knocking again. "Could you open the door, Miss Barrett?"

"What is it, Nora?"

"I've your breakfast."

Unable to argue, unable to think, Eden managed again to go to the door. She let Nora in and tried to hide her face while the maid set the tray on the night table. Nora had been told to get a good look at Miss Barrett to make sure she was well, and nothing would deter her. She gasped. Eden put a finger to her lips to silence her. "Please don't tell anyone about the bruise. It looks worse than it is. You might bring me some ice if we have any and a comfrey poultice, but don't let His Lordship see you. I intend to hide until the swelling goes down. I don't want to frighten the children needlessly."

"His Lordship'll be wantin' to know why you'll not come down."

"If he asks, tell him I need to be alone for awhile to sort things out. No, perhaps you should… Oh, I don't know. I don't know anything."

"I'll do my best."

When Nora left, Eden shot the bolt on her door again, then moved over to the sitting room door to check its lock. The maid hurried down the stairs to her master. He had sent her up and was waiting for her report.

"She is awake?"

"Yes, milord."

"When will she be down?"

"Not today, milord."

"The entire day? Is she ill? Should I send for a physician?"

"Yes and no."

"Yes and no? What does that mean? What is it? Why won't she come down?"

"She said she'd like to be let alone to sort things out."

Colin had never struck anyone in his life, but the thought crossed his mind briefly that he was going to strike this girl if she didn't say something sensible soon. "If that is all, why do you look so frightened? You're hiding something."

Nora knew which side her bread was buttered on, and she had veiled her answers as much as she was able. It was time to have the truth out, "It's her face, milord."

"Her face! What about it?"

"She tells me it's not as bad as it looks."

He took the stairs two at a time. In a moment he was at Eden's bedroom door. His knock was infinitely more demanding than Nora's. "Who is it?" she called weakly from within. As if she didn't know.

Colin controlled his voice. "Come to the door, Eden," he said gently.

"What is it, my lord?" her voice was closer now.

"Open the door," he commanded, his voice tinged with exasperation, as he rattled the door handle.

"I won't"

"Why not?"

"I wish to be let alone."

"You'll be let alone all you please just as soon as you open this door and let me see your face."

"I am perfectly well."

One could hear Colin's reply on all four floors, "Damn your impudence, Eden! Open this door!"

"Go away. Make a fool of yourself shouting all you like. I'm not opening the door."

"If I have to have an axe brought in, this door will be opened so it will never shut again!" he bellowed, pounding on the door for good measure.

Eden knew he certainly would have the door destroyed if she did not comply, so she unbolted it. She stood looking at the ground. He took her chin in his hand and forced her head to tilt up. She winced. He pivoted abruptly on his heel, turning away from the painful sight. Clenching his fists, he said very coolly and resolutely, "I will kill him."

She took his forearm and urged. "I was afraid of that reaction. Don't even think it. It's not worth it."

"I will find him, and I will kill him."

"No. 'Vengeance is mine says the Lord.'"

"Excellent. That Lord may have him after this one is finished with him." He took a step, but she grabbed his arm with both hands now.

"Don't descend to his level," her voice of reason told him.

"What shall I do? Stand idle while that…that…thing! How could I be so deceived? How dare he! Insolent scum! On my own grounds! You hid this from me. Why? He'll be repaid! Let go of me!"

"I beg of you, don't go in this state."

"Good God, woman! Will you not think of yourself, then?"

"But I am thinking of myself. If I allow myself to hate him, then I become his slave. All my time, energy and thoughts would be marred, wasted in feeling self-pity, injustice, insult, anger and plots of revenge toward him. Those only aggravate the wound and allow it to fester so that it never heals properly. I refuse to be bitter for one moment.

"Forgiveness strengthens the spirit, allows it to continue on its path instead of lingering in an ugly place. I must forgive so I can forget. I must forget so I can get on with my life. I must suspend all judgment and trust God's will or die inside."

"Rot!" He pulled his arm sharply from her grasp and strode out the door, down the stairs, and out toward the stables. He called to Patrick to have his horse saddled and brought round.

He walked back to the servant's hall and ordered the staff to see that the children be kept away from Miss Barrett and entertained elsewhere. He told Nora to wait hand and foot on Eden, and John to find the doctor for her. When Joseph came to say his animal was ready, Colin left the house, mounted, and set off at a gallop telling no one where he was going or why.

Colin rode out with a heart filled with hate and a mind seething with revenge. He entertained imaginative thoughts of what he would do when he caught up with Dorian. A fistfight would be most satisfying to his thwarted emotions. He could imagine himself pummeling the man's face until it was no more than a mass of red pulp. How dare that grinning thing profane his property in such a way and on his own estate land! He thought of her as his property; entrusted to his care, his very own. How dare that swine insult that innocent face with the slap of a hand - and such a slap! Then his mind ventured on thoughts that made him ill. If she had hidden this much from him, what else might Dorian have done that she was unwilling to reveal? His stomach hinted at retching. She had said he had not reached his goal. He would have to hold on to that. He turned his mind back to vindictiveness to get it off what Dorian might have done. His muscles tensed in exquisite anticipation of the revenge they would be privileged to wreak.

Galahad maintained his steady gait until a white lather began to form over his neck and chest and turn his silver-gray coat to a steely black. When the animal's breathing became labored, Colin was roused from his sadistic reverie to think of another's welfare. He pulled the horse back into a trot and then a walk. The steady churning movement of the animal's gait served to soothe Colin's nerves so that rationality could find its way into his thoughts.

Dorian had a full ten hours ahead of him. But surely he had put up at some inn for the night, and bothered to breakfast before setting out again, unlike himself. Would he be able to find him in time? He was supposed to board a frigate. That he knew. What was the name of it? Why had he not paid closer attention to the details of Dorian's concerns? What if it set sail before he arrived? What then? What charges could he bring against Dorian without involving and further upsetting Eden? He would have to obtain the direction of his commanding officer.

If he arrived in Portsmouth to find Dorian's ship to have set sail, what would he have accomplished? He had left his staff in an anxious state, his sister would be worried, and Eden... At the appearance of her name in his thoughts, he was seized with regret. He was inflicting a further pain on her by being here, by his behavior to her. He should be adding to her comfort, aiding her recovery. Damn her wisdom! There was more sense to what she had said than to what he was doing here. Repaying evil with evil only doubled the amount of evil done. *Go home now!* The thought came vividly into his mind almost as if he could hear the command.

But Dorian must not go unpunished! The idea inflamed his emotions again. He urged Galahad into a canter. The horse obliged his master until he stumbled and almost fell completely. Colin dismounted and led the animal off the road. Galahad favored his right foreleg. Colin examined it and found a large stone lodged between the shoe and the hoof. He opened a leather pouch on the back of the saddle and found a metal hoof pick in the instruments there. He worked at the stone, swore, and worked some more. In dislodging it, he loosened the shoe. The bruise caused by the stone was surely painful enough. With the iron shoe loose, there was no way he could ride his horse now.

Colin felt the greatest of fools. He did not know this road well. He had no idea where the next farmhouse might be, let alone a smith or another mount. By looking over the slopes before him, he was able to make out a stream of smoke rising from a clump of trees far in the distance. Hopefully, it was coming from a fireplace and not a campfire. He took Galahad's reigns and started toward the smoke on foot.

Hours later, Colin knocked at a farmhouse door. There was no smith there, but the farmer could fetch one. The earl saw that Galahad was given a portion of mash and rubbed him down with towels. He paid the farmer well for the use of his stall and the promise of seeing to Galahad's needs. He pledged a second reward when his servant came to fetch the horse. In the stable, Colin found a donkey, a sway-backed old nag, and a young bay gelding. He offered to pay handsomely for the use of the gelding. Galahad would serve as collateral. The farmer pounced on the offer.

While the farmer's son saddled the horse, he warned Colin that the animal was skittish. A rabbit crossing the path or a branch hanging too low could cause it to shy. His wife offered the earl some buns and cheese to eat along the way. Colin suddenly remembered his empty stomach and thanked her profusely. The farmer and his son stood in front of their cottage and watched the earl ride out. Satisfied that the stranger knew what he was about on a horse, they turned to enter their gate. On the opposite road, four men on horseback, two dressed as soldiers, bore down on them. When they were close enough, one of the soldiers asked, "I say. Can you direct us to the Southampton road? We've got ourselves all turned about here. We can get to Portsmouth from there. Wouldn't be good form to miss our ship, you know."

* * *

As John was riding in search of a doctor, Mrs. York and her husband were helping Mother Grey down off the grocery dray in front of her daughter's house in town.

They then rode on to the marketplace to examine the wares displayed on market day. Mr. York headed toward the cutlery and pans being shown by a caravan of Romanies; Mrs. York went to look at the fowl. As she was debating about a coop of hens, a sailor excused himself to her. "Don't know if y' recall me, Mum, but you 'ired me 'bout six months back."

Mrs. York looked at the man. There was something familiar about him, but she couldn't place him. "Me an' me boys swep' a chimney for you," he said. "Oi member you said that Barrett lady 'ad no roight to take me boys. Oi was wonderin', Mum, is they still there?"

"Yes they are. I shouldn't be talking to you, though. Not after what you did to Miss Barrett."

"Oi swear Oi was only troin' to scare her, mum. Oi wanted 'er to take me where me boys were and she wouldn't budge. Oi didn't mean no 'arm. Ow'd you feel if someone took your toykes?"

"That's what she said at the time. How do you come to be dressed like a sailor?"

"Oi'm in Navy, Mum. Joined up some months ago. Made me some money, too. We took two French ships, brought 'em back and sold 'em. Split the toikings. Oi want to give some money to me boys. Oi missed 'em sumpfin awful, Oi did. Oi was wonderin' if Oi could see 'em before me ship puts out. Never learnt to write or Oi'd do 'em a letter wiv the money and give it you to give 'em. Me ship leaves again in three day's toime. Oi'll be 'avin' to go tomorrow to reach it. Don't ye know a way oi could see 'em? Oi'd make it worf your while."

"Don't want your money. Master said no one's to allow you on the estate. The gatekeeper could recognize you. I couldn't send the boys all the way here; never have before."

"Oi could 'ide under the tarp in your wagon and jump out oncet oi'm inside the grounds."

"Only how will you get out again?"

"Oi know a place where Oi can crawl through the wall. Oi'll figure sumpfin."

"I could have my husband stop at Mother Grey's cottage. I'll tell him she told me she left something she needs. Then I can leave the door unlocked when I come out. You jump out right when he stops. I'll cough real hard and start to stand. That way, he won't feel the movement in the springs in the back. Hide in the tall grass until we leave. Wait there till I can send the boys out there on an errand. It probably won't be till tea-time. Then the gamekeepers and groundskeepers will be eating. The other servants don't know the old lady's gone yet. I could give the boys some stew to take to Mother Grey."

"Don't let 'em know oi'm 'ere, yet. Let me surproise 'em. Oi'm changed so much, Oi bet they cawn't recanize me. Oi put on weight, oi 'ave, and me skin's gone all brown."

Mrs. York agreed. She led the way back to the grocery dray. Crane crawled in the wagon and sat between the baskets while she pulled the tarp over him and loosely tied it. When Mr. York returned and started to check the ropes, she said, "I checked 'em. Everything's right and tight. Let's go. I'm tired."

* * *

When the doctor recommended leeches on her face, Eden had her doubts. But after only four leeches had engorged themselves on the blood in her bruised cheek, the tightness was gone as well as much of the discoloration. Eden allowed the application of several more leeches without complaint. The cool poultice he applied to her skin helped a great deal too. He left an order for cook to prepare a nourishing mashed vegetable stew that she could swallow without chewing and a recipe for a physic to reduce pain. Finally, the physician recommended a long soak in the warmest water she could stand, and he showed Nora how to massage Eden's neck and back to further sooth the muscle tension.

When her treatment was completed, and Eden had slept most of the day, she awoke feeling like a new woman and famished. As Nora went to get a tray, the governess began to ponder something that had been bothering her waking thoughts. The earl had whispered that he loved her. She had so wanted to reciprocate the tender sentiment, but a shyness and doubts had clamped her mouth. *What did he mean? That he loved her as a good friend? It had sounded like so much more; was that merely because she wanted it to? If he did mean something more, how could he also love Cassy? Could a man be in love with two women at once*? She could not imagine ever loving anyone one else as much as she loved him. He took up her whole heart, her very breath.

"Don't you dare!" Nora cried, "You're not allowed in here. Doctor's orders."

Diana shoved past the maid and ran through the door. Nora struggled in after her, juggling a tray of food and the keys she had just used to unlock the door.

Diana flopped on Eden's bed and grasped her hands. Her expression was first one of distress, but after getting a good look at Eden, it metamorphosed into one merely of puzzlement. "Miss Barrett, you look well. You've a little cut on your cheek, and your face is red and blotchy. What do you have? I was afraid you were dying. The doctor was here so long. No one would let me see you, and they wouldn't tell me what was going on. Everyone had a different story."

"I'm fine. In fact I'm sure I'll be in the schoolroom tomorrow. I've been sleeping most of the day. I was running home from Mother

Grey's in the dark last night, and I slipped and there was this big hard root sticking out of the ground..." *So far everything is true.* "Stay and talk to me while I eat. I'm starving."

Though she looked like she would explode with information, Diana waited until Nora had arranged the tray of soup over Eden's lap. When it looked as if the maid intended to stay, Diana said, "Nora, could you leave us? I have a private matter to discuss with Miss Barrett." After the maid left, Diana hemmed and hawed until Eden encouraged her not to be afraid to tell her anything.

"I thought you were dying, and I thought of the lies I've told, and how nice you truly are, and how you didn't deserve to die not knowing the truth." Diana searched her mind for a way to say what she felt she had to say. Eden schooled her expression to keep from discouraging the confession. Diana continued, "You remember what I said ... about Daniel... the other day?" Eden nodded once. "Well, you see, now I know... how it is. I thought it would be such a shame if you...and Colin...never knew... I think Colin loves you, Miss Barrett. Or at least he would let himself if I hadn't told him... you were engaged to a soldier."

"You told him I was engaged? Why, Diana?"

"I didn't want you and him... always running off to be alone together, like he did with Miss Austen. Miss Barrett, sometimes I've been so lonely, but not since you are here. Most of the staff here is single or so old their children are grown, so there's been no one my age to play with. Father was sick with the gout and grouchy a lot before he died. He hardly ever went anywhere or did anything except have stuffy old friends over for stuffy dinner or music. The only time I had a friend or a comrade was when Colin came home on holiday.

"He's a lot of fun, Miss Barrett. He listens to a person like you do. He even likes to play and make believe and make jokes. But then Father got Miss Austen for me, and I liked her, but so did Colin, and they kept leaving me with Nurse Warren who I don't like at all, or they would 'accidentally' meet on the grounds and tell me to 'run along and play'.

"That's when I found out about my powers. I found I could control them and use them on someone on purpose. I willed her away. I hated her and wished she'd never come here, never existed. One night I wished and wished, and the next morning she was gone - her clothes, her books, everything. She left no note or message, and no one would speak of her. It was as if she had never been."

"I'm sure there is some explanation," Eden lifted her tray to shift it, and Diana took it, placed it on the window seat, and returned to the governess's bed.

"It was me. I know because I already made someone else die by wishing."

"What do you mean? Who?"

"Kathleen Stagg, the head groom's wife. She laughed at me and made me mad. I felt like a fool. She was always laughing at something when I was in the stables. She said my pony was too fat, or stupid, or I couldn't sit a hobby horse properly let alone a pony. One day I said, 'I'm going to put a spell on you so you can't laugh.' Then I willed her mouth to be closed. She got lockjaw that night and three days later she died. She never laughed again."

"Purely coincidence. Your brother told me she cut herself with a rusty knife."

"It's not coincidence. I've tested it. I can make smaller things happen. I think I've had this power since birth. What if, when I was a baby, I wished my mother dead? It hurts the mother to give birth. It must hurt the child too. It cries when it comes into the world. Maybe I wanted to hurt her back. My mother might have died because of me."

Eden reached out to embrace her, "No, Diana. I don't believe it. Nurse Warren said she was healthy for several days afterward. She blames your mother's death on the physician cupping her and accidentally bleeding her too much. Where did you get this idea of willing something to happen?"

"It's in the Bible. Nurse Warren showed me. It says if you have faith the size of a mustard seed, you can command a mountain to jump into the sea and it will."

"It is talking about believing in God and not about wishing evil upon people; that is not what God would want from you. You were not responsible for what happened to any of those women. Life is fragile, people die everyday without you willing it. I do believe in the power of thought, but not in this case. You have been blaming yourself for a long time for something you did not do."

"I hope you're right. I wish I knew what happened to Miss Austen."

"I'll try to find out for you, sweetness."

Diana disentangled herself from Eden's embrace and left the bed to pace. "You may not call me that once I'm finished."

"What else?"

"I lied to you too."

"About what?"

"Colin and Cassy. I know what they're doing. Colin told me because he didn't want me to misunderstand. He said I should tell you too, but no one else. But I didn't tell you. And that's almost like lying. They're all gone now, and it's over, and you'll probably find out anyway. Colin has been pretending to be Cassy's beau so that Jeremy could talk with her, and they could plan. Lady Bradley and Major Bradley thought Jeremy was beneath Cassy's touch because he has no title and little money. They wouldn't grant him admittance to their house, and wouldn't let her recognize him at social events. But they wanted to plan an elopement. So Colin escorted Cassy to places where Jeremy would be going, and he invited them both here. She was nineteen yesterday; she reached her majority. Jeremy and Cassy were married by special license in town early this morning before the rest of the house was up. Colin stood as Jeremy's best man. Colin came back for breakfast, but then he rode out again before he even sat down to eat. He didn't answer when I asked where he was going. Do you know?"

"I'm not sure exactly where, but I feel he's on a spiritual journey. I've been praying for him, that he'll choose the right, the good: life, and return to us here as soon as he can."

"What does that mean?"

"It means he'll explain it to you when he gets back."

"Will you forgive me for lying to you?"

"Absolutely and completely. I love you too much not to. Come and kiss me. All is forgotten, but leave me for a while, love. I have much to pray about."

"Should I tell Daniel and Thomas you don't want to see them? Mrs. York sent them to take Mother Grey her supper. They said they would come up to see you when they returned if they're allowed. They were worried about you too."

"Is Mother Grey still at home? I wonder what happened."

"What do you mean?"

"She told me she was going in to town to stay with her daughter this morning."

"I didn't know that. I wanted to walk with the boys to see her too, but Mrs. York said I was not to leave the house all day, Colin's orders."

"I think I'd better go see if there was a problem. I can pray on the way. And I'll bet I can get the story of Miss Austen's whereabouts out of Mother Grey. You stay here. I'm hoping your brother will be home soon."

CHAPTER XXIII

"Come on, son. You haven't drunk enough to kill the pain." The gin burned his throat and made his ears pop and his stomach feel like a hole was burning through it. He gagged on it, but one of the surgeon's assistants held his arms while the other one kept tilting the bottle to his lips.

His mother had lied to him, or the surgeon had lied to her. She said the doctor was just going to examine him; he had a new medicine to take care of it. But when the doctor came in the room, he came with two burly male assistants and his knives.

The physician had said if his painful problem didn't go away, a surgeon would have to cut it out before it went to the rest of his body and he died a painful death. They had done nothing then because they had no money to pay. But now, Vicar Barrett said he would foot the bill for the operation.

Timothy Crane cried and howled. There was nothing else he could do. He bawled right there in front of those three strong men who wouldn't let him go. He pleaded and screamed, "Oh God, Oi'd rather die. Please don't do this to me."

"There's others had this same problem, and this same operation. Scrotal cancer is a too common hazard for sweeps. But you'll get used to it son. It won't hurt forever, and at least, you'll go on living. If we don't do this, you'll die," the surgeon warned. "You're lucky the cancer's contained. We just cut it out and it's all gone. Other cancers can't be cut out. One day you'll hardly think of it."

"'Ow cawn you 'elp thinkin' 'bout it when you pulls your pants on every morning? Please don't cut me there. Just let me die."

"Then who'd care for your mum?" the surgeon said. The other assistant grabbed his legs and tried to lay him out on the table. Tim kicked as hard as he could, but he felt so weak and so queer, as if his mind had drifted away from his body, and he was going to puke soon. "Oh God, Please, no! Oh God, no!"

Crane woke from his familiar nightmare kicking and writhing. He sat up on the couch and caught his breath. Sweat poured over him. He looked about the cottage to get his bearings and bring himself back to the present, to reality. He had lived after the operation. It had felt like a huge horse had kicked him in the groin about ten times, but he had lived.

It was a painful, lonely existence. He could never take a wife. Didn't really want to, but there was no one to touch him after his ma died. He remembered how she used to stroke his hair sometimes and hug him and tell him she couldn't make it without him. When his little sister and brother got the typhoid, he'd take care of them at night so his ma could get some rest. But they wasted away and died anyway, and then his ma got it, and he was on his own at fourteen. Then the only caresses he got were the strap or the back of a hand if his master wasn't happy. He had sworn to himself he would never treat a kid that way when he grew up, but somehow you sometimes did things you didn't like yourself for in the morning.

Crane rose from the couch and walked about the dark cottage. He bumped into something and drew back. What the heck was that post doing in the middle of the room like that? It must be supporting the sagging ceiling. He looked at the base of it and saw a long rope knotted about it. He bent to untie the rope.

* * *

The sun was a brilliant red globe above the horizon when Daniel knocked at the door of the cottage. It opened slowly to reveal his old master in sailor's clothing. "'Ello, me boys. What 'ave ye brought your ol' da? Goodies?"

Before he could say another word, both boys turned tail and ran. Daniel set the basket down as he went. Crane had Thomas' arm before he could run three steps. Thomas yelled. Daniel turned around. He picked up a rock. Crane saw the action. "You throw that thing, and Oi'll break 'is arm loike a toothpick. What's a matter wif you boys? Ain't you glad to see me? Oi missed you." He tugged the smaller boy into the cottage. "Bring that food in 'ere. Oi'm sharp set, ain't ad naught to eat all day," he told Daniel. The older boy decided to bide his time. Crane would hurt Thomas if he ran for help. He picked up the basket and walked to the door of the cottage.

"Come 'ere little Tom. Oi've got a present for you," Crane was saying. He pulled the child into the little kitchen where he had stockpiled some ropes and rags and a shovel he had found leaning against the wall outside. "Oi'm just gonna toi you up real gentle loike so's you don't bolt out the door when Oi lets you go. Oi wants to enjoy moi meal."

Thomas put his hands together behind his back for Crane to tie. "At's a boy. Don't give me no fuss. See, Oi don't want to 'urt you. Oi just wants to visit. What you fink of your ol' da now? I'm a Navy man, Oi am."

"Ain't my da."

"'Ere, don't talk loike that. Oi'm closest thing you got. Sit down, Tommy boy." Crane pushed him down on a stool in the center of the kitchen. "Come 'ere, Danny boy, bring your Da 'is supper." Daniel stood glaring. Crane continued, "Oi promise, Oi won't touch you. Just don't run off 'till Oi've said what Oi come to say."

Daniel stepped inside and handed Crane the basket. The man busied himself with finding a pewter plate and piling it up with the stew and rolls Mrs. York had sent. "So boys. Don't Oi look good? Me skins most as brown as a Colonies' native or a Rajah. Oi put some meat on me bones. Should a joined up years ago. Noivy 'grees wif me. Getting' to see the world. Oi misses you boys though. Toimes there ain't much to do but loi around. Oi misses you readin' me them stories, Danny boy. 'Member how we loiked them mysteries and them scary ones?"

Daniel nodded, trying to keep Crane's eyes on him. He could see Thomas easing the ropes around on his wrists. "Tom's too little to take on board, but you ain't, Danny. Ow would you loike to go to sea, Danny? Ship's captain is lookin' for a new cabin boy."

The boy stood tensed, ready to explode into any movement necessary. Crane kept urging, "Oi know we read about some ships 'avin' bad captains an' bad food an' all, but this one's run good. She's a beauty too. You'd get to see the world, Danny."

"I can't do it. I've got to stay here," Daniel said. "I have to take care of Tom, and I have a job I like in the stables, and His Lordship says he's found my real parents. He says they are coming a long way from India to get me."

Crane was momentarily taken aback. His brow furrowed, and his chewing slacked. Then he shrugged it off and grinned. "You're spinnin' tales, that's what you are. Allus could spin a good yarn. Tellin' me about the Romanies and the rich Daddy and the racehorses. C'mere, boy. That's dreamin'. This is real." He rose as he said this and took a step toward Daniel, reaching out a hand as he did. Daniel ran to the threshold, standing half out, half in the cottage. Crane grabbed his shovel from his pile of loot. He raised it in the air over Thomas. "You wouldn't want me to 'urt 'im would you?"

"Don't you dare!" Daniel screamed and rushed at Crane. The man stepped aside, grabbed Daniel's arm and swung the shovel over the boy's head at his back. The boy groaned and jerked and fell to the ground with Crane still holding his arm. Tom scurried into the darkness of a corner.

"My God! What have you done!" Eden screamed.

Crane dropped the boy's arm and turned his full attention on the cottage door where Eden had just entered. "Well, look 'oo's 'ere," Crane greeted her.

"Stand aside," she commanded, walking directly to Daniel and stooping over him.

"Oo, Miss Bossy, Bossy," Crane teased. He picked up a second rope, placed the shovel on the floor, grabbed Eden and wrestled with her. She struggled with him, guiding him away from the boys. She had seen that Daniel was breathing. The sweep got one of her arms pinned behind her back and jerked upward. The pain was excruciating. He shoved her forward and fumbled with the rope at her right wrist.

When she felt what he was attempting, she relaxed. She must keep his attention on her. Daniel might come awake any minute, and he and little Tom could escape out the kitchen door. Then she felt the wood against her back. He was tying her to the support beam Mother Grey always tied her dog to. She tensed and twisted her hands, writhing gently until he had them tied to his satisfaction.

Crane walked away from Eden and sat down on the couch. He had to plan this out, make this revenge exquisite. He had hoped to meet her again, but this was too good and too easy. He had her completely at his mercy. He could draw it out and wreak all sorts of vengeance on her. He sat grinning at her. The long, thick, yellow nails of his right hand began methodically clawing at a boil on his neck.

Eden could see his decaying teeth as he caught his breath. She saw Daniel behind him on the floor moving his head very slowly to look back at her. She lifted a determined jaw and straightened to her full height against the post. She kept the movements of her hands small so that he would suspect nothing. She saw Daniel motion to Thomas and begin to crawl slowly toward the kitchen.

"So, you've decided to be brave, eh?" Crane asked her. "That housekeeper said you were a holier-than-thou; wouldn't you loike to be a martyr too? Tied to that post loike that, you puts me in mind of that French lady, that Joan of Arc. 'Cept she cut her 'air short loike a boy's and wore armor. She thought as she was all high and mighty too." Crane was looking around the room. His eyes lit on a sewing basket next to the couch. He picked it up, put it on his lap and began to rifle through it. "Lookie what Oi found," he said as he held up a pair of scissors. "Now you can be Joan of Arc."

Crane came over to her and tugged at a wad of hair that was already falling from its prison of pins. Eden felt the cold metal against her neck and heard the crunch of hair being cut. A lifetime of hair growth fell to the floor. *He wants to wound my pride. Well, he's doing a good job, but I have to keep him here.* "Why do you do this to me?"

"So's you can get to 'eaven, Miss Bossy. Oi'm gonna send you to 'eaven where all the pretty angels floi around all day long just strummin' on their 'arps." Crane pulled at the rest of her hair, not bothering to take the pins out, until he had loosed enough of it to clip it all off at the nape of her neck. Eden could no longer see the children, but they could be trapped in the little kitchen if the door was not unlocked.

Dear God, he's insane. His Lordship was right. Protect those children, Father, and don't let him hurt me. "Please, Mr. Crane, you're only making things worse for yourself. I told the staff I would be out here. They'll watch for my return. They know the children are here as well. They'll be looking for us soon, and if we're late, they'll come to find us. I don't know how you got in, but the gamekeepers were just finishing their tea as I left the manor.

They always come to check on Mrs. Grey first. They'll surely be coming this way with their dogs soon."

"There ye go. Ye looks just loike that picture of that saint oi saw in school. Oi did go to school, you know, till your da sent me to work."

"I didn't know," she said conversationally, attempting to stall him from thinking up something devious to do to her. "Tell me how you knew my Father."

"Picture's not roight. Got to 'ave wood about your feet for burnin'." Crane pulled the box of firewood from beside the fireplace to the center of the room. He tilted it and dumped it at her feet. "Now all we needs is a torch, and we'll 'ear your prayers, pretty lady. Then you can go to see old God and your da and tell 'em bof to stick it for me."

Crane was now winding the lace antimacassars and linens Mother Grey used to protect her chairs and tables around a stick of kindling. Eden tried to think clearly. *How does one reason with a madman? Should I try to make him think I'm not afraid, or will that only infuriate him more and make him more dangerous? Shall I encourage him to continue what he's doing, so he'll be contrary and stop what he's doing? Do they think that way?*

Before she could decide how to act, Crane had lit his torch from the embers in the fireplace. His rotten teeth gleamed in the light as he grinned maniacally. He extended the torch toward her face.

"I don't know what my father did that has caused you to hate him so," Eden reasoned, "but I am sure he acted in what he thought was your best interest. He just didn't know it would harm you. The boys have told me you were not a bad master. They said you even abstained from eating so that they could eat. But here at Chadilaine they are being educated for free, and Daniel's parents have been found. They are rich, and I am certain they will want to reward you for keeping their son safe. And you, Mr. Crane, you seem to have fallen on good times. You look so much healthier than when I saw you last."

His grin faded. He was listening to her, "Aye, His Lordship had me carted off and pressed into service in Noivy..."

The voice of Mrs. York invaded the room and disturbed the tense stillness of captive and captor. "What the blue blazes are you doing! You're stark raving mad! You said you wanted to give the boys gifts. My God! You're insane!"

Mrs. York ran toward the sweep with her arms out, reaching for the torch to wrench it from him. He swerved and touched the curtains with it as he held it away from her. The cloth went up in flames. "Give me that, you idiot!" Mrs. York commanded and grabbed his arm. Crane shoved her down and ran to the other side of the room. He picked up the shovel with his free hand.

Mrs. York got to her feet and came at him again. He tossed the torch on the couch and took the shovel in both hands. She grabbed up an arm table for a weapon, but when she threw it at him, he just dodged and giggled. Then he came at her with the shovel raised high. She ran around the now blazing couch and out the door. Crane followed her, tripping to his knees on the threshold.

* * *

Colin took pains to become adjusted to his excitable mount. In an easier frame of mind, he rationalized that Dorian would be forced to see action in Spain. *So far the swine has managed to maintain an easy position in the war office. A real battle or two or three might be punishment enough for the coward. Maybe he'll be wounded and die a slow, painful death. Then they'll give him a medal and laud him, but I won't care as long as I never have to bear his smirking face again.*

It was quite dark when the horse and rider stopped at the gatehouse. The gatekeeper rushed out to unlock the iron gates and push them open. The closer Colin came to the end of his journey, the greater his impatience to see Eden again. He urged his mount into a gallop.

The moon was new, so the tall poplars that lined the path cast great spectral shadows across it. It was foolish to ride at this rate in the dark on a skittish mount unfamiliar with the terrain, but the desire to determine that all was well had caused a nagging doubt that it was. Suddenly the horse reared, plunged, and flailed the air with its hooves, emitting an ear-piercing neigh at the same time. A figure unseen to the rider had darted across the road directly in the animal's path. The person was struck on the head and back by the pawing hooves. The human scream was drowned out by the horse's sounds.

As soon as Colin could control the animal, he dismounted and tied it to a branch. In the dim light, he found his way back to the crumpled form. He couldn't tell at first if it was a man or woman. He thought to go back to the horse to get a flint out of the saddle, but he didn't relish wasting the time it would take to produce a light. A shovel was clutched tightly in one of the stilled hands. Colin rolled the body over and recognized Crane. Dread entered Colin's gut and caused it to clench.

"My lord, is that you?" It was Mrs. York's voice. "Oh, thank God Almighty! Is he dead? I hope he is! What are we to do? The boys and Miss Barrett are tied up in Mother Grey's cottage, and ..." As she looked back toward the little house, she screeched and clutched her chest. Bright orange flames reached out the window and lit the night with their mad dance.

Colin ran back to the horse, mounted and gave it a kick. He spat several choice expletives when he realized the poor animal was still tied. He had to dismount, untie it, and mount again never letting go of the reins. The horse shied and backed and pirouetted until Colin applied his boot heels viciously. "Damn you! I don't have time for your silliness!"

The horse fought all the way, snorting and tugging for control of the bit, but he got Colin there. He jumped down and pulled at the iron door handle, burning his hands as he did. Flames leapt out as he cracked the door open. He lurched backwards to avoid burning his face and fell. The thatch roof was crackling, popping, and pouring out thick black smoke. The heat outside the house was too great to bear. *What must it be like inside*? He was up again. Smoke filled his nostrils and burned his lungs as Colin tried to find an entry. "Dear God, don't do this thing!" he shouted. "Help me now! You've got to save her, God! I can't do this alone!"

No prayer was ever more heartfelt, nor answered more expediently, for Colin heard music in the air. Music in the form of her voice calling him. "My lord, we're over here. There's no one in the house. Come away from the fire. We're safe."

He turned and saw Eden, Daniel, and Thomas about a quarter of a mile in the distance. The light of the cottage fire just reached them. Great racking coughs split his sides as he stumbled toward them. He fell to the ground. He looked once more to make sure his eyes were not playing tricks the first time. She was there, closer now and coming to him. He relaxed and lay his head down in the grass and tried to fill his lungs. His chest felt like an anvil sat on it. His palms began to remember they were in pain. They would be a mass of blisters tomorrow, but he didn't care. *She's alive. She's safe. Thank God, she's safe. Dear God, thank you truly!*

"Catch his mount, boys. Are you alright?" she asked, kneeling over him.

"Just getting my breath," he choked out, smiling to see her and coughing because he had spoken aloud.

"Did you see Crane? He's here. He ran after Mrs. York with a shovel!"

"He's dead. That horse collided with him. Mrs. York is fine. She thought you… How …did… you…"

"Escape? You can thank your sister for that."

"Is she here too!"

"No. It's something she taught us in class about the Natives in the American Colonies. A trick for escaping from ropes. Thomas used it too. And, when Crane struck Daniel, he pretended to be knocked unconscious like in your sister's plays."

"So I was completely unnecessary? What the deuce have you done to your hair?"

She smiled brightly, "Crane was playing barber. Do you like it? It's my new summer bob."

He sat up slowly and moistened his mouth. As soon as he was able, he intended to kiss the face clean off that cropped head.

"Your Lordship!" the boys shouted in unison. "The fields are on fire!"

As Colin rode the skittish gelding to the chapel, the reins cut into his burn-sensitive palms. Grasping the scratchy hemp rope to ring the bell for the alarm was a further punishment. At the sound of the deep bell tones, servants began to file quickly out of the manor and surrounding buildings in various stages of dress and in complete confusion. It had been ages since they had heard the warning for a fire.

Hours passed before the flames could be extinguished satisfactorily. There was no fire-fighting equipment more modern than tarps and the leather buckets of water on the fire wagon on the estate. Colin made a mental note to rectify that situation in the near future. When the last ember was drowned, the staff cheered. Colin told them to all go in for a round or two of something strong and to start as late as they pleased tomorrow, or better still, no work to be done tomorrow except feeding the animals and the humans. They cheered again.

Then there was the business of loading Crane's body onto a wagon and bringing it back to the house. Joseph and two of the maids washed the body and laid it out in an outgrown suit the earl donated to them for that purpose. It was quite the finest thing the sweep had ever worn.

It was late into the night when Colin trudged upstairs to his bedroom. She would be asleep by now and he would have to spend another night alone in that giant four poster. Perrin was in the earl's suite with copper kettles warming by the fire in case His Lordship wished a bath before retiring. The slender, middle-aged valet helped the earl out of his travel clothes and bathed him since Colin's pain-filled hands could not manage a cloth. He dried the earl off, dressed him in his nightclothes, put salve on his hands, bandaged them, poured him a snifter of brandy, and watched him drink it down.

"What would I do without you?" Colin told Perrin as he dismissed him. When his valet was gone, he managed to pour himself another drink and downed it as well. He could have lost Chadilane tonight if he had not been there to go for help. *Thank you, God, that I did return in time. But I would gladly have lost it all in exchange for her love.*

He slipped his robe on and fumbled with the belt. He would just go and stand outside her room for a while to be near her. As he padded down the hall, he saw light shining from beneath her door. Had she had her fire lit in this warmer weather? Or was she up, with her lamp lit? He leaned his head against the door, and it opened. She was sitting up in bed gazing ahead at nothing. When she heard the door creak, Eden pulled her coverlet up to her neck and began to look about the room.

With both bandaged hands, Colin picked up her wrapper from the back of a chair, "Is this what you need?" Then he saw water glistening over her lashes and asked, "What's wrong, Eden?"

"What's wrong? Surely you jest. This entire night would not have happened - the fire, the boys, Crane - if I had not..."

"Hush. Stop blaming yourself. There were a few others involved... myself included. It hasn't turned out so badly."

"A man died."

"An accident... it was his time. It had nothing to do with you. Here, put this on. I won't look." He handed her the robe and turned his face to the wall.

Eden slid out of bed, pulled the garment on, and tied it. She went to him and touched his arm. "Your hands, do they hurt much?"

He shrugged, "I'll live." He turned to face her and opened his arms to enfold her. "Come here." She went into his arms like a mountain stream flows into a vast lake. He gingerly clasped her with his aching hands.

"I have so much to say to you," he began. "I had memorized a little speech on the journey home, but the ensuing events and the nearness of you have driven it from my brain. First, let me say your face looks vastly improved since this morning."

"I thank you. Your physician knows his business." Eden considered saying something about the leeches, but decided now was not the time. "My hair is another matter...I believe you prefer it long."

"It'll grow back. Until then, you look an adorable pixie. You're safe; that's what counts. The next thing I simply must tell you is I love you, and I want you to marry me, and I won't take 'no' for an answer. Now what? I didn't know you were such a watering pot. I'm sorry the news distresses you. I never meant to open your floodgates."

Eden sniffed and employed her handkerchief, wiping at the brine that streamed over her cheeks. "Can't help it. Tears of joy, though. I thought you were marrying Miss Bradley."

"Good Heavens! That would be like marrying my sister! I told Diana to... My fault. I should have explained what was going on myself. Forgive me?"

"Always."

Colin kissed the salty water on her cheek and moved to take her lips, but she turned her face away. He schooled his voice to eliminate the annoyance that teased at him. After all, he had her in his arms; that was heaven enough. "You did say joy, didn't you?" he asked.

"I do want your caress, but I'm afraid."

"Of me?"

"Of your kisses. My jaw still aches. It won't take much pressure."

"Ah. Then you will have to do the kissing, and I will try to control myself."

She chuckled and tentatively traced a finger across his smiling mouth. Her slender fingers found their way to the raven locks at the back of his neck and entwined themselves there. So much eager happiness shone in his eyes as he beheld her, Eden was amazed. Was she really the cause of such bliss? She looked deep into his eyes and saw a hint of color in his irises, a pale blue like the dawn sky. Then Eden could see her own face reflected in those watery depths. She was small and far away, but there inside of him.

He lowered his head, and their lips met in a dozen feather-gentle caresses. Then he crushed her even closer to him and covered her hair and ears and neck with kisses. Her body responded in a heavy lethargy. It was right; it was what she wanted; what she had been created for. He began to tremble, and it frightened her. "My lord, get hold of yourself." He took a deep breath and did as he was told.

He released her, and took her by the hand into her sitting room where he sat on the couch and pulled her down onto his lap. Eden curled up against the warmth of him and listened to his deep voice saying, "You will marry me. I don't ask; I insist. You'll marry me just as quickly as it can be arranged. Tomorrow, if possible. I won't allow you time to change your mind now that I've made it up for you.

"I purchased a special license at the same time Jeremy arranged for his. The new curate at St. John's awaits my message. We'll have no audience. This will be between you and me and God, Who, by the way, has gotten on better terms with me lately, especially by protecting you. We can put on a show for the others later. We'll marry twice and double the knot that binds if you like. Answer quickly."

"You haven't asked me anything."

"No, and I won't. I won't give you the chance to refuse me, for I've asked your Father in Heaven for you. You tell me his answer is 'Yes' or 'I have something better for you'. You see, I do listen to what you say - when it serves my purpose. Since nothing could possibly be better than having you for my wife, the answer must be, 'Yes'. Now give me His answer through your beautiful voice, and remember the word 'yes'."

Eden thought she would burst. She could not find her voice. She could hardly breathe. Colin filled the pause. "Oh, Eden, I do love you with all of my ability to love, and that grows greater each day because of your patient instruction." To prove this, he planted kisses indiscriminately about her head and neck being careful not to injure her jaw. "Answer me, woman. You're silence is torture. Here is my heart torn beating and bloody from its place of hiding. It's yours to govern, yours to teach, yours to conquer by surrender. You've taught a bitter, melancholy man to hope. Say you return my love, and you will teach me joy as well."

"I do love you."

"Glorious! Say it again."

"I love you, Colin."

"You use my name. Sweeter still. I may now live. Once more and I must be content."

"I love you with all my heart and soul."

"You swear to keep to me and be my soul's possession to love always?"

"I swear it." She presented her puckered mouth in expectation of a reward for her admission, and a seal for her commitment.

He shook his head. "You can't know what you're asking. If you allow me to taste that sweet, generous, petal-soft mouth again, you put yourself in great danger."

She was all shy coyness. "I'll take my chances."

He obliged her. Assured of her love, he was a connoisseur: languorously savoring her mouth; venturing from it to bestow soft kisses beneath her earlobes. She melted against him, enjoying all the exquisite sensations he aroused in her. He pulled his head up and teased, "Young lady, you have had lessons."

"A few."

His expression sobered. "You mustn't make me jealous."

"I wasn't trying to."

"Did this young man happen to teach you anything else?"

"That's about as far as we got."

"Good. Because I reserve the right to teach you the rest."

"You're the young man I'm talking about. Have you forgotten the little incident by the lake?" With feigned innocence, Eden could not resist batting her eyelashes while adding, "You mean there is more?"

"A great deal more, as you well know, but that is for after the vows and the witness's signatures."

"Why do you say, 'as you well know'? I know nothing of..."

"Ah, governess - my sister tells me all. What were my favorite words that evening? Ah, yes: (at this point, Colin gave a humorous imitation of Eden's voice) 'God has given a pleasurable sensation to the marriage act. One you will long to share with your partner...'"

Her eyes grew as round as dinner plates. She placed her fingers on his mouth to shut him up. "I can't believe she told you that. You were listening at doors."

He kissed the fingers that rested on his lips. "Oh yes she did, and I can't believe that I am the one who will be privileged to teach you these 'pleasurable sensations'."

"Behave."

"I am."

Then Eden thought of Miss Austen and an uneasy thought niggled at her. She took her lower lip between her teeth and swallowed. "Teaching requires prior knowledge of a subject. Are you saying you have knowledge of the intimacies of marriage?"

He shrugged. "Some."

She could not help but look away. She was disappointed and wished she had not pressed him with the question. She had not wanted to share his body with some phantom. Now he could never be wholly, exclusively hers.

He felt her cooling in his arms: drawing away without actually moving. Quickly, before damage was done, he amended his answer. "Only what knowledge I could garner from books and conversations at the club."

How quickly she warmed to him. "Are you saying you have no… um…practical experience?"

"Only to you will I admit the truth. I have no experience whatsoever. I have the same urges as any man, but I am a romantic. I wanted my first to be my only and my always. I thought I'd save that for my bride on our honeymoon."

"What an exquisite wedding gift for her: you can discover together."

"We can discover together, Eden, and you are too innocent of the ways of men for you are provoking me beyond control." He pushed her off his lap and onto the couch beside him. "Sorry, my love, but we stop the kissing here unless you wish to continue in there." With a nod, he indicated her bedroom.

"I can wait," she said.

"Cruel. In my mind we are married already. We have repeated our vows to each other. But, I'll do it your way with the parson and the words of magic. I'll marry you every day of your life if you like."

"We'd best make it tomorrow and put you out of your misery. And once or twice will be enough ceremonies for me."

"So understanding."

"Before you go, I must ask you something. I know it's not my concern, but it is very important to your sister."

"Ask."

"What became of Miss Austen?"

"Miss Austen? Now there's a non-sequiter. You mean Diana doesn't know?"

"She thinks she willed her into oblivion."

"She what? Well, in a way, she did, but I certainly never told her that."

"No one would tell her what happened."

"They wouldn't tell me either. It really wasn't so much, now that I look back on it. I was infatuated. I was nineteen; she was six and twenty. We spoke of marriage. We knew my father would never condone it. He wanted me spliced to a peer with connections, property, the usual. I was at home on school holiday. I guess I fobbed Diana off on her nurse and ran off with her governess once too often. I was a foolish youth. It seems little sister mentioned it to our father.

"That night, he sent me to London to pay a gambling debt for him. Then he gave Jessica two hours to pack everything she had and vanish from the face of the earth until she read the announcement that his son was married to an heiress. In recompense, he would pay her a hefty sum each year. She took the money and ran.

"Father assembled all the staff and warned them never to speak of her again. In fact, they were to act as if she never existed. They were quite loyal to his command. I tried for days to pry information out of them. Finally, I went back to school. A letter awaited me there. She explained the whole and apologized for being so weak, but money in the hand was sure, and she would hold to the stipulation my father had put down. It hurt like hell for a time, but I got over it. And now, I'm overjoyed it happened. I am free to marry a far worthier and vastly more handsome woman. But I warn you, I will never get over you."

"I'll tell Diana about Miss Austen tomorrow. She'll be extremely relieved."

"I'll tell her about us, though I fear it will be the hardest thing I've ever done."

"The hardest thing I'll ever do will be telling my mother she was right." After explaining this, Eden asked, "You bought a special license and spoke to the curate. What would you have done if I had said, 'No'?"

"Other arrangements were made for that possibility."

She cocked her head, amazed. "What arrangements?"

"A coach with shades drawn, a team of fresh horses, a loaded gun, a gag, a blindfold, soft rope."

"What!"

"I'm serious. I fully intended to abduct you at gunpoint and carry you off to Gretna Green, ravishing you on the way, so you would have no choice but to marry me to save your honor."

Eden gasped, but the gleam in his icy irises belied his words. She teased, "In that case I made the right choice… I think."

"We could always try it that way if you like."

"I'd prefer an unloaded gun. Good night, my lord."

"Colin."

"Good night, Colin, my love."

"Must we part?"

"We absolutely must."

But, neither had the will or the energy to move, so they talked about anything and everything until they could no longer stifle yawns or think clearly. Then they were quiet together until they fell asleep. When a log in the fire shifted, Colin awoke to find his intended asleep on his breast. He would have been content to serve as her pillow the entire night, but his feet were complaining intensely of needles pricking them. "Wake up, love," he coaxed, kissing her crown. "Can't have the servants finding us this way in the morning." Eden uncurled and sat up. Her eyes were open, but she was dazed. "All the way up," her betrothed encouraged.

With his help, she managed to stand sleeping, head hung down, while Colin stomped his feet to get the blood running back to them. He guided her to her bedchamber door. Eden pushed the door open, entered, and shut the door. Colin lingered a moment, listening, half afraid that in her automaton state, she might trip over something before she reached the bed. He heard the bolt being slid into place.

CHAPTER XXIV

Eden did not awake until the sun was well up and the birds' calls were past and the noises of the staff upstairs having a little impromptu party could no longer be ignored. She woke with a sense of excitement, newness, and vigor. She dressed quickly, but carefully, taking extra time with teeth cleaning and evening out the trim job her hair had been given. She fluffed the hair and fussed with it and had to agree with the man in her life that it was not an unbecoming style for her. She had never known her hair was curly.

Eden hoped there was still some tea and perhaps something to eat in the breakfast salon. She'd never been so hungry in her life. When she arrived there, she found the room empty, but the wonderful smells of food emanated from the covered dishes on the sideboard. Had he dined and left? Two cups were still inverted in front of the coffee server, and it was covered with a cozy. The tea service was likewise arranged.

As she stood deciding which beverage she preferred today, the tall figure of Lord Edmund filled the doorframe. His hair was slightly disheveled and his eyes were pinched. "Good morning, Eden. Quickly, if you care anything at all for me, pour me a coffee."

She did so, remembering he took it black. He tossed the hot liquid back as she had seen some men take spirits or medicine. He handed the cup to her and said, "Another, please." This cup he drank almost as quickly. When he had put the cup down, he focused his eyes on her. "How dare you look so good in the morning?" When she attempted a rejoinder, he placed a finger over his lips, and she was silent. "I have something very serious to ask you," he said. "You must promise to answer truthfully."

"You know I will."

"Did I, or did I not ask you to be my bride last night?"

"You did not."

"I beg your pardon?"

"You insisted I would be your bride. There was no asking involved."

"And how did you reply to all this?"

"I said I would."

"Thank God. I thought it was all some fantastic dream I had, although I could never remember actually sleeping... except on the sofa...with you." He advanced upon her and encircled her waist with one swift move. His eyes gleamed. "From today forward I take my coffee with sugar. You will give it me now."

She laughed and resisted, turning her head. "Is this the type of speeches I am to be treated to? Surely a member of the House of Lords can do better? Unhand me. I have much to do. I will not sit on your lap gazing into your eyes and listening to you degenerate into sentimentalities. We did that last night." As he looked a little displeased, she added, "Much as I might like to."

"You are still in my employ, ma'am, and I will employ your time as I see fit. Now I will have that sugar." Eden could not resist this treatment, or she could have, had she wanted to. She gave him the sugar he was longing for until they both heard a male servant clear his throat. Colin released his intended with a quick step away from her. The two stood side by side like a pair of very naughty children feigning innocence as York, Nathan, and Joseph brought in more dishes and removed the covers of all. Each servant expressed his best wishes and exited discreetly. Eden thought she saw a smirk on Joseph's face just as he closed the door behind him.

"Who told them?"

"Probably Perrin."

"And you told him?"

"Had to. He figured it out himself. You see he is my hands these days and somewhere about my person he planted one of your bridal gifts at my request. I think it's in one of my waistcoat pockets. You'll have to find it yourself."

"Where is Diana? Does she know, yet?"

"She knows and she approves. She has gone with Patrick and Daniel and Thomas down to the lake to feed the swans. I was up early, and told Nora not to wake you. Took care of a few things and went back to sleep. You are not the least interested in your gift?"

"I don't need gifts to make me happy, Colin. I am delirious as it is."

"You need this one. Now find it."

Eden approached the smiling earl tentatively. He had already accosted her once this morning. He held his bandaged hands out at head level to indicate his non-dangerous state to her. "I feel so vulnerable with these," he said.

"Keep them up there, and I will search your pockets," she instructed.

As her fingers found his right waistcoat pocket, Colin squirmed. "It tickles." Eden extracted the little box and opened it. "It was my mother's ring," he said, "and my grandmother's before her. If you wish, I will have the stones put in a new setting, something more to your liking."

"It's gorgeous. Don't think of changing it. This is mine?"

"To prove that you are mine. Put it on yourself; I would love to help, but…"

Eden slid the ring on her finger. It was a little loose. She accosted the earl, pulling his face down to receive her kiss. "You have another gift waiting for you in the stables," he told her. "It arrived yesterday while I was behaving like an idiot. Come, you must choose my breakfast. Kippers and eggs for me, and one of those pastries. Serve yourself plenty of whatever you like. We must build up your strength."

"And why is that?"

"A number of reasons come to my mind, the most expedient one being that I want you to try out your new mount soon. Her name is Willow. I have been negotiating with Lord Beaumont for three months for her. He didn't want to give her up. I've found the very mare you described to my sister in the first hour of our meeting seven months ago. She is everything you said she was, and she is yours. Galahad approved of her the first time he met her; he thought I was buying her for him. She has a sweet gait and a tender mouth - not unlike you."

"Colin, you are the most romantic man alive," Eden said, and accosted him again.

Once they were seated across from each other, and Colin was practicing balancing his fork on his curled fingers, he said in a quiet, serious tone of voice, "You were wise last night to bolt your door, Eden. Never have you been in more danger from me than then. I thought I knew what loneliness was, but knowing that you were in another bed in this house and that you loved me but I could not be with you was pure torture."

She answered as seriously, "I didn't bolt the door to keep you out, but to remind myself to stay in."

His answer was ominous, "Oh my, I'm wedding a seductress. You shall be paid in full for your wicked thoughts."

Eden lowered her eyes and ate her breakfast.

* * *

Their first wedding took place several days later and was attended by several more people than Colin originally planned. The pair had decided to wait until her face and jaw no longer ached and his hands gave him less pain. In the meantime, a white satin bridal dress was made up for Eden and the servants had a field day cleaning the chapel and decorating it with a profusion of hothouse and wild flowers. His Lordship brought her the Edmund veil from its storage place, but told her he would just as soon see her in a wreath of Baby's Breath to echo the wreath she had been wearing by the lake. Eden contrived a headdress that incorporated both.

The afternoon before the first wedding, Lord and Lady Darrow and their daughter arrived. They were shown to the green parlor where Lord Edmund, Lady Diana, and Miss Barrett were introduced to them. Lady Darrow was thin and drawn. Her face had a haunted look, but it resembled Daniel's face so closely there could be no mistake. Daniel was sent for immediately. When Daniel appeared at the door, his parents stood up. Daniel's eyes locked on his mother's face first, then his father's. His body shrunk. His face contorted. Finally, a quavering voice cried, "Mamma? Pappa?"

He ran straight into the arms of his parents as they stood in the center of the room. There was not a dry eye or relaxed throat in the room for quite a while. Lord Darrow caught his son and lifted him off the floor. "I would have known him anywhere," Lady Darrow cried. "His face has hardly changed in eight years." When things were calmer, Daniel was introduced to nine-year-old Sabrina, his sister.

Little Thomas had followed Daniel and experienced much anxiety until Lord and Lady Darrow were introduced to him. When Daniel explained to his parents how much Tom meant to him, they promptly invited the boy to become part of their family if he liked. He liked.

While the company was talking nineteen to the dozen, Diana begged her brother to be excused a while and slipped away. She went to the kitchen to see if any stale bread was left in the bin used for that purpose. Helping herself to a basket full of rolls, she went to the stables and had John saddle her pony and ride with her to the lake.

Lady Diana Ashton knew her halcyon days were over. The Darrow's had accepted an invitation to stay at Chadilane, but they would not stay forever. They would go home to their estates and take her true love with them. And Colin and Eden were disgusting. Always laughing and smiling into each other's eyes and touching hands and talking low. They included her in their conversation when she was with them, but one could not help feeling odd-man-out when in a room with two newlyweds-to-be.

Diana dismounted close to the lower pond and handed John the reins. The swans were near the rushes making a display of dipping their heads, arching their long necks, and fluffing out their feathers so that their bodies seemed twice as large. Diana tossed a few pieces of bread. The birds paid no attention. She called. They ignored her, completely engrossed in their courtship rituals. She hurled a whole roll at them. They glided further away and took up their display again. "Stupid birds," she said, and crumbled the remaining bread on the ground for smaller wildfowl, saving one roll for the pony, which promptly devoured the offering. At least Tony loved her.

The thing was done; the vows were pledged; the two became one. The next morning in their chamber, Eden confided to Colin that she now knew it was he who was the true artist in the family. Then the wedding was performed all over again on a grand scale for the family, friends, neighbors, and tenants in two week's time. Within a month after their marriage, Eden's mother and siblings that remained at home were ensconced in the dower house on the estate. One of the first pieces of mail to come to Chadilane addressed to the Hon. the Earl and Countess of Edmund was an invitation to the wedding of Mollie and Jem. The earl and the countess promptly replied with an affirmative. As Eden found her duties as Lady Edmund to be vast and overwhelming, she soon employed a secretary to keep track of appointments and elevated

Nora to lady's maid. Eden threatened her husband that she intended to hire a hefty old hag to act as companion and confidant to his sister in her place, since he displayed a distinct propensity to fall head-over-ears for each of Diana's governesses, but in the end, she let Diana do the choosing. Diana chose Eden's younger sisters, Faith and Hope, and they became sisters to her as well.

When her husband was called to London, Eden went with him. She was delighted to act as sounding board for him whenever he prepared to attack or present some bill in the Lords, and was even suffered to suggest some terminology to be included. She was presented at court and engaged in the social whirl whenever it served her husband's political needs, but the Ashtons preferred museums to routes, and quiet evenings at home with each other to just about anything. In the next year alone, husband and wife worked side-by-side overseeing the expansion and updating of the two orphanages Colin already headed and also planned and instigated two free schools-for-trade, one for young ladies and one for young men.

In the spring, seven downy, gray cygnets trailed the pair of swans on the lower pond. By the following Christmas, Eden was able to present Colin with a unique gift: an heir to the earldom of Edmund. When the infant was first placed in his mother's arms, Eden pronounced him quite the most amazingly beautiful thing God had ever created out of the love of two earthly beings. Her husband agreed wholeheartedly.

LaVergne, TN USA
30 November 2009

165539LV00006B/39/P